# BiG SNEAKY BARBARiAN

## BOOK 2

# BIG SNEAKY BARBARIAN

## BOOK 2

### SETH MCDUFFEE

Podium

Podium

# BiG SNEAKY BARBARiAN

## BOOK 2

# THOSE ARE MY PIES!

**S**he moved through the trees like a shadow.

Mind you, not the dark and evil, unwavering specter of inky skulking that many people might assume a shadow's passage might be—no, this was more of the silent, unnoticeable movement of a friendly prey animal's shade on a midday stroll. This was a mission of a different sort from something nefarious or perilous, and there was no immediate danger to her. Currently.

She was scouting.

Her long limbs might've seemed ill-suited to this work, but she was dexterous and stepped along the soft, weedy earth with grace and intention. She was an elf, and this sort of meandering was second nature to her kind. Further, she was a Lotus elf, and theirs was a long history of confidently performing tasks just like these with finesse.

Well, most of the time.

Her boot found a gnarled, uprooted tangle of plant, which shattered with a loud *crunch* under her weight. She stumbled.

"Shit!" she roared, catching herself on the trunk of a sapling. But her momentum was too great and unwieldy. The sapling cracked. She hit the ground in a heap, the top half of the fledgling tree in her hand.

"Oof!"

Just like that, she was covered in dirt and shame.

*At least the ground isn't hard here*, she thought gratefully.

She stood, brushing herself off and checking her sword belt to ensure she'd retained her full complement of tools and weapons before continuing again through the wood, wholly embarrassed but relieved no one else had seen her display. She'd been tasked with this mission with reluctance, and she did not want to be the cause of any future woes to her people. However, neither did she want to return empty-handed of valuable information. Whether or not reconnaissance was in her people's nature, this particular Lotus elf had something to prove. But don't we all?

It was her third day out there alone, directionless and unsure, stomping through the muck and grime during daylight and combating the painfully chilly air in the evenings. She'd made good headway, though, she liked to think. She was also learning a lot about herself in the process. For instance, she *really* hated having only a thin cloak to shield her body from the wind, rain, and whatever else this region produced from its temperamental skies. Precipitation had never bothered her much in the past, but being unrelentingly subjected to the harsh whims of the elements had a way of changing a person. In fact, the constant presence of the miserable *most likely* autumnal climate weighed on her so much that she was just beginning to consider turning back.

That was when she noticed the dirt road cutting through the wood.

After last night's lovely little torrential downpour, *mud road* would have likely been a more appropriate description. It appeared to be well traveled, something her Tracking Skill confirmed, dotted with countless foot-, hoof-, and miscellaneous other prints swaggering to and fro along its length as it slithered through the trees and bent away into a smudge of darkness in either direction.

A little while later, after bravely skirting the edge of the path she'd only recently realized was there, she saw a tower. She'd spotted it jutting over the tops of the unfamiliar trees and, at first, worried it was nefarious—as seemed to be the case of most structures there. However, after watching and waiting within the trees for hours, she began to sense that this tower was not holed up in some fortress of malicious intent but was, in fact, a regular old run-of-the-mill building. Though she thought she saw a faint blue glow emanating from its peculiarly hooded head. Even later, as she watched the occasional creature waddle toward it down the road, she realized the tower belonged to a *village*. The scope widened further in her mind as she neared, saw the well-made walls and squat stone buildings, and decided it wasn't a village at all but a *town*. One teeming with people.

She let out a squeal of joy before stifling it reluctantly. She would do well to be careful, even in her glee, to make sure no one spotted her before she was ready to be seen. That was practically Scouting 101, and she knew that. If the simulations she'd run countless times in her past were any indicator, bad things happened to excitable stalkers who couldn't help but *eek* and *hurray* their way into conflict. It was tricky, though, because this revelation *changed everything* for her and those back at the base. Plus, it was exhilarating and a bit relieving on a more-personal level.

What was more exciting and even *thrilling* was that she saw quite a few humans within the curvature of the open portcullis. Grubby, boisterous, awful, *beautiful* humans!

She'd almost vaulted from her hiding place, arms wide and shouting for them to notice her, but then remembered that she was an elf and a foreigner. Her instincts bid that it wouldn't be wise to stumble into their sight without any idea of how reactive they could be. Additionally, of course, she had *just* reprimanded herself—however lightly—for almost making a joyous peep, and this could be *much* worse than that. It would not do to trot back to the others with an arrow-riddled body. That would be uncomfortable.

So, she planned to wait a while longer. *Planned* being the operative word, because she *didn't*. Despite her knowledge that it could be *incredibly* perilous and perhaps even stupid to do so, she couldn't help herself from popping out of the brush like some woodland hobo and entering the wonderful little town.

She encountered no difficulties upon walking through the gateway, just a handful of stares and a few confused eyebrow raises. She paid it no mind, though. She was positively *alight* with awe, her eyes wandering along the contours of every perceivable scratch of land and architecture. It was all so breathtakingly remarkable.

She saw bustling, hustling, and a whole lot of tussling all around her: individuals of myriad races and apparent cultures rushing here and there, groups of children and adults alike gathered together, living their lives quite sonderously within the confines of this quaint microcosm.

She continued along the main thoroughfare, absorbing everything with a fiendish delight—a tapestry of mismatched buildings and cobblestoned streets. The streets, she found, were surprisingly wide, and further on she saw large, unfamiliar beasts and oversized carriages that called out to one another or passersby as they made their way down the avenue. The buildings themselves were an eclectic mix of styles and sizes, some tall and grand, others small and squat. The rooftops were adorned with strange symbols and sigils, many glowing with an otherworldly light. These structures making up the bulk were crafted of craggy brick—though she didn't know what material precisely—and seemed to be sturdy. It was ancient stuff, too, by the look of it, pockmarked by age with cracks that may have held thousands of stories as to their origin. The tattooed roofs, too, were a mishmash of styles, with some favoring the classic thatched design she'd seen in many iterations of invention in her life. In contrast, others consisted of slate or even clay. Despite the mild chill, most windows were open to let in the midday sun, and they had no sense of insulation. She reasoned they'd likely be frigid winter palaces come snowfall.

The tower, she'd come to find, was actually a *water tower*, and it occupied the area she had to assume was roughly the center of the town, easily visible from any vantage she found herself in. Though when she noticed she was the only one staring at it like a hungry wastrel, she quickly reined herself in, hoping to blend in among the denizens of the lovely place and that she'd not given herself away as a tourist.

Even further in the distance, the elf could make out a grand . . . Was that a castle? Perched on a hilltop. It was a glorious and imposing sight, even from afar. The walls were tall and thick, built of a dark, almost-black stone that seemed to absorb the light. Turrets and towers surrounded it like a group of jealous lovers, each reaching high into the sky, their pointed tops disappearing into the clouds. Whatever this castle was, it had a certain air of age and mysticism about it, as if it had stood there for centuries, watching over the town below.

*I wonder who lives there? Maybe the mayor?*

But as grand and mysterious as it was, it was easily forgotten as each new stimulating experience assailed her senses with charm.

The most surprising aspect of this town came as she continued through its twists and turns. The elf had been venturing past various businesses—most seeming to be taverns, inns, eateries, or some configuration of each—when she heard a shout. Moving out of the way—so as to not be crushed—the warning had announced the arrival of this city's finest. A mounted town guard patrol went by, moving in formation throughout the street atop the backs of humongous, armored tortoises.

The elf woman, being an elf after all, should have been used to seeing all manner of strange and fantastical creatures in her travels, and she wanted to play her part well—but this was something else entirely. It was odd, exciting, and perhaps, she thought, just a little silly. In fact, she couldn't help but let out a chuckle as the turtle-mounted guards clomped past, their armor shining in the sun and their expressions as serious as a tax collector.

As she looked up at the towering figures astride their giant turtle steeds, she couldn't help but to muse at their expense.

"Well, I suppose it's better than horses in some ways—at least they're less likely to leave a dump on the streets."

And with that, she continued on her way, still chuckling to herself as she rounded a block of buildings and entered a different stretch, still thinking about the absurdity of the scene she had just witnessed.

The guards, for their part, had seemed completely unaware of the absurdity of their mounts, or the elf woman's amusement, as they went about their duties of protecting the town with utmost seriousness and professionalism. Yep. Just another day of fine guarding.

A handful of stalls lined this drag, and people fluttered around them like hungry birds as the vendors cried out to passersby to sample their wares.

"Double-baked mince pies," she heard one of them shout from behind the cavalcade queueing up in front of a yellow awning. "All the way from the towns of Kess! Warm from the oven! Only five coppers!"

"Which Kess?!" a human man shouted nearby.

The vendor paused for a moment, and it seemed to the Lotus elf that he was seriously considering his answer.

"Erm," he finally said, sounding unsure. ". . . East?"

There was a collective groan as roughly half of the patrons in line abandoned their places and walked away.

"I mean West—er, *both!*"

This caused another exodus of disappointedly muttering folk until the Lotus elf found that she was the only person standing in front of the stall, a smile plastered on her face.

"Hello!" she said exuberantly.

The vendor was a squat, middle-aged dwarf with a mane of silver curls who had propped himself up to stand on a steam trunk. He looked down at her from his lofty position with surprise. Then he shook his head, righting his mind, and slipped back into his sales-friendly persona.

"My, my, miss," he said. "You've come to sample the most tremendous treat known this side of the Fury River?"

She was about to respond when another voice shouted.

"There's a Kess on both sides of the Fury, you charlatan!"

The dwarf blinked, ignoring the comment and hoping that the woman would as well. He plastered a look of pure, blissful ignorance onto his friendly visage as if the shouter was speaking to some other mince-peddling swindler.

"Um, yes," the Lotus elf said. "Please."

"Well, right-o, miss! Let me grab one for you—as I mentioned, they're right out of the warming oven."

The dwarf hopped off from his perch on the trunk into the mud and yanked open the top to reveal a pile of parcels wrapped in parchment paper. Despite the afternoon's chill, no steam escaped from this particular steam trunk.

"The producer of these fine morsels of tongue-exciting scrumptiousness is a little lass with whom I have an exclusive contract. It's a special recipe—fully secret, mind—that she developed herself and one that I have the pleasure of being the sole proprietor to administer the labor's fruits of!"

The dwarf snatched one of the top bundles from the pile, slammed the top of the trunk back in place, and hopped atop it again. With a grin, he unfurled the paper to reveal a lumpy mass of bread bleeding with dark gravy. The Lotus elf stared at it for a moment but then found her manners had faded and smiled up at the dwarf.

"Lovely!"

He winked.

"Now. Usually, I charge five copper apiece for these. But, for a charming beauty such as yourself—who clearly has a discerning eye for quality pies—I'll give you two for eleven copper."

He smiled in a perfect display of genuineness.

"But that's more than if I were to buy two separately," the Lotus elf said kindly, hoping that he'd made an error and not saddled her for an easy mark.

The dwarf stiffened and then cleared his throat.

"My! She's beautiful, *and* she's a whip at arithmetic! Fair enough! Ten for the both!"

The elf woman chuckled.

"Can I just have one for now? I'm not that hungry."

"Oh, but after just one taste, you'll be glad you had another in reserve, miss. One never does it all in, you understand. Two is the way to go—trust me on that!"

She blinked, unsure how best to approach this interaction. It wasn't clear what would be considered rude, but she knew she only had a little bit of coin on her. Spending more than she wanted on something as trivial as badly abused pastries was probably not the best way to start her journey. She still had to make sure she could buy any supplies if she blundered into any.

*This is not like the simulations,* she thought.

Seeing her hesitation, the dwarf nodded and hopped down from the trunk again, sloshing in the mud. He disappeared from view for a moment before returning, holding a rusty spoon in his hand.

"Here you are," he said, holding it out for her to view. "Thought I'd sweeten the deal for you. A genuine Dimlocke food dipper. Best way to get your fill of the mince, if I do say so myself! I'm a bit of an expert on the subject of consumption!"

He patted his gut with a laugh.

The elf examined the object.

*It's just a spoon . . .*

"What does it do?"

The dwarf gave her a curious look and then brightened.

"My, it is a wondrous tink for procuring the best experience in your food devouring needs! You just stick that shovel end into the pie and—"

He stuffed the spoon into the center of the pastry and dug a portion of its sloppy innards out from the crust. Then he proffered it toward her.

"See? A real meal on the go. I hear it's quite the dandy of a device down in Malort. All the noble ladies are using one," he said. "Though I can't imagine *your* like beating a path down there, miss, seeing as it's a nasty cesspool of a rotting dung heap—but I'll keep my personal politics to myself. As you please, then."

He flipped the spoon around so the handle faced her and smiled wide.

*But . . . it's a spoon! Is that a fresh new technology here? If that's the case, I'm going to blow their minds with some of my own neato . . . What was the word he used? Tinks?*

She accepted the spoon with all the grace she could muster and nodded.

"Thank you so much, but I think I'd still like just the one minced pie."

A few minutes later, the Lotus elf found herself walking through the town again, a minced pie tucked under each arm and a spoon in her belt. She glanced down at her haul with a sigh and continued on, feeling ever much like easy pickings.

Over the next half hour or so, she perused the many vendors and brick-and-mortars that dotted the roadways. There were different varieties and flavors of use and necessity, all with that cozy, quaint, archaic flair that filled her with a strange sense of nostalgia for something she had never personally experienced. Eventually, she wound her way into a road with a dead end and a handful of building fronts that seemed more interesting than the others. She had no way of knowing that she'd stand out like a sore thumb in this particular stretch of town. Or, at the very least, be regarded with suspicion. But that was irrelevant to her at the moment: she was *browsing*. One shop bore a wooden sign with flecked and fading purple paint and the symbol of a foot freshly applied in silver paint. Inside the deep glass panes of the window, though, all she saw were lit candles.

*Odd,* she thought.

Another was clearly some sort of tool shop, with a marquee above the wide, open door that said TOOLERY.

*I wonder if they have spoons in there.*

Still, another had an equally chipped wooden sign as the "foot" one but depicted what looked like a bovine animal of some kind—though with a single horn instead of two—standing on its hind legs. She couldn't see within this building, though, as heavy, wine-colored curtains obscured the view, deterring any unsavory sorts from having a bit of a gawk. She was just about to enter that one out of curiosity when she heard a commotion behind her.

"Stop, menace!"

She balked.

*What in blazes?*

To her extreme confusion, she saw a figure that confounded the fabric of her mind and struck her with the immediate fear that she had burst something loose from her brain. *Herself.*

A nearly perfect copy of *her* rounded the corner, cheeks flushed and puffing out dramatically as she raced along in the mud, splashing and sloshing in her haste.

*I'm definitely losing my mind! Unless I crossed some magical barrier that causes hallucinations?*

The elf wasn't sure exactly what was happening, but she had a sneaking suspicion that there would be an overripe helping of complications because of it.

The duplicate elf didn't even seem to notice her as she approached at top speed. The copy looked over a shoulder and suddenly hurled something behind her that exploded as it hit the ground—filling the area with smoke.

*A grenade?*

Then the doppelganger moved past her and into the shop she'd just been preparing to enter herself, dashing into the darkness within.

The elf stood stunned for a moment before shrugging her shoulders.

"That was strange," she said aloud. Then, thinking that perhaps she ought to get a little bit more information about this predicament, she took a step forward to follow. That was when she felt a cold point press into the back of her neck. She froze.

"Don't even think of moving, scoundrel," the same gruff voice from before commanded.

"Uh, what?" she asked, her back still to whoever it was behind her. Whoever it was, she was most decidedly *not* interested in disobeying a command like that, as this particular someone was clearly not happy.

"I don't have much money," she continued, staring directly ahead at the shops on the other side of the street from her. "But you can have whatever is there. I don't want any trouble."

"It's a bit late for avoiding trouble, dwarf," came the sharp reply.

*Dwarf? Is he blind? I'm a tall, thin, lightly garbed elf. There's literally nothing dwarvish about me.*

"I'm sorry," she said hesitantly, "but you might be mistaken. I'm not a dw—"

"Quiet, dwarf," the man barked. "We already know you use illusory Arcana. Not to mention we *saw* you change right in front of us. You must have quite the high opinion of yourself—or an extremely low one of us—if you think we would fall for your trickery."

*Illusions?*

Something clicked into place then, and the elf furrowed her brow. The vendor with the mince pies. He had been the only dwarf she'd seen so far, and the sole person she'd really chatted with since arriving—other than this fine gentleman behind her with a sharp point inching into her spine. He must have used Arcana to disguise himself as her and escape from . . .

She saw two armored individuals round the same corner her double had come from.

*The town guard,* she thought, anxiety spiking in her heart.

"Please believe me," she began, her voice taking on a tone of desperation. "I'm not really certain what's going on here, but it seems like I've been framed. The dwarf you're chasing must have disguised himself as me to throw you all off."

She sighed, wishing she'd dumped at least a few more Points into Charisma, or had picked up a Diplomacy Skill like Saban had.

"I am not involved," she continued, taking a risk and turning her head to the side and gesturing to the building before her. "You have to believe me. He just ran into that shop right there . . ."

She blinked. The storefront she'd just been preparing to enter—and where the dwarf had escaped into—was no longer there. In its place was a dilapidated structure with an entrance barred by thick, wooden planks. The windows no longer remained and were instead ghosts of what she had seen: the glass was shattered, and the curtains were either torn or moth-eaten where they existed at all.

"Sure thing," the voice behind her said, but it was clear from the way he said it that he didn't believe her. The elf could hear the thick clank of something metallic behind her.

"I suppose he leaped right through that shattered pane and didn't leave so much as a print in the dust."

The man chuckled.

"Or did you forget, *dwarf,* that you're carrying some minced pies yourself?"

She frowned, the weight of the pastries feeling tremendous now that they were apparently some sort of accessory to a crime she did not recall committing.

"I bought these," she said quietly.

"Sure you did," the man said. "Because they taste so good and are just *flying* out of that chest."

"I'm not the dwarf," she found herself saying, but knew it was useless. The guard seemed to have made up his mind, and based on the looks his companions were tossing her way, they agreed with his assessment of the situation. This wasn't good. It would be very bad if she couldn't get back to the others.

"Enough of your lies, dwarf. Your disguise is flimsy at best. Why would an elf be here, of all places? You'll come with us now, and then you can argue about who you *are* or *aren't* with the headsman."

*Shit,* she thought. *If I don't return soon . . . the whole camp will be at risk. And Alpha . . . well, he won't even bother to try to send people out to look for me. I'll be done for.*

Then she felt a powerful and painful blow to the back of the head, and everything went black.

# CHAPTER ONE

# LEGS FOR DAYS

I moved through the streets like a shadow.

You know—like some dark and evil unwavering specter of inky skulking. I was one with the night, and the night—she be spooky. I felt like this comparison still worked . . . even if it was technically only early evening. With the long shadows and general hum of end-of-day caterwauling, twilight was the perfect time to unfurl my powers of nefarious misbehavin' and get up to no good. I was naughty by nature and in the business of cloak-and-dagger. And business was good. Or it would be once I got the hang of acrobatics.

Despite having an Acrobat Skill of E-Rank, Level One, I hadn't really grown into my own with it yet. It was still a bit . . . awkward. I raced along the cobblestoned road, feeling my heart cudgel-crunching in my chest as I struggled to suck air into my lungs. Man, I was neither coordinated enough nor in shape enough to keep this up for long, but while I was able to, I would make my night like a hot dog—and relish it.

*Spirit of an athlete, body of a mathlete.*

I heaved, diving toward a low ledge on the outer city wall, and grasped it. I dangled for a moment, feeling like a big ole chub before hefting myself up and over onto the lip. I took a moment to catch my breath, staring out at the valley beyond the town. Then I took another deep intake of oxygen and turned toward the backside of the buildings. I leaped *fatly* from the wall onto a roof, smirking as I did. I loved the feeling of being able to slip about mostly unnoticed while the rest of the world lived on beneath me. I climbed—boy, did I climb—to the top of the roof and perched my meaty haunches upon it to look down at the lively settlement below as my lungs screamed and my loud bellows of breath echoed off of the rooftops.

*Tallrock.*

As the last rays of sunset stretched into the cracks and alleyways of the town, I felt a surge of glee. I was *actually* up in this bitch—this new world. Here with new rules, new dangers, and a huge new orc body.

Before all this, I was just a short, overweight teenaged dipshit named Gabe. I lived with my outrageously aggrieved aunt and uncle, caused trouble for the local authorities, and spent the vast majority of my time listening to metal and being useless to society. But, don't worry, *ladies*—my sex appeal gets even better. Even if it had only been a handful of days since I'd arrived in Regaia—well, a little longer if you counted the bullshit time dilation in a dungeon that had forced me to lose almost a week—I was starting to feel as though I was getting a grasp on what it meant to be a Sojourner.

I chuckled.

*Sojourner.*

The term didn't really mean anything to me before arriving. Hell, it didn't mean much to me now. To be fair, I'd always been pretty ignorant of words that didn't directly involve insulting someone hilariously. But even so, I don't think I'd even heard the term before being vaulted gooch-over-forehead into this annoyingly charming and unendingly dangerous fantasy world. A fantasy world that revolved around goddamn *Dungeons and Dragons* number-crunching, no less.

Yet, despite that, the word *Sojourner* was now one that described me. It was a badge I didn't want but would have to learn to deal with—like when I had to go to that stupid mixer for my Uncle Luke's law firm's anniversary celebration. I'd gotten in trouble for writing *Jonathan Schlongburg* on my name tag and introducing myself as "Schlong-John," but it had been worth it. I was a contrary lad, all the way down to my gigantic, stubborn bones. Satisfaction with doing what was expected or requested of me was nonexistent. When life gives you lemons, you ask for apple juice. If life gives you the apple juice you asked for, you hurl it to the ground and demand a refill.

As I watched the townsfolk toot around several dozen feet beneath my perch, I wondered about the *other* Sojourners I knew were there. The crew of stupids I'd arrived with from my own reality by way of screeching train derailment death. I had to believe my recent badass and cinematic boss fight deep within the Dreadnaught Lord's Crypt had yielded the truth, as it wouldn't make sense otherwise. That being: Ocho—whose real name was Frey, I think—had confirmed my former high school classmates were also slung up with the same shitty fate I was . . . you know, right before he'd been speared through the heart.

I didn't know where the others from my former world were exactly, other than a vague direction the posthumous pisslicker had given me, but I'd find them. For now, I'd just have to be satisfied with resting my substantial laurels near a crooked weather vane atop a nameless building in some town in an alternate world.

We'd only arrived in Tallrock yesterday, and I hadn't quite gotten a chance to check it out, considering we'd immediately had to find a doctor—or, I guess, *healer* was the word used here. One of my companions, Jes, required urgent care, as his bones had been broken all topsy-turvy and upside down by Ocho. We'd been worried that we weren't going to make it before the damage was permanent, and had busted our asses to arrive within the narrow window Stinky had indicated we had in order to rescue most of his body. It didn't help that we'd taken the time to have ourselves a bit of a nap after our arduous journey through the butthole of the earth—but, to be fair, we were sleepy. Demolishing a baddie deep within a dungeon pit was tiring work, and we'd just barely made it out with our squishy bits intact—so I'll ask you not to pass judgment.

Now we were here, and there was a little bit of extra excitement for me: there was a Quest to complete. The first Quest I'd received shortly after arriving was to find some schmo named Edwig Quintham and deliver a fat pouch of false goblin ears I'd lifted off of the corpses of some ratmen I'd exploded. Apparently, he was part of some "Mages' Order" and needed them for research. I hadn't thought about it much, but I supposed now that I was, it was actually super fucking gross to be walking around with a bulging envelope of rotting ears this whole time—and a little impressive that they hadn't been eviscerated by one of the many harrowing shitstorms I'd been a reluctant participant in. Once I figured out where Yosper Hall was, I could deliver the desiccated skin trophies and be on my way, paid in full and ready to pop bands with the best of them.

There was one problem: my Reputation.

I was an orc. As such, the locals tended to frown upon my extremely badass background, labeling me "Untrusted." So, before even arriving inside the town, I'd gotten a notification that my Reputation would be much like the song "Bible Basher" from American death metal band Deicide—poorly received. This universe was weirdly racist when it came to certain groups, painting them with broad brushes of varying contempt. Apparently, orcs were known for being world-class pillaging, destructive assholes, and I guess that was a little bit of a bugaboo around there—for some reason. I hadn't thought anything of my Reputation before, and to be perfectly honest, there wasn't really a reason, as far as I was concerned. I hadn't traipsed into any towns until now, so there'd never been an opportunity to gauge the bigot barometer to divine exactly how much I was magically disliked. Boy, was my face red!

While my companions Stinky, Frida, and the aforementioned hyper-injured Jes had just waltzed right into Tallrock, I'd been forced to wait until dark and then sneak over the wall like some sort of leper gymnast. I'd been steaming mad and really wanted to just run through the streets, shouting swear words. But after calming down a little and considering my options, I decided that the consequences might be too harsh for that level of dramatic misbehaving. I hated rules, especially exclusionary authoritative ones, but rather than a fine or some jail time there in Bubonicburg, the result for my hilarious misdeeds might actually end up in me being tarred, feathered, and launched over the hills from a trebuchet. So, I respected the temperature of the townsfolk and sought to be a good little automaton. For now. Plus, silver lining: it gave me the opportunity to climb buildings and show off my stock-pile of sweet new stealth maneuvers.

I'd snuck out of town just before dawn that morning and used the daylight hours to bop about, exploring the wilds—then spent a while bathing once I'd found a river. Our accommodations in town had some sort of bathhouse, but it wasn't connected to the room and required a communal soak. It seemed like a bad idea to successfully creep inside the town only to be caught *being an orc* during rubber-ducky time. Right now, I was waiting for it to get well and truly dark, so that I could meet up with the others outside the healer's place of operation, check on Jes's condition, and then go with Frida to try and locate Yosper Hall to finalize my Quest. Until then, all I could do was wait.

So, with nothing else to do, I found myself plopped atop a rooftop at dusk, overlooking the twisted streets of Tallrock.

The view was a mix of the mundane and the bizarre. The streets were lined with all manner of shops and businesses, not that I'd be allowed in, but with a healthy dose of weirdness thrown in for good measure. The buildings themselves were all mismatched in a confusing collection of styles and sizes, some big and boring, others *small* and boring. I did notice while clambering around up on the housetop all Jersey Devil–style that a lot of the roofs had strange, glowing fantasy symbols etched into them—but once I screwed around with them a little and discovered that they didn't make me immediately explode, I lost interest pretty quickly.

As the sky darkened, the streets came alive with flickering lanterns and bonfires, casting a warm orange glow on the cobblestones. It was kinda pretty, actually. The distant sound of music and laughter drifted along through the air, and—especially with my FOMO kicking into overdrive—I couldn't help but feel a sense of wonder and curiosity about this unique town, despite my initial *extremely warranted* anger.

But, under that contentment, there was something else. I couldn't shake the feeling that there was something *off* about Tallrock, like a sinister underbelly or villainous machinations lurking just beneath the surface. I mean, I'd seen the goddamn guards roaming around mounted on fucking *turtles*, for Christ's sake.

That was fucking weird, right? They were big bitches, too, but not like the Teenage Mutant Ninja variety. Just, like, hyper large. As big as horses.

Furthermore—yeah, I'm using it—*furthermore*, I was pretty sure I hadn't *seen* a single motherfuckin' horse the whole time I'd been there. Did they even exist? Not that I was missing them or anything, but it would just be a bit absurd, ya know? It would make sense, though, since most of the bindlesticks I'd come across seemed perfectly happy to go without any convenient mode of transport in the slightest. Though I supposed I couldn't blame someone for abstaining from the hoof life—it ain't for everybody. Perhaps, like me, they preferred the freedom afforded to them by using the tried-and-true, ole reliable *feet*—nature's horses.

*Shit, that reminds me. I gotta get myself some boots, or . . . fuckin,' I dunno, some slippers or something. Running around barefoot is* not *the move out here.*

Anyway—back to the guards. Those turtle-jockeys could usually be found patrolling the streets with an air of arrogant authority, and the citizens seemed to be living in fear of them. I guess some things are the same no matter which bullshit universe you get farted into. AGAB or whatever.

Still, in light of all this, I'd decided I was gonna keep an open mind and explore more of this town as long as I was left unmolested. Who knew; it might be fun? Though if anyone was under the misconception I'd be keeping my nose clean, well, then *oof.* If there's one quirk about me I'd kept as a personal keepsake after crossing over, it was that I couldn't *wait* to see what kind of trouble I could get into in this place.

After a little more voyeurism, I found that, much like when I did any activity, my attention span waned, and before long, I decided it was a good time to review my statistics. You know, cuz I hadn't done so in a while and it was probably an alright idea to check out what I had goin' on inside my body before anything popped off. Not encountered anything deadly in over a day had me on edge, and *perhaps* it was making me a little paranoid.

*Loon:*
**Race: Orc***
**Class: Barbarian**
**Level: 10**
**Profession: Unassigned**
**Health: 410 / 410**
**Arcana: 85 / 85**
**Max Stamina: 175**
**Reputation: N/A**
***Current Settlement Reputation: Tallrock [Untrusted]**

*Sodality*
**Assignment: Cult of the Capricious**
**Cult Rank: Initiate**

*Attributes*
**Remaining Points to Allocate: 12**
**Strength: 12**
**Constitution: 29**
**Dexterity: 12**
**Wisdom: 10**
**Intelligence: 8**
**Charisma: 6**
**Luck: 15***

*Skills*
- Camp (F-Rank Level 1)
- Hunting (F-Rank Level 1)
- Improvised Weapons (E-Rank Level 2)
- Improvised Shield (F-Rank Level 2)
- Insight (E-Rank Level 2)
- Intimidate (F-Rank Level 2)
- Knowledge [Nature] (F-Rank Level 1)
- One-Handed Weapons (F-Rank Level 3)
- Perception (F-Rank Level 4)
- Simple Weapon Proficiency (F-Rank Level 6)
- Simple Armor Proficiency (F-Rank Level 1)
- Sneaking (B-Rank Level 4)
- Survival (F-Rank Level 1)
- Two-Handed Weapons (F-Rank Level 6)
- Throwing Weapons (F-Rank Level 9)
- Unarmed Fighting (E-Rank Level 2)

*Active Abilities*
- Armorless Defense (E-Rank Level 6)
- Battle Born I
- Enduring Perch I
- Eye of the Saboteur I
- Darkvision I
- Primal Rage (E-Rank Level 1)
- Pernicious Volley I

- Natural Resilience (F-Rank Level 2)
- Uncommon Consumption (F-Rank Level 1)
- Warchant I
- Blackout Warchant

*Passive Abilities*
- **Outsider**
- **Unfaltering**
- **Wildling**

*Perks*
- **Adventurous Tastes (First Perk Bonus)**
- **Aegis Synthesis**

*Aegis*
- **Calden's Hang Time**
- **Loon's Bombastic Beatdown**

*Esper Nodes*
- **Emerald: 1**
- **Sapphire: 1**
- **Topaz: 1**

I roosted for a little longer and tried to go back to watching the milling and meandering of the townsfolk blissfully unaware of my nefariously shrouded presence—thanks in part to the Trespasser's Veil clasped around my shoulders. . . . until I got bored and started looking into windows.

I know, I know: nobody likes a peeping tom. But, to be fair, I wasn't trying to see anything scandalous; I was just hoping to spot something interesting enough to keep my attention until nightfall. What was the use of all this sneaky if I couldn't use it with reckless abandon?

I crouched along the edge of the roof, huddled under the stealth-enhancing cloak and peering into a few homes while moving slowly. Most of the scenes I caught glimpses of were pretty dull: a human couple sharing a meal and looking lovingly into one another's eyes; a gray-skinned humanoid with a green beard sipping an amber liquid from a glass while scratching notes into a ledger; an empty bedroom with a dog sleeping on the bed. Nothing out of the ordinary at all. It was actually *strangely* ordinary insomuch that this was a gosh-darn dark age fantasy world, for fuck's sake. Nobody was practicing magic spells, or inspecting their evil alchemy vials, or summoning a mummy from the void—just basic-bitch shit.

*This is dumb*, I thought. The sun had finally gone to bed and my Darkvision had activated on its own, immediately bathing the area in hues of gray, white, and black. It also made looking into the windows a bit of an actual pain, as the dim illumination from rooms with light were like blinding brands of retina-gouging sunlight. I decided it was much too painful while I was eye level with the windows, so I focused and switched my sight back to normal. There was a moment of adjustment, but then I was able to easily see without wincing like an old man who'd left his "readers" at the bank, and began my path back to where I'd initially climbed up. Then I stopped. A light had appeared in a previously dark window, and within the frame of the sill I could see a small silhouette. A child.

Normally, I wouldn't have cared—there wasn't much interest a kid's life had. But I had paused because it was very clear that their gaze was on me.

The child stared at me not with shock or fear but a look that seemed . . . amused. The boy—I think—looked to be about five or six, though I couldn't know for sure, and followed me with his eyes as I slowly crept forward, a little smile fastened to his lips. Then he waved at me.

*Ah, what the hell.*

I chuckled quietly and then returned the motion. This seemed to excite him and he began frantically gesturing at me and waving more. He said something, but he was behind the thick glass pane, so I couldn't hear him. I made a theatrical show of shrugging and then pointed at my ear to indicate I didn't know what he was saying. He nodded and pointed at me once, then mimed looking around wide-eyed and craning his neck before returning my shrug.

*I think he's asking where I'm from?*

I smirked. Then I gestured in a wide arc over my shoulder, pointing beyond the hills and wiped the air with my hand in the "away" motion.

The boy nodded again almost urgently, then pointed and made a sort of "fisticuffs" fighting stance and boxed the air before looking back at me. I grinned big. I thought that he might have been asking if I was a fighter or a hero or something like that. Far be it from me to disrupt a child's first instincts on the type of person I was. So, I curled my arm into a bicep flex and slapped the muscle while nodding, one eyebrow raised like the Rock. I could see the kid found this hilarious, as he'd started laughing. The act looked weird, though, almost like he was hyperventilating. Oh, well, I'm not gonna knock him for having a bizarre chuckle.

*The current public opinion might be pretty anti-orc*, I thought. *But I'm going to personally change the minds of the next generation—one heroic pose at a time.*

I heard a loud scratching and paused. It was a strange sound and close. I glanced around, but it was pretty dark without my extra-special night vision.

*Huh. Strange.*

I looked back to the kid, pointing to myself and waving goodbye. He frowned but returned the wave and I flexed again—you know, to give him something to remember me by—then started skulking away. I hadn't made it five feet before I heard the manic pounding of glass. I snapped my head back to the boy and saw that he was frantically beating his little pudgy fists to get my attention.

*The fuck? Jeez, kid, don't be so clingy.*

As he saw I'd noticed, he began gesturing wildly to a spot on the roof behind me and shouting. I could *sort* of hear it, though muffled, and I sighed and turned fully around. The roof was still dark, so I put my thumb up to cover the window from my vision and reactivated Darkvision. Once again, the world grew brighter but colorless. However, *now* I could see there was something new in the mix that immediately spiked my heart rate. Perched at the top of the roof thirty feet away from me was a huge, dark shape. It was maybe fifteen feet tall and curled like a serpent—except *unlike* a snake, this thing had a multi-sectioned armored body and dozens of insectoid arms. It looked like a massive centipede save for one horrific feature: it had a bone-white human-like face. Dark, empty eye sockets peered out, framed by thick black circles, and its blood-red lips were open in a terrifying snarl. I could see at least two rows of long fangs surrounding the dark void of the inside of its maw. It was utterly and truly jacked up beyond belief.

"What in the *Silent Hill* fuck is this?!" I shouted.

That, it turned out, was a phenomenal mistake.

Apparently, it hadn't noticed me before I loudly bellowed, but it had now. Its entire face turned toward me, and it released a piercing screech that echoed out into the night. I took a step back, clamping my hands over my ears as the wail continued. Then it stopped, and I instantly grabbed the double-bladed boomerang-like weapon tucked into the waistband of my kilt. I held the haladie out, ready to hurl it if need be, but then saw something that made me almost puke. Two more forms rose up from the other side of the roof, scritch-scratching along as countless legs pushed them into view.

*More centipede creatures!*

I looked back to the window where the boy was staring, frozen with fear, and saw another of the monsters scurrying along the outside of the building.

*They can climb walls! Fuck!*

In the distance I could hear the toll of bells and cries of alarm. Apparently, this wasn't just happening to me. That was a little bit of comfort, I supposed. But not much.

Then a message appeared in my vision:

**Citizens of Tallrock,**

**This settlement is under a monster attack. This is a C-Rank Assault and poses a danger to Health, Resources, and Structures. Please take the necessary precautions to limit destruction or Tallrock will suffer negative consequences, Conditions, and Debuffs. Good luck!**

I scoffed at the message and turned my attention back to the monsters.

*So, that's it? No explanation of how to do anything or—*

My train of thought was interrupted by another message.

**You have been offered a Quest!**

**[Mission Quest] A Multi-pronged Assault**

*Goodness gracious! Monsters called oomukade have invaded Tallrock, and boy, do these guys know how to stir the pot! They are attracted to sources of water to lay their brood of ooey-gooey egg sacs and won't stop unless they get their way or are killed. This act typically poisons the water and is a surefire way to kill off a substantial amount of the population. You need to survive this [C-Rank] attack and safeguard the town from destruction or suffer the penalties!*

**Goals:**

*Defend or Escape Tallrock without being killed*

*Defense Priorities:*

- *Keep Total Settlement Destruction (TSD) below 30%*
- *Stop oomukade horde from reaching Settlement Resource [Water Tower] and finishing their birthing cycle.*
- *Kill 80% of the invading oomukade*
    - *Remaining oomukade [70 / 70]*
    - *Percent vanquished: 0%*

*Escape Priorities:*

- *Exit Tallrock before 10% of TSD.*

**Defense Reward: Reputation, Additional Reward(s)**

**Escape Reward: Unknown**

**This Quest is not optional.**

*Well, fucking goddamn shit!*

So, my two options were fight or flight. It made sense, but obviously I wasn't going to run away. I had shit to do there. I sighed.

"Well," I shouted at the monsters still clacking their disgusting mouths at me. "Looks like I'm going to have to body-blow you guys into submission. It's nothing personal, gang. You're just really gross and nobody likes you. Guess you're about to find out if there's an afterlife for gigantic, sickly—"

*CRACK!*

One of the monsters had shot at me faster than I could follow and blasted me hard with one of its spindly appendages. Before I knew what was happening, I was spiraling from the roof and down toward the cobblestoned street below.

"Fuuuuuuuuuuuuuuuuuuuuuck!" I roared.

## CHAPTER TWO

# A RIPP-ROARING GOOD TIME

Ripp's day had been quite awful, and very unfair—if he did say so himself. He'd spent the afternoon playing in the streets with his best mates, Pomondus and Tiffy, whiling away the hours with one of their invented games they simply called "Hit With a Stick." It involved hitting anything they thought was interesting with a thick branch they'd found. Ripp—or Rippelyn, as his parents unerringly referred to him—thought this new world-renowned pastime was thoroughly enjoyable and had no end of promise until Tiffy went and changed the rules. She'd decided that Pomondus and Ripp would also qualify as "something interesting" and could therefore be swatted whenever the little human liked. Ripp had complained that it wasn't a fair game unless he and Pomondus could hit *her* with the branch as well, but Tiffy had explained that she did not count, as she was the eldest. It was at that moment that Ripp decided he didn't care about points.

As Tiffy ran crying to her parents—her hand clamped tightly over the reddening welt on her arm—Ripp knew that he was in a pot of boiling trouble.

Though he was already seven years old, Ripp's parents still treated him like he was just a child. After—in his esteemed opinion—a lackluster dinner of erta and potato stew, willowberry dumplings and a heel of bread drenched in butter and turnip gravy, he was under express orders to receive *no* dessert and head straight up to his room to think about how he was meant to treat his friends. This seemed very unfair to Ripp, as he'd wanted to stay up with his older sister while she read to him from her book of adventure stories. No matter how much he begged, pleaded, or pounded on the floor, they were resolved to teach him to be kind. And so, without any other options, he slumped toward the stairs that led to his room, his head down and fists clenched as he cursed Tiffy *and* Pomondus (who'd tattled on him as well.)

Ripp retired to his room for the evening, feeling very much like a prisoner. Though, he reasoned, prisoners likely received dessert. It was then that he decided he had it far worse than any prisoner and set about planning how best to suffer the remainder of his night now shunned from the world in a family that did not love him. He'd activated the magelight in his room (a minor bit of arcane spellwork his grandmother had rigged together) and pulled up a chair to the window.

He spent only a few minutes watching the darkness creep into the neighborhood before he felt a yawn intrude upon him.

*Oh, no,* he thought in horror. If he went to bed now, he'd have spent the last of his waking day being scolded, and he didn't want to go to bed and learn any sort of lesson without a period of disobedience first. That just wouldn't do. He resigned himself to staring out the window, willing his body to stay awake. Perhaps, he thought, he could trick his mind into waking up if he pressed his forehead to the window. It was no longer summer, and the evenings *were* getting chillier. So, he did.

It was at that moment, his brow smashed firmly against the glass, that Ripp noticed movement on the roof across the alley from where he was. It was easy to pick out, even in the darkness, as the boy was a quarter ovid—a near-human race typified by a similarity to lesser shades—on his mother's side. What the boy saw was very peculiar: a large, bulky man—or maybe some sort of beefy, mutated hobgoblin—hunched over and clattering along the shingles. He had a dark hue to his skin, peppered with an assortment of dots, like his Auntie Belara's party dress. He was also dressed quite oddly, Ripp thought, with a bandolier of belts across his chest, and rather than pants, he wore some sort of skirt. Draped around his shoulders was a black cape that seemed darker than the world outside. He was also barefoot.

*That must be uncomfortable,* thought Ripp.

The creature paused, noticing the boy noticing him, and Ripp thought that it would be polite to give a little wave. So, he did. To his great pleasure, the beast across the way returned his motion.

*He's a friendly sort of hobgoblin,* thought Ripp. Then, suddenly, a shape loomed up behind the man on the roof. In the moonlight, the boy could see a massive body wreathed in legs and a very frightening face constructed of bone-white horror. Young Ripp did not have the life experience nor the necessary linguistic capability to read that would allow him to recognize that this was an oomukade. Had he borne either trait, he'd have been able to see the postings all over town from the local Exhibition Guild requesting aid in combating a nest of the creatures not far from the town. As it stood, Ripp could only figure these had crawled straight from his nightmares.

Ripp began shouting and gesturing wildly to the beast on the roof, who seemed blissfully unaware of this new threat. The man gestured to his ear, a clear notion that he was unable to understand the boy. From far below him, likely from the sitting room, Ripp's father called out that under no circumstances were his outbursts appropriate, and were he not to stop, he'd face additional consequences. Ripp choked back his fear, pointing to the man again and looking around, begging him to understand that he needed to peer around his person and awaken to the danger just behind him. He didn't know what else to do, so he shrugged. He could feel his heartbeat quickening and thought that it would be his fault were he not able to inform the stranger across the way of the impending doom.

The man nodded, and a pang of hope resonated deep within little Ripp. He'd understood him! *Watch out!* the boy wanted to scream, but knew that the noise might cause the slowly uncoiling monster not far away to attack him. Or, worse, he thought, it might bring his father upstairs to take away *tomorrow's* dessert.

The stranger waved directly toward the oomukade, as if to ask if he should turn around.

*Yes!* screamed the boy in his mind. He nodded. Then, another idea came to his seven-year-old mind, and he began swiping at the air with his fists. The stranger needed to fight! The hobgoblin—or maybe he was some sort of trollkin—smirked and flexed at the boy. Then he slapped his doughy limb— devoid of any muscle that Ripp could see—and cockily raised an eyebrow at him with a wide grin.

*Oh,* thought Ripp. *He's an idiot.*

This sent the boy spiraling into a fit of panic. He suddenly felt as though he couldn't catch his breath, and he sucked in deep lungfuls of air, tilting his head back to try to breathe normally and calm himself down. Then he caught a glimpse of the oomukade slinking forward, its many legs scratching against the surface of the shingles as it boosted itself up, growing taller than before—a sure sign it was soon to strike.

Pushing down his anxiety, the boy grew cold as he watched the trollkin—or perhaps shrimpy ogre—wave him goodbye. His heart fell and he tried to urge the stranger to notice with a wave of his hand, but the fool just scuttled away, ignorant to the forthcoming death.

*No,* thought Ripp. *I am Rippelyn Watervane, son of Tanzal and Big Quincy Watervane—two of the best accountants in the whole of Tallrock. I cannot let someone stumble unknowing into their own demise. Especially if they are simple.*

The boy raised his fists and pounded on the glass. It seemed to work. The shrimpy ogre—or was he an out-of-shape sahuagin?—turned, seeming annoyed. But it didn't matter. Ripp roared and pointed right at the horrifying sight, which caused the stranger to finally notice. It also had the unfortunate side effect of sending his father into a state of annoyance, and though he was only vaguely aware of it, the boy heard his stern paternal figure's heavy bootfalls on the stairs. His attention, however, was firmly affixed to the scene outside his window.

The stranger, though clearly a bit soft in his head meat, seemed incensed by the presence of the many-legged monster. Ripp had a bad feeling about his chances, though. The creature was several sizes bigger than the stranger. Then more of them arrived, and Ripp's young mind calculated that the man's odds of survival had gotten even slimmer.

*I have to rescue him!* the boy thought. So, while every other being was distracted, he took a deep breath and slid his pudgy, uncoordinated fingers underneath the window and tugged it upward. In his mind, if he could get it open, the stranger could leap in to escape. It didn't occur to Ripp that the window being open would likely allow the enemy to enter his room as well. Without that foresight, however, he continued.

As he budged the window open a few inches, Ripp's mind was suddenly invaded by a voice. It was soft and emotionless, without a discernible sex, and reminded the boy of one of the healers of the mending house speaking to a patient. Most importantly, it was familiar.

As previously mentioned, Ripp was too young to recognize the symbols required to qualify one as being able to read. As such, the system that spoke to the denizens of Regaia through the medium of floating messages and displays had protocols in place to ensure all who dwelled within the confines of the world could access the information they needed. For those individuals who were blind—or otherwise without sight—had too-immature minds, or were simply too stupid, the system deployed its critical instructions through verbalization directly into the mind. Ripp had encountered this only a few times in his short lifespan, and typically this had happened when he was sick or injured—save the one time he was given a Quest to find his sister's pet frog. However, he'd never been imparted with a message quite like this.

It began with a calm monotone of caution, informing the townsfolk that they were under a monster attack. Ripp was unsure what a "sea-rank" assault was but assumed that it probably had something to do with pirates. Perhaps some ocean-trekking ne'er-do-wells had unleashed these monstrous blights into the town to steal the citizens' belongings? In any case, the boy thought that this was redundant and very silly information, as it was plain as day they were under attack. However, his underdeveloped sense of reason had not considered that others within Tallrock were not privy to what he was currently witnessing outside his window.

After a moment, the voice continued, and Ripp was left a little speechless by what it said.

*Rippelyn Watervane, you have been offered a Quest. You must run or hide from the big, bad monsters attacking Tallrock. Find a safe place with your family and do not worry; surely someone will come along to help scare them away. It is important that you let the adults handle this situation, or you might get in trouble. Now, hurry along and get somewhere out of harm's way. Your reward for completing this Quest is unknown, but rest assured it will be a really great one.*

Ripp wasn't sure how to approach this situation. On the one hand, he knew it was important to do his best to complete any Quest that the system in place offered. He'd been told his whole life that it was the most efficient way to start on the best foot when he came of age and began racking up Points and Abilities. However, he felt that his circumstances were unique in that he had a front-row seat to seeing a potentially heroic battle between a monster and a . . . whatever the stranger was. An upright alligator? He knew if he ran away now, he'd miss his one opportunity to behold something that in his mind was very neat.

So, Rippelyn Watervane, known as Ripp to those who knew him best, called "Ripp the obnoxious" by his frustratingly unkind cousin Marvill, brother of Sandarya Watervane, finder of frogs and breaker of old Miss Hatterink's garden gate . . . stood to watch the battle unfold.

He'd just managed to prop the window open halfway when he saw one of the monsters on the roof shoot forward with incredible speed and clobber the dim-witted stranger, knocking him off the roof.

"Fuuuuuuuuuuuuuuuuuuuuuuck!" he heard the man roar.

Then, before Ripp could blink, he saw the man *stop* falling. He froze in mid-air just as he passed the edge of the roof. It was as if the pull of gravity no longer worked as normal, and the man floated high above the street, a grin plastered on his face.

*That must be some kind of heroic Arcane Ability!* Ripp thought, his mind racing with the possibilities. He hoped to one day gain something similar when he got old enough to gain Levels.

Then the stranger let out a loud *Ha!* and turned to glare up at the centipede-like monstrosity that had assailed him.

"Lesson one," the stranger shouted. "*Never* try to sucker-punch a man who knows how to take a hit."

He shook his head and then grasped the ledge with both hands, heaving himself up onto the roof again.

"Lesson two," he continued, standing up as the monster regarded him curiously. "Don't dunk on a dude with methods to counteract falling."

He cracked his knuckles and raised a strange, double-bladed knife thing, using one of the tips to point right back at the oomukade.

"That's right, motherfucker," he said, mistaking the monster's hesitation for shock. "I got *features*—and I kinda know how to use 'em!"

The monster that had hit him before took another swipe, but the stranger saw it coming and darted out of the way. However, the oomukade's follow-up blow caught him in the top of the head, knocking the stranger back a few paces. He rubbed his head with a loud *Ow!* and took another few steps back. Then the big, green rapscallion suddenly went still. His voice grew louder and more authoritative as Ripp noticed something in the air had changed. The boy behind the window wasn't sure, but he thought that the man was activating another Ability of some kind. It reminded him of when his mother used *Revolving Gate* to stop him and his sister from running away from their chores. However, in this instance, the man's body began to morph. His muscles bulked, growing more defined. Even from this distance, Ripp could see the veins under his skin bulging, straining to escape from his fleshy body. His entire form transmogrified, if only in size and muscle mass, becoming more intimidating to behold—to the boy.

"Three," the stranger bellowed, his voice taking on a dark, intimidating tone that made Ripp frightened. "I'm getting fuckin' *pissed*."

He growled, which turned into a roar, and the boy watched as the man's body flashed for a moment with red-hot light that sprang from him like a wave of heat. Ripp took an unconscious step backward. As he did, he bumped right into something soft and turned to look behind him to see his father. Big Quincy was standing stock-still in the middle of his room, staring wide-eyed at the scene unfolding outside his youngest child's window. Ripp looked back to the roof and saw the stranger suddenly bolt toward the monster, swinging his double-bladed weapon like a farmer slicing wheat with a sickle. The edge connected, cutting deep into the oomukade's leg, and the monster screeched with pain and anger. Then it set to its revenge and began pummeling the stranger with strikes from its many *other* legs.

The stranger fought back, sliding until he was once more at the edge of the roof. Then he hurled his weapon through the air, cutting through one of the monster's legs as it passed by and arced off into the night.

*That seems bad*, Ripp thought. The stranger drew something out of his bag—a dented skullcap helmet. But instead of placing it on his head, the man slid it over his clenched fist and launched forward, connecting his encased punch against the segmented body of the oomukade.

Ripp felt his father's strong hands grab him around the shoulders.

"Rippelyn," Big Quincy said, his tone as grim as a gravestone. "We need to go, lad. We've a need to get somewhere safe."

"But, Father," Ripp started indignantly, "I want to see!" He pointed to the window where the battle was still unfolding.

His father shouted and wrapped his arms around the boy just as the window they'd been staring out of exploded in a shower of wood and dust. Ripp felt himself hit the ground, though softened by his father's body. It took only a moment for him to get his wits together to see what had happened. From the floor Ripp could see the towering specter of the stranger, standing back up after being hurled directly into his room. The boy couldn't make any sound, only watch in frozen fear and fascination as the stranger coughed, blood spattering against his bedsheets.

*That's going to need* two *washes,* Ripp thought absently.

The stranger's back was to them as he stared out through the newly created fissure in Ripp's bedroom wall. The boy heard a whoosh of wind and watched as the double-bladed weapon spiraled through the opening and slapped right into the stranger's open hand.

"Amazing," Ripp muttered quietly, the only noise he was able to eke out as the quiet of the moment fell on him, heavy and awe-inspiring. The stranger roared, shaking the walls of his bedroom, and Ripp felt his father's embrace tighten around him as Big Quincy lifted his son from the floor and began speeding away.

*I want to see!* Ripp thought, but his father was much bigger and stronger and whisked him toward the doorway and into the hall. The last thing Ripp saw before they rounded the corner was the monster from the roof forcing its way into the hole in his bedroom wall as the stranger roared once more and vaulted forward.

*I can't wait to tell Tiffy and Pomondous about* this!

# CHAPTER THREE

# ALLEY-OOPSIE

I stood up. Then I coughed out a gob of bloody phlegm and wiped my mouth.

**Warning!**
**You have contributed to the TSD of Tallrock! Your actions, whether intentional or otherwise, have caused the settlement to incur [ 0.045 ]% more destructive damage!**
*Total Settlement Destruction: 1.3%*
*Remaining oomukade [70 / 70]*
*Percent vanquished: 0%*

*Shit!*

Not only were other people allowing the town to get an unsolicited dick-walloping, but I'd been careless enough to get myself involved in contributing. After narrowly avoiding tumbling off the roof by smashing my *oh-shit* ability, Calden's Hang Time, I'd been very rudely Spartan-kicked through a wall by this *oompa loompa* or whatever the hell it was called. Now my anger was an unbridled, seething squall. It was odd; though my Primal Rage was meant to be a clouded, maddening express train on a single track of rampage, I felt more inner calm and purpose than I typically did. In fact, it seemed like every time the effect had activated, my mind could work more clearly, as if the focus of the tyrant fury was where I truly belonged. It had to be a feature of the Ability, I imagined. Still, as I stood in front of the Cronenberg centipede, huffing in a room full of wood shavings and sawdust, I was in my element.

I released a scream of joyous aggression and barreled toward the beast. It screeched in reply, daring to test its might against *me*, devastation personified.

I was the avatar of brutality, the scion of bloodshed. I would crash against this monster like a plague of flaming—

I hit the ground again as the creature moved its entire middle section out of the path of my strike and hit me with two legs at once. I bounced a little and rolled to my side, guessing that the creature would follow up with another attack. The floorboards crunched as my prediction turned out to be accurate and two more legs pierced the ground where I'd been.

*So, they've got stabbies on their bashies. Good.*

There was a bed near me that looked like it belonged to the kid from the window, based on its size. Normally, I might've worried I'd smeared the boy into mush when I was hurled indoors, but my Primal Rage didn't spare any thought for that at the moment. He was a whisper of a worry as I grabbed a wooden leg of the bed with my un-helmeted hand and heaved myself up. The monster screeched and tried to strike at me again, but I punched the leg with Berg's skullcap and heard a crunch and a wail. I delighted in the feeling. Then I grabbed the bed by the headboard and wrenched it up. I heard a few springy *thwacks* as the centipede attempted to get at me, but my new slumber shield had protected me from the onslaught.

*Coming. Soon. Hurry. Coming.*

I was only partially paying attention as faint voices entered my mind. A few more dull strikes hit the mattress, and then I felt a stab of pain in my side as one of the barbed limbs found its way around my barrier and buried itself in my flank. However, the Primal Rage transformed what would normally have been a potentially debilitating blow into a symphony of searing euphoria, and I felt my lips twist into a cruel smile.

*Fucking bring it!*

I dropped the helmet from my mitt and grasped both sides of the frame before charging forward, wielding the bed like a battering ram. I crashed against the monster with all the force I could muster and felt it yield instantly. I kept going. On the other side of the barricade, the monster slid backward, screeching with anger. But I wasn't done. I pulled back for just a second—long enough for the thing to become unbalanced—and then I slammed forward again, thrusting the beast to the wall and out the hole it had used me to create.

*Time to go night-night!*

Then I fell.

With the child-sized bed between us, I rode the monster down as we fell to the cobblestones below. A moment later, I crashed against the underside of the frame as the beast beneath connected with the hard ground. It had begun to screech but was overwhelmed by a loud *splat*—announcing its body had popped like a zit. Bug juice splattered my sides as the monster's gore exploded everywhere.

*Total Settlement Destruction:* 1.3%
*Remaining oomukade [67 / 70]*
*Percent vanquished:* 4.3%

*Huh. Two more are dead. Looks like the town is finally fighting back. Bully for us.*

I didn't wait. I was up in an instant, knowing I didn't have long before my high-octane anger would fade. I was a lion, roaring with its fresh triumphant kill, and only mildly aware of the notification announcing its death and the amount of experience I'd stacked. I glanced up, seeing that the creature's three ugly sisters were converging on me from up high. At the end of the alley, two more suddenly appeared, scurrying down either side along the outside of the buildings.

*Shit-fuck!*

That was when Primal Rage dispersed and the true magnitude of the situation hit me like five AM diarrhea after an all-nighter pounding pizza rolls and energy drinks.

*There are too many, and they're coming way too fast.*

The monsters closed in, and I activated my trump card—Blackout Warchant. The Ability would render most arcane effects functionally useless for a brief window, allowing me a few extra moments to knuckle-drop my foes into kingdom come. Unfortunately, if there was nothing magical in front of me, it had no effect. That was how I learned that these . . . umamis? Ummagumma? Nevermind. *They* had no magic affecting them. They just kept on truckin', unresponsive to my incredibly baller anti-enchantment howl. So, I hurled my haladie at the three above and backpedaled, seeking some avenue of freedom. I needed a better vantage point so I could bring the pain on these disgusting super larvae, but this alleyway was a straight shot down either side to the streets beyond.

*Ugh.*

The haladie pinwheeled away, missing one of the oomies by inches, and I had to hope I'd get one of them on the reach-around. I hated to do a runner, but I needed to even the odds. So, despite my extreme aversion to anything even remotely resembling cowardice, I booked it as fast as I could to the end of the alley, hoping I could think of something along the way that would give me the edge in this confrontation.

I got about ten feet before one of the monsters crashed to the ground in front of me, screeching from its kabuki-mask-like face.

"Ew, fuck! That's gross as shit!"

I didn't stop. I saw a spot to the creature's right that looked appropriate, so I tried to bypass it by parkouring up the wall and to the other side.

"Alley-oop!" I shouted smugly, leaping into the air to press off the wall with my foot and hop through the opening. But my bare foot immediately slipped, and I slammed forward hard, smashing my head against the building and collapsing to the cobblestones in a heap.

"Shit!" I groaned. "What the fuck? It's an alley-oop! It should work *in an alley!*"

The monster towered over me, releasing horrendous sounds from its double-stacked, fang-filled maw. I scrambled backward, my head pounding, feeling trapped. From the other side of me, the four remaining oomies clattered into view. I'd been wrong a moment before. *Now* I was trapped.

*PING. PING. PING. PING.*

The sound of rubbery recoil dropped into my awareness like a care package of glee. Now that I wasn't an inferno of anger, I could recall hearing the voices earlier that had entered my mind. My heart swelled.

"Well, ladies," I said loudly, wanting to leave a good impression. "Looks like you're about to learn lesson four: don't—"

*PING. PING. PING. PING. PING. PING.*

Four pink-white pearls shot over the head of the monster blocking my initial exit and literally sprang into action. Like a wildly malfunctioning pinball machine, the bouncy orbs ricocheted from the ground and off the walls and struck four of the monsters before rebounding and landing around me in a protective circle.

I glanced down, my chest swelling with pride. Each orb was actually a spherical egg creature, roughly a foot tall, with glowing red eyes and large, grinning mouths full of uncomfortably long teeth. They chittered, their stance on this one-sided fight clear. I had to imagine they seemed as incomprehensibly vicious to the centipede monstrosities as they'd been to me when I'd first encountered them in the Crypt only days ago. They were possessed roe, and they were my homies.

*Jumpy, Clucky, Slappy, Mortimer,* I said to them mentally, *that was awesome! But remember, guys—always wait 'til I finish my one-liners before launching in to attack. It'll make your arrival more impactful. Plus, it's like holding in a sneeze, otherwise.*

*Sorry. Sorry. Apologies. Sorry,* they responded.

*It's alright,* I continued. *I can deal with a bit of zippy-comeback blue balls as long as we get out of here alive. We'll workshop it.*

The monsters surrounding us seemed to hesitate, unsure what to make of this new development.

*You guys ready to do what we practiced?* I asked the egg creatures. Rather than a verbalized response, I just *felt* them all agree with me. It had to be due to the fact that I shared a lifeforce with them from my reincarnation, but it was still bizarre—and, honestly, pretty fucking cool.

*Remember,* I continued, *no sticky.*

*Yes. Yes. Yeah. Yup.*

I stood up fully, suddenly wondering why my haladie hadn't returned to me yet.

*Aw, man. Did it get stuck in the branches of a tree again?*

I pushed the thought out of my mind and reached into my pack, removing a small silver-lined wooden shield. I grasped the handle and raised it up in a warding gesture, facing off against the monster standing solo on its side of the battle lines.

"Now!" I shouted, and darted right at the centipede. At the same time, I heard the bouncy *pings* as my egg allies launched into their own assault. The sound was slow at first, like a few flutter kicks on a bass drum, but even before I reached my foe, I heard a sound like a machine gun firing dodgeballs at a high velocity. I didn't have to look. Yesterday, the egg boys and I had discussed some arguably dumb-as-fuck maneuvers I had in mind. They'd been *more* than a little game, almost in a frenzy of excitement at the prospect of being useful in combat. It seemed like they were deploying one of them right then with what I could only assume was a moderate level of expertise.

I hit the summa cum laude with the Guardian buckler and, since my buddy, the haladie, hadn't returned yet, used one of the only other actual weapons I had available to wield: my paring knife. The dull, rusty blade scraped against the flesh of the monster with all the ease of trying to pierce a tank with a toothpick. It slid away, and the beast was unscathed.

"God fucking dipswitch!" I shouted.

At least my buckler had administered a bit of force damage with my swing—but *bit* was being generous. These things must have been made of Kevlar and rhino hide, because other than my enchanted double knife, nothing seemed to hurt them much. Then I remembered self-torpedoing the one into the ground a moment ago and smiled.

*Oh, yeah,* I thought. *That too.*

However, my current prospects did not seem to be very cash money. Plus— the monster wasn't interested in just taking its licks passive-aggressively. Nope, these guys were fighting back—aggressive-aggressively. I struck as the oomie tried to lash out at me, connecting and crunching a leg with the small shield before batting away another. Yet still, some of the creature's attacks were getting through my unbelievably perfect barrier, and it was more than just pinpricks.

Those barbed ends on their limbs hurt like a motherfucker, and each time they connected, the nonconsensual body piercings sent a shiver of pain all the way through me. A few more bops and stabs, and I had to leap backward to stop the onslaught of ouchie carnage. I was bloody and bruised, and I'd hardly made a dent in this dumb son of bitch. I turned to look at how my four captains were faring—and found that it was a lot better than me.

One of the moves I'd devised earlier was being executed with no small amount of badass pluck: Jumpy, Clucky, Slappy, and Mortimer were ricocheting from wall to ground to gigantic monster and back, but at a speed that was nearly impossible to follow. They circled through the air and around each other in a perfect display of synchronicity that reminded me of motorcycle cage riders at a circus performing the Globe of Death. I saw a splash of dark blood and finally realized that my companions weren't just *following* my "foster chaos" strategy—they'd *improved* it. On each pass, the eggs were ripping into the oomies with their long, dagger-like fangs. Sections of monster flesh lay open like display meat at a deli counter, and it was driving their opponents crazy with rage.

The huge bug monsters couldn't move forward, because the bouncing inertia of the roe kept rebuffing them. And they couldn't counterattack, because each time they tried, they got a hot, sloppy eggload of evisceration from the tooth tornado. All the centipedes seemed capable of doing was gnashing their awful, ghostly humanoid faces in pain and frustration. I watched as one tried to snatch Slappy out of the air and received a missing stump in response.

I cheered.

I realized that I'd not been paying close enough attention before: all four of the oomies were missing at least one leg, and most were missing several. I knew they had plenty to spare, but it was breathtaking to see them literally succumbing to death by a thousand cuts from my little pink pals. They looked like really terrible chainsaw jugglers.

A screech behind me caught me by surprise, and I pivoted just in time to see that the overgrown insect I'd been tangling with was barreling down on me. I tried again to parkour the wall and this time was able to stick the landing and shove off into the air. But I wasn't as slick as I thought, because the monster caught me mid-leap and slammed me into the ground.

My Health bar flashed, and I found it was around the halfway mark now.

*Dammit, I can't keep this up for long! I gotta do something quick—but it also has to look cool!*

As much as I was growing to like the zany, zigzaggy zygotes—I couldn't let them outshine me. I was sort of like their boss and needed to lead by example. But how? The monster was above me, and all I could focus on was its disgusting, pale face as it loomed closer—perhaps to bite my nose in half. Eyeless black sockets seemed to peer into my soul, and its rows of fangs dripped with saliva. I gulped back the sensation of vomit. I wasn't scared, just a bit annoyed. How the hell was I supposed to take one of these things out without a magic weapon or really high fall? My paring knife had been knocked out of my hand and was lying somewhere in the alley. All I had were the buckler and my bare hands . . .

*Fuck it.*

The porcelain monster mask launched forward, aiming for my delicious face. I yanked the Guardian's Buckler up and smashed it right into its open mouth and then slammed the thumb and index finger of my free hand into its eye sockets. I struck and pierced something soft and fleshy just as the creature released a muffled screech. It reared back and away suddenly, taking the buckler with it.

"Aw, piss!" I shouted. Then I looked down at my fingers, seeing an oily, black residue had stained them. The goop was a little sticky, and I noticed a long, thin trail of inky snot connecting my hand to the white face of the oomie like a slice of pizza in one of those old Domino's commercials.

"Gah!" I shouted, and began shaking my digits with reckless abandon to free myself of the mess. I didn't do much but break the thin membrane bridge so I scraped what I could off my fingers on the cobblestones and stood. Instantly, I was hit in the back by something small and springy, and shuffled forward at the force. Slappy sprang into view, bouncing against the stone and glaring up at me. I got the sense from him that I'd messed up his sick moves.

"Sorry," I said quickly, then jabbed a finger behind me. "Try again. I don't have time to console you."

He made the roe equivalent of a sigh and leaped away, disappearing from my view. I rushed forward, intent on continuing my assault on the centipede I'd . . . blinded? Though I wasn't sure if it counted if they didn't have eyes to begin with. Regardless, I caught up to it as it was still thrashing and tried once more to do my cool-ass acrobat leap. I kicked off from the wall and launched myself into the air right at the monster. I grasped the edge of the Guardian's Buckler and tried to yank it free with the weight of gravity. But this thing had a cast-iron clench on my shield, and instead, I was left dangling from its mouth—refusing to let go as well. I tightened my grip and set both bare feet on its midsection, pulling hard to dislodge the buckler from its maw.

I heard a crack and saw a shower of razor teeth as I succeeded in freeing the shield, but only had a moment to enjoy my victory as I crashed against the ground. My body reflexively turned it into a backward roll over one shoulder, which counteracted a lot of the damage I'd have likely sustained. It still wasn't graceful, and I completed my roll by landing hard on my knee and skinning it.

"UU-AGH!" I shrieked.

Man, no matter how many times you get stabbed, burned, sliced, or pierced—few things still hurt as bad as surface-level flesh wounds.

Fortunately, I was in a much better situation than the monster. I only had a boo-boo on my leg knuckle; *he* had eye sockets full of orc fingernails and a bunch of broken teeth. But the thrashing continued, so I knew he had a bit of fight left in 'im.

"Fine by me," I declared to no one, and raced forward, raising the shield. "The bigger they are, the harder they—"

I was interrupted by a *swishing* as something metallic separated every single leg on the monster's left side from its body. I slid to a stop as I saw the glint of a squarish blade, and then a fraction of a second later, the same weapon bit into the torso region of the oomie as it screeched bloody murder. There were several more chops before the beast finally slumped and died, crashing to the ground in a huge heap.

An imposing figure swaggered into view. She was tall, encased in dented silver armor and hefting the weapon she'd used to fell the centipede: a simple woodcutter's ax. Her face was unhelmeted—typical—so it was easy to see who it was even if I hadn't recognized her fully bolstered Guardian outfit. Brown skin, short black hair, and blue eyes that seemed to almost *glow* in the darkness and danced with an inner light as if she was the only one clued in to some private joke. It was one of my party members. Frida.

"Ach, Loon!" she said in her Scottish-ish burr as she moved forward, raising the ax. Her eyes darted from my face to the scene of carnage being gradually implemented behind me. "Fig'ered ye'd be the 'un over here makin' a clatter. Takin' yoor time t' draw out enjoyment?"

"Frida!" I shouted, my grin unhideable. "About time you showed up! I was holding them off 'til you got here because I'm a goddamn *gentleman*—you're welcome, by the way. I knew you'd be ten kinds of pissed if I took all the kills!"

I used the buckler to indicate her ax.

"Where'd you find *that*?" She'd destroyed her original, super baller-ass head-trimmer in the fight with Frey.

She shrugged.

"Nicked it. Proud o' me?"

I raised an eyebrow and then gestured for her to hold it up so I could scan it. Then I activated Eye of the Saboteur and watched the details pour in.

**Ecliptic**
- **Rarity: Unique**
- **Item Class: One-Handed/Two-Handed Weapon**
- **Durability: 141/610**

- Weight: 2.1 lbs.
- Damage: 81–93 Chopping
- Bonuses:
  - x2 Damage Versus Solar Arcana
  - x2 Damage Versus Lunar Arcana

*Oh, you're looking for an ax? Well, you've stumbled upon something much more extraordinary! Bask in awe, my precious little piglet. This unassuming piece of wood and steel ain't just a tool for chopping logs; it's a weapon of mass destruction against those foolish enough to wield the arcane forces of solar and lunar.*

*Forged by a blacksmith with a grudge, Ecliptic has the ability to deal twice as much damage against any Arcana of those kinds. Go ahead and wield it if you dare. Just don't come crying to me when you can't handle the power!*

*The eversteel blade is sharp as a razor, and the luxurious handle is made of dragoneye ashwood—sturdy enough to withstand the most vise-fisted dunderhead. But the true magic lies in the engravings of a sun and moon on its blade, a subtle hint at its true power. Bet you missed that, though, didn't you?*

*So, grab hold and let the hacking begin!*

*Yikes. I forgot how much more smug and wordy the descriptions are now with Eye of the Saboteur.*

If I'd put a hand on the Ecliptic—or any body part, really—Eye of the Saboteur would have given me even *more* information, but I didn't really need to see its weakness or material components, so it would be a mystery for now. I wasn't sure what exactly Solar and Lunar Arcana were, but I figured Frida would probably have a good understanding—why wield it, after all, if you didn't grasp its properties? I mean, someone would have to be really *stupid* to do something like that, right? It also seemed to average nearly four times as much damage as my haladie, if I remembered correctly. Fortunately, despite not currently having the weapon in my clutches, Eye of the Beholder had an adorable little function embedded within its sultry depths that allowed me to store the details of items I'd scanned like a fucked-up, medieval Pokedex.

So, just to be sure, I glanced at my own double-bladed butchery-bequeather's information and found, to my surprise, I was mistaken.

**Enchanted Haladie**
- **Rarity: Uncommon [Exotic]**
- **Item Class: Throwing Weapon**
- **Durability: 99/200**
- **Weight: 1.0 lbs.**

- **Damage: 55–62 Piercing / 55–60 Slashing**
- **Bonuses:**
  - ○ **+8 versus Suskin**
  - ○ **Return**

*The Enchanted Haladie returns to the user who has bonded with it when thrown.*

**???**

*A weapon discovered on a corpse! Look at you go, grave robber, you! This double-bladed throwing dagger is the perfect accessory for those who want to do a bit of wet work from a distance! You'll look very intimidating, hurling this bad boy from the shadows. You know, where no one can see how scared you are!*

*THIS ITEM CAN BE UPGRADED WITH ADDITIONAL ENCHANTMENTS.*

*Well, god damn. I was* way *off.*

I coulda sworn it was only rocking somewhere in the high twenties or low thirties for damage, but apparently, it was almost up to snuff with Frida's new toy. But that couldn't be right, could it? There's no way I'd been so far away from the mark on how strong it was. Plus, I distinctly recalled that it had originally only offered a plus-one to whatever the hell Suskin was, and now it was *eight?* In fact, the only sections of the haladie I could see that might *not* have changed were the name and the suspiciously accusatory description toe-tagging it.

*Huh. How about that? Curiouser and curiouser.*

I looked it over again, scowling at each word as if they'd suddenly spring up and start rearranging themselves. Was the mention of "upgrading" the culprit? I wasn't sure what that entailed, despite the vague "enchantments" mention at the end. Had it somehow been upgraded when I wasn't paying attention? A definite possibility, considering my track record with attentiveness. Well, that was *neat.*

I remembered I was in the middle of a conversation and quickly got my shit together, adopting a frown and pretending to be disappointed.

"You know how much I abhor the idea of wanton criminality, Frida. Some-one probably needs that to, like . . . I dunno—chop down a tree or something?"

"Looks like ah'm doin' m'own part, then. You know, saving the river forests and all."

"You know it's *rain* forests, Frida," I sighed. "And I never should have told you about environmentalists from my world."

"Well, ye did, and ah'm a fan," she stated as if to end the discussion. "Now, then. What sort o' mess have ye shackled me to?"

"Oh, just some monsters," I said casually. "The boys are taking care of 'em, though, so don't worry—we can keep quipping at each other."

"Nay," she said, turning her gaze fully away from me toward the remaining foes. "Your banter's right shite. *This* seems much more interesting. Oh—"

She paused, looking down at her belt and reaching for something.

"Almost forgot," she continued. "Found this for ye."

She held up the double blades of my haladie and then lofted it in my direction. I caught it and smirked.

"Thanks! Where was it?"

She shrugged.

"Stuck under a chimney cap."

"Dammit," I whined, looking dejectedly at the weapon and directing my next statement to it. "You gotta stop embarrassing me like this, dude. People are going to start making fun of me."

I looked up at Frida then, seeing her raised eyebrow.

"What? You gotta scold your items if they act disobediently," I said. "Jeez, have you ever even *been* to a magical world before?"

She snorted.

"Besides, I need it to work well with me if I ever hope to become big and strong like you and take 'em down one-hitter-quitter-style."

"Well, ye'd prob'ly have a better go o' et if you played to yoor strengths."

"Whatcha mean?"

"Yoor always leapin' an' bashin' when ye *should* be skulkin' and stabbin.' Ye said ye had a bit o' sneak on ye, so use et."

I ignored her comment. Instead, I nodded toward the remaining monsters still being punked out by the eggs. "I take the right, you take the left?"

"Nay," she said again with a grin, turning back to the fight and leveling her ax. "How 'bout *ah* take 'em all out and you see if'n you can get to any before ah cover the walls in their vile guts?"

# CHAPTER FOUR

# VOLLEY BALLS

*Total Settlement Destruction: 8.5%*
*Remaining oomukade [51 / 70]*
*Percent vanquished: 27.14%*

**W**ith Frida's help, the fight was over almost instantly. She was Level Sixteen, and I couldn't hold a candle to that—yet. So, after the choppy-death variety show was finished, she, the egg boys, and I made a hasty path toward the healing house, which was the whole reason Frida had grabbed me in the first place. It was being overrun, she'd told me, what with a bunch of juicy injured folk inside for the monsters to nibble on. The oomukade (I'd finally remembered) seemed to think it would be an easy meal, and they were likely spot-on. Unfortunately, our companion and party leader Jes, was still not one hundred percent hunky-dory and trapped inside the building. Despite her cavalier exterior and suspiciously sexy blood lust, Frida was a caring individual, concerned about the elf. She'd known him for hundreds of years—mostly on account of being trapped in the dungeon in a time dilation for that long—but had definitely been traveling with him for a perceivable while beforehand. They were friends and siblings-in-arms. She didn't say it out loud, but I knew she was really worried about his recovery, and him getting eaten by a bevy of big bedbugs wouldn't help matters.

We rounded the corner, spilling out into the street where pure, unfettered anarchy was taking place. It was an odd juxtaposition to the cozy environment Tallrock usually offered, with its warm, amber lanterns arrayed along the paths. Instead, droves of townsfolk were running and screaming, with gigantic centipede monsters trailing along horrifyingly in their wake. Some of the people were fighting back, but it didn't seem like there were many in the vicinity with the necessary capabilities to fend them off for long.

As we dashed forward, I threw my haladie at one of the oomukade chasing a family of tiny gnome-like individuals, buzz-sawing through the top of a leg and forcing it to wheel in my direction. When it got close enough, Frida chopped it down with a few swings and left it to die in the street. The roe, ever my constant companions, were taking the rear and engaging any monsters that got too close to our backs. We ran in single file, with me in the lead, hurling my weapon with a gleeful ferocity usually reserved for deranged psychopaths. We were a death parade of punishment and pain, killing any monsters that had the misfortune of crossing us—or leaving them crippled enough for others to finish them off. At Level Ten, I wasn't much of a powerhouse at the moment, but I more than made up for it with my sassy demeanor and lawnmower-bladed taunting, luring the beasts close enough that the others could do the bulk of the dirty work.

I liked to imagine that this scene would have been excellent over the soundtrack of Gaerea's *Mirage* album. In fact, right at that moment, I was envisioning the frenetic guitars and explosive double bass of their track "Salve" blasting through the town as I clipped another oomukade with my haladie, watching as the weapon arced and sliced another bug monster vertically through the creepy-ass face as it returned to my beefy fist. The beast slumped and was dead before it hit the ground.

**Author's Note: How about y'all go ahead and bring that track up right now and get down to some hot, nasty riffage?**

Then, right when I was turning back to brag about my dope-ass maneuver, my Experience notification popped up, announcing my kill. Unfortunately, before it could minimize, there was just enough time for another of the creatures to try and sneak-attack me—like it had somehow known—and caught me unawares before I could react from the distraction. It came flying from within my fucking blind spot. I brought the haladie up to block as much of the blow as I could, but just before it connected, I heard Frida scream out some phrase, and the oomukade suddenly jerked backward in the air, a silvery band of magic around its upper torso—right behind its face. It looked like it was floating for half a moment before, all at once, it was yanked down, slamming its back against the ground. The monster shrieked and began a fruitless attempt of snapping at the arcane leash to release itself. Then Frida was on it, chopping away until it was nothing but pork knuckles.

When her spontaneous meat-merchant impression was through, she rested her ax against its . . . well, not *corpse*, exactly, but, yeah—its bits—and turned her face up to me. Her smile was radiant, and even covered with blood spray—or maybe *especially* covered in it—she really knew how to light up a room. Or, in this case, a cobblestoned road.

"Hey there, Loon," she said. "Worried ah'd be a step behind and ye'd have te start wearin' fash'nable masks te cover ye maimery."

"Nope," I said, breathing heavily—more out of relief than any exertion on my part. "No . . . you, as always . . . delivered a surprising attack . . . with perfect . . . dramatic . . . timing. What was . . . that?"

"Aw, nothin' te be bleedin' yer heart over," she said, still beaming. "Just one o' the new tricks ah picked up when ah Leveled. They're both situational, but growin' on me. Ye like it?"

"Yeah . . ." I breathed, my heart still thundering. "It was . . . *super dope*. Did I hear . . . you right? Did you shout . . . Slipknot . . . Sepultura?"

"Ye mostly got et," she said, nodding at the silver. "Et's called 'Slipknot Sepulcher.' Glad te find out et works on these bastards—wasn't all sure, on account o' them being neckless an' all. Pounds through a shite-barrel's worth of Arcana, but et's a grand once-in-a-while treat. Fig'ered ah'd snatch up the Spell while ah could. Ah was a bit of a lack without a Snare."

It had been hard to make out while I was reacting to my assassination attempt, but it had *definitely* sounded like she'd cried out the names of two badass metal monsters beforehand. I really shouldn't have been surprised by what the Spell was called, but I was. I mean, I knew what a slipknot was, of course—especially the one I was more familiar with. One was a type of hangman's noose. At least, I thought so. The other was, naturally, an all-around ass-beating Midwestern metal band—AKA, the hardest thing to hit Iowa since the day the music died. Some people called them nu metal, but I think *those* people were probably missing their eardrums. Not to mention brain cells and teeth. Still, I wasn't one hundred percent on what *sepulcher* meant.

Now that I was thinking about it, I didn't think I knew what Sepultura meant, either. I mean, I knew it was probably something in . . . What language do they speak in Brazil? Brazilian? That sounds right. Anyway, their prefix was the same, so I had no doubt that it directly translated to *godlike groove-thrash*. Ultimately, it didn't matter. Frida had said it was a snare, so, in all likelihood, it probably meant "snare."

"'*S'nare-y* a day goes by that you don't do something that impresses me," I said to Frida, winking as I butchered any hope of her ever finding me cool with that world-class pun.

To my surprise, she chuckled.

"Yoor gettin' *funnier*," she said.

"Yeah, it's a new thing I'm testing out," I said.

"Keep et up," Frida said. "Ah like a man that can make me laugh."

*I vow at this very moment to never say anything serious ever again.*

We wrapped up the mayhem in that spot and set off again at a run, duplicating our previous efforts as we went along. However, it wasn't long before I saw something off: there was an explosion of light in the sky. I actually slid to a stop for a moment, causing Frida to collide with my back.

"Ach, Loon!" she shouted, annoyed. "Now's nae the time for a breather. We've gotta beat to the healer's."

"Who the hell is that?!" I exclaimed, gesturing at the sky. A human-shaped fire was soaring above the rooftops, sending targeted blasts of flame down to connect with the monsters' bodies, incinerating most on contact.

"Dunno," Frida said, her tone filled with wonder. "She's strong, though."

"You can tell that's a girl?" I asked, baffled.

"Nae a girl," Frida corrected. "A *woman*. And o' course! She's nae loudly braggin' 'bout her kills or tryin' te make a show of et, is she?"

"What are you talking about?" I asked, starting to run again. "They're literally a flaming torch *flying* through the sky shooting fireballs! That is the precise definition of a show. Plus, you're a lady type, and you're *always* boasting about your kills!"

"Ah donnae boast!" Frida returned with a wink. "Ah just want te make sure yer payin' attention to me."

I swallowed my response and darted down another alleyway that was *probably* a shortcut to the mending house.

*Whoever that person was, they're seriously strong. The power of flight and napalm death? That's somebody I've gotta meet . . . from a distance.*

I pushed the humanoid military drone from my thoughts and focused on navigating through the next round of streets. We killed a few more centipede nightmares, rescuing a few more townsfolk as a result, and finally reached the avenue leading to the healer's. I knew that Stinky was likely there, as Frida had briefly mentioned he'd offered to hold off the attack while she went to find me—which was not exactly in character for him. It didn't matter, though. If there were a healthy horde of these things exacting fucky nonsense on the sick and wounded, I'd have a few words for them. Mainly *fuck off* and *die*.

Before I could even catch a glimpse of our end zone, I knew exactly where it was. There were at least ten of the buzzkill asshole bugs swarming the streets, combating something I couldn't see. I kicked it into high gear, and when I was within about a hundred yards—I think—I launched my haladie as a preemptive strike and turned back to Frida. The Guardian was barreling along behind me, her eyes locked on the scene ahead. I nodded at the buildings.

"You go ahead; I'm going to try something!" I shouted, then looked to the roe. "Jumpy, Clucky, Slappy, Mortimer: follow Frida and keep her safe!"

Frida nodded and then hit a burst of speed I didn't know she was capable of, zipping right by me and rushing toward the fray outside the healer's place of business. The roe bounced after her, not as quick but seemingly determined to make good on my orders. I, however, was going to take the scenic route.

I dashed off to the right, aiming myself at a pleasant little building with an expanse of ivy climbing up the outside of the wall, and, without slowing down, leaped into the air and snatched the first leafy vine I could. It broke almost immediately, but I was already climbing, wrenching myself upward toward the roof, digging my bare toes into any crevice I could find. It took a little longer than I was anticipating, but eventually, I made it up to the overhanging slate acting as shingles and pulled myself up. I rolled once as I cleared the edge and was up and running again. The haladie returned to me, and I urgently stuffed it into the waistband of my kilt—lamenting again that I hadn't yet found a Batman-esque utility belt. I reached the end of the roof and jumped, grasping a handful of beautiful stone as I made it to the next building and hauled my ass up again, continuing my sprint.

After a few more of those beautiful moves, I was right where I needed to be: directly above the undulating horrors wreaking havoc on the outside of the mending house. From this vantage point, I could see that at least a few of the bastards had managed to gain entry through a hole in the wall they'd *definitely* made.

Ignoring that for the moment, I peered over to see what all the hubbub was about.

Below, I could see Frida striking out wildly with the ax, tangling with three of the beasts at once. She dove out of the way as one swiped at her, and landed hard on the ground on her back. Another tried to pin her down with its legs, but she moved too quickly and slammed the ax head right into its ghostly face. She used the momentum of it trying to retreat from her wound and allowed it to pick her up off the ground. Then she wrenched the ax loose by way of a well-placed leveraging boot, and blocked a bite attack with the handle of her weapon. She shoved back, and the oomukade recoiled, tearing the ax from her grasp. That was when Slappy hit the creature in the face with his body, causing it to send the ax clattering to the cobblestones. Frida spun, ducked down, snatched the ax up from the ground, and was back in the fight in an instant.

Curiously, I couldn't see Stinky—which fucking figured—but I could see another individual battling it out with some of the centipedes. A small blue-skinned creature in a flowing robe of electric green was spinning around, dodging attack after attack from the oomukade. At first, I'd thought it was a child, based on its size, until I noticed a fluffy orange goatee adorning his face. I couldn't make out any other physical features, but I didn't really need to to appreciate his dazzling display of skills. He whirled and twirled, deftly avoiding any of the humongous bug monsters' strikes as the creatures screeched in anger. Then he performed a beautiful—really the only word to describe it—flip and landed on one of their heads. His tiny blue fingers formed several Naruto-looking hand seals, and a brilliant, glowing arcane symbol appeared in the air. The symbol flashed and the little blue man swiped his palm down onto the oomukade's dome piece. Its whole body lit up like a hillbilly bottle rocket and exploded with a level of force I'd reserve only for the mightiest of Chipotle toilets.

Chunks flew everywhere, including the roof I was currently standing on, and I brought up the Guardian's Buckler to keep the goo away from my face. It didn't save the rest of me, though. I was absolutely covered in gore and centipede ichor as the disgusting deluge of the oomukade's insides splattered my outsides.

"Ugh!" I groaned, and tried to shake myself like a dog to remove the muck, but it wasn't very successful. I moved back to try to find the little blue terrorist, but all I could see was chaos.

*Time to do this.*

I chose my target: a cluster of oomukade not far from the ledge that were converging on Clucky and Mortimer. The roe had been backed into a corner and were keeping the monsters from advancing on them by sheer force of their bounce.

*Perfect.*

I placed the shield back in my pack and then reached down and grabbed a slate shingle from the edge of the roof in each hand. Then I opened my menu to double-check that I hadn't misunderstood anything about my newest Ability.

**Pernicious Volley**
*Trading accuracy for sheer, raw power, you can increase the damage you output with all manner of projectiles. For [8] seconds, Pernicious Volley allows you to target multiple foes and unleash untold aerial hell upon them with the chance to cultivate exponential damage with each successful strike. However, trier beware: this caterwaul bombardment packs a doozy of a punch to your Stamina and will exhaust [10] points per [1] second. The outcome for efficiency is Strength quotient + Throwing Weapons Skill.*

*Caveat: If the user chooses a nontraditional weapon, then the Throwing Weapons Skill will be substituted with the Improvised Weapons Skill. This is*

*the perfect Ability for those who value a less-measured approach or just want
to see what happens when you decide to sow a little chaos.*

*Yup. Just what I thought.*

I'd hit Level Ten after my fight in the dungeon but had waited until we were
on the road to actually look at what I'd earned to find that I'd been gifted this
wonderful little bliss feature. It was perfect for me. To use video-game terms,
it gave me more area damage at the cost of accurately hitting a single target. I
was absolutely fine with that. Being precise wasn't really my jam. I liked the idea
of hurling whatever I wanted into a massive cluster of enemies and just *seeing*
what happened. There'd be a little bit of loss in effect from using my Improvised Weapons Skill over Throwing Weapons, but only a *touch*. They were both
E-Rank but separated by a single Level within.

*Clucky. Mortimer,* I commanded with my mind, *get back as far as you can.
Daddy's home.*

I activated Pernicious Volley and felt as though my limbs were suddenly
filled with pistons. As I saw the two roe strike and use the force of their hit
to bounce away, I chucked the first heavy chunk of slate down. It flew from
my palm like I'd fired it from a potato gun. The shingle rocket hit the group
of oomukade like a faulty freight elevator, and I heard it explode against the
cobblestones, immediately filling the area with smoke and debris. I didn't wait
for a reaction; I frisbee-tossed the next one, and it followed like a lightning
strike. It was only as I was reaching for my next two spice missiles that I heard
the agonized screeching of the centipede cluster.

A notification popped up and just as quickly minimized, as I supposed the
system seemed to think I was in combat.

*I mean . . . they are,* I chuckled to myself.

I'd been able to see the words *Sneak Attack* in the message, so I wasn't too
worried about the rest of its content. It was just helpfully informing me of how
badass I was being.

Two more shingles followed the initial pair, and I was able to crack off a fifth
and final toss before the Ability faded. When the dust began to clear, all that
remained of the formerly monstrous creatures was a big pile of goo and body
parts. Dark blood streaked the street where they'd been, and I laughed. Not a
single one remained.

"Holy SHIT!" I exclaimed.

*Why the hell had I just been sitting on this Ability?! Imagine what I could do
if I combined that move with my haladie! I could probably pull off two of those
attacks if it returned to me fast enough.*

To be fair to myself—which I usually was—it was a fresh new feature and I had
completely forgotten about it while I'd been combating the dangers in the town.

However, I didn't have any more time to gloat—my self-aggrandized shouting had drawn the attention of two more oomukade, and—undeterred by my recent explodening of their companions—they began to advance toward me. They reached the building and started scuttling up the wall, their kabuki faces turned up toward me, screeching. Through the hole in the healer's, I could now see there were at least two oomukade within, striking out at what appeared to be an old man and a little girl, who were trying desperately to beat them back with a piece of the broken wall.

*Dammit, where the hell is Stinky?! Or one of those shell-surfing town guards? Anyone, really.*

As much as I loved to be the hero, I was all the way up *here*, and they were all the way over *there*. It wasn't convenient, but it didn't look like any of the outside defense units had noticed. I let out a big dramatic sigh.

*Guess it's up to me.*

Looking down, I saw that the pursuing centipedes had almost reached the rooftop.

"Aww, shit," I muttered. I would be trapped up there with them if I didn't find an expedient exit path. I really wasn't keen on using Calden's Hang Time if there was a good chance it would come in handy later. So, unfortunately, my options were limited. Fortunately, they were *great* options.

*Alright, boys,* I projected to the roe. *I need some ground support. Comin' in hot!*

I didn't wait for them to mobilize; I just swan-dived off the roof, making sure to steer clear of the monsters scurrying up the drainpipes toward me. I'd have to trust either they'd reach me in time or that I'd be able to survive striking the ground at a speed that would obliterate a golf ball.

I saw a flash of pink as Clucky and Mortimer—the two closest to my location—organized themselves beneath me, and I curled up into a ball just in time for them to take the brunt of my collision, springing me back up about fifteen feet. I landed again and took off at a sprint toward the hole in the side of the mending house.

*To me!* I shouted in my mind to Clucky and Mortimer, and heard the telltale *ping* as they followed.

My bare feet pounded against the pavement as I raced along. An oomukade appeared to my left, its barbed legs poised to strike. Before I could even shift to avoid it, Mortimer smacked hard into the monster's face, distracting it enough for me to continue. So, I did. I kept pumping my legs, my focus locked on the hole in the wall and the two desperate individuals inside nearing big-bug dinnertime.

*I've gotta get to them. No other option.*

Another monster flung itself at me to my right and I dived into a roll, avoiding its spooky horror face. Yet a third dropped down in front of me, only to get a surprise bounce attack from Clucky and then a blast of magical beatdown from the blue man, who'd suddenly appeared again. He slapped a palm on the creature's flank, causing it to convulse with something akin to electrical energy. I leaped over the portion of the creature's segmented back that was horizontal and kept moving.

Duck. Dive. Pivot.

I slid beneath one oomukade's arced belly that was being chopped rather mercilessly by Frida and pushed myself up, crossing the final few feet to the hole in the wall and hurling myself in. The monsters were occupied with their potential snack and had their backs to me at the moment.

*This is gonna be so fucking cool. I'm going to look like such a stud when I save these two!*

I yanked the haladie out of my waistband and stabbed right into the back of the oomukade nearest me. It reared with a screech of pain as I pulled the blade out and ran at the wall.

*It'll work this time! It's gotta work this time!*

I leaped into the air and kicked off from the wall, swinging my weapon in a sideways arc.

"ALLEY-OOP!" I roared as I jammed the blade into the oomukade's horrible face.

It went limp instantly—dead as fuck—and fell against its companion, who'd still been obliviously trying to reach the old man and little girl. The bug screamed as the corpse of its buddy pinned down the coiled portion of its own body, and immediately tried to attack it, not realizing it done *been* attacked. I took that opportunity to launch my haladie like a spear right into its vicious face. The blade sank all the way to the handle, and that was all she wrote. The beast was done. It slumped lifelessly atop the other monster like two intertwined lovers.

I retrieved the haladie and flicked the dark muck off of the blade. However, I hadn't looked where I was aiming and watched as the viscous liquid splattered all over the two exhausted humans staring wide-eyed at me. They both blinked.

"Uh," I said. "First of all, *my bad.* Second: you guys need to find a safe spot *away* from this mess. I'm not an expert on . . . giant insects with people faces, but it seems like you should probably be out of the line of sight with *anything* that is planning on eating you. I'm Loon, by the way."

They both continued gawking at me wordlessly.

"Yeah, like I said, sorry about that. But the doom is still very much impending, so y'all need to skedaddle. *Now.* Like, *now* now."

Neither of them had moved, still partially cowering behind their laughably fragile barrier of broken wall. I was about to launch into a whole thing about how I'd just risked every part of my luscious body to rescue them, when the old man finally spoke. His tone was ragged, like he'd just pulled a full sixteen-hour shift at the laryngitis factory.

"Orc . . ." he whispered, his eyes never leaving mine. I noticed he'd put a hand up to provide extra protection for the girl, whose eyes were just as engorged with fear.

"That's right, bay-bee," I said, hoping to alleviate some of the tension with a bit of nonchalant declarations. "I'm an orc! But, believe it or not, you don't need to be afraid of me—I'm on *your* side. Pro-Tallrock—et cetera. So, if you could set aside your racism for a couple seconds and toddle off to somewhere more secure than *an open crack in the wall next to monsters*, that would just be real, real *neat*. Savvy?"

They both blinked at me. I sighed.

*"Move it!"* I roared, jabbing a finger at a hallway to the left. The two of them instantly obeyed, hurriedly shuffling toward the direction I'd indicated. I had been planning to ask them where the rest of the sick and infirm were, but based on our singular interaction, the two seemed like they weren't the best representatives for their peeps. I noticed the little girl kept looking back at me, and her impression was slightly less severe than the elderly bloke shoving her forward out of fear. I gave my best approximation of an innocuous smile, but she didn't react.

*Eh, I'll take what kindness I can get. At least neither of them are screaming.*

Once we were finally in the hallway, I pointed to a door.

"Can you hide in there? It's probably gonna be a bumpy night for a bit yet, and I don't want to have to rush back in here and save you until it's unavoidable."

The old man nodded, backing away slowly and keeping his eyes locked on me as he reached out to blindly grasp the doorknob. I sighed again.

"Have you seen a matau? Bald head, scarred yellow skin, three mouths? Shitty attitude?"

The old man seemed more intent on entering the next room rather than assisting me in literally anything. However, the little girl looked up at me and nodded. She couldn't have been more than four or five, and when she spoke, it sounded like a tiny little chirp.

"Yes," she said, looking up at the old man and then back to me. "They went to the water tower."

"They?" I asked.

"The m . . . yellow man and his elf friend."

"He took Jes with him?!" I exclaimed, startling the girl. "Sorry, sorry—I'm not yelling at you. I was just surprised. Were they going to defend it?"

Jes was injured. Like *super* injured. So, why did Stinky think it was a good idea to bring him along to go to the water tower? I knew that it was the final destination of the oomukade, but it didn't make sense that the two of them would have abandoned the mending house to trek across town to stop the monsters from reaching their future birth palace—especially when one half of them could barely move. We'd literally had to carry Jes to Tallrock, and unless magic there was advanced enough to fix broken bones in a *day*, it didn't seem like that was a great decision. There had to be something else going on.

The little girl shrugged as a response, and the old man finally got the door open and wrapped an arm around her to usher her away from me. They entered the room and slammed the door. I heard the *clack* of a lock sliding into place, and I shook my head sadly.

"You're welcome!" I called exasperatedly through the closed door. Then I turned and dashed back out the hole in the wall to rejoin the fight.

# CHAPTER FIVE

# CURLY AND SURLY

*Total Settlement Destruction: 18.5%*
*Remaining oomukade [43 / 70]*
*Percent vanquished: 38.57%*

This go-around with the oomukade had been a little more perilous, but between Frida, the egg boys, the tiny blue stranger, and myself—the fight was . . . pretty much over with the moment I stepped back out into the street.

I'd scanned my notifications to learn that the majority of the monsters ranged in Levels between eight and eleven—which I figured had to be the case, considering that not a single one had offered up an Esper Node. Those floating magical baubles only appeared when I killed something at least five Levels higher than what I was, and changed color in exponential increments of five as they got stronger. Apparently, it happened only occasionally with the normal, in-world-bred residents of Regaia, but as one of the lucky few individuals from *outside*, my Sojourner powers unlocked them with a suspicious regularity. I'd racked up experience from combat but not nearly enough to warrant Leveling up again.

Those of us outside the mending house reconvened once the bugs were annihilated, and I hastily explained to Frida what the little girl had told me.

"Why'd they leave?" the Guardian asked, wiping her ax blade free of blood with the leather portion of her gauntlet.

"Dunno," I said. "But we should probably catch up. Whatever their reasoning, they aren't exactly stupid—well, Jes isn't, as far as I know. There'd have to be something majorly obscene for him to hobble off into danger like that. And Stinky wouldn't just volunteer to help. He's not much of a participator."

"Yer mind is mine," Frida said thoughtfully. "Should make haste, then."

"Definitely," I said. "Since it looks like the mischief is managed 'round these parts, it's probably safe to kick rocks. Let's goose it."

I paused, though, looking at the little man who was slowly walking back toward the mending house without saying a word to us.

"Hey, blue Yoda," I called. "Thanks for the help! I wouldn't have made it inside if you hadn't Force lightninged that one big bad into a seizure. Appreciate it."

The man turned and gave me a nod.

"It was no issue," he said. "This is my mending house, and the onus is on me to defend it. I should be thanking the six of you, instead."

"You own this joint?" I asked. "So, you're what, like the chief of medicine here?"

He gave me a curious look and then nodded.

"Yes, though that is not the term we use here."

I balked.

*Wait a second . . .*

"Loon," Frida said, pointing off to the north—I think. "Let's beat. Ah need to chop more o' these filth to ribbons, an' Jes is a frolickin' toad out there."

"One sec," I said, and looked back at the man, but he'd already gone. I frowned, turning back to my friend.

"Well, hm," I muttered thoughtfully, and then switched gears. "Yeah—alright, Frida—damn! Let's get goin' already!"

We made quite the scene as we continued on into the night, choosing speed over an unhealthy display of violence as we purposely bypassed several instances of oomies moving through the town on their own, only stopping if it looked like they were attacking folks or doing more than cursory damage to the structures. We were now in a time crunch, and that meant we couldn't just drop the smackdown on every single monster we came across. So, as much as it pained me to do so, we mostly left the creatures to enact petty delinquency in whatever way they saw fit.

It took us nearly ten minutes of full-on dusting it to get near enough to see the entire water tower. Once we had, I slid to a stop. My lungs were pounding and my Stamina bar was nearly depleted—which was doing *wonders* for my self-confidence. Despite having an actual, quantifiable metric at my fingertips with which to gauge my progress, I was still vastly out of shape. To make matters worse, it was now very clear that anyone close to the tower was going to be *boned*, as at least two dozen of the oomukade swarmed around the base. I could see a cluster of tense fighting as they attempted to climb up the huge structure.

But, at that moment, I couldn't even *try* to push it to the limit. My heart was thundering and felt as though it was gonna explode. I crashed against a wall dramatically to take a quick rest.

"Loon, are ye well?" Frida asked, peering at me from a dozen feet away.

"Uh-huh . . ." I wheezed, totally not selling it. "Just need ta . . . grab . . . a quick . . . time . . . out. Gonna be . . . good . . . in a sec."

The woman just watched, as if expecting me to keel over even more than I already had. The roe seemed a bit winded as well, leaning against one another and puffing out their cheeks—something I didn't know they even had.

*Weird. They use their bounces to propel them forward. It must take a lot outta . . . Ah, shit.*

As I cleared my throat of phlegm, the roe did the same, and I suddenly realized that they weren't worn out at all. They were copying me.

*Fakers!* I razzed in my mind.

*Fake. Copy. Mimic. Pretend,* they returned.

"If yoor square an' good here," Frida said, glancing away from me and up at the tower and the battle taking place, "then ah'm goin' 'head. Ah donnae think *that* bunch can spare t' manpower. Ye'll be good if I pace et?"

I waved her away.

"Go . . . ahead," I huffed. "I'm right . . . behind you."

She removed an object from the belt at her waist and handed it to me. "What's this?"

"Health potion," she said. "Yoor a tad under, by t' looks of ye. Use et."

"Won't you need it?" I asked.

She flashed me such a lovely grin that I felt off-balance.

"Nae," she said. "Got 'nother on me. Found 'em both in the road, 's'well as a few potions o' sleep. Ye'll get better use out of et than ah would."

She winked.

"Plus, this gal's not as easy te hit as the big orc. Better at fighting, most like."

Then she took off without another word, faster than she'd been moving than when I was alongside her. Apparently, she'd been slowing her pace for me, which sort of made me feel bad. I pushed it out of my mind.

*Her Stamina is probably five times mine. Catch your breath, you heap of pudding, and then make up for it with untold decimation of your enemies.*

Internally, I spoke to the roe.

*Stay near her unless you see Jes, then help defend him. You guys remember Jes, right?*

They bounced up and down excitedly, as I knew they would. For some reason, they were obsessed with him and probably liked him even more than they liked me. They were a curious bunch.

*Good. He's probably still pretty hurt, so try to keep anything from attacking him. Now go. Do me proud!*

They sent out a feeling that they would do their best and then shot off toward the water tower after Frida. I still didn't know what Stinky was thinking—dragging Jes up there like that. I guessed I'd get to the bottom of it once I wrangled in a spare breath or two. In fact, I was already starting to feel like I could probably hop back up and join the fight in another few moments.

So, of course, that was when I was very abruptly greeted by a familiar face. It smirked at me under a tangle of curls.

"Good evening, Gabriel."

*The woman from the train.*

I hadn't seen her in a few days, but it seemed like a lifetime back. Which, now that I was thinking about it, *was* my first day in this world. She'd also been the one to usher me from my *old* world by appearing on the train I'd been riding on just before it flew off the tracks and brought me to Regaia.

Man, she really sucked. When last she'd shown her face, she was dressed in more "modern American" clothing. Now, however, her style was much more en vogue with the current environment. A leathery combo of thick jacket and pants, both lined with animal fur and covered in an assortment of belts. She also had on a pair of too-large gloves and clunky boots, trimmed with fur as well. It wasn't really surprising, considering she'd been able to skip on over from my world to this one without so much as a hair out of place. Wherever she'd just come from—or was heading *to*—it was probably very cold. She looked like she'd just finished vacationing in a dark-ages ski resort.

"A bit warm for that getup, isn't it?" I greeted her.

She chuckled, but the humor didn't reach her eyes. Those remained deadly cold. Unfortunately, she was still smokin' hot, which was as baffling as it was frustrating to my sensibilities.

"I see you are acclimating to the world well," she returned, nodding her head to my own clothing. "A kilt? That is a very bold look. I see *someone* is attempting to make a statement."

"What do you want?" I shot back, not willing to pretend her presence was anything short of infuriating. She was the whole reason I was there, and every time she appeared, things had gone to shit shortly afterward. I could only imagine what would follow *this* encounter.

"My, you do enjoy cutting straight to the point, do you not? I'd have assumed you would try to stab me at the very least."

"Yeah, well, you were wrong," I said. "I exhausted myself a couple days ago, kicking your lackey's dick inside out, and still haven't fully recovered. Oh, yeah, and then I killed him."

I knew she'd had something to do with Ocho, the illusion-obsessed assassin I'd fought on top of a giant bird statue in the dungeon. He'd been trying the best he could to injure me to the point that he could take me back to his home base and turn me into Sojourner butter, but we'd bested him. Unfortunately, not before he'd killed most of Frida's companions.

*My friends.*

I pushed that back deep inside my brain. Rather than making me angry, it made me extremely sad, and I couldn't afford to feel that way right now. I'd gotten very good at blocking out painful memories back in my former life, and I'd successfully adapted to that here so far as well.

"As I recall, you were not the one to land the final blow," the woman said, waving a hand to the water tower. "I believe that honor belongs to your companion."

She was referring to Stinky. He'd been the one to hurl the broken haft of Frida's ax into Ocho's stupid chest.

*That's a worrisome comment. Is she planning to get revenge?*

"Yeah, Stinky put him out of his misery after I pounded him into a fine mist. And trust me, that was more mercy than he deserved."

"Yes, of course," she said, her tone clear about what she'd decided on the matter. "Regardless, I am not here to twist the knife about what transpired between you and Frey in the Crypt—though I *am* interested to learn the full detail of accounts . . . eventually. I am here on business of a different matter."

"Spit it out already," I said, standing up. "Lemme guess. You're here to finish the job that *he* couldn't complete and drag me back to your lair. I will literally kill myself if you try to do that, and then you'll have to try again. But guess what? I'll *kill myself* again. It'll be an endless cycle of seppuku, and you'll be pulling your perfectly curled hair out trying to keep track of it."

I didn't mention that I'd already signed a contract with some devil-like creature that dictated if I died, I'd have to spend the rest of eternity as a prisoner—but she didn't need to know that. Or maybe she already knew and didn't care about what I'd said. I wasn't sure which was worse.

She shook her head.

"No, *Loon*," she began, wielding my name like a cudgel. "You misunderstand. I do not want to whisk you off to some far-reaching fortress of tormented agony. Contrary to what Frey may have indicated, doing so now would be premature. That man is so irksomely impatient. It is fortunate he failed. Had he been successful in acquiring you, I would have been forced to destroy you anyway."

"*Was*," I said.

"Pardon?"

"He *was* impatient. He's dead, remember?" I smirked.

She wrinkled her brow but then a smile crossed her lips.

"Ah, yes," she agreed. "He *was* impatient. But as to that point, you are not suited to our necessity as you are now. A lifeforce as fragile as the one you are currently displaying is less than worthless to the designs we seek to achieve. My goals are only met once you have grown far, *far* stronger."

"Wow," I said. "Stellar comment. A-plus. Really. It's good to know that villains are the same on every plane of existence."

"What do you mean?"

"What do you mean, 'What do you mean?' You're telling me you've been to my world and you haven't watched any movies?"

"Ah," the woman said, tapping her index finger on her chin. "Unfortunately, I did not have the occasion. I saw an episode or two of a . . . television program? In passing. I recall the name was *Young Sheldon*. It was . . ."

She raised a hand to give a so-so gesture. I snorted despite myself.

"Yeah, you really fucked up there. Not the best introduction to a representation of our media. Wait—shut the fuck up. Don't try to distract me! Why are you here?"

The woman raised a single eyebrow and then gestured toward the climactic fight I was missing out on. Behind her I could see bright flashes of light and hear a whole lot of screaming from both monstrous and humanoid throats.

*Ah, diss. That looks fun as* fuck.

"*That*," she said, still indicating the water-tower throwdown, "is not an endeavor you'll be participating in."

"The *fuck* I won't be," I spat. "You can't tell me what to do, lady. I'm an adult."

"Hardly," she said. "But your level of physical maturity is irrelevant to this affair. You will not be joining the defense of the water tower, because you are needed elsewhere."

"Listen—" I said, jabbing a finger at her. That was a mistake, because she snatched the tip of my digit instantly and, with seemingly zero effort, twisted it to the side. She grasped my elbow in her other hand and forced me to turn my body to stop the wrenching pain.

"Agh! Fuck! Ow-ow-ow-ow!"

"*You* will be the one to *listen*," she said calmly, her icy glare boring into my soul. I could feel power wafting off her like a stink. It was overwhelming. For the first time in a long time, I was *afraid*. I gritted my teeth, but the pain was nearly unbearable. She hadn't broken the arm or finger, but she didn't need to. To make matters worse, because I had to curl my body to the side to not only stay level with her movement but also remain standing, I wouldn't even be able to attack her if I wanted to. I was totally and completely powerless.

"Fine— Fucking— Agh! Jesus! Tell me what you're talking about and let me go!"

She released me instantly, and I tucked my whole arm to my chest, cradling it like a wounded bird.

"You're prepared to hear me out?" she asked, though I doubted she cared about my answer.

"Just tell me how you think you can convince me to abandon my friends, so I can tell you to fuck off and then go join them anyway."

She seemed to consider my words and then sighed.

"You will not be joining your *friends*, because you've another that needs your assistance much more desperately."

"Huh? What the hell are you talking about?"

The woman pulled an object from . . . nowhere, and I realized I'd seen it before. It was a small copper clamshell. It fit neatly in her palm, and I couldn't help but think of how closely it resembled an antique makeup mirror, complete with little clasp in the front. I recalled she'd been peering into the same item right before she'd summoned the blue lights that somehow threw the train off the tracks. I cringed.

"Here," she commanded, and the top of the clamshell popped open with her command, revealing a blue light within.

*Nothing good can come from that thing.*

I wanted to recoil but restrained the urge and forced myself to lean forward to look into the swirling blue patterns. Slowly, they shifted and formed a solid image. A building. Based on the way it was designed, it had to be a structure here in Regaia.

"Where's this?" I asked, but as soon as the words left my mouth, I saw an oomukade slithering by. I realized with a start that this building wasn't just in Regaia but *there in Tallrock.*

*At least it's not a long trip.*

"When you say *friend* . . ." I began, but the woman cut me off.

"One of your fellow Sojourners is here in the city. In that building, to be ineffaccably precise. And yes—as you will likely think I am drawing your lead in a ploying orchestration—it is one of those who were on that outworn rail carriage with you. You will find speed is most critical, as you will need to reach them before—"

Suddenly, three oomukade returned to the scene inside the mirror. As if by some compelling force, the monsters began slamming themselves against the outside wall of the building. The foundation began to crack, and one of the windows shattered. Despite the fact that the woman was looking at me and not the mirror, she seemed to know exactly what I was seeing.

"You had something to do with this attack, didn't you?" I demanded. "*Gah.* I fucking *knew* this wasn't a regular . . . *monster* . . . attack. It's hard to tell what qualifies as normal in this godforsaken place, but this ain't it."

She shrugged.

"I wish that I were able to tell you I had the prescience to concoct these machinations," she admitted. "But alas. I am not the architect of this scheme. I simply saw the opportunity and struck out to capitalize on it."

I glanced at the skirmish by the water tower. It was hard to make out finer detail, but it looked like one helluva hoopla. Then I turned back to the woman and glared at her.

"What's in it for you?"

*Shit! I just engaged in the predictable* What's in it for you? *trope. I've fallen right into her contrived, clichéd designs! Curse my loveable yet inquisitive mind!*

"It is in both of our best interests for *all* of the Sojourners to gather together. This individual can assist you in rejoining the rest of your lot. And before you ask: dying—in this particular ordeal—will do more to place your companion within that building in peril than to benefit them. If you choose to ignore the danger posed to them and they were to expire and return to their place of origin, they would suffer. Fantastically so. And at the fingertips of a hand far crueler than even what you consider mine."

She'd done it. I didn't think she'd be able to, but she goddamn *did*. She'd presented me with a compelling argument for abandoning my friends. It was alright, though. Despite my reservations, they'd likely be just peachy pressing back the oomukade *and* defending the water tower from literal impregnation. At least for as long as it took me to get back to them. I sighed.

"What do I need to do?" I asked, defeated.

"Well, Loon," she said, leaning forward with something resembling excitement, "how do you feel about assisting in a prison break?"

# CHAPTER SIX

# THE WORLD'S WORST PRISON BREAK

*Total Settlement Destruction: 22.8%*
*Remaining oomukade [35 / 70]*
*Percent vanquished: 50%*

As the last centipede fell, I whooped loudly, flicking the dark ichor from my blades and pushing on through the hallway of the jailhouse.

The inside of the place was a wreck: broken furniture, gouged or missing sections of wall and floor, and blood—so much blood. Most of the gore belonged to the corpses of the oomukade that had had the misfortune of coming across me. It wasn't a brag. Outside—with plenty of space—they were proper terrors, having the unrestricted freedom to flail, bite, and scurry around all menacing-like. Inside, however, was a different story.

I'll admit, when I first entered, I'd gotten the snot jostled out of me for a minute. However, despite not giving Frida her deserved response earlier, I *had* taken her words to heart. She'd said I should focus on what I was proficient in, so I decided to lend some weight to that idea. Outside, I was in constant danger of fucking myself over with my uncoordinated slapdashery. But in *this* environment . . . well, I could be a bit more of a bump in the night.

The interior of the building was dark, which allowed me ample opportunity to possess the shadows like a phantom, tapping into my Sneaking Skill in a way I didn't know was possible until now. When I first clambered into the jail, I didn't know what I was doing. However—as previously established—taking a few opening licks from the baddies jarred me into a sense of "Fuck this bullshit, for real," and I had to improvise. Sneaking was a B-Rank Level 4 Skill jumped up *very* swiftly from my incredibly long and very painful accidental Slip 'N

Slide past a fat lot of soldiers in a militia camp. It had been objectively hilarious but also a little frightening, considering the Redmark were full of elite-level ragamuffins. I'd only used Sneaking sparingly up until now, as most of my fights involved huge, cavernous rooms without much cover. This was different.

Without light, the corners, hallways, and other tight spaces turned every encounter with the enormous beasts into a meat grinder—and I was the king of the butchers. Bone, muscle, flesh, and sinew were transformed into mist as I peppered the monsters with attacks from every perceivable angle with my blade. In my haste to rescue whichever one of my unlucky fellow boxcar children had gotten themselves ensnared by the local authorities, I was forced to actually utilize the tools at my disposal. It wasn't what I'd initially envisioned for myself when I arrived, but I would lean into it for the sake of brevity. And wouldn't you know? It turned out just *aces*. By the time I finished my enthusiastic massacre, it had looked more like the inside of a knife wound than the hallway of a jailhouse.

The guards—if there'd ever been any—had abandoned the imprisoned to their fates, presumably to help defend Tallrock from attacks. This was my assumption, anyway, considering I didn't see any roughly humanoid dead that weren't prisoners. Unfortunately, several of the poor bastards had already been devoured by the bug monsters by the time I'd arrived. Partially eaten bodies were splayed out inside their cells or dragged from them, the bars wrenched and twisted to form oomukade-sized snacking holes. With a sense of macabre relief, I knew that none of them was who I was there for. This was because despite refusing to tell me the identity of the Sojourner trapped here, the woman *had* told me their pen was on the second floor.

So, after Loon's Hallway of Consequences, I moved up the stairs to the second floor. I was intent on making this a quick little errand so I could get back to the water tower with enough time to get a single punch in. The moment I stepped into the hallway, though, I noticed things were different. First, orbs of amber light dotted the wall near the ceiling at even intervals, giving the area a cozy allure. This made it look more like the entryway of a day spa than the upper floor of a prison. Second, I could see several *large* shadows stretching from around a corner to the left. But they weren't moving. Either the oomukade were frozen in fear, or something else entirely was waiting for me once I hung around the bend. I thought about this.

Mindless centipede monsters were one thing—they could be duped or circumvented quickly enough. But something that *knew* I was there would require a different tactic than usual. So far, my experience in this world had not allowed me much time to plan or reflect, and I'd just been chiefly reacting to whatever challenge revealed itself. This was, of course, super badass, considering I was still alive and had only died once. Apparently, we Sojourners were able to expire at an incredible rate and still be brought back to life. But my whole motif was different because of making my unintentional deal with Pontivex—a creature that looked like a demon but acted like he was a judge on *The Great British Bake Off.*

*Alright,* I thought. *There's a few of them, and if they aren't those fucking murder worms, they're at least as big as 'em. The hallway is the same size, so I can still do some fancy footwor—*

I was interrupted mid-thought by a voice.

"So, what's the plan, then, eh? Gonna sit around and stare at us with them threatening insects?"

*Insects? So . . . it is the centipedes. Or maybe another kind of monster that is also a bug? Or a secret third thing. Who's that speaking, though? Is this the person I'm supposed to rescue?*

I hated not being privy to the party. Still, if there was some fuckery stewing, I was definitely interested in sticking my beautiful orcish nose into the soup. I found that, in life, you learned your best bits of juicy hot goss' while dropping eaves. So, endeavoring to do just that, I slipped forward silently—haladie at the ready—and snuck up to the end of the hallway.

"You'll just need to pipe down in there, my friend," another voice returned. This one was friendly and male, sounding closer to my location than the other. "Unless, of course, you want to wind up lining the bellies of these stately chaps here. Just sit quietly, if you'd only be so kind. You're likely to stress the poor things to ulcerative malcontent."

"Pah!" returned the original speaker. "You should *hope* that I stay talking, *shrimp.* If I'm talking, I'm still friendly. Let me out, and I'll show you exactly how *un*friendly I can be."

"My, that is quite the endorsement for *not* releasing you if I've ever heard one," the friendly voice said. "Alas. I don't believe I'll be doing so—my apologies. I'm here for someone else, but perhaps the next dwarf intent on springing a wretch from the clink will take pity on you?"

"Afraid, are you? Pah! I don't blame you. Who are you breaking out of here? The elf girl? You lecherous bastard! But I suppose I don't blame you for that neither."

I snuck a glance around the corner to see what I was dealing with. It turned out I was right about the oomies—sorta. Two of the beasts clogged up the walkable area of the passage, nearly as tall as the ceiling. They were different from the others, though. Rather than the pale spectrum of color I'd grown accustomed to, *these* centipedes were varying dark hues. Mostly black. Rather than barbs on the ends of their appendages, they had broad, flat scythe-like blades. Another uncomfortable difference was that rather than white horror faces pressed into their segmented bodies, theirs were crimson. However, they still had the eyeless sockets rimmed in black eyeliner.

*What the actual shit?* I thought. *What fresh new hellspawn are these? As if the classic version wasn't gross enough, they went and made some limited-release repulsive monstrosities.*

These *extra* goth editions weren't moving, just standing there as if waiting to see how this interaction would go down. Worse yet, they flanked a smaller figure—presumably the friendly speaker. This had the effect of making him seem a lot less wholesome than his tone indicated.

He was a dwarf—that much had been easy to figure out from context clues—with silver ringlets of hair and a short beard that was neatly trimmed. He wore what might have been considered fancy clothes if they weren't so wrinkled and dirty. This, combined with how he spoke, gave off the vibe of a sleazy salesman, like the kind of guy manning one of those novelty T-shirt kiosks at the mall. Based on the two giant mountains of evidence on either side of him, it was clear *this* guy was the ringleader of this batshit-crazy circus. Or heavily involved, at the very least.

I couldn't see who he was speaking to from this angle, as they were obviously in one of the cells on my side of the hall. But I could see into the ones on the opposite side. It was only now that I realized that the configuration of the drunk tanks on this floor was different from the simpler ones below. These were more complex, with thicker bars and no doors I could see. Along the outside wall to the right of each alcove was what I could only refer to as a magic symbol shimmering with red light. I had to assume this was akin to an arcane lock, if that was even a thing? Maybe this floor was where the town kept their bigger, more *magical* problem children?

The dwarf continued speaking to whoever was in the cage, drawing his lips into a placating smile.

"Oh, I do wish you'd be quieter, friend," he said. "My affairs are of no concern to you. Just rest in silent repose, and let me be about my business. I'll only be a moment."

Then I caught sight of someone in a cell on the opposite side of the hallway as they moved forward to press themselves against the bars of their cage. A woman—elf, it looked like—with a very pale complexion and flowing red hair. She was staring at the dwarf with open disdain as if he'd been the one to put her there. She seemed out of place, and not just in this jail. Something about her didn't fit with this vibe, but even more importantly, she seemed familiar to me. At first, I thought maybe she reminded me of Ocho, what with the cascade of crimson hair and all—but that wasn't it. She seemed familiar in a different way. Whatever it was, my gut told me *she* was the one I was there to rescue. Everybody else was just frosting on a very terrible cake.

"Oh, my" the dwarf bellowed, also taking note of her. "Glad to see you well! I realized I undercharged you for the delicacies I parted with earlier. I was hoping you'd be willing to make up the difference."

She continued to scowl at him but didn't say anything.

*Well,* they *obviously have a history. Maybe he really* did *get her arrested?*

"Not an opportune moment, then?" the dwarf continued, undeterred. "Pity. Ah, well. Perhaps another time. You do seem awfully occupied for now. I'll tell you what—write me upon your release, and I'll gladly swing back here and retrieve the coin you owe."

The elf woman seemed to be quaking with rage, something I knew a lot about. She opened her mouth. Then she looked as though she couldn't find the words and shut it again.

*Ah, shit,* I thought. *She's catatonically angry. Nothing worse than being so mad you can't think straight enough to respond.*

Really, when experiencing a fury of that magnitude, it was like trying to suck the words out of your brain with a coffee straw. Whatever he'd intended with his cutting words had apparently been wildly successful.

"However, I am not here for you, either, which I am sure you're upset by. We did have such a wonderful rapport, if I recall. A more-robust shame doesn't exist. But, unfortunately, there's only one empty seat on this escape carriage, and it has already been claimed by another."

"You'd do well to leave her be, dwarf," the first voice said, finally reappearing after a few moments of silence. "It's one thing to mock *me*—your little flowery speech isn't uncouth enough to rattle *my* cage. But she isn't bothering nobody. So, either unfetter me so I can fill your orifices with silverfire, or get out of here and let us prisoners enjoy our dutiful reprimand."

I couldn't figure out why this dwarf was standing around, taunting and teasing people, either. If he had some great deed to accomplish, it didn't make sense to bully folks who couldn't fight back. Power trip much? He and his two monstrous goons were giving me the creeps the longer they loitered, and unfortunately, I was trying to be cautious for once.

"I'll make an ironclad promise that I won't be bandying here longer than I have to be, my friend. Trust me on that. I just need to wait for—"

"Asshole."

It was the elf. She'd finally managed to say something, and though it was quiet and shaky, she'd done it.

*Get it, girl.*

Everything was still for a moment. The dwarf turned back to her and tilted his head.

"I'm sorry, miss," he said, "but, did you say something?"

"I said . . ." she managed, rage still choking her, "you're . . . *amotherfuckingasshole*."

The last part came out in a rush as if she'd had to will it to happen, and the words spilled forth all at once. The dwarf seemed like he had a response, but now that the clot was unclogged, she was flowing freely. Her next words streamed out of her like there was a hole in her brain.

"I can't believe you charged me for your stupid *fucking* gross, *shitty* fucking pies and got me thrown in fucking jail. You asshole. You're an *asshole*. You stupid fucking shit-ass, dumb son of a fucking bitch. Fuck you . . . ass. You . . . asshat. Fuck you to death, fucker—and fuck your mom. Fuck your grandma. You assholey . . . asshole *bitch*. You dumb fucking fuck. *FUCK!*"

Damn, she was goin' *off*. She'd punctuated her curse-word hurricane with a final swear so full of exasperation that I felt terrible for her. Being pissed was clearly not in her wheelhouse—nor her lexicon. But, as a connoisseur of foul language, I was actually kind of impressed. She lacked finesse and complexity, but she more than made up for it with the sheer volume of expletives she'd managed to vomit up in such a short amount of time.

"Wow. That was . . ." breathed the unknown occupier of the other cell. "You . . . uh, alright in there, gal? I'm not a virgin to that sort of language, but, uh . . . well, *wow*."

The dwarf cleared his throat.

"You're clearly navigating quite a *trying* time in there, so I'll ignore—"

"Shut the hell up!" the woman snapped, jabbing a finger in the dwarf's direction. "*You* got me thrown in here. *You* are going to get me out. You're obviously fucking waiting around for some dumb, shitty . . . *thing*, so . . . maybe . . ."

She let out a growl.

"Agh! Just . . . fucking . . . get me the fuck *out of here!*"

The dwarf dropped his hands, seeming to consider her request. However, an instant later, his head snapped to attention as if at a dog whistle only he could hear. A smile crossed his face. Then he apparently caught himself and plastered over it with a mask of concern.

"Oh. Unfortunately, miss, that will have to wait. It appears that my time in this cesspool has come to an end. As jolly as my company here is, I have a duty to attend to, and I'll not miss my *very* narrow window to achieve my ends."

"What are you talking—"

The mystery prisoner had begun to speak but was interrupted by the screech of the two dark oomukade. It was at the moment a notification appeared.

Quest Update!

[Mission Quest] A Multi-pronged Assault

The Settlement Resource [Water Tower] has been reached by the oomukade horde! This is considered exceptionally good if you are an oomukade but very, very *bad* if you are anything but. Because Tallrock failed to defend this portion of the Quest, consequences will be administered. However, new Priorities have been unlocked:

Stop the oomukade queen from reaching Settlement Resource [Water Tower] and laying her eggs.

The way is cleared for Her Majesty to make her way through the settlement. She brings along her oldest children. Congratulations, this [C-Rank] Mission has advanced to [B-Rank] and therefore has more significant consequences upon failure.

New Defense Priorities:

- Keep Total Settlement Destruction (TSD) below 70%
- TSD: 27.1%
- Stop the oomukade queen from reaching Settlement Resource [Water Tower]
- Kill 100% of the invading oomukade
- Remaining oomukade [115/150]
- Percent vanquished: 23.3%
    o [Updated] Quest Reward: Reputation, Additional Reward(s)
    o [Updated] Quest Reward: Reputation, Additional Reward(s)

*They failed.*

The realization hit me like a ton of dicks, and it was honestly a little terrifying.

*Did the bugs just get past their defenses? Was it too overwhelming, and they had to fall back?*

Then another thought festered through my brain, and my stomach fell.

*Were they dead?*

No. I could still feel the party's connection through whatever vague sense I had. So, they were still alive, but I could tell they were weakened. Whatever they'd been dealing with over there was obviously pretty difficult.

*I need to go to them!*

That was equally stupid at the moment. There was some certified fuckery happening right there in front of me, and I knew I *had* to rescue my fellow extraterrestrial. My companions were all the way across town; besides, they were all higher-Level than I was. If I raced to them, I'd only be in a big hurry to get to my funeral. As much as it sucked, it wasn't over: they were still alive. Not like . . .

I shook my head.

*Focus, thick-head. Focus.*

I needed to figure out a way of getting that elf lady outta there without involving myself in whatever bizarre soap opera was being reenacted in this hallway. I switched my fixation to the dwarf, but he wasn't where he was supposed to be. I craned my neck around the corner to see him marching down the hallway toward a cell at the end, the oomukade trailing behind. He raised a hand, holding up a . . . Was that a fucking wand?

*I'm so sick of wizards.*

The dwarf gestured with the stick and shouted something in a language I didn't recognize. Bright light burst out of the tip like an over-exuberant virgin. It filled the passageway with blinding pink magical energy, and I winced. When the illumination faded, the cell door that had once been sealed was open, looking as though something had wrenched it free from its hinges. From the arcane smoke stepped a large figure.

He was a tower of muscle as tall as the doorframe he ducked beneath. A shaggy mane of gray-black hair fell to his shoulders, and dark eyes peered out from behind the curtain of bangs covering his face. Weeks, or maybe months, of scruff covered his face, split by a smile much too charming to belong to a person who looked like a deranged anime supervillain. I mean, he wasn't even wearing a shirt. I could see some sort of burn gracing the top of his hip bone, but the majority of it disappeared beneath the waist of his tattered pants.

*Is this the fucking bug mommy?*

"Whoa! Look at the pecs on that guy!" said the prisoner that I couldn't see. "What are you, part gorilla?"

"It's good to see you, Velton," the now ex-prisoner intoned, his voice rich and strangely stately as if he hadn't just spent at least a fortnight in the slammer. His tone reminded me of a debonair noble who spent his nights out-womanizing Casanova and not at all like what he appeared: Jack the Ripper's bodybuilding cousin.

"I apologize, Rafe. We can exchange pleasantries afterward, but we've a need to make haste. Our timetable is limited by—"

"The monster queen," Rafe—apparently—finished for him. "I know. I saw the message. You'll have to tell me sometime how you managed to take control of them."

"I promise to explain it in most ample detail once we are clear of this town," Velton, the dwarf, said. "For now . . ."

He gestured to the oomukade flanking him once more.

"You're not suggesting that we ride these?" Rafe asked, sounding more amused than disturbed.

"Any port in a panic, Mister Crowmoon," Velton said hurriedly. "Now, shall we . . ."

He'd trailed off as Rafe—fuckin'—*Crowmoon* stepped past him toward the other prisoners. What a goddamned name, though. It was the edgy sorta moniker an eight-year-old would give the bad guy when playing with his action figures.

"Rafe?" Velton asked.

"You gonna let us out?" asked the person I couldn't see. "I'd be in your debt if you did, considering I've got a whole lot of things to do. You know, business . . . et cetera. Your dwarf friend was really rude about it. Vulgar, even. Though I can tell you're the *real* intelligence behind this operation, Mister Crowmoon."

Crowmoon tilted his head to the side as if planning to ask an important question but then just smiled and shook his head.

"Oh . . . afraid it's too late for that," the giant man said. "You've heard names as well as other pertinent information. Unfortunately, we'll have to make sure you never leave this place. I'm genuinely very sorry."

I swallowed a lump in my throat. Was I going to have to fight this guy? The prospect seemed insane, considering he looked like he could push a needle through a tractor engine with his fingertips. I mean, I *would*. I'd fucking *die*—but I'd do it.

"Pah! Just try it, scum!" the voice shot back virulently—was that the right word? Angrily? Whatever—he was defiant. "Unlock this cell, and I'll zap your shriveled bits into butterfly food!"

I had to hand it to the prisoner dude: he was plucky, whoever he was. I could admire that.

Crowmoon chuckled.

"Damn," he sighed. "Now I'm *really* going to feel bad about it. You're a hoot. It seems like you're a great time.

"I *am* a great time!" the voice continued. "Having one, too! Open her up and find out for yourself! Don't be fooled by the arcane seal on this cage; I'm angry death in a sweater vest."

I knew I'd need to engage, but this new dude was built like a battering ram with abs and was at least a foot taller than *me*. Taking him down would be tricky, but I was notorious for outmaneuvering even the diciest of circumstances. . . . Wasn't I?

*I've just gotta wait 'til he turns his back,* I thought. *Then I'll use my badass sneakery to sidle up behind him and* cap his ass.

Quickly, I glugged down the potion that Frida had given me, then stuffed the bottle back into my pack. My Health immediately shot back up to a comfortable level. I sighed.

*I gotta start preparing better.*

"Sorry," Crowmoon said, looking genuinely apologetic. "But as I said, you fine folk can't leave. I'll have to kill you."

Then he did something that stopped my heart in its sexy tracks: he flashed a glance right at me. He smiled wide.

"All of you."

# CHAPTER SEVEN

# JAIL-O

The big man, Rafe Crowmoon—god, that fucking name—kept his eyes on me as he dropped his thematic-hydrogen-bomb comment. He'd spotted me or knew I was there the whole time. It was a tad rattling, but the big grin on his chiseled, handsome face started grinding my bladder, you know? This dude must have scored an A-plus on all of his vision exams, because seeing me should have been *hella* difficult to do, considering the Rank my Sneakery was at. Did none of these goddamn Skills mean anything at all? This was, like, my one good feature in this shitty, world and he was acting like it was as simple as the first page of a *Where's Waldo* book.

*You smug motherf—*

"I think you mean '*both* of you,'" the voice in the cage said suddenly. "There's only two of us trapped in these cells. Truly, I am reconsidering my position about your being the mastermind in this if you can't even grasp something as remedial as basic grammar. Maybe the monsters are the brain trust here?"

The voice paused, then shouted to get the attention of the two oomukade.

"Hey, bugs! You the smarts of this outfit?"

Crowmoon turned to look at the man.

*Oh, fuck the hell out of this!*

I reached into my bag and snatched up an object that had saved me against powerful dickheads before: the indestructible orb. I whipped it at the big dude, drawing my haladie backward to time my follow-up attack as well as I could. Then I hurled the blades end-over-end and rolled myself into a shadow on the other side of the hallway.

Crowmoon didn't even flinch. While still staring at the mouthy individual in the cell, his hand flashed forward, and he caught the orb overhand. He turned to regard it for a moment before seeming to sense the haladie and brought the impervious stone up almost casually to smash the spinning weapon out of its flight. This sent it rocketing into the wall, where one of the blades stuck in. Deep.

I gawked at his speed.

*Shiiiiit.*

I'd just handed an immovable object to an unstoppable force. I was so utterly and completely *porked.*

"Whoa!" came the person from the cell. "What the hell was that? Are you under attack, big guy? Let me out, and I'll help you, mage's promise."

From my new position in the shadows, I could see what the prisoner looked like—and let me tell ya: I was not prepared for it. The individual who'd been so aggressively playing both sides of the battlefield was not a creature I recognized. He was about five and a half feet tall—or in the neighborhood size of one pre-transported *me.* But that was where the similarities ended. Instead of flesh, this creature had outsides resembling yellow gelatin. Though he wasn't entirely formless. Despite having a rough approximation of torso, limbs, and head, his general body shape could be described as *best guess.* There were eyes, similar in consistency to the rest of his . . . everything, and he wore open robes over a sweater vest. Whatever he was, I was wholly confused by his physical alignment—and a little interested in knowing more. It's not every day you encounter a gummy-bear demon.

Crowmoon ignored the creature's comment and hefted the orb, continuing to look at it perplexedly. I waited, unsure of how to proceed. He'd so handily given my attack the slip, so I needed to do some deep introspection to see if I had anything at my disposal that could aid me. I could *maybe* get mad enough to go into Primal Rage, but based on what I had just seen, I didn't think that would be enough.

After a moment of quiet contemplation, the gigantic man smiled and looked directly into the shadow I hoped would shield me.

"'Now, where did you get something like this, my sneaky orc friend?"

"An orc? Pah! Where's there an orc?!" the blob man demanded, pressing his face close as he dared to the bars of his cell to scour the area. His eyes protruded a bit, elongating in his search. It had the effect of making him look a little like a slug.

"If there's an orc, it's even more reason to release me! I've got a few spells up my sleeves that'll murder an orc quicker than they deserve! Just point me at it, and I'll make short work of the beast!"

*Ouch,* I thought. *I've got feelings, you stupid melted Jolly Rancher.*

Keeping in character with what I'd seen so far, Crowmoon didn't acknowledge the statement, instead choosing to keep staring at me. His grin was very friendly, and it was hard to marry that image with the comments he'd just made about killing people so they wouldn't narc on him. But he'd obviously not been fooled by my maneuver—so, it appeared the time for hiding had passed. Now bravery was going to have to be on the menu.

"That's mine," I said, stepping out of my stealthy not-so-safe space. "Can you give it back? Sorry, I, uh, dropped it right at you."

"Dropped it, eh?" Crowmoon said, amusement playing at his features.

*Yuck it up, chuckles.*

"Yeah. I'm a bit of a Klutzy Chloe," I continued, and held out my hand. "A little help?"

To my surprise, the big dude actually nodded, then lightly tossed the orb back to me. I fumbled the catch but managed to hold on to the smooth, round object without embarrassing myself too much.

"Is that the orc?" the thing in the cell asked. "What's with the spots, orc? You sick or something?"

"You speak well for one of your kind," Crowmoon said.

"Why do people keep saying that?" I asked. "Has *no one* in this place ever even *met* another orc? We're perfectly nice! Pleasant, even! Invite one to tea sometime."

"No, they're not!" the gelatin prisoner exclaimed. "Orcs are awful, actually. Rarely hear one speaking the common tongue, though. *That's* new. More an exception than the law of the gods, really. I've heard about some of the dreadful atrocities they've carried out. A group of orcs wiped out Lorelai Village a couple summers ago. Hardly anyone survived."

"Yeah, well . . . did you ever stop to think that maybe the villagers were being big, fat racists, so they finally had enough and torched the joint?"

"What?" the creature asked, clearly confused.

"What brings an orc such as yourself to this place?" Crowmoon asked, resting his hands on his hips.

"Field trip," I said. "Just need to collect one of my fellows and get the hell out of here. I'm not trying to get wrapped up in . . . whatever the fuck is going on, though. So, feel free to pretend I wasn't here, and I'll do the same."

Crowmoon gestured to the cell where the elf woman was, though I couldn't see her at the moment.

"You mean *her*, I assume? You don't seem on familiar terms with the illisinaf, so it would have to be her. Am I right?"

*Illisinaf? Is that what ole Slimer's race was called? That sounded like a name you get by randomly smashing letters on a keyboard.*

"Rafe . . ." the dwarf finally said. "I don't think we should be spending the time—"

"In a moment, Velton," Rafe interjected, seemingly transfixed by my presence. He held his hand up in the air to quiet his friend and then spoke directly to me.

"An elf and an orc being friends? I feel like *that* is a story worth hearing."

"Yeah, well, there ain't much to it. We're from the same *hometown*," I emphasized, hoping the occupant of the cell would pick up what I was putting down. I didn't know *who* they were from my old world, but it didn't matter. Even though it seemed like a terrible idea to follow any direction given to me by the curly-haired asshole who'd brought us there—this elf was my best chance to meet back up with my crew. Plus, I'd been informed that I should specifically *not* allow her to die, since that would be all sorts of bad news for her.

My statement seemed to have done the trick. I saw a pair of slim hands wrap around the bars of the cell, and the elf woman's eyes peered out from her confines to rest on me. She seemed hell-bent on figuring out who I was or if she'd even heard correctly.

"Well, if that's all there is to the story, I guess I'm a little disappointed," Crowmoon said, taking a step forward. I leaned back, ready to pivot and perform a series of awesome—but ultimately pointless—escape actions. "Well, nameless orc. I suppose it's time to bid our goodbyes. You've made this quite interesting."

"Take another step and you're toast," I said, mustering all the intimidation factor I could into my voice. "I'm not just some regular orc."

"Oh?" Crowmoon asked, taking another step forward.

"Nope," I said. "I'm a *special* orc— NINJA VANISH!"

I immediately rolled backward into a somersault, intending to hop up and book it for the doorway downstairs. But, despite how quick I had tried to be—Crowmoon was *faster*. Before even reaching the ground, I felt his strong hands scoop me up by the armpits and lift me into the air. But I didn't wait for him to do anything else. I swung back with the indestructible orb, cracking it against his face.

It felt like I'd been electrocuted. The force of my connection created vibrations that shot through my arm with searing pain. The orb flew out of my hand and slammed into the wall, leaving a large gouge as it continued its journey down the hallway.

I froze.

"Oops," I said. "There I go, bein' clumsy again."

"That wasn't very sportsmanlike," Crowmoon said. "I gave that back to you in good faith."

"Hey, man," I said, still dangling from his grasp like a newborn baby. "I dunno what to tell you. It's a condition I was born w— HIYAH!"

I tried to kick at him, but he just released his grip, and I fell to the ground in a heap.

"This would be adorable if you weren't a fully grown adult," the big man said. "As it stands, it's just a bit sad."

"You're one to talk," I wheezed from the ground. "If I'm fully grown, you're obscenely ripe. They shoulda taken you out *way* earlier from whatever vat they grew you in."

He just stared at me as I struggled to stand. Then he lifted his foot and lightly pushed me back to the ground. I was already unbalanced, so I fell *very* unprofessionally onto my side.

"Hey! Not cool! You don't have to be mad. All I'm saying is: you're a *healthy boy*. Congratulations, you beat puberty. Now, if you don't mind, I'm trying to beat your ass. Hold still."

I stood up finally, albeit shakily, and raised my fists. If I could just keep him distracted long enough with my pseudo-pathetic antics, I could maybe think of a way to get out of this without getting my head popped like a grape.

"You're not doing an excellent job of that," Crowmoon chuckled. It was really annoying how he was equal parts terrifyingly monstrous and unyieldingly charming.

"Just wait," I said. "I'm about to uncork the hurt of a lifetime on you—emphasis on the *orc*."

"That's right, orc!" the gelatin man in the cell urged. "Take him out behind the woodpile! Or, better yet: let me out, and I'll help you tan his hide."

"What Level are you, friend?" Crowmoon asked.

"A million!" I shot back. Then made to wind up a punch to his stomach. Instead, I pretended to biff it and tripped on my own feet, tumbling back to the ground.

"Aw, man. Orc—you're killing me!" Baron von Jiggle shouted.

I looked at the elf woman, still observing quietly in her own chamber, and shot her a wink.

"Rafe," Velton said again. "The time—"

Crowmoon shot a hand up again to quiet his friend, but his demeanor was different this time. His body was rigid, his jaw set tightly. I could see that his attention was locked not on me anymore but on the hallway I'd entered from.

*What the hell? Why does everyone in this goddamn place have to be so dramatic?*

"Rafe, what is it?" Velton continued, taking a cautious step forward. The big man chopped his hand once as if to demand obedient silence, then dropped his arm. It had me curious, so I glanced down the hallway as well. Finally, I heard a sound.

*Footsteps.*

Then a shape emerged from the stairwell.

She wasn't big—probably about average height for a human—but she was muscular, wearing form-fitting leather armor with a big metal . . . shoulder-guard thingy on one side. On her hip was a scabbard, and though this was definitely the type of situation to call for it, she hadn't removed her sword. The woman stepped forward with purpose, her short, light brown hair seemingly caught in an updraft of some variety as the ends danced. It reminded me of those photos you see of someone's 'do standing on end right before getting struck by lightning. Except the motion on this lady's follicles was a lot more elegant.

*Who's this, now? Man, this world keeps on introducing baffling new elements into my general field of vision, and I'm just supposed to . . . what? Deal with them?*

"You're out of your cell," the woman said. It was a statement, and one that didn't hold any sense of surprise or worry. She carried herself confidently, and it almost felt like I was in trouble just witnessing the exchange—but, like, in the same sense as a cop pulling you over not only for driving without a license but for also being ten and having stolen your aunt's Subaru.

*Sorry about that, Aunt Ella.*

"The environment doesn't suit me," Crowmoon returned. His tone was playful, but his eyes were deadly. "Thought that perhaps I'd make my way to a nicer one."

"Who's this now? She sounds tough!" the illisinaf shouted. "Can you guys move your confrontation over to the right a bit? I wanna see what's going on!"

"Go back to your cell," the woman said firmly to Crowmoon. "I should have guessed you'd have something to do with this attack on Tallrock, but I didn't think you'd eschew decorum so flagrantly."

The woman closed her eyes and rolled her shoulders.

"Now," she continued, "I'm much too tired to try to convince you with words. If you refuse to return to your confinement, I'll be forced to put you back in myself. Again."

"You are more than welcome to try," Crowmoon said, and I felt power begin to radiate off of him. "But you won't be able to fool me with your tricks this time, Captain. Nor—it seems—will you have the assistance of any of your lackeys. Even with the wretched *bridle* you've planted in me—I imagine *I'm* the one with my thumb on the scales here."

*Captain . . . so, this must be what? The head of the town guard? Did she say she put him here before? Goddamn, she must be strong as* fuck. *Will the wonders of this world never cease?*

The captain sighed, and I watched as power visibly gathered around her as well. The hair dancing on her head began to writhe, and bright flickers of . . .

was it magic? . . . swirled around her. I flinched back instinctively as suddenly, her whole body caught fire.

"Whoa!" I exclaimed, and rolled backward.

*Did she just fucking* immolate *herself?*

"What was that?!" the illisinaf demanded, trying to stretch to view the scene. "Orc! What am I missing?"

I didn't respond to him. I was too busy backing away from the two super-charging Gokus. Plus, even if I wasn't concerned with staying the hell out of the way, I wouldn't know what to even describe this as.

The woman didn't scream, and in fact, the flames seemed to die down after a moment, surrounding her like a bodysuit. It covered her from head to toe in vibrant arcane fire, leaving only a pair of smoldering eyes untouched by the Spell. Then it hit me.

*She was the one flying around earlier, shooting fireballs at the oomukade! Dammit, Frida was right! She* was *a lady!*

Armed with this new knowledge, I knew I'd need to blow this popsicle stand before things got real *scorchy*. I backed up a bit more, locating the indestructible orb, and scooped it up before finding a pleasant little dark shadow to slink into.

Then the fight started in earnest.

All I saw were two blurs flying at one another and connecting with such a loud crash that it made my eardrums go numb. I winced. Then I saw my opportunity and took it. I vaulted forward into a roll as the two mortal enemies became visible from their cartoonish violence cloud for a moment, now out of the way of where I needed to be.

I shot back up and sprang to the wall, grasping the handle of the haladie embedded in the gaps between two bricks. I yanked hard, but it wouldn't come unstuck.

"Goddamn shit!" I roared, tugging harder.

Then, as if things weren't weird enough, I heard a voice in my head. It was raspy, dripping with venom and an intent to do harm.

*My children. I arrive. Your mother approaches.*

The two oomukade were suddenly screeching, and I covered my ears.

"The fuck?" I muttered, looking around, but in all the chaos, I wasn't sure what was actually happening.

*Was that the queen? She sounds . . . well, gross.*

I felt more magical energy fill the space. I glanced up to see that the dwarf—Velton, I guess—was raising a hand and muttering under his breath.

"Not today, honey," I said. I spun and whipped the orb at him, socking him right in the stomach, and he bowled over with a groan. However, this had the unfortunate side effect of making the two oomukade he controlled go absolutely *bonkers.* They began thrashing about, slamming their giant bodies into the walls.

*"Jesus!"* I yelled, completely confused by everything happening all at once. Everywhere I looked was pure pandemonium.

"Orc!" shouted the illisinaf.

I turned to look at the blob creature.

"What?!" I shouted.

"Watch out!" he shouted back. I turned just in time to see one of the oomukade barreling down on me.

"Oh, you gotta be fucking kidding m—"

# CHAPTER EIGHT

# ELF BY HERSELF

The fight began, and the elf in the cell was utterly baffled as to how things had gone this majorly off the metaphorical rails. She'd known things were going badly, but it seemed like the moment she'd lost her temper, that was indeed when the ship had sailed on sense and order. However, if she was honest with herself, there was nothing typical about the ordeal since the moment she was arrested.

To start, the guards hadn't allowed her any opportunity to defend herself upon arrival. They were wholly convinced that she was the very same dwarf who had swindled and framed her. No matter how she insisted, they were deaf to what they considered excuses. She supposed she understood that. If she *had* been him, casting an illusion to evade the authorities, she'd have continued professing she was *not* the culprit of whatever crime or plot the dwarf had apparently been involved in—which was also a mystery.

Then there'd been the somewhat strange creature imprisoned in a chamber across the way. He'd been an alright-enough sort as far as unsolicited housemates went. He was respectful and understanding of her position—even if he frequently requested to know if she had some method of springing them from confinement. However, at her Level, she didn't think there was any chance of being useful in extricating herself—let alone the both of them—from this dire strait. Still, it hadn't tempered his enthusiasm in developing exponentially wilder ideas about what she could do to free them from this snare. This was up to and including suggesting she wedge her head between the bars, wail for the guards to rescue her, and subsequently fight them off—all while stealing their unsealing implements when they made the rescue attempt. After a while, she'd actually been considering it. At the very least, it would offer a change of pace, which she now felt was necessary for breaking up the monotony of compulsory captivity.

This plan, of course, had been abandoned once the notification announced that the town was under attack. Until then, the elf mused, she hadn't even known the *name* of the place she'd been . . . visiting. She supposed it was, despite the circumstances, good information to know. Every guard in the facility seemed to have rushed out the door in their haste to defend Tallrock, leaving her and the creature across the way alone. Though she suspected there may have been another on this floor based on the heavy surveillance previously placed at the thick metal door at the end of the hall.

Not long afterward, there was crashing from below. The screams echoing through the building turned her stomach to ice. Even the creature in the opposite cell was quiet while they awaited their likely demise.

However, what arrived from the stairwell while the horrific symphony played from below was not what the elf expected. The millisecond the dwarf from the marketplace had appeared, swaggering through the passage, she'd been overtaken by rage. Worse still, and as if to add insult to injury, he carried her confiscated mince pies. Her anger in this life was much the same as in her previous one—it strangled her. She'd always considered herself to have quite the high boiling point, rarely getting upset, even as the world had tried to wallop her down with its many attempts to break her spirit. However, when she *got* worked up, rather than finding a proper way to release the percolation under which she was inconveniently subjected, her body stoppered it, like a tightly clamped lid on a pressure cooker.

It was the same there. Despite the dwarf brazenly displaying the fruits of her mistake, she couldn't do anything but quietly fume.

However, the dwarf seemed not to notice her presence. In fact, the man was so thoroughly fixated on the room at the end of the hall, she wasn't sure he'd even realized she would be there. Perhaps he'd assumed she'd somehow escaped? Whatever the case may have been, soon after stepping into view, he'd begun digging his fingers into the pies, removing a white marble from each. The remains of each pastry were discarded as the dwarf mumbled words under his breath. Then a bright flash forced her to shield her eyes.

When the light faded, two gigantic centipede-like creatures stood stockstill next to him. This was . . . curious to the elf, for lack of a better word. She considered that perhaps she could have been shocked, appalled, terrified, or even—as some are prone to be—taken by a mad, hysterical fit. This wasn't the case. Instead, something about the entire scene was just . . . embarrassing. It was a high cringe of the secondhand variety to her sensibilities to watch a dwarf—who'd readily outwitted a threesome of town guards—dig his stubby fingers into two long-cold baked goods and pluck monster eggs from them. It was a pathetic sight. This shame at witnessing such a display began to roil within her, and she became even more enraged at her status. Somehow, this oafish nincompoop had hatched a plan involving illusions, imprisonment, and, worst of all, sullying the good name of savory confections. This had ultimately resulted in the elf being trapped in a cell in a town she'd only just learned the name of, being forced to watch as he literally fat-fingered his way through some scheme.

It was incensing. The fury blossoming in her heart grew so large, it choked her, and she couldn't do much more than watch at a quiet boil behind a cracked dam. The analogy, it would seem, was mixed.

Of course, this changed when he'd actually spoken to her. His condescending monologue, thinly disguised by the veneer of gentlemanly rapport, was too much. The dam had been cracked, but now it had broken. Words tumbled forth, spilling from her so violently that she didn't think she'd be able to rein in the geyser of verbal turbulence unless her bottom jaw fell off.

Indeed, the only thing that seemed to stop her from stripping him fleshless with her barbs was the arrival of the system notification. Of course, she wasn't surprised that the half-witted defenders of this town had failed to beat back the danger. Still, the inclusion of the queen of . . . whatever an oomukade was seemed *quite* reasonable—all things considered. Everything about this world had passed the sniff test as possibly the worst form of a gamified reality, and this new information was no different. If you fail, the odds get worse. Poor design, by any metric.

Of course, the dwarf was not there for her, saying as much and rudely releasing another prisoner from captivity instead—a powerfully built macho sort. This felon's demeanor was . . . strange, possibly the only thing that had set her off-balance since being plopped into jail. But, as predictable villains often do, Mr. Big Macho threatened to kill her and the nice-but-persistent fellow across the way. Though, when it came to the matter of her own demise, the elf had no worrisome reservations. Her assumption was that if she were to be unceremoniously culled, she'd return to where they'd arrived upon entry into this world. At least, that was what she'd picked up from the unending questions the Messenger had answered. Sojourners, as was her understanding of what her type of people were called here, could be revived. The exact methodology and mechanics of the process were unknown to her, nor was it accessible knowledge to anyone else at her home base—even Tartarus. But it would still likely not be very comfortable. Death rarely was.

But then, as if whatever gods existed there had the strangest sense of humor, there was a new arrival. An orc. Though he was large, he'd foolishly baited the only creature within his immediate radius that was *larger* than he was. It didn't seem bright. She was sure she would have just slipped away quietly if she'd been in his position. But this orc did not appear to be someone who knew a bad idea from a good one, and so, he set out to apparently piss off the likely end-game boss without considering the further ramifications.

Despite being, by all accounts, a full-sized orc, there was something . . . off about this stranger. Chiefly that he didn't seem very *strange* to her at all. He was big but moved about like he was much smaller, as though his body was new to him after a tremendous growth spurt. His manner, too, was odd. From every manifestation of orcs she was aware of, they tended to default to an intimidating stance on any issue. But it was as though *this guy* seemed to delight in laboring to showcase precisely how *very opposite* of intimidating he was. His general actions were boyish, as if he were far younger than he appeared.

It was, however, when he opened his mouth that the elf woman knew exactly who this orc was.

The cadence, the delivery, the unrepentant *brashness* of his cavalcade of swears. The familiarity she felt solidified. This big, mouthy, semi-sneaky, spotty-skinned, fast-talking, ridiculously garbed, *clumsy* orc was, in fact, someone she knew quite well: her former classmate from the old world, Gabe Skelter.

There was no mistaking it, and once she knew what she was looking for, the energy of the encounter shifted. She was no longer angry. Like a lightning rod, Gabe had always absorbed all of the anger in the room. Even when he was pretending to be anything but, the undercurrent of it clung to him, embedding itself deep in his bones. You couldn't be upset when Gabe was around, because he took all the rage for himself. Even just *knowing* he was there, whether or not he himself was angry, was all it took for her own bubble of bad feelings to disintegrate.

His conversation with Mr. Big Macho, appropriately named *Rafe Crowmoon*, confirmed his identity. He announced, with extremely transparent codification, that they were from the same hometown, even saying he was on a field trip. Gabe had always been bold, but he was never someone you'd accuse of being particularly clever. Though, considering the functional intelligence of most of the folk she'd come across in this world, perhaps it was a successful venture in obfuscation. The two exchanged more words and a handful of poorly timed attacks on Gabe's behalf . . . then the mood changed again.

Another individual had arrived, and it was at this point precisely that the elf woman believed things were getting quite ridiculous.

*Player Six has joined the game,* she thought to herself.

Player Six and Mr. Big Macho began to fight about something that must have happened earlier offscreen. More discord, as loud chittering filled the air. It was as though some deep bestial god had been torn from its slumber and filled the woman's mind with its primordial howling. Then the oomukade began to wail and undulate, using their bodies to crash hard against any surface they saw. This was quite bizarre, since they'd been practically docile up until now. A hot fire of fury must have burned its way deep into their tissue, thought the elf, and while the orc—formerly Gabe—was distracted, one of the monsters bolted right at him.

"Oh, you gotta be fucking kidding m—" Gabe roared. Then the beast was on him, knocking him to the side as it charged past and down the hall toward Mr. Big Macho and Player Six. Gabe slammed against the bars of her pen with an angry oath. Still, he didn't have time to sit in commiseration, because the damnable dwarf—Velton—had pulled another wand out of his sleeve and pointed it at him.

"Duck!" the elf shouted. Fortunately, she was quick and capable of grasping Gabe by the cape at his back and giving him a solid yank. He hadn't fully risen, so the movement was enough to overturn him and send him tumbling to the ground just as a glob of spherical lightning whizzed into the bars where his head had just been.

However, concerning the frustratingly resistant barrier surrounding the elf's cell, it was a surprise blessing. The Spell hit the bars and rebounded, the crackling energy shooting across the hall, where it hit the creature across the way's cell and ricocheted again. It bounced back to the elf's cage once more before zipping toward the dwarf who'd initially cast it. Before any opportunity to turn his fortune, Velton found the self-guided missile was blasting him in the chest and bowling him into a backflip. He landed on the ground with a cry.

"Yeah!" the illisinaf in the other cell cheered. "That was a good one! He didn't know the arcane seal would rebuff his Lightning Ball! Now finish him off, orc!"

"Ugh," Gabe groaned, picking himself up from the floor and rubbing his head. She'd indirectly caused him to bash his temple on the bars in her haste. The orc turned to look at her.

"Hey, I'll—"

*BLAM!*

The unattended oomukade slammed against the cage as it had tried to target Gabe but misjudged its strike. Undeterred by its comically inaccurate blow, it slashed out with its bladed legs. Unfortunately for the beast, Gabe was nowhere to be seen. He'd disappeared.

*What in the world?* the elf thought to herself. But all was disrupted as a huge shape flew by her cell from down the hall near the entryway, slamming into the far wall.

Apparently, the oomukade attempting to engage in the fight with the two elites had not fared well. One of them must have tossed it away from them— giving the elf an entirely new measurement by which to gauge power. The beast was still moving, however. It straightened and, seeing its sibling battling something unseen, made haste to join the fray. In seconds, both beasts were slicing at the air in front of the elf, her only saving grace the bars of her prison. This left her unable to do anything but back away, hoping they didn't manifest a way of getting inside.

Then, as if to make matters worse, a *third* oomukade appeared.

*How is this happening?* the elf wondered.

"Fucking *seriously*?!" she heard Gabe exclaim, echoing her own sentiments in a much more colorful fashion. She couldn't help but grin, despite the extreme circumstances. There were very few constants in this new world, and she was happy for once that there was something akin to a physical law—regardless of what plane of existence you happened to be toiling on. No matter the body, irrespective of the circumstances, for good or for ill, Gabriel Skelter wasn't ever going to be anything but *Gabe.*

*But how is there a third monster?* she wondered. The oomukade trio was now congesting the jail hallway so mightily that moving room seemed scarce. *I think I'd have noticed if the dwarf had suddenly brought another pie . . .*

"Oh," she said aloud—even though she hadn't meant to. *That tricky son of a buck.*

"Ga— Uh, orc!" she continued, deciding against using his real name in mixed company at the last moment. "He—um, *the dwarf guy* uses illusions! One of those monsters is a *fake!*"

Though she couldn't see him—still an odd thing, now that she was thinking about it—she heard Gabe laugh.

"Illusions?! Oh, *mama.* You done fucked up now, shortcake! I'm great with those. Check out *my* illusion!"

Suddenly, the elf saw him. He stepped out from a shadow and leaned back with his chest puffed as if he was holding back vomit.

"What is he—"

She was interrupted once again as the orc snapped forward, his jaw so wide that it looked like it would become unhinged. With a roar like a wild beast, colorless force erupted from his jowls in a wide cone, blasting into the three oomukade in front of the bars of her cell. Strangely, whatever Gabe had just done had also caused the barrier to flicker as if powering on and off again. The instant the blast hit, the rightmost oomukade's body melted away, leaving a very confused-looking dwarf underneath. The illusion had vanished. However, the other two oomukade remained very much in existence.

*Makes sense,* she thought. *Whatever Gabe did demolished the dwarf's magic, but he'd said he would use an illusion. That—*

"That wasn't an illusion!" shouted the illisinaf.

"Semantics!" Gabe said just as he appeared behind the dwarf and grasped the hair on the top of his head. "Hey, buddy! Nice wig!"

He quickly gathered up Velton's silver curls in his fist and wrenched him backward.

"Ah!" Velton screeched, his hand diving into his pocket as he was pulled to the wall.

"Huh," Gabe muttered. "Not a wig, I guess. I would have bet my—"

"He's going for another wand, orc!" the illisinaf shouted.

Gabe wasn't quick enough. As he reached for the dwarf's arm, Velton pulled the wand's wood tip from his pocket and fired another Spell at the orc. A hot, orange flash filled the chamber, and the elf could feel it even in her cold, dreary cell. Gabe took the attack full on as a fireball struck him dead center, sending him flying into the ceiling. He hit with tremendous force and dropped straight to the ground on his stomach, looking as though he was unconscious. The two oomukade were still up and about, screaming as loud as they could, poised to strike.

*Oh, no,* the elf thought. *Get up, Gabe.*

"Aw, man," said the globular man in the cell across the way. "I was really pulling for him, too. Ah, well— Hey, dwarf! Mind letting me out of here? Just wave your little wand around and unlock this contraption. I'll make it worth your while."

The battle raged down the hallway, shaking the entire building as the two masterfully powerful individuals pummeled the dickens out of one another. The elf couldn't see precisely what was going on from her vantage, but it did seem incredible, from all the rumblings and magical flashing.

The dwarf kept his wand at the ready and slowly approached Gabe's inert form. He held his hand up to the two giant bugs, keeping them at bay for the moment as he examined his victim.

"Hey, did you hear me, dwarf?!" the illisinaf demanded, pressing his face against the bars. "I said I'd—"

"Would you be *quiet*?!" Velton suddenly spat, his bumbling, friendly exterior finally shattered by the other creature's incessant pestering. The dwarf glared daggers at the prisoner before continuing his rebuke.

"You are *never* getting out of there, do you hear? Once my companion has finished with the guard, we'll dash both of you to tatters. In fact, I am going to finish you off my—"

The elf saw that, in his anger, the dwarf had stepped too close to Gabe's prostrate body. One of the orc's eyes popped open. This startled the elf but not as much as what happened next. Her classmate glanced upward for a fraction of a moment before he pivoted in place and snatched Velton's leg in his massive hands.

"PSYCH!" Gabe roared.

The elf heard a loud snap as the leg in Gabe's meaty grasp was wrenched so hard, it broke. Velton screeched but aimed the wand in front of him as he fell backward, firing off another ball of flames. It hit the orc once more and sent him blasting away to the left, clear from the elf's view.

The oomukade stopped screaming. In fact, other than the *alternate* fight happening at what sounded like the other side of the building, the only sound was the grunts of pain as Velton struggled to stand. Hunched over, he let out a loud breath and eased his broken leg into something resembling the usual configuration.

*Slap-slap-slap-slap.*

The elf heard bare feet racing along the stone floor the moment before she saw it: From stage left, Gabe zoomed back into view at a full sprint toward Velton, who was only just becoming aware of the orc's presence. But even as the dwarf raised his wand again, Gabe launched himself into the air, both feet off the ground, performing what could only be described as a double dragon kick, colliding with the dwarf's unprotected torso.

"Expelliarmus!" Gabe shouted as he connected with a booming *crack* that undoubtedly broke most of Velton's . . . everything. The move sent the dwarf sprawling, his wand flying through the air to land on the ground next to where Gabe crash-landed. Not waiting, Gabe was up again, the rod in his hand. He pointed it right at the screaming figure properly diagnosed as Velton, and his look grew grim. His eyes clouded over, and the elf thought she saw his pupils darting back and forth as if he was reading a system message.

*Can he see the stats of the wand?* she wondered. *That would be a game changer.*

Then Gabe's eyes returned to normal, though his expression was still terrifying.

*Oh, Gabe,* she thought sadly. She'd been pairing the image of this orc with her knowledge of who he was inside that costume. But at that moment, she saw something else. He was burned pretty badly, his skin blackened in places and red-raw in others. Dozens of cuts and gouges peppered his body in a horrifying mural of the fight—and earlier, it appeared. It was as if the outsides of her classmate had now morphed into what always lived within, kept just beneath the surface. A terrifying specter of determination, pain, and anger. It frightened her.

Gabe stared at the dwarf, his brows knitting into a single line of concentrated frustration.

"You ready to yield?" he finally said. The dwarf couldn't move. He could only lie in his tangle of broken bones and scream.

Quietly, the illisinaf spoke.

"I . . . think you got him," he said. "Real nasty-like, too. He was a killer, though. That much was clear. Don't spare any pity for a miserable mistake like him. In fact, it would probably be a waste to put him out of his—"

There was a blinding flash as Gabe unleashed a column of flame from the wand that engulfed the dwarf. There was no recoil from Velton, no dispute or other response. He simply dissolved inside the fire.

"Fuck you," Gabe said to the blaze.

Then he turned to the two oomukade and raised the wand again. Now that he was facing non-humanoid creatures, his features transformed, and his grin returned. This was a much more terrifying prospect than she had just seen, and the elf felt her breath catch. It was like he'd banished the last moments from his mind, as if the battle was returning to the usual tempo, and he was cavalier once more.

"Hey, motherfuckers!" he shouted to the oomukade, his smile so wide, he could have split his own face in half. "Say *cheese!*"

Then he released another blast of flame right at them.

When the smoke cleared, Gabe stood by himself in the hallway. Coughing. The elf was witness to a flash of light as orbs she hadn't even noticed began circling around him and were suddenly sucked into his body.

*What were those?* she wondered. *A Spell of some kind?*

"Ah, gross!" the orc said, fanning away the cloud of burned oomukade corpses erratically. "I'm never making s'mores like this again."

The elf stood silently, still processing the calamity born of a positively preposterous happening. The two impressively powerful individuals had continued stomping one another elsewhere, leaving them alone for the moment. Still, she had no words—and her head was spinning. However, the illisinaf on the opposite side of the hallway was more than capable of picking up where she was unable.

"Wow!" he exclaimed, slapping his gelatinous arms together in ovational celebration. "That was really something, orc! You just . . . just fried them into char. I'm really proud of you, you know? I know we just met, but . . . would you consider letting me—"

"Jee-zuss," Gabe emphasized, wheeling on the prisoner. "Are you a malfunctioning AI or something? You've only got, like, six words in your vocabulary, all of which revolve around being released from captivity. I get it—being in jail *sucks*, and I'd probably be pleading for the same thing if I were in your position. In fact, I know I would. But goddamn if it isn't annoying as fuck when you're trying to slap the ol' beatdown on a baddie and somebody's constantly begging for yard time. I'll let you out if you promise never to ask me for anything ever again."

The illisinaf looked gobsmacked. Then a wide grin appeared, and he nodded vigorously.

"You've got yourself a deal, pal!"

"Alright," Gabe said, glancing around his immediate area, then turned back to the creature with a sheepish grin. "So, uh . . . how do I do it?"

"The dwarf had a wand of supreme unlocking on him—it's what he used to spring the big 'un from his room. It's probably still on him . . . somewhere."

He said the last word with much less confidence as he eyed the ashen remains of the dwarf scattered around on the floor. Gabe shrugged.

"Don't mind if I do!"

He dropped down and began sifting his hands through the silty pile before coming up a moment later with a triumphant hoot.

"Ha!"

He directed the wand at the illisinaf's cage, but before he could use it, the creature shouted.

"Stop!"

Gabe lowered the stick with a confused expression.

"Huh? Why? I thought you wanted out."

"That's not the correct wand," the illisinaf said, wobbling his head in a manner that must have been an intended shake.

"Whatcha mean?" Gabe asked, staring down at the magical item in his hand. He touched the tip experimentally.

"I *mean* that you're holding on to one of the *additional* wands he used during the fight. Remember when he cast that Lightning Ball Spell?"

He noticed the look the orc gave him and sighed.

"The one that narrowly missed your face when your friend pulled you out of the way."

"Oh," Gabe said, nodding. "The *buzzy blasty one.* Gotcha. So, that was this bad boy, eh?" He flailed the object through the air and made zapping sounds, punctuating each noise with a wrist flick.

"Zzzzap. Zzzzzzaaaap. Zap. Zap. Zzzeeeyap."

"If you'd used *that* wand on the cage," the creature explained, "it would have rebounded like *his,* and you'd've been blasted into pieces. From the state of you, I don't know that you could handle another attack."

"I'm *excellent*, thanks," Gabe said. "Gonna take a lot more 'n that to dissolve *me.* So, it looks like there's one more of these I've gotta fish outta there, then? Fine. Foraging I go."

It only took him a moment to find the proper wand, and after confirming with the illisinaf, the orc aimed and fired at the bars. The pinkish light erupted from the item and seemingly absorbed the entirety of the metal that kept the creature locked away. The illisinaf immediately slid out from his alcove with a whoop.

"*Gods,*" he gasped. "I don't know if you've ever been held prisoner for an extended period of time, but it is *phenomenally* tiresome. I was prepping to make your elf friend there get her head chopped off from a failed prison break just for some entertainment."

The elf started, then narrowed her eyes.

"You thought they'd kill me? And you convinced me to do it *anyway*?"

"Yeah . . ." the illisinaf said, his tone apologetic. "Sorry about that. Not my proudest moment. But, to be fair, I didn't think *either* of us was getting out of here, and it seemed like I'd be doing you a favor. Those guards aren't known for their kindness."

"Alright," Gabe interrupted, pointing the wand at the elf woman. "Cool it for a second. You guys can keep flirting once I get you out of your kennel."

He stepped forward, leveled the wand again at her cell, and then released the Spell. The bars dissipated, and suddenly, she was free. She smiled, finally realizing that she might yet make it out of her predicament. Still, the bothersome fact was that she was rather unintentionally participating in what could be confused for an honest-to-goodness damsel-in-distress situation. This was something she'd never needed to worry would happen to her in her old life. Indeed, *only* in this world did she feel she'd have met the typical criteria for the trope. She let out an audible sigh. She'd take her wins where she could, all things figured into the equation.

Gabe nodded, then glanced down the hallway.

"How long do you think we have 'til they come back?"

"You think *both of them* are coming back?" the illisinaf asked, turning to look down the hallway as well. "That's optimistic."

"Let me guess," Gabe began, rolling his eyes. "Despite not being able to see jack shit in your cell, you have opinions on their skirmish?"

The illisinaf nodded eagerly and unironically.

"I'd say that fight is fairly one-sided. The big brute will likely come out on top."

"I dunno," Gabe muttered. "That chick can turn into a human torch and fuckin' *fly*. Don't count her out yet."

"Hard to fly indoors, orc."

"So what? She can explode a hole into the roof and blast off into the sky. Listen, I'm not a *magic surgeon*. I am just telling you what I witnessed her do. All I saw the other guy do was . . . *be big*. That's not nearly as impressive."

"*Big isn't impressive*, says the big one," the illisinaf returned. "Your perspective's a little wanting on that front, I'd say. Also, wasn't he the one tossing you around like you were made of wet hay?"

"Anyway . . ." Gabe said, turning back to the elf. "We need to get out of here. Like, quick."

"Uh, okay—uh, I mean . . . yes," she said. "Thanks, by the way."

"No problem at all," Gabe declared smugly. "Just another service I offer as your fellow good-natured ass-beating classmate."

"You two schooled together?" the illisinaf asked. "Which institute did you both attend? Pragstas? Kalome?"

The creature squinted suspiciously at the two of them.

". . . Berringdale?"

"Sure," Gabe said. "All of the above— Listen, we don't really have time—"

"Don't tell me it's Grellini?"

"What? Oh," Gabe said. "Isn't that a type of pasta? Actually, never mind— shut up for a sec, will ya? Where we got our . . . uh, learnin' on doesn't matter. What *is* important, though, is that we haven't seen each other in a while. And . . . uh, she is gonna . . . take me to our class reunion."

"Class reunion?" asked the creature.

"Yeah . . . that's a thing that definitely exists here, and we're going to it. So, we gotta skedaddle."

"I've never heard of it. What is it?"

"Jeez, you ask a lot of questions, huh?"

"I am a researcher, after all," the illisinaf said proudly.

"Neat," Gabe said, clearly uninterested. "Hey, could you—uh, give us a minute to catch up real quick? It's been a hot second, and I want to discuss some private matters."

A conspiratorial look crossed the illisinaf's face, and he chuckled.

"Oh! Sure, sure. Take *all* the time you need, lovebirds."

"What? No. Ew," Gabe said. "Don't make your face do that. It's . . . well, it's unsettling. Alright, I'm going to talk to my friend here, okay? Then we will goose it outta this joint and probably get killed—but we'll be outside, so . . . well, just a minute."

He jerked his head to the left to indicate they should move away from their current position, and the elf woman nodded. When they were out of earshot— they hoped—of the strange sweater-vested individual Gabe sighed.

"Oof! The mouth on that guy, am I right?"

"Gabe, what are you doing here?" the elf whispered angrily. "We thought you'd been killed or sucked out of the train during the transfer or something. Now you're suddenly here—fighting giant centipedes and making enemies of super-powerful warriors? What the hell? Where have you been? Why are you here *now*? How'd you know I was even in this place?"

Gabe shrugged.

"Yeah, I went off the beaten path a bit; that's for sure. It wasn't my choice, though; that crazy lady from the train separated me from the rest of you and dropped me in *the woods*. At least, I *think* it was her. She was there when I appeared anyway, so chances are good . . ."

He paused.

"Wait, you already know who I am?"

"Of course I know who you are," the elf intoned, glancing back at the illisinaf. The creature smiled and nodded, giving her a three-fingered salute that must have been this world's equivalent of a thumbs-up. She groaned.

"Even if you weren't the only one unaccounted for in the camp—and even if you hadn't made those *terribly* obvious references to knowing me—it was clear who you were from the start. *Zero* other people I have ever met talk like you or are pigheaded enough to waltz into danger like this and—"

She broke off, startling the orc as she suddenly wrapped him in a hug. Gabe froze, unable to process this sharp turn down Affection Alley. He just stood there, accepting the embrace like a chastised dog.

"I'm glad you're okay," she whispered, releasing him from her arms and shaking her head. "It's good to know you're alive, man."

"Uh, yeah . . ." Gabe said, clearly uncomfortable with the unsolicited kindness. "Well, I'm pretty hard to kill, I guess. Though—oh, man, you guys don't even know yet. I have a *shitload* of stuff to tell you."

He paused again.

"Once, uh . . . I know who you are."

"Ah . . ." she said. Now it was her turn to be uncomfortable.

"Lemme guess: Abbie?" Gabe offered with a big grin. "That red hair is a total giveaway."

"Um . . . nope . . ." she said. She had been dreading this. Gabe's reactions were never predictable, but when they were bad, they tended to be . . . well, fairly *explosive*.

"Well, *damn*, don't leave me hanging," he said with a smile. "Though I will shit my kilt if you're Emma Stokes. Can't even imagine the idea of her *knowing* what an elf is, let alone being one."

The name registered with the elf, and she felt an icy lance to her stomach.

"Gabe . . ." she said softly. Sadly.

"What's wrong?" Gabe asked.

"Emma didn't make it."

"What do you mean? Like, what? She's still back in the other world, or something?"

"No . . ." the elf said. "She . . . *didn't make it.*"

"Huh? You are a goofy goose, elf gal. You know we come back from the dead, right?"

"I mean, I suspected that was the case—you confirming it is nice to know, I guess—but no . . . she was . . . dead when we got here."

"The *fuck*?"

"I didn't think you guys were close—"

"We weren't, but . . . well, *goddamn.* How the fuck does something like that happen? That's goddamn awful. Any ideas on a culprit?"

"Nah . . ." the elf said, her eyes down. "We, uh, buried her . . . once we could stop freaking out about everything going on. It took a while to figure out who was who—especially because not everyone could speak to us. Race restrictions with language, I think."

"Okay, we have *got* to slow down," Gabe said. "You can't hop from *dead classmate* to sussin' out which people forgot to upgrade their Duolingo account. Those are two *wildly* different subjects with drastically unequal importance."

He took a breath.

"But . . . let's put a safety pin on that diaper. There's no opportunity at the moment to unpack all of that. There's still an active Quest and some larvae queen slithering around, talking in people's heads."

He sighed.

"So, who are you?"

*Here goes nothing*, the elf thought. Then she took a deep breath.

"You'll probably be surprised to know . . ." She paused. "That I'm . . . *was* . . . Mike, uh, Cutsford."

There was a momentary pause as the orc seemed to process this information. The elf felt an icy stab of pain in her stomach. It was like waiting at the top of a rollercoaster for too long before the drop. Then excitement.

"Holy *shit*!" Gabe exclaimed, slapping her on the shoulder. "Fucking whoa, dude! I was *not* expecting that!"

Some of her tension eased a little, and she was preparing to continue, but he steamrolled on.

"Jesus, man. That's *wild!* I, uh, think you may have misunderstood the assignment, though. You know that whatever you choose is permanent, right?"

"Uh . . ." she said hesitantly. "Yeah, I do. That was, um . . . kind of, I dunno . . . the point?"

Gabe blinked at her. The elf felt as though all the air had left her lungs as she awaited his reaction.

"Oh," he said, almost absently. Then she physically saw the realization dawn on his face.

"*Ohh.*"

She winced.

She wasn't sure what would come next. It was old hat now at their base, yet still, some people had some holdover opinions or ideas from the previous world. Gabe was the first person she'd actually explained it to in almost two weeks—since they'd initially arrived. Even the passive way she'd revealed it to the orc was exhausting because of the severe emotional drain it took to work up to it.

She waited, careful not to say anything else before he did. She didn't think it was necessary to explain—or worse—defend herself. If he wanted to investigate her reasoning or rationale, she wasn't sure she'd have it in her to fight back. She was happy with what had happened, and the longer he was silent, the more defiant she became about his potential adversarial response. She clenched her jaw. If he didn't like it, he could take a fucking hike. She wasn't there to coddle anyone into—

However, Gabe finally spoke, and it was as though the knot she wasn't aware was clumped inside her chest released from her body. She let out a breath.

"So, what do I call you now?" Gabe's tone was respectful and friendly. There wasn't a single hint of any malice or disgust.

". . . Rua," she said.

"Well, Rua," he said, pointing down the hallway, "I'm Loon now—pleased to meet you. Let's stop piddle-shitting around, though. You can tell me all about what those assholes are up to once we are *way* the fuck outta this prison and standing on top of a mountain of dead oomukade queen. Let's pace it."

"Pace it?" Rua asked.

"Yeah," he said, seeming to consider the words reverently. "One of my friends always says that, and I think I'm going to start using it—mostly to annoy her."

"Friend . . . ?"

"Not the time, Rua! We gotta go!"

"Uh, well, lead the way . . . *Loon.*"

"Oh," he said, nodding with a broad, mischievous smirk plastered on his face. "Lead the way *I shall.*"

# CHAPTER NINE

# WHOA, MAMA!

*Total Settlement Destruction: 29.8%*
*Remaining oomukade [113 / 150]*
*Percent vanquished: 24.66%*

It was an all-out *sprint* from the jailhouse shortly following my super cool and not at all hilariously eventful heroic rescue. I'd broken some baddie bones, zapped some giant bug monsters, and even picked up a few cool new toys along the way. Three wands, to be precise. I'd used Eye of the Saboteur on them each before my acquisition and learned that they were the *very* appropriately named Wand of Lightning Ball, Wand of Flames, and Wand of Supreme Unlocking.

*Gee willikers. I'm not a namesmith by any stretch, but how about a little panache in your branding?*

Whatever. At least they were direct and clear names that wouldn't have me mishandling them because somebody decided to call it "Wand Jeremy" or something. Though I supposed I *did* already almost mistakenly bukkake myself with lightning just a moment before. Regardless, the wands were now mine and I would wield them recklessly and often.

I'd banished Velton and the bug boys to the afterlife with the magic sticks already, and though I'd felt myself losing control during the encounter, I'd been able to rein myself in. Killing someone was miserable business, but I didn't have time to consider my feelings on the matter, nor what type of person that made me. I'd shown the dwarf mercy, at the end. More than he probably would have given me. However, that was better reflected on in a quiet place with soundproofing. If I let even a sliver of the memory of his death penetrate my thoughts while embroiled in chaotic battle . . . well, it would be bad. I could think about it later and have myself a nice long sob. There'd hopefully be time for that when there wasn't a sputtering sprinkler of physical conflict surrounding me.

I'd also, funnily enough, picked up a new mode of mayhem.

**Congratulations! You have gained an Ability!**
**Wanderlust I**
**Wanderlust**
*You can now wield wands! Whether wizard, warrior, werewolf, waif, or whelp, with wand wielding, whatever wild, wacky or winsome wiles one wants to weave will wax or wane with worthwhile wonder! What a whimsical way to whip a whimpering weakling or ward away wanton wounds while otherwise weaponless and weathering wayward woes! Well, well, well, what are you—a warlock or what-have-you?*

*Well, would you look at that! Guess I'm getting my letter to Hogwarts after all!*

Somehow in the middle of it all, though, I'd lost track of Rafe Crowmoon and Captain . . . uh, well . . . let's just call her Captain, for now.

They'd duked it out unrelentingly in the hallway for a New York minute, but during my super dope rebuke of my enemies, they'd disappeared from view. Which was really strange, because the amount of force they were unloading on one another made it very hard to believe they could hide their rock 'em sock 'em throwdown. Yet somehow they had. I didn't know if they were still in the building or out in the streets, partaking in Bum Fights: Fantasy Edition. What I *did* know was that we had to bust the hell outta the slammer and join my friends in defending the town. Oh, yeah, and probably fight the big mama insect that was *still* occasionally projecting her bullshit sentence fragments into my mind.

Rua as I now knew she was called—seemed *more* than happy to follow me as I dashed down the stairs, through the murder hallway on the first floor, and out into the street. I didn't much care what the loudmouthed slug man did, but as I exited the building, I found that he'd been right behind us.

I stopped in the road to catch my breath and gawk at my wounds. I'd taken a fuckin' *beating*; that was for damn sure. My entire body hurt, and I could see countless battle blemishes adorning my typically nubile orc flesh. Catching a bunch of bites, stabs, and Spells—most of them in the face—would do that, I supposed. To make matters worse, my soiree with Velton's seemingly never-ending magic missiles had chopped my Health bar down to the dregs—and I had *just* upped my intake with Frida's health potion. It seemed incredibly unfair that I was so susceptible to being spit-roasted by any dumbass Gandalf with a nipple duct's worth of magical ability that wandered into my pasture. Bullshit of the highest order, if you ask me.

Fuck, I hate wizards.

I must have taken too long glaring at my undeserved beauty marks, because the man-sized Sloppy Joe in a sweater vest thought it was a good time to *opinionate* about my state of well-being.

"Gods, friend," he said, his gelatinous eyes bulging. "I couldn't really tell in there, but you just got handed the throttling of a lifetime, didn't you?"

"What? These party wounds?" I asked, adopting a nonchalant air. "Nah. I've definitely had worse. You should have seen me after I tangled with the, uh . . . whaddya call it? Oh, yeah: the cosmic chaos monstrosity. Turned me into mulch. This, though? Nothin' to worry over. I'm fine."

"Cosmic chaos monstrosity?" Sloppy Joe asked, moving closer to me. "What in the realm is that?"

"Oh, huh," I said smugly. "Thought you'd have heard of it—you know, being a *researcher* and all. I guess when you're as well traveled as I am, you—"

"Shouldn't we be getting out of here?" Rua asked, clearly sick of my grandstanding. "Let's not forget that there's an active Quest happening right now. Seems like something we should be making a priority, right?"

"Damn," I said, shaking my head. "Sorry, I only just *broke you guys out of prison*. Figured I could take a moment to get my lungs back in working order, but I guess it's too much to ask to—"

"If you actually need a breather, that's fine," Rua said, interrupting me. "But I'm not trying to be out here in full view when one—or both—of those assholes returns. We should keep moving."

"One of them is a much better prospect than the other," I said. "We should hope it's Captain What's-her-face that crawls back from that fight. She seems a lot more reasonable."

"Eh, maybe you should reconsider that, Loon," Rua said, shaking her head. "As you just mentioned, we're escapees now—and she's the head jailer. She's not going to be happy that two of her prisoners just waltzed out of captivity."

I snorted.

"Heh, yeah, that's right. Y'all would be in *big* trouble."

Rua leveled a cool gaze at me.

"Why are you laughing? *You* were the one who broke us out. You'll be in just as much—if not more—trouble than we would be."

I froze.

"Oh, *shit*," I breathed. "You're right—we gotta get the fuck outta here *now*!"

I didn't even wait; I just started running.

It was another few minutes before I stopped again, realizing I had gotten completely turned around during the flight and had no idea where I was. I pumped the brakes, skidding to a halt in front of a building with a busted-down wagon out front that had a sign by the door advertising "cartwright services." Whatever the hell those were.

"Why'd you stop?" Rua asked, padding to a stop right next to me.

"I don't know where I'm going," I admitted.

"Seriously?" she asked, seeming incredulous. "We're on a timetable, man!"

"Fucking— Yeah, I know!" I said. "But you got me all riled up on law-breaking anxiety and I didn't really think about it."

"Shit, Loon," she said. "Well . . . never mind. Even if we don't know where we're heading at the moment, at least we are farther away from the jail. I don't even want to think about how much I don't want to return to that place. Let's just get our bearings together and then figure out—"

"I know where we are," said Sloppy Joe, *sliming* right up to where the two of us were, looking quite pleased with himself.

"You do?" I asked, incredulously. "I swear to god, Jigglypuff, if you try to turn this into an opportunistic—"

"Pah! Calm your balls, orc," Sloppy Joe said with a grin. I think. "My conduct in the cell was one of necessity. I'm not going to needle you for coin you clearly don't have or favors you can't repay to achieve an end that also assists me in my goals."

"Wait, what do you—"

"Jigglypuff?" Rua asked, perplexed. "How is *he* a Jigglypuff? He doesn't look anything like one."

"What?" I asked, completely confused by how that was relevant at the moment.

"Jigglypuff—the Pokémon—is a round, pink creature that sings songs. Do you even know what you're talking about?"

*Fuck.*

I'd forgotten how much of a *nerd* Rua was in the old world—guess she hadn't dropped that particular charming branch of her personality.

"I don't give a shit about Pokémon," I said. "It was the first name that popped into my head. He's jiggly and puffy, and so I went with it."

"That's a bit rude," Sloppy Joe explained.

"Regardless," I continued. "I can't have you out here correcting my insulting references on technicalities—no one here knows them, and it makes me happy to confuse the shit out of people."

"I . . . I'm . . ." she started, trying to find the words that would be her apparent anchor in her sense of bafflement. "Like, there's a *bunch* of other stuff you could have called him that makes *way* more sense than Jigglypuff."

"Oh, yeah?" I asked. "Name *one*."

"I dunno," she said, considering my question. "Like . . . slurm worm?"

"What the fuck is a slurm worm?" I demanded.

"From *Futurama*? The big, mucusy slug aliens? He kinda looks like one of those."

"Whoa, hey," Sloppy Joe started. "Now, that's not—"

"That's too complicated," I said, ignoring him. "If you have to *explain* what it is, it loses its bite."

"What? How is that complicated?" Rua asked, placing her hands on her hips. "It's descriptive *and* it rhymes."

"I don't think—" Sloppy Joe tried to interject.

"Yeah, but *I* don't know what it is," I explained. "I mean, I do *now*, but I didn't before you took the time to regurgitate its Wikipedia page. Listen: you say, 'He's like a slurm worm,' and I go, 'What's a slurm worm?' and already we've lost time we could have better utilized if we'd stuck with something simpler—*whether or not it was entirely accurate.* All because you wanted to be pedantic."

"Jigglypuff doesn't make sense," Rua continued. "Maybe I'm splitting hairs here because I love Pokémon, but—"

"See? There's your problem," I said, shaking my head in disappointment. "Too close to the source material. You don't care about the joke; you only care about being *right*. We could have moved on *long* ago, but now we have to have this whole conversation where I'm going to have to explain to you how humor works and you—"

"Shut up!" Sloppy Joe suddenly erupted, sliding forward to put himself between us.

I paused, staring down at him.

"Whoa, easy there . . . *slurm worm*," I said, giving Rua a wink. "What's with the outburst?"

Then realization hit me and I wheeled to face Rua again, my finger in the air.

"Okay, you know what? You're right," I said to Rua. "*Slurm worm* is definitely better than *Jigglypuff*. Plus, it's fun to say and just *sounds* like an insult, you know?"

"Right?" Rua agreed.

"I said, 'Shut up!'" Sloppy Joe repeated, bulging his eyes out grossly. "Stop calling me Jigglepuss, or whatever else—"

"Ha!" I laughed sharply, cutting him off again. "*Jigglepuss!* Holy balls! That's great. I love that so much more than anything so far."

"It's definitely unique," Rua said, nodding and smiling, "but also sorta creeps me out. It almost sounds . . ."

She paused, trying to find the right word.

"Unwholesome?" I offered.

*Man, I feel like I've been using that word a lot as of late.*

"Yeah, maybe," she said with a shrug. "I don't know. Yeah . . . I guess? The imagery that word conjures up is uncomfortable."

"Well, it doesn't matter!" Jigglepuss explained matter-of-factly. "Stop with the *wildly offensive* nicknames. I'm an illisinaf, and what's more, I have a name."

I chuckled.

"Okay, what is it, then?"

"Pah! How about you tell me yours first?"

"What are you talking about? We've been using each other's names since we ran into one another. You not paying attention? I'm not trying to play games, man, so if you have a name, why don't you—"

"You haven't acquainted yourselves!" he exclaimed. "I know you're probably not used to certain modes of address—being an orc as you are—but in polite society, we make *introductions* when we meet someone!"

"Whoa, easy there, me boyo," I said, raising my hands in a placating gesture. "There's no reason to get upset—we were just having a little fun. She and I haven't seen one another in a while, and excluding someone is one of the best ways to bond over an extended absence."

I sighed, dropping one arm to my side and extending the other in greeting.

"Here," I said. "We can make nice. I'm Loon; pleased to meet you."

The illisinaf hesitated, staring at my hand for a moment. However, it was short-lived. His frown morphed into a friendlier alignment, and he nodded eagerly before extending one of his own limbs and wrapping it around my wrist.

"Pleased to meet *you*, Loon. I'm Quintham, Edwig Quintham."

He turned to Rua, taking on a much more . . . self-important tone. As though he was trying to impress her.

"A pleasure to meet you, as well, my dear," he said sincerely. "Edwig Quintham, Undermagister Researcher of the august and venerable Mages' Order at Yosper Hall."

Rua seemed to feel the shift in his address and wrinkled her nose.

"Rua," she said.

"Wait," I said, realization dawning on me. "Edwig Quintham?"

The creature paused, and then nodded slowly, as if suspecting some dreadful result.

"Yes . . ."

"Holy shit!" I shouted, and both he and Rua jumped. I dug into my pack, not saying anything else to follow up. After a moment, I found what I was looking for and withdrew it triumphantly, propping the thin scrap of parchment into the air like a long-overdue discovery.

"A*ha!*" I exclaimed.

"I'm sorry . . ." Edwig began. "What is—"

I slapped the paper down against his chest with a flourish. It wasn't an aggressive move; I was just excited.

"This you?" I asked.

Edwig stared down in surprise before slipping a gummy appendage up to slide the note out from where it was pinned between his torso and my fingers. He lifted it to read, then nodded at me.

"Oh," he said. "Yeah, this is me. You found my request?"

"I *did indeed*," I said very pointedly, grinning and nodding in what I later thought had to look pretty unhinged. Then I shot back to my bag, pilfering through my belongings with gleeful abandon before finding a fat leather envelope that squished as I palmed it. Then I lofted it at Edwig. The envelope slapped against the creature and tumbled to the ground in front of him, the contents spilling out.

"What the hell is that?" Rua demanded, pointing at the pile of flesh that had poured onto the cobblestones.

"False goblin ears," I said proudly. "A whole bunch of 'em, too. Bagged and tagged and ready for distribution—or whatever you were going to do with them."

Edwig regarded the gift with a strange expression I couldn't read at first. *Fear?* No, he wasn't afraid. Was that . . . guilt?

**Congratulations! You have raised a Skill!**
*Insight [E-Rank Level 3]*

"Oh . . ." Edwig said, his unease clear on his strange gelatinous features. "I, er . . ."

He seemed to have trouble forming the words he wanted to use. However, I'd never been much for patience—pesky thing, it is—so, I tried to assist.

"So . . . you wanna pay me *here*? Or do we need to go to a bank? I'm not sure how much people typically carry around on them. The request said it was a silver per ear, and just a rough estimate on my part put it at . . ."

I stared at the collection of pointed, gray flesh.

". . . a fuckload."

Edwig kept grimacing, and now I was getting concerned.

"Hey, wise guy," I said, "don't tell me you're broke or something. I went through a lot of trouble to . . . uh, well, to *bring* those to you. Don't ask me about the hunt, though, 'cuz I'm not willing to go into the details."

Truthfully, I hadn't yanked the ears off the goblins myself and was, in fact, only the courier in delivering the gross, squishy package. Upon arrival to this world, I'd killed some rat men and found the note *and* the ears. It had almost led to my being carved like a Thanksgiving turkey, too, by a fellow Sojourner once she found out about it. Well, sorta.

Edwig was silent, and when he looked up at me finally, his countenance was completely different. It was as though he was suddenly trying to pretend everything was normal. But I was on to him.

"Well, all appears to be in order, then," he said, not even bothering to pick the envelope up. "Why don't you hang on to those a bit longer, orc? Once we finish defending Tallrock, we can head back to my—"

"Oh, no, you don't," I said, jabbing a finger at the blob man. "I'm not lugging those things around anywhere else. This is the final stop. I know *this* game, friendo, and I'm not going to get fooled so easily. You're planning to leave me with them and then sneak away without paying, aren't you? If you think—"

"Uh, guys," Rua said.

"—I'm just some dumb orc you can trick into—hold on a sec, Rua—carting your belongings around just so you can piss off into the ether . . ."

"That's not it at all," Edwig protested. "I just don't have the coinage on me at the moment—like you said. I was hoping you'd keep them safe a bit longer so that I *didn't* get separated from you, and then have you think I'm some sort of—"

"Guys!" Rua tried again.

"Nope!" I exclaimed, getting close enough to the gelatin man that I could smell his strangely pleasant perfume. "*You're* going to have to buck up and keep your little bindle together, Jigglepuss. I'm not—"

"FUCKING *LOOK*, YOU ASSHOLES!"

I stopped my argument with Edwig and turned to Rua as the illisinaf did the same. But she wasn't looking at us. She was staring at something . . . *above us*?

"What're you . . ." I started, but then turned to look in the same direction, the words falling out of my brain as I did.

In the distance, taller than even the roofs of the buildings, was a massive shape. Now, when I say it was big, I mean that this thing was *fucking big*. It looked like a gathering storm looming over the city structures, and what was worse, it was moving. I gaped as it drew closer, and even in the darkness, some of its features became more alarmingly clear.

"So, gang . . . remember what I said earlier about a mountain of oomukade queen?" I asked no one in particular. "Well, I'm going to go ahead and say that the statement was some . . . unintentional foreshadowing."

Really, I had never in all my two lives seen something so large that was also . . . alive. Moving just within the boundaries of the edge of Tallrock was the biggest, ugliest, *orneriest*-looking fucking centipede you could ever hope not to witness. Its body was a dark, menacing crimson, with horrifying ichor-colored splotches lining several choice sections of its tough-looking carapace. Dozens of limbs as long as trees danced in the air around its lengthy, seg-mented body, each ending in cutting scythe-like barbs that seemed like they could slice a mining dump truck in half. Worse yet was that it moved practi-cally silently. You'd think a monster the size of a FIFA stadium would smash and crash its way through the terrain like a wrecking ball, but it didn't. I had to imagine it was because where I *could* see its legs connecting to the ground, they moved like a conveyor belt, effortlessly coasting the gigantic body across the earth.

But that wasn't all. The clear front-runner for most pants-shittingly terrify-ing feature of this beast was that where the rest of the oomukade had placed their fucked-up featureless white kabuki maws, this thing had what could almost be described as a huge, humanoid face. I mean, it looked like a person. A grotesque, wildly mutated, and super huge one but a human face nonetheless. It had fuckin' cheekbones and eyebrows and everything.

The oo*mama*kade had shown herself, and she was a horrible bitch to behold.

"You've got to be fuckin' kidding me!" I roared, just as the creature opened its mouth to release its own monstrous peal. The sound it made then shook the foundation of the very town we stood in. It was a bodacious bellow, and I had to smash my hands over my ears to block out the blood-splitting decibels she was coughing up. Then, in my head, I heard her voice.

*Children. I arrive. Make haste to me. Clear the way to my birthing grounds. Elder children . . . release.*

"Ah, fuckin' *horse dicks!*" I yelled, but I'm pretty sure her screech had deaf-ened anyone and everyone within a ten-mile radius and nobody could hear how *totally over this shit* I was. Looking at Rua and Edwig, I could see they were dealing with this even worse than I was. Both of them were on the ground, clamping their arms and jiggly appendages over their hearin' holes and scream-ing as they convulsed on the ground.

*Why are they getting the worst of this?* I wondered. *It sucked, but it didn't knock me on my ass. This master bug should be bothering us all the same, right?*

Then I realized that what I'd just thought wasn't exactly true. Quickly, and still reeling, I opened up my Abilities and found the selection I was looking for and let out a surprised grunt.

"Huh," I said. "Whaddya know?"

The Ability was Natural Resilience and, as it turns out, it actually *did* make me less susceptible to them. Well, more specifically, all insects, but I wasn't going to split this particular banana to make a dessert.

**Natural Resilience [F-Rank Level 2]**

*As Barbarians are more inclined to the outer workings of the world, it is within their domain to receive more than the usual trove of forces acting against their best interest. You show marked resistance to some of Mother Nature's most curious affronts. This Ability will continue to offer rewards the more it is employed.*

- *+5% Resistance to Insects*
- *+2% Resistance to Weather Conditions [Cold]*
- *+1% Resistance to Weather Conditions [Heat]*

I didn't have much time to stand and gloat; the overall effectiveness of my Barbarian capabilities was not worth losing time over. The oomukade had said she was on her way to what I can only assume was the water tower, and that meant—based on her size—there was only a handful of minutes until she would get there.

I took a moment after her screams had abated to yank Rua and Edwig up from the ground and then pointed up at the towering centipede still backlining the town.

"We've got to figure out some way to kill it before it gets to the water tower!" I exclaimed. "And we have to go *now*!"

Rua seemed to have gathered her wits about her before ol' Jigglepuss, and she was smartly up and at 'em right after my proclamation. The illisinaf, however, was still moving around, shaking his head.

"Whoa," he breathed. "That was a real head-spinner. I don't know if I can handle another one of *those*."

"Well, grab some damn earmuffs or something, cupcake, because we've got a job to do! She's heading off to give birth to a whole pile of these things, and if *that* happens . . . well, actually, I don't know what the ramifications will be—but they probably aren't good!"

Rua made to grab something from her back but then froze, looking back the way we'd come from.

"What is it?" I demanded.

"I don't have any weapons!" she announced. "All of my stuff is back at the jail!"

"Fuck!" I yelled. "Well, we can't go back now. Screw it. Here."

I pulled an object from my waistband and after confirming it was the right one, tossed it to her. She caught it, glancing down at it and then back up at me incredulously.

"One of the wands?" She wondered.

"Yes, one of the wands!" I said.

"But I don't know how—"

"Listen, it's easy," I said. "I figured it out, and you're way smarter than I am. Just aim that puppy at anything with more than two legs and say the word *unleash*. It'll go like gangbusters."

That wasn't actually true. You didn't have to say anything specific, as the wands' descriptions had specified you just needed intent and any sort of triggering word or sound, but I felt like saying that word would add an element of brutality. I thought she'd have a follow-up, but she just steeled herself and nodded once in confirmation.

*Damn, you are way more confident now,* I thought. *That can only be a good thing.*

"Jiggly—er—Edwig," I said, looking at the illisinaf. "You're a mage or something, right? So, I hope to fuck that means you can cast Spells."

Edwig took a moment to register my question, as he was busy staring at the H. P. Lovecraft waterbug, but when he did, he nodded as well.

"Good; I was worried you were going to tell me you left your bag of tricks in the jail as well," I said. "Alright, gang. We've only got a couple of hot seconds before the queen's army of jacked-up offspring come barreling through the streets, so we need to move fast."

"Wait, how do you know that?" Edwig asked.

"Because—fuck, man—weren't you listening? She telegraphed her whole playbook just now. She's . . . releasing her *elder* children, so I'm going to imagine they're going to mess up our bell curve on wins and losses."

They both looked at me as if I'd just drunk a canister of gasoline right in front of them.

"What?" I demanded.

"All I heard was screeching . . ." Rua said.

By Edwig's nod of agreement, I knew he thought me equally as crazy.

"What the fuck are you talking— Oh. Shit."

It had happened again. Just like in the dungeon a couple of days ago with Pontivex, I'd understood something that nobody else could. I had precisely one idea as to how. Just before entering the Crypt, Zeol had "gifted" me with a potion that had allowed me to understand any language spoken in my near vicinity for twenty-four hours and learn the basics of it as long as it was uttered for a whole minute.

"Do either of you know what Ancient Chitinus is?" I asked.

"That's a language, right?" Edwig asked.

"Yeah . . ." I said thoughtfully. "I think it might be a bug language. Or a demon language? Or both?"

"You know more than I do, then," Edwig admitted.

"Chitin is a polymer in the exoskeletons of arthropods," Rua offered. Then, when I just gaped at her, she sighed, rolled her eyes.

"*Centipedes* are arthropods," she clarified. "Come on, man; we took the same biology class."

"Sister, I took that class *twice*, and I still don't even remember what the room looked like. But, thankfully, you're a gigantic fucking geek and now we have solved this mystery. I think you get to be President of Science Club again."

"What?" she asked.

"Remember, on the train?" I asked, trying to jog her memory.

She just shook her head.

"What the fuck; you remember *Arthur*pods but not a conversation we had less than a week ago?"

I interrupted myself before she could answer.

"You know what? Never mind. Now's not the time! I don't know why a word from Ancient Rome would be relevant to—"

"It's Greek, technically," Rua said.

"What's the difference?"

"Are you serious?" she asked.

"They both wore togas!" I exclaimed.

"Actually—"

"Shut up, shut up, shut up," I said quickly. "It doesn't matter. I can speak the language of bugs, which is weird and, uh, also cool, I guess—in this particular scenario. But it doesn't matter! We've gotta get to the queen before *she* gets to the water tower and—"

I checked to see if I could still feel all of the lifelines in my party. They were there. Weak as shit but holding on.

"—the other people defending it."

"What do you suggest, then?" Edwig asked. "You're beaten all to hell, and the elf doesn't have anything other than that little blasting twig. Additionally, I don't know that any of us is fast enough to get to the big beast, considering she's all the way over *there*. Even at a sprint, that's not a bet I'd take."

I stopped. He'd made some valid points, but that wasn't what caused a hiccup in my hitch. I had let my eyes wander around as he was talking, looking for anything that might aid us in this instance, and my vision had rested on the building next to where we stood and the contraption gathering dust in front of it. Then I looked in the window.

*Oh . . . So,* that's *what a cartwright is.*

An epiphany began to bubble up then, and I shook my head.

"Well," I began, trying to figure out how I'd go about suggesting what I was planning on suggesting. "I might have an idea."

"Might?" Rua asked, looking concerned.

"Yeah," I said. "But it's a really, *really* stupid one."

# CHAPTER TEN

# A TERRIBLE, HORRIBLE, NO-GOOD, VERY BAD THIEF

Orville was good at hiding.

He always had been. When he was but a pup, he'd effortlessly won the sneaky games he and his friends would play, especially when it involved wedging himself betwixt objects secretly, awaiting being found. The young Orville would perform this task with glee, spending—at times—hours without anyone discovering his whereabouts, and that made him feel quite good. Even when the other children would grow bored with searching and abandon the game for another, he would often keep hiding, happy to know that his ability to remain unseen was so absolute.

As he grew older, he practiced his stealth more and more. Eventually, when the system categorized him as an adult, he began gaining Ranks. In fact, he spent so much time exercising his Sneaking that it was at the cost of many other more balanced Skills he could have cultivated. But Orville was not the type to be outclassed—nor, it seemed, to reflect on the consequences of his actions. To be fair, he *was* outmatched, and quite often at that, by virtue of his disregard for anything not involving the hobby of stealth. This included ignoring his more-detailed deficits like Intelligence, Wisdom, Strength, and just about any Ability or Skill that fell under those surveillances. But he had his Sneaking and was more than happy to labor through life with it as his primary mode of interaction with the broader world.

Orville's clandestine skill set had aided him on numerous occasions: for instance, escaping punishment from his parents (as when he'd accidentally broken a window while playing with a dog he thought he'd befriended), avoiding being chosen for tasks at the mill he'd been *strongly encouraged* by his father to apply at, and even outwitting bullies that took issue with his general existence and inferior communication style. It had even helped him remain unscathed during his brief tenure in His Majesty's Army, attaining a position for a time as a scout—even though his martial prowess was abysmal. It didn't matter. He was never seen during his precisely eight instances of missions. Though what *did* matter was that his memory was absolutely dreadful, and he could never accurately recount the events he saw during his ranges. When he *did* remember, he mixed up the details so terribly that the information was functionally corrupted. And so, with his battalion leadership deciding that he *wasn't very good at his job* and worried that his mistakes would one day get good soldiers killed, maimed, or captured . . . Orville was discharged.

Then it was back to the mill—a fine-enough place to waste away the remainder of his youth. In the decade since returning, he'd even gotten a promotion. He was now the substitute lead quern stone rotator's assistant. It was an honest job; if he was being forthright, it didn't require him to do much. Additionally, because of his perceived elevated station, he had access to as much grain as he could steal. Which he did only rarely, on nights when there were few other workers and the moonlight was low. Of course, his foreman knew of his misdeeds but never said anything. Despite Orville being talented enough to go physically unnoticed in his theft, he had never considered the residual evidence he'd ignored. This included the fact that the grain always conveniently went missing on nights he'd loudly declared he would be "waiting around for a little bit longer" after his shift had ended.

That was alright, though. The foreman never had the heart to tell him that the grain Orville was surreptitiously absconding with was mostly chaff and other useless bits of leftovers the mill would end up binning anyway. However, for Orville, each time he made away with his quarry was electrifying. The adrenaline from his heists kept him excited to continue working, and the foreman believed it was a good thing, as it kept the man adequately motivated. Before he'd begun stealing, he was a touch of a mope—lamenting about his lot in life and frequently waxing ad nauseum as to his "time as a scout—you know, in His Majesty's Army."

Orville used his ill-gotten grains uniquely. He'd bring them to his brewer friend working at the Treacherous Tankard, a tavern in the city that served—in his opinion—the finest swill he'd yet in his life imbibed, but unfortunately had *the* most menacing clientele. The brewer, Malthparlek, used the grain to make 'Orville Ale,' and the two would split the profits. Fortunately, despite the terrible taste, it was *potent* and quite often . . . poisonous. Though Orville was naive to this dreadful fact, this meant those who tasted the fruit of their labor likely wouldn't return anytime soon to harry the two crooks over the results. For the brewer, this kept the overhead low. For the ignorantly unscrupulous Orville, it meant that his namesake brew always seemed to have a fresh flow of new customers. Then the two would use their profits to buy more booze from the tavern and celebrate.

That had been the way of things for quite some time, and Orville thought his life was quite lovely, all things considered. Which is why it was such an unfortunate pain when the monsters attacked.

All night long, it seemed, the . . . oomukade had been swarming the town, and that was something terribly inconvenient for Orville. He'd been on his way to the tavern for the evening, a burlap sack full of his acquired haul over his shoulder, when he'd been accosted by two terrifying creatures. The man couldn't help but think they looked very much like overgrown caterpillars. To make matters worse, that damnable system kept jabbering in his ear to alert him to what he already knew: Tallrock was under attack.

Using his overqualified Sneaking Skill, the man immediately dropped his sack of stealings and hid in the shadows, waiting a long time for the monsters to grow bored and move on. Then, knowing the excrement had indeed hit the rudders, he retrieved his spoils and moved stealthily through the streets. Orville knew he'd need to be careful to avoid any more of the foul beasts running amok in his glorious hometown.

As was mentioned, Orville was a wonder at hiding. He had no issue routing around the dangers until he found the tavern. Upon his arrival, however, he discovered that, curiously, the doors were locked and the windows shuttered tight. Even after several minutes of prying, he couldn't find a way in. And so, heaving a great sigh of disappointment, he began looking for another tavern to drown his evening inside. He thought it was monstrously disrespectful of the establishment to make itself unavailable on a night like this one.

However, every tavern Orville thought of engaging on that fateful eve resolved to be much the same as the Tankard: closed.

Orville had never in his life been so in need of a drink and so incapable of retrieving one. While he may have had a great many flaws, the man was not one to balk at the challenge of finding a dry place for wet swill. Undeterred, he endeavored to continue his quest, his satchel of stolen animal feed slung over his shoulder and a dream in his heart. So encouraged was he by the thought of forthcoming ale, he didn't even notice when the gigantic queen arrived within the confines of Tallrock. When he'd recovered from being knocked to the flagstones by her roar, he'd glared at the clear night sky, believing the weather had also turned on him.

Really, the only thing that even caught his attention in any form was the auxiliary monsters that would sweep by periodically, forcing him back into hiding. Eventually, as he made his way back to his home, the thicket of oomukade became too dense to ignore successfully. So, he decided to hide along the main thoroughfare of the western side of town behind a large rubbish dumpster and wait out the whole business. That was, of course, when everything turned very strange indeed.

There was a loud *snap* and a *boom*. Though the crowd of monsters continued to grow in the streets, even Orville's perception deficit could make out a shape moving along the road in the distance. Most critically: it was traveling quickly. He heard another loud, banging racket, followed by a crackling that sounded to the man like hundreds of pebbles being scattered over metal. In his hiding place, he watched and waited as the shape in the distance grew, joined by flashes of light.

Someone was performing Arcana unrepentantly and flippantly right there in the streets; he was sure of it. Was there no decency to the folk of this town? Didn't they know someone could get hurt? These were all thoughts that Orville had swimming in his mind as he watched. What big thing was shooting across the stones and causing such a fuss?

Then it became abundantly clear. It was a cart.

Firing at top speed through the street Orville could see a large wagon, unburdened by any beast and lofted along by Arcana, it appeared. Within the open top of the four-wheeled vehicle were three figures. One was a comely elf woman with fire-red hair, waving a stick in the air and casting—what appeared to be clustering bolts of lightning—at any behemoth caterpillars that happened into her path. Next to her was an illisinaf, and though Orville had not seen many in his life, he knew one on sight by the amorphous general shape they assumed. This one was clad only in a sweater vest and producing identical bolts as the elf with minute motions of their appendages. Together they blasted all of the enemies around them in a frantic sort of way.

The third member of the carriage crew was a massive humanoid, and Orville wasn't sure what he was at first. He appeared orc like at initial glance, but he was dressed in a strange motley of skirt and bandoliers. Just as strange was his skin. Though it was hard to tell in the dim light, the orc appeared to have the usual green-gray hue to his flesh, but there was an oddity: he had dozens of shimmering spots adorning the entirety of visible skin. When lightning would flash, the spots would glimmer brighter as if made of mirrors, and Orville wasn't sure but thought they might be pink. That couldn't be accurate. Could it?

The orc was at the back, wielding a branch similar to the one brandished by the elf. However, he was not using it to attack any nearby creatures. Instead, he was facing backward, eyes cast to something beyond that Orville hadn't yet noticed. The man peered out, trying desperately to make out what the large, terrifying individual was viewing. He didn't have to wait long.

As the group approached, Orville saw what looked like a writhing shadow giving swift chase to the cart. After just a breath, he could make out arms, or rather, legs—lots of them—and large caterpillar bodies. However, these versions of the oomukade weren't like the ones he'd been dodging all evening. No, these were *much* larger and vastly more numerous. As they came into view, Orville could see that they were, in fact, much more menacing than their easy-to-flee counterparts. Whatever they were, Orville knew they were a bad omen and trouble of the highest order.

That was when he realized the orc's role in this encounter. As the horde of oomukade drew closer to their quarry, the enormous creature let out a sound that was more animal roar than scream and lifted the branch. Then he fired a plume of flame from the end of the stick. The cart lurched with the blast and heaved forward, moving faster than it had been and carrying the group narrowly away from the monsters' clutches.

Orville was aghast. This party was somehow using arcane fire to propel themselves along the road at high speeds to outrun their pursuers. That seemed monumentally inventive and unique to the man hiding bravely near the garbage. In fact, he was so awed that before he'd even realized it, he'd stepped out into the roadway, revealing himself and flagging down the group with a cheery smile and friendly wave.

"Oi!" He shouted. "Big 'un! Can I catch a ride on your sorcery craft?!"

# CHAPTER ELEVEN

# ACHY BREAKY CART

oon!" Rua yelled from the front of the wagon.

"A little busy!" I yelled back, firing another blast from the wand to keep the disgusting higher-level oomukade from catching up with us.

"There's a man in the street up ahead!" She shouted. "He's waving at us!"

"What?" I demanded. "Tell him to get outta the way and, I dunno, *hide* or something! This ain't a parade, goddammit!"

There was a pause, and then Edwig responded. "He wants a ride!"

"What?!" I shouted. "That's stupid! Tell him to *git*! We can't stop this ride, or we'll fuckin' die!" I glanced over my shoulder, and sure enough, there was some dumbass dude with a sack slung over his back, waving like a damned fool in the fucking *middle* of the road! "What the fuck? Tell his ass to *move*! We're gonna blast right into him!"

"He doesn't seem to realize that!" Rua yelled back to me.

Growling, I looked back at the quickly gaining mass of super oomukade we'd been outmatching for the last few minutes. Then, rolling my eyes, I wheeled in place and stuck my head over the side of the cart, careful not to shift my weight too much lest the whole thing topple over and give us a medieval road rash.

"Hey! Dipshit!" I roared at the man still stupidly gesturing at us. "Get outta the fucking way! We can't stop!"

He moved to the right a little, which *may* have been enough to divert himself outta Splatsville, but I couldn't be sure. Then he waved again.

"Take me with you!" he shouted. Despite his demand, he didn't seem to realize the danger he was actually in, as he still had a goofy grin plastered on his face.

*Is this guy a for-real dumbass?* I wondered.

"Loon!" Rua called. "Even if we don't hit him, he'll get trampled by the oomukade!"

She didn't need to say anything else, because I knew the implication in her tone. The elf was saying that this schmuck was doomed either way. Worse yet, the silly little shit-for-brains didn't seem to realize the predicament he'd gotten himself into.

I let out another growl of pure disappointed contempt. I hated this sort of shit. Wasn't it bad enough that we had about as much window of opportunity to escape this fiasco as a third party had of winning a meaningful election in American politics? Now, despite just *barely* holding the lead on these monster fucks, I'd have to do something to help *this* guy out, too?

"Fuck!" I roared, and turned back to the man in the road. He was still fucking waving.

"Put your hand out!" I exclaimed. The man paused, then pointed stupidly at himself.

"Me?" I could see—but not hear—him ask.

"Yes, *you!*" I shouted. "We can't stop, so I'll pull you onboard as we pass!"

The man nodded and stuck his hand out like he was hailing a taxi.

I grumbled, anger building in my chest. I already knew I was going to regret the shit out of this.

"Get ready!" I yelled, and flashed a look at the horde behind us. They were closer.

"Shit! Alright! Rua! Edwig!" I called. "Both of you guys lean on the left side. I'm gonna try grabbing this guy, and we don't need the whole cart flipping over. Ready?"

I shifted so that I was on the right side of the cart. I braced myself with one hand and waited as we neared. My fear—you know, other than immediately smashing face-first into the ground—was that we were moving too fast and I'd turn this guy into paste—like when I hit that Redmark soldier after falling off a cliff.

"Here goes nothing!" I yelled. "Okay! Ready . . . LEAN!"

From the corner of my eye, I saw Rua and Edwig slam themselves against the other side of the cart to balance us. I leaned forward, my arm outstretched, fingers reaching out to the moron in the road's hand.

*WHAM!*

*Ah, fuck!*

The absolute douchenozzle had stepped forward just as I was about to snatch his wrist up, and I'd accidentally *slapped him in the head.* He went down. Hard.

"SHIIIIIT!" I roared.

I whipped back to look at Rua and Edwig, my eyes wide. I was too shocked to say anything. Fortunately, so were they. Their expressions mirrored my own, and none of us could make a sound as we all realized what had just happened.

It was Edwig who broke the silence.

"You . . . coldcocked him . . ."

"He—he, uh, well . . ." That was all I could say.

Thankfully, I was interrupted by another voice behind us, full of confusion.

"Help me!"

As one, Rua, Edwig, and I all turned. There, dangling from the back of the cart, was the man I'd just finished administering a rocketing sucker-slap to. He was dragging along behind us in the street, clinging desperately to one lifeline: his big sack of whatever-the-fuck. Apparently, when he'd fallen, the bag must've gotten snared by the poorly made edge of the rough wood as we passed, and this numbskull was *just* covetous enough to not let go. It had saved his life, but now he was in a whole new pot of nonsense as the sack itself was beginning to rip apart where it was hooked up to our ride. Wang rod there was in danger of being left in the dust—you know, directly in the path of the big-ass centi-stampede.

"Well . . . fuckin' *oopsie!*" I exclaimed.

I was tired. It was well into the evening, and despite my sleeping in the woods giving me a Well Rested status, my exhaustion was beginning to set in. This was both a good thing and a bad thing. Suppose I got Fatigued, as in the world's mechanical trait associated with my stats. In that case, I'd gain a boost to Strength, Constitution, and Dexterity, but it would be at the cost of just about everything else. I hadn't yet received a Fatigued condition, but it had to be coming soon, and it was making me cranky.

Because of this, I was possibly a little pricklier than I would have been otherwise. I mean, let's be honest: I'd been forced to rescue this guy because he didn't understand the concept of right-of-way. *Learn to fuckin' signal or something, bone brain!* I reached over and stuck my arms out to try and grab him. Still, before I could do anything, the pesky, perturbing pedestrian began floating in the air. Like *whoosh.*

"Ah! He's a witch!" I exclaimed, reeling back. "Kill him!"

"Oh, he is *not!*" Edwig exclaimed with a loud sigh. "I'm just using a Spell!"

The illisinaf's appendages were a-wavin' in the air, gesturing in configurations regular limbs would never be able to reproduce. Now I could see the thin sheen of a magical aura surrounding the newcomer as he was plucked from his precarious position behind the cart and lazily plopped into the vehicle's bed. He staggered and swayed for a moment, getting his bearings, before panic snared his eyes. He lunged toward the sack still dragging behind us.

"My TREASURES!" he wailed, sounding like a damn maniac, his desperate fingers grasping for his goods.

"Oh, no, you don't!" I boomed, and snatched him by the back of the neck. I physically twisted his whole body in place so that he faced the front of the cart. "You got saved, and you're *stayin'* saved. *Now* you're gonna earn your keep."

I pointed ahead of us at the mildly congested roadway.

"Navigate," I commanded. "Now."

I paused before deciding it might be best to give a little context to his task.

"We're trying to catch that big motherfucking bug."

At that, I turned myself around quickly. I fired another blast from the wand, a fireball erupting from the end and launching us forward faster. The cluster of up-jumped oomukade in our wake had been gaining on us, but my magical speed flame had pushed us out of their reach a little farther. The sound of crackling lightning announced that Rua and Edwig had picked up their attacks again as the world whipped by us. However, our newest passenger was silent.

"I don't hear any *navigating*!" I called in a threatening singsong.

The man cleared his throat nervously, and then the cart shifted slightly as he moved to the front.

"Er, yes," he began. "Well, move it straight forward, lads. Keep it stead— *Corner*— CORNER!"

"Left or right?!" I yelled.

"Uh . . . left!" he yelled back.

"Rua! Edwig!" I barked, and immediately felt the both of them shift to one side of the ride as I switched my wand to the right with another flame gout to give us our momentum. I looked over my shoulder, grasping the carriage's sides and leaning to the left to apply the proper amount of weight to force a turn as I roared in concentrated effort. It was close, but we made it.

"Alright, newbie," I yelled, "that was almost *bad*! You only get *one*!"

"One?!" he exclaimed nervously. "One *what*?"

"One near miss," I said. "Next time, you're getting tossed out of here on your ass!"

"Loon, be nicer to him," Rua admonished.

"No!" I returned. "We ain't gonna survive if we worry about nice! Now— new guy!"

I paused for a moment to shoot another fireball.

"It's Orville," he answered.

"What? Who cares?!" I returned. "You know these streets, right?"

"Well, yes," he began. "This is my hometo—"

"Great!" I interjected. "Do you want to live?"

"What? Of course I want to live!"

"*Magnifico*," I said. "In that case—you see that gigantic uncomfortable conversation in the distance, lording over the buildings?"

"What?" he called back.

"The huge fuckin' monster!"

"Oh, er, yes!"

"Wonderful!" I continued. "Keep us—"

Another blast from the wand.

"—on a path toward that thing!"

"You want to get *close* to that terrible monster?!" the newcomer asked, evident horror in his tone.

"Baby, we ain't just gettin' close," I said. "We're—"

Blast!

"—gonna be *all* up in her grille."

"You're planning to fight it?!" came the man's terrified response. "That's madness!"

"Yup! But he's as crazy as a . . . well, a loon," Rua confirmed.

"Suicidal, he is!" Edwig continued, building up my insanity lore with further support. "Likely to take us all with him, too."

"That's right!" I said. "You're on—"

Blast!

"—the express train to Nuttyville, newbie! Now—"

Blast! Blast!

"—I ain't got a ton of charges left in this thing, so I need you to use *every single* shortcut you know about to get us—"

Blast!

"—to that big ol' bitch in the quickest route possible."

The man was silent.

"Goddammit, this is life or death, newbie! Do you understand or not?!" I roared.

"Yes! Yes!" he yelled back. Then he paused again. "I said my name was Orville, though. Perhaps you didn't hear."

"Oh, I heard. Don't give a shit!" I exclaimed.

Orville frowned, then turned forward.

"We've got a detour up ahead, I think. I hid from some people here once when—"

"No backstory!" I yelled. "Just direction! *Do. You. Comprehend?*"

Man, it wasn't often I felt smarter than someone. However, with this guy, I will admit I felt a little smug about the difference in our intellect. He seemed pretty simple. Hopefully, saving him wouldn't bite us right in the cheeks.

"Corner!" Orville suddenly announced. "To the right!"

A prompt suddenly appeared, and I'd be lying if I said I had ever thought it was something I'd see, even here in this world.

**Congratulations! You've gained a new Skill!**
*Leadership [F-Rank Level 1]*

I smirked. Then I fired another blast and *leaned*.

With the new guy's help, it took us less than an additional five minutes to get to where we wanted to be: staring down the barrel of catastrophe incarnate.

There she was in all her glory: the oomukade queen mum, and my oh my, was she a terror beyond reasonable comprehension. She was a vulgar, repulsive creature and a towering affront to whatever it is that passed for normalcy, even in this world. But before long, despite the firm and unmistakable sensation of wanting to be literally anywhere else, we were soaring into a direct confrontation with her. Regardless of the situation and the building bile in my esophagus, I couldn't help but smirk. I felt alive.

We rocketed along the avenue, having—for the moment—a perfectly straight shot toward Madam Gross-and-Terrifying, with the nest of nefarious ne'er-do-wells eating up the distance behind us. I squinted as I saw movement up ahead in the street. At first, I thought, *Ah, fiddlesticks*, because it almost looked like an additional cluster of centipedes gathering near her . . . base— where her legs were. But, as we drew near, I found that wasn't actually the case. A few large shapes—three, to be precise—moved jerkily alongside her, making aggressive maneuvers as if they were some type of shambling mega-zombies. Anyway, they looked quite a bit different from the segmented nightmare serpents we'd been battling all the live-long evening. In fact, it was now evident to me that them weren't no bugs. Them were *other* monsters.

First of all, one of the creatures looked like a huge, bipedal polar bear made out of crystalline stone, with glowing red eyes that left afterimages like the goddamn Terminator as it moved its massive head from side to side. Another resembled a four-foot-tall toad, except it shimmered with irradiated-green energy like it had just gotten back from sunbathing in Chernobyl. Both of these beasts seemed to behave like actual animals, prowling along—albeit a bit strangely—with very little in the way of communicative agency. It was the third monster that was actually the scariest. It wasn't as tall and girthy as the crystal bear, nor was it as nuclear-powered-looking as the toad; instead, it was vaguely humanoid in shape and covered in . . . Was that fur? Hair? I dunno. They looked like a sasquatch, kind of. But like his younger, *svelter* sister. Either way, it looked like whatever the third monster was, they were capable of *commanding* the others. Bigfoot Jr. gestured with long limbs, and the monster pair followed their master's indication immediately.

*Uh-oh, SpaghettiOs.*

"Shit," I said aloud. "Guys—the mommy bug's got friends!"

"We're surrounded by her friends!" Edwig called back from his post at the left side of the cart.

"Not that!" I shouted, pointing ahead. "I'm talkin' about *those!*"

"Oh, *gods!*" Edwig returned, spotting the group of new horrors. "We're doomed in a big, big way."

"Can we find an alternate route?" Rua asked. "You know, one that doesn't send us right into their midst?"

I glanced around the streets and the impressive lack of alleys or substitute roadways.

"Ah, fuckin' piss!" I shouted. "Nope! Nothin'. Get ready to fight."

"Fight?" Rua asked. "We've only got these wands!"

"Well, we're just going to have to hope we're lucky and it turns out they're allergic to magic," I declared, removing my haladie from my waistband. ". . . and, uh . . . blades."

I realized when I said that, that I hadn't checked my Luck stat in a while. I knew that it had a tendency to shift around, either in the positive or the negative, and I had to hope to fucking *fuck* it wasn't dipping below zero. I opened my menu and searched for the Attribute.


**Luck -4**


*Ah, poop. This is bad.*

Edwig scowled at my previous words, shaking his blubbery head.

"Pah! We're definitely dead."

"Wait!" Orville exclaimed.

The man had been silent for the last few minutes, so this was a surprise. As one, the three of us turned to face him. When he turned around, he had a big goofy grin.

*Great, he's gone feral.*

"We're not doomed," he finally said.

"We're not?" Edwig asked, looking back and forth from Orville, to Rua, to me, and back.

"Nope!" Orville declared.

"You better start making sense right now, home slice," I hissed. "What. Do. You. Mean?"

"Those creatures aren't on *her* side," he continued with a single nod. "That's Bonnie and her friends."

"What?" I barked. "Who's Bonnie?"

"Just a gal I know," he said smugly. "She's the middle one. But she's not in league with the monster. Look."

He gestured back to the group, and I squinted to get a greater gander at the goings-on. Sure enough, as I watched, the trio of rejected Chuck E. Cheese animatronic cast members began *attacking* the oomamakade, striking out at her legs and undercarriage. The crystal bear slashed out with gigantic rock claws, while the toad leaped into the air and vomited out a glowing tongue that connected with one of the centipede legs. Sassy Quatch began yanking cobblestones out of the street and hurling them up toward the larger monster's mass.

"Oh, hell, yeah," I said, then smirked. "Guys, *we've* got friends!"

I could ask later as to the nature of how this doofus knew a crazy cryptid creature; for now, I was perfectly swell with being ignorant as long as I knew they'd be batting for Team Loon. Instead of questions, I mustered up my muscle and reared back with the haladie.

"Alright, gang," I said, preparing a toss. "Things might get a little shitty, but we're here. Time to bring these beasts back from the babysitter."

I pointed at the still-gaining oomukade at our rear and adopted a gruesome grin. Luck be damned. I was going to make my own fortune. Zeol *had* said it was high-risk, high-reward, and all I'd have to do was make it out the other side of this encounter. I pointed at the monster still traipsing through Tallrock.

"She ain't gonna know what sucker-punched her. How about we swing by and say hell— OHH SHIT!"

I'd seen movement out of the corner of my eye and, turning my head, discovered that we were not alone. You know, other than the horde of bugs behind us, the giant one ahead of us, and the three big, friendly goonies. This was a distinctly anti-monstrous figure, racing along next to our speed wagon. Uncomfortably tall, laden-down with inflated-looking muscle, and with a face like a CW DILF, this four-thousand-RPM roadrunner was none other than Rafe Crowmoon himself.

*What in the Kentucky-fried fuck is* happening?

I was about to scream at Edwig and Rua to blast him to holy hell, but I didn't get the chance. Before a single molecule of air could leave my lungs in alarm, the colossal man turned on a fucking pin and slammed his whole body against the side of the carriage, sending us careening off the road and into . . .

All I knew was pain. I'd hit something hard when I'd been thrown and crashed into another hard thing before landing on . . . something else that was hard and coming to a stop. Eyes closed, my senses congealed into one incredible ball of agonized confusion. However, even in my stupor with my lids tightly clamped, I could still see my Health bar. It was a deep, flashing crimson and indicated that I only had three points of life left in my body. I had an ability that allowed me to drop to negative nine for up to one minute, so it wasn't as dire as it would have been for others, but it still wasn't good.

"Jesus fuck . . ." I heard myself moan. There was a loud crunch and something like creaking, and I finally gained enough sense to open my eyes.

I was lying amongst pieces of the wrecked carriage in a smoking hole of rubble and debris inside what appeared to be somebody's house.

*Shit, this is the second time this has happened tonight. I'm becoming a menace.*

Then, my senses fully returned, and I recalled what had just happened: Crowmoon had pitched our entire wagonload into a building. It had happened so fast that I hadn't had any time to react. I frantically looked around to see if I could locate Rua and Edwig. However, the dust that kicked up from my spontaneous home inspection made it difficult to see anything. Worse yet, I was still in an assload of pain and could see the notifications informing me of my Fractured condition.

*Great,* I thought to myself. *Blind, dumb, and in an orc costume filled with broken bones. This is going to go great for me.*

That was, of course, when Rafe Crowmoon decided to reveal himself.

He stepped into the cloud of destruction, his handsome silver-fox features curled into a smile. There were open cuts and scrapes along his face and arms, as it appeared the fight with the captain had been challenging even for him. However, considering he was standing in front of me and she was not, it wasn't hard to imagine who'd finally been crowned the winner of their Tekken tournament.

"Hello, there," Crowmoon said, his tone just as frighteningly friendly as before. "What a wonderful coincidence to find you here."

"Oh, fuck off," I said, trying—and failing—to lift myself up from the ground. "You're a real piece of shit, you know that?"

"That's not a very—"

"Man, shut *up*," I interrupted. "Why the hell are you even pretending to be polite? You're a fuckin' murderer. Or, at least, you're an attempted murderer. Whatever; you've got murder in your heart, making you one whether you've successfully completed a homicide or not."

"I have," Crowmoon said casually, shrugging a little. "It's not that difficult to kill when everyone is weaker than you."

"You are the human equivalent of a gooch punch, do you know that?" I asked rhetorically. "I just thought you were kind of a dick before, but now you're bragging about using your superior strength to make other people suffer?"

Crowmoon shrugged again.

"They rarely suffer," he said. "I tend to make it quick—over with before they know it. I don't delight in torture or prolonged anguish."

"What a fuckin' hero," I said. "And how many of the people you've killed were just minding their own business like we were?"

"You were not minding yourself, orc," Crowmoon said, chuckling. "As I recall, you were slinking around in the dark, trying to stick your nose into the business of others. I understand you were there to rescue your friend, but unfortunately, it was simply terrible timing. So it goes, as they say."

He hefted something in his hand, and I felt a sharp pang of dread.

"I think you dropped this," the balloon-muscled behemoth said, revealing the indestructible orb's milky-glass texture in his palm.

*How the hell did he get ahold of that?*

I quickly looked from side to side and noticed that my pack had been abso-lutely ravaged by the forceful jettisoning. A wide array of my belongings had spilled and scattered along the floor. Fortunately, it seemed that most of the objects I'd had on my person were still intact, and with a pang of relief, I found that I could feel the weight of the Dreadnaught trinket and Merra's amulet in the pouch of my kilt. Though how I hadn't sliced my hip bone into sashimi with the haladie was a miracle unto itself. I'd landed *right on it*, and it was currently wedged under me, out of reach.

*Well, fuckin'* gulp.

"Thought I might return the favor from earlier," he continued, tossing the orb repeatedly in the air and catching it.

This was bullshit. I could see the threat in the gesture: he was planning to bludgeon me to death with that rock because I'd tried to do that earlier to him. A natural douchebag move.

"I thought you didn't like people to suffer," I spat defiantly from the floor.

"Yes, I did say that . . ." he said thoughtfully. "But you're very annoying. I think you deserve it."

With that, Rafe Crowmoon raised the orb and advanced.

# CHAPTER TWELVE

# HOMEWRECKER

I was in an entire universe of shit.

As Rafe moved toward me, I frantically began to scrabble away. It was essentially useless since I was too busted and broken on the inside to do anything other than lie there and grimace. If I was planning to do anything, now would be the time. I couldn't just lie there and die unless I wanted to be some dumbass demon's favorite dino nugget. Worse still, my Luck was in the negatives, meaning my odds were supremely stunted when it came to anything helping me out of my situation other than little ole me.

*Fuck this,* I thought. *I'm not scared of this obnoxiously polite gutter pumpkin.*

Even facing an impossible and inescapable nightmare, I was reminded of something my Uncle Luke used to say. He was apparently an *okay* lawyer, but he had a terrible case of stage fright any time he'd have to . . . MC for his clients during court, or whatever you called it. He'd always be up late the night before a trial, no matter how menial the charges—and they were usually *pretty low-stakes*—because he was so nervous about having to go to work and command the attention of the whole courtroom. Whenever I asked him how he got through it, he'd say the same thing. *"Impending doom is only as powerful as you allow it to be. Don't give it the satisfaction of seeing you cower in fear."*

I didn't know if Uncle Luke had read that in one of those fantastical British novels he was always lost in or if he'd conjured it up himself. Either way, I'm fairly certain he'd never had to face a maniacal beefcake Super Shredder while trying to keep his innards from spilling out all over the place.

Crowmoon approached casually, as if the horrible deed he was about to exact on me was just another task on his Sunday-afternoon to-do list. Was it Sunday? It struck me, oddly, right there in the thick of potential manslaughter, that I didn't even know how days of the week worked there or if they even had them. Let's pretend it was Sunday. Regardless, the way he was so lackadaisically meandering toward my demise really pissed me off, ya know? It wasn't enough that he was bigger, stronger, faster, and handsomer than me; he had to go ahead and treat me like I wasn't even worth respectfully murdering. Like I was *just some dude.*

*I'm motherfucking Loon, asshole.*

I was dragged into this fucking place against my will, only to have to literally fight for survival since the very first nanosecond I arrived. I'd almost died numerous times, *actually* died once, and taken more bites, scratches, kicks, and head punches than a first-year mall Santa. This jugheaded taint-tickler thought he could kill *me?* I am not the one.

*I goddamn promise: you're going to take me seriously, motherfucker.*

Plus, his narrowed brows and squint were really . . . Wait. Crowmoon *looked as* though he was probably human, and it seemed like he was having a hard time seeing too well in the dimly lit interior of the destroyed building.

*Interesting . . .* I thought. *This guy's a bit impaired in the low-viz department. Well, what do you know? I'm not.*

I needed to hold him off for as long as possible, but he wasn't the type to get rattled by well-placed insults or hilariously clever barbs. But maybe I could use this? So, as he got close, I did the only thing I could think to do: I started goin' *fuckin' bonkers.*

I slammed my fists on the floor next to me, writhing in place. I howled, making sounds like the Tasmanian Devil, then switched between absurd sex moans and unhinged laughter. Then I started growling, which turned into barking. I thrashed my legs around, and despite the pain of having more broken bones inside me than a KFC sandwich, I began hip-thrusting and doing a really awful backward worm. I was just going with whatever came to mind—I mean absolutely straight-up apeshit stuff. I think I even started singing "The Star-Spangled Banner."

There's one thing that's true no matter how tough someone thinks they are: *nobody* wants to fuck with crazy.

I could tell I'd really made Crowmoon pause, because rather than get any closer, he sort of took a tentative step backward, his face twisted in horror. I'd surmised he was probably at a disadvantage in low-light environments, and I was so incredibly stealthy . . . So, that was when I flipped the lid off my masterwork Tupperware of tricks: I scooped some dust up from the ground and threw it right in his eyes.

Being stubborn may not always be the most graceful quality, but it sure comes in handy when you're trying to stand your ground.

"Ninja vanish!" I roared.

"Gah!" Crowmoon bellowed, clawing at his sockets with his free hand. Apparently, even super strong demigods like him couldn't stop the ole iris-itchies. Then, while he was momentarily distracted, I grabbed the first weapon in my immediate vicinity: the wand of flames. I brought it up, fired it right at Crowmoon's stupid face, and released a guttural, pig-squeal death growl.

"Brrrreeeeeeee!" I exhaled, trying to mimic the swine-like noise as best I could.

It was when I saw the color of the blast I realized I'd messed up.

Magical *pink* energy shot from the end of the rod—indicating I *hadn't* grabbed the fiery magic stick. When wielding the wand of flames, it spat out fireballs. I'd instead just used the wand of supreme unlocking. You know, on a person.

It didn't matter anyway, because Crowmoon's Spidey senses were apparently incredibly well-developed. He brought the indestructible orb up to cover his face, and the Spell rebounded, ricocheting right back at me. It hit my body, which swiftly grew warm before fading as the magic dissolved. I'd halfway worried it would blast all my clothes off and I'd be harmless, flailing, *and* naked. But it didn't appear anything was wrong with me, so I adopted my former hostile-insanity act and laughed.

Crowmoon wiped the last of the dust out of tear-filled eyes and scowled.

"What's the matter, sweetie?" I asked. "Is the big, strong predator not used to getting a taste of his own medicine? Here's a lesson for you: sometimes even the mice fight back."

"You are—" Crowmoon began, but didn't get a chance to finish his sentence because, at that moment, there was a flash of light from my crotch.

Purples, blues, and pinks erupted from the pouch on my kilt, swirling and sparkling in the air like a magical STD firework. The plume flashed again with an internal light before twisting and shriveling into a much smaller form. It shrank to the size of a two-liter bottle of soda, the vaporwave color scheme becoming transparent as the shape continued to transform.

During this, I saw Crowmoon's eyes. They were as wide as saucers, and he looked at me silently with voiceless wonder as to what I'd just done. I returned a shrug. It was weird that we were suddenly unified in bafflement, if only briefly. The thing undulating amorphously near my nethers looked like a Miyazaki monster until it suddenly began shifting into a new configuration. It was now roughly the size of a teddy bear, with spindly deep-violet arms and legs. It had a round little onion head with glowing electric-blue eyes made up of spirals. Around its body was a very thin, translucent garment the color of illuminated spider web. From its head, long, fluorescent pink hair cascaded down and dispersed amongst the body wrap like a waterfall disappearing into a river's misty surface.

*Is this a fucking alien?* I wondered. *What the hell is this creepy little thing? It looks like a haunted American Girl doll.*

Nobody said anything for a moment as the creature that had just appeared seemed to take in its surroundings. Then it pivoted where it floated in midair, resting its LED gaze on me. I couldn't even stare right into them because it was not only unnerving but also painful and left afterimages in my vision as I looked away.

"You know what's funny?"

The question had come from the creature, its tiny mouth issuing the words in a high, dreamy voice. It had delivered the line quickly, as if it was excited to get them out as fast as possible.

No one said anything in response to this bizarre specter; both Crowmoon and I were apparently too shocked to make a sound. The creature continued.

"I have had a song stuck in my head the whole time I was in there," the creature continued. "And can't figure out what it is."

Then the thing floated toward me lightning-quick, and I let out a little gasp. It got right in my face.

"It goes 'Doo-da-doo, doo-doo-da-da-dum. Dum-da-doo, doo doo,'" it sang, its eyes forcing me to look away. "You know it? Ringin' any bells? I think it's a love song . . ."

The creature paused, thoughtfully bringing its little arm up to its chin before staring off as if recalling some profound universal truth before continuing.

"Or maybe . . . a song of *war* . . ."

"What *are* you?" I wondered aloud in an awed stupor.

The creature flew closer, its mouth open in what I thought might be a mimicry of me.

"I don't *know*," it said in the same flabbergasted tone I'd used—though considerably higher-pitched.

I needed to recap the last few seconds. The Spell had hit me, and then light had ejaculated from my pelvic region and the pocket of my kilt where I kept precisely two items: Merra's amulet and the figurine I'd liberated from the dungeon. Based on the description of the little trinket that Eye of the Saboteur had offered, I was uncomfortably convinced as to who this specter actually was.

"Rexen?" I asked, using the name of the apparently super powerful . . . What was the word? Thoombatoom? Whatever, I think it was a type of necromancer or something. Rexen Gravetongue was not only the purported creator of the Crypt of the Dreadnaught Lord but was, in fact, the Dreadnaught Lord himself. More importantly, according to my Ability, his soul had been trapped inside the figurine. Which I'd just accidentally used an unlocking Spell on.

*Fuck, I hate wizards,* I thought for the second time tonight.

The . . . former sorcerer seemed to brighten at my use of his name, a happy little smile curving on his diminutive lips.

"Good! You're caught up. That will save loads of time!" Then he actually looked critically at me and took in everything happening around us. I absolutely *hated* when people tried to figure me out with a glance.

"Wow, you really got the stuffing pulled outta ya, huh? How'd that happen?"

I raised a finger indignantly and pointed right at Crowmoon.

"He did it."

Listen, I know that no one likes a tattletale, but it just felt right in the moment, you know? If *anything* could get me out of this predicament, it would be the bizarre spectral anomaly floating in the air before me. He was supposed to be powerful, right? Maybe he could turn him into a frog?

*Or a corpse.*

Rexen followed my gesture and stared at Rafe Crowmoon. The man still seemed perplexed but no longer as shocked as he did a moment before. Now he appeared pensive, as if he was working something over in his mind.

"You some kind of bully boy?" Rexen asked him suddenly in his fast-paced way. It was an accusatory question but not exactly threatening.

Crowmoon smiled wide.

"Not at all," he said with his usual honeyed tone. "I was simply preparing to execute this orc here because he saw something he shouldn't have. It won't take but a minute, if you'll just pardon me."

"Oh, okay," Rexen said, nodding sagely.

"What?" I shouted. "You're just . . . cool with it? That doesn't bother you? He's a murderer!"

Rexen gasped, but it seemed like he was almost . . . delighted?

"I've never met a murderer before! I'm not sure how to react. What do I do with my hands?"

Then the creature raised his limbs, staring at them in horror.

"I haven't got any hands!" Then he released an exaggerated exhalation. "That's a relief."

Perhaps because, at that moment, I was so low in Health that I was practically pounding on the door of hell's Port-o-Potty, I didn't fully appreciate the unique humor of this bizarre encounter. It was hella weird.

"No," I exclaimed. "No, no, no! Fuck this. Rexen, you're here because of me. I rescued you from—"

"I am sorry," Crowmoon interrupted. "I must get on with my escape, but that requires cleaning up this mess first. I'll ask that you forgive me for the necessity of—"

"—that stupid fucking toy wizard's tower," I interrupted right back.

*This asshole ain't talking over* me; *that's for damn sure.*

Crowmoon had stopped speaking the moment I'd started again and just smiled at me like a proud dad. It was disgusting. This distraction wouldn't hold for long, so I had to think of something else. But my Luck was low. I was on borrowed time, and if, somewhere in the cosmos, there was something like a chrono-bookie, it was going to send someone to break my legs any second. I quickly looked from side to side, hoping to catch a glimpse of my wagon companions as the dust finally settled.

*There.*

Edwig was lying on his . . . side? Back? I dunno; his body was weird, so it could have just as well been his gelatinous face. Either way, he wasn't moving, which was worrisome. Rua was twenty feet from me, her back resting against a wall with a suspiciously elf-sized crater. Blood stained her cheeks, and her eyes were closed. The new guy . . . was nowhere to be seen.

*Well, he's almost definitely dead. Probably got blasted to bits the moment we flew in here.*

I knew I'd have to help the others, as they looked pretty worse for wear. Fortunately, Rua hadn't turned to mist yet, so she still had to be alive. Who knew *what* the fuck went on with Edwig's kind, but it had to be more challenging than that to kill a living Jell-O, right?

I guess I wasn't exactly blessed with a depth of knowledge about whatever the fuck illisinafs actually *were.* Still, he had to be made out of sturdier stuff if his whole blobby body could hold an upright shape regularly. I mean, he wasn't a puddle, so he was, therefore . . . alive? I'll admit that I was probably grasping. But if I'd learned one thing since getting there, it was that I should never assume I know what the fuck I'm talking about. When he was safely in that cell, he'd seemed so confident about his odds against Crowmoon before. Was that all just misplaced bravado?

That was enough pondering. If Crowmoon didn't kill me now, odds were—based on my abysmal Luck—that the whole place could cave in on itself soon, crushing me and everyone else.

*Wait a minute . . .*

There was a chance! I quickly delved into one of my wonderful little Abilities: Eye of the Saboteur. I knew I'd only have seconds, but maybe that would be enough time to give Rafey-boy the ole razzle-dazzle.

**Crofter's Building**
- **Rarity: Common**
- **Item Class: Residence**
- **Durability: 1,208 / 5,000**
- **Weight: N/A**

Material Composition: Stone, straw, wood, glass, metal
- Stone [80%] - The walls of the building are made of roughhewn stone, providing strong, durable support.
- Straw [6.5%]—The roof of the building is thatched with straw, providing insulation and protection from the elements.
- Wood [12%]—The doors, window frames, and other features of the building are made of wood, which is strong and easy to work with.
- Glass [0.2%]—The panes of the windows are made of glass to keep out the elements and allow visibility at the same time.
- Metal [0.8%]—The hinges of the doors and nails in the wood are made of metal.
- Other (Miscellaneous) [0.5%]

*Ah, the poor crofter's building. It stands here, battered and broken, a testament to the cruel whims of fate. It was once a humble dwelling, nestled amongst the beauty of urban Tallrock. But now its walls are destroyed or otherwise cracked, and its roof is caved in, the victim of some sudden, brutal force. It's hard to say what could have caused such destruction—a rampaging monster, perhaps, or a gang of bandits? Whatever the cause, it's clear that this building has seen better days.*

*But even in its ruined state, the crofter's building has a certain charm. Its walls are made of roughhewn stone worn smooth by the passage of time. Its roof is thatched with straw, now torn and tattered by the elements. And despite the damage, it still stands, a testament to the resilience and resourcefulness of the crofter who built it.*

*So, let us pause a moment and pay our respects to this humble dwelling. For even in its ruined state, it is stubbornly refusing to fall.*

I'd still not gotten used to the fact that I could glean all of this information about something with Eye of the Saboteur as long as I was looking at it as a whole. I had experimented a bit in the last day or so and discovered that my intent was more important than anything else, but knew I had to touch whatever it was I was trying to get the blueprints on.

Speaking of: a mental map had begun forming in my mind, showing me the sort of detail I'd initially been seeking. It was like a hazy outline drawn by an eight-year-old, but it worked for what I needed. Within the graphic I could see several red dots, showing me the weak spots and damaged areas, and the dots were bigger based on what was least structurally sound—at least, that was what I'd been able to figure out so far. I was pretty sure there'd be more detail and information if I was ever able to Level this Ability up, but I had to work with what I had at the moment. I was also hoping there was a way to shut off the *extra*-long descriptions the Ability provided. I mean, don't get me wrong, having access to all that crap might be helpful to someone who *wasn't* me—but for this particular orc, it was just more dung to plod through.

This was the same strange superpower that I'd used to demolish the statue in the dungeon just a few days before, saving my ass at a crucial moment. I'd found the structure's weak spot and delivered a beautiful punishing blow to the honey zone, causing it to collapse on top of Ocho, the friend-killing fuckhead. I could see now, above my newest enemy's head was a spot that *might* work, if only I could figure out a method to get to it. Though, based on the flow of my encounter so far—I might've already been fucked.

Strangely, Rexen hadn't said anything for a moment, seemingly digesting what I'd told him.

*Pfft. If you start thinking what I say is important, little spirit dude, you're gonna have a bad time. I'm notoriously—*

"That's enough, then," Crowmoon said jovially, as if he was a lenient baby-sitter telling his charge he'd have to stop playing with his Beyblades and get to bed before his parents got home. Man, it was *super* irritating how friendly he seemed. The tank of a man strode forward, brandishing the orb.

"I've let you keep me here long enough," he continued. "Though I tip my hat to you for waylaying me this long with your frequent detours."

"Fuck off, neckbeard," I hissed. "Why don't you—"

He struck. Crowmoon's arm snapped into a pitch, hurling the orb at a speed that would have landed him a spot as history's greatest baseball player back in my world. I flinched away, closing my eyes and letting out a low peep of surprise. I didn't move, waiting to feel the force of a thousand paintballs and ultimately fucking die. But the blow never came.

I opened my eyes.

Crowmoon looked shocked. He was gaping down at Rexen, who was now floating in place with a big smile on his tiny face. The little spirit was holding the goddamn indestructible orb.

*What?* I wondered. *Don't tell me—*

"My shiny!" the creature cheered, hugging the stone tightly to himself, his eyes closed and both arms wrapped around its smooth curvature. "I missed you!"

"How did you do that?" Crowmoon demanded, clearly dazzled by this unforeseen twist.

Rexen was silent for a moment and opened his eyes just the barest amount, giving a mischievous glint.

"It's mine," he said simply. "So, I took it back."

"Remarkable," Crowmoon breathed. "Truly astonishing. Is there a limit to your range?"

"If I can see it, I can be it," Rexen said. "But, sometimes—as long as I know where it is."

Then the spirit turned to face me, its sunny vibe returning.

"You were the one who released me? For truest true?"

"Uh, yeah . . ." I said, unsure of where this was going. Was he going to be happy about it? Pissed off that I interrupted some unknown ritual? Some other mysterious third thing that would be bafflingly stupid?

"Ooh, okay!" he said. Then he lifted an arm into the air like a superhero in some big-budget cinematic cash grab. "Then I'll allow you to form a Pact!"

"Guh-wha, now?" I asked.

"Yes or no," he stated soberly. "I can help you. But you gotta decide now. Time's running out for you to—"

"Yes!" I interrupted. "Yes, yes, yes! I accept. Do it n—!"

Time stopped. At least, sort of. Everything physical seemed frozen in place: Crowmoon, the dust in the air, and Rexen himself. But that wasn't the weird part. No, it was that the moment I'd started my agreement, not only had everything paused but the world was instantly filled with pinks, purples, and blues. The colors swirled in the air like I'd tumbled into a reality dreamed up by a manic peyote demon. I could also not move, only watch, as Rexen's entire . . . everything flared with brilliant, blinding light. Symbols appeared in the air, arcing this way and that, forming intricate designs made of pure color.

I wanted to shout or do something—anything at all—but I was fixed to this spot, left wondering silently in horror and intrigue. Worse yet, I had the sneaking suspicion I'd just made a very bad decision. It wasn't until now I'd really considered the word he'd actually used: *Pact*.

Had I just accidentally formed *another* contract with a devil? Well, I suppose this wouldn't be considered "accidental" and likely counted as *fucking stupidly*. The symbols floated above me in their strange aerial-serpent entwinement for only a moment longer before flashing again, making me wish I could blink. Then my body was hit with heat. It felt like a hot fork was burrowing its way into my bones and muscles to lay some little utensil eggs. I wanted to scream, but I could only exist. I was imprisoned unmoving inside myself as I was subjected to the new torment of zany beams of nuclear color.

*Fuck!* I screamed inside my own mind. *This must be what locked-in syndrome feels like!*

Then the pain faded. Like, fucking *gone*. Nothing remained of the experience but a memory and raw eye sockets from holding back my tears. I was instantly reminded of when I'd whacked my Strength and Dexterity up to ten after wingmanning the collapse of the Redmark camp. That had hurt like holy fucking murder as well but had disappeared just as quickly.

*Wait.*

It wasn't just the agony from the spectral glyph torture that had gone away but *all* of my pain. Nothing hurt anymore. The broken bones, the bashes, and gashes—none of it. What the hell had just happened?

Before I could even finish being confused, the world whirled back into normal time, all the color sliding away and replaced by the dimness of the partially demolished crack den in the middle of the night. Crowmoon, too, was back to business, except he had taken another step in the opposite direction, like when I'd been flopping around on my back, acting all crazy. He'd sensed something—I could see it in his eyes. That alone gave me no end of hope.

But, even more, as I'd just discovered: I wasn't hurting anymore. However, when I checked my Health, I nearly shat my heart out of my dick.

It was . . . full.

Like, nothing gone at all. Moreover, the usual green color of the video-game-like bar was now behind a sheen of winking purple sparkles. As though it had been messing with one of those face-morphing Snapchat filters and was now *extra purdy.*

*Well, huh.* I thought. *This weird sumbitch just healed me!*

A notification flickered in the corner of my vision. While I usually would have ignored it—this seemed pertinent to the party. I opened the message and read over what I realized was a new addition to my already grossly overindulgent arsenal.

**Congratulations! You have formed a Pact!**
**Contractor: Rexen Gravetongue, the Dreadnaught Lord**
**Contractor Type: Arcane Entity**
**Duration: ???**
**Abilities: ???**
**Cost: ???**

*Uh-oh,* I thought. *Goddammit, Loon! Can't you get your shit together for five minutes and* not *suddenly make everything wildly inappropriate?*

Rexen was beaming at me now. His bright eyes swirled happily on his face. What was more, now I could *feel* his presence. It was like when I'd connected to Jes's party, but it felt more . . . intimate. Like we shared a magical umbilical cord or something. The little creature floated over to me, resting a handless arm on my forehead.

"Yes," he said, nodding as if bestowing me with some as-yet-unearthed secret of the universe. "This pleases me. Now I will always know exactly where you are."

"What . . . what just happened?" I asked, feeling very strange inside.

"Oh, nothing," Rexen explained, shrugging his little shoulders. "I just *own* you now. That's all."

*Fuck.*

# CHAPTER THIRTEEN

# CROTCH POCKET WIZARD

I am such a buffoon.

So far, I'd been at the mercy of pretty much every jacked-up, slack-jawed local yokel with an ax to grind, and had been lurching idiotically from danger to exponentially more irritating danger with the diplomacy and focused decision-making intensity of a drunk toddler. It sucked. But, ultimately, wantonly abandoning my . . . agency to rub shoulders with some sort of witch-ghost would likely prove to be . . . maybe one of my worst moves. Who knew? What I *did* know was that this spooky, spectral spell-slinger was claiming he could Watson my Sherlock. Unfortunately, I didn't have many other options. Like, zero.

But, regardless of what I felt about the situation, I had to just look at the facts. There was one shiny silver lining to this eternal storm cloud hanging over my head like the sword of . . . what was the term? Democracy? Dermatitis? Man, I don't think that's right, but fuck it—the fact of the matter was: I was friggin' *healed*, baby!

"I don't care *who* owns me!" I declared, doing a kip-up and landing in a crouch—before losing my train of thought because I couldn't believe I had landed such a maneuver. I stared down at my bare feet and smirked.

"Fuck yeah!" I said, looking back up at Crowmoon. The handsome bodybuilder was still watching with careful curiosity, as if he wanted to engage but was thrown off his game by my world-shattering super move.

"There's more where that came from, sweetheart!" I said, answering his unasked question and raising my arms for fisticuffs. "I'm all *kinds* of hopped up on healy-wheelies, and I could take on the fucking *sun* right now. Let's dance, ya dweeb!"

Crowmoon just stared at me, obviously too terrified of the monstrous display I was whipping out in front of him to do anything but gawk.

*That's right, Precious. Take it all in. I'm ready for round two—or three, or wherever we're at in the score.*

"You ready to rumble, wide boy? Don't tell me you're scared! I'm freshened up, so if—"

*CRACK!*

I went flying.

I smashed into the wall, my back breaking a chunk out of the wood and a piece tumbling from above and bopping me on the head. My chest felt like it had just been bashed against the front of Aunt Ella's Subaru.

*What the fuck just happened?*

Crowmoon was turned in a different position, so I got a good look at his Hollywood-esque side profile. He wasn't even looking at me; instead, his focus was claimed entirely by the little specter who'd just revitalized me. God. Damn. He'd hit me so fast, I wasn't even sure what *with*. His fist? His foot? I didn't know, but this brawny motherfucker really packed a punch. I glanced at my Health and saw it was still full, but a little fissured crack-like symbol was above it. Selecting it mentally, I saw a notification appear.

**Pact Boon [Bone Warrior]**
***While this Boon is active, the user cannot suffer the Fractured Effect.***
***Charges remaining: [1/2]***

*Whoa, that's a badass Boon name! I am already starting to like ole RG more than Zeol or Sababo. Looks like I've been blessed with bones of steel! But also: Boon? What the hell does that mean? Another ridiculous new-world bullshit metric, that's what.*

Apparently, this state-of-the-art overpowered-as-fuck Ability had protected me from getting one-hitter-quittered by Crowmoon's dazzling surprise attack. Though I thought about how sweet it was that I now had a trait that made me temporarily invulnerable and another that made it impossible to break my skeleton. I was going to be unstoppable!

I'd eventually need to find a primer with all the information I needed for continued navigation in Regaia, because this shit was unending. Fortunately, I'd just stumbled onto a millennia-old magic spirit who probably knew a thing or two about all this silly nonsense and might be able to shine a black light on the uncomfortable knowledge stains hiding in plain sight. Once Rexen was done with his parlay with Crowmoon—and I could stand again—I was planning to pick his brain mercilessly.

I sat in the dust for a minute, massaging my bruised titties and contemplating my life choices. Crowmoon still seemed unable to make a complete sentence as he gaped at RG, the ghost wizard, and I took the lay of the land. I wasn't far from Rua, who was beginning to stir from her stupor, her mouth curved into a grimace. At least she was alive—though to what level remained to be seen. On the other side of the expanse of shattered wood and rock, Edwig still rested, unmoving. I was less sure about his fate.

*You better not die before I can collect my money, asshole. And, uh, 'cuz that would be sad, too, I guess.*

I still hadn't clocked where Orville the Annoying Stowaway had gone. Regardless, he was less critical to the overall success of my mission. I still had to get out of there and whip the queen oomukade's ass back into whatever ant farm she'd climbed out of and save the day. Even now, I could hear the rumble of her passage out in the city beyond—and what was more, I could also make out the distinct din of combat.

*Ah, shit! I'm missing a dope-ass fight sequence!* I thought sourly. *Well, that's just wonderful. I'm in here facing off against a shirtless goon who seems really proud of his Caesarean scar. Everybody else gets to gang up on the uber-bug using the power of friendship. This just won't do—it's time to finish this.*

I quivered to a standing position, helping myself by resting my hand against the wall and sighing deeply so that the world knew I was a heroic figure in need of worship.

*That's right, folks! He goes through hell, takes a whole load of ass-beatings, and* still *comes back for more! Bow to your new god!*

My due respect would arrive eventually, I was sure. I'd just have to tackle the last roadblock in my path: Crowmoon. I noticed the exhaustingly polite piece of shit had begun speaking, so I paused my dramatic return to the battle for a moment to listen to him.

"Truly? You're Rexen Gravetongue? The infamous thaumaturge?"

*Thaumaturge—that's the word! But wait . . . what the hell was a Thoomba-toomba, then? Did I make that up? No way; that's gotta be something!*

"Yep!" Rexen answered peppily, pointing a thumb at himself. "In the flesh—er, well . . . you know what I mean! I'm here, and I'm *me!* You should be very impressed!"

*Man, this dude was worse than I was.*

"Oh, I am indeed, O Gravetongue," Crowmoon said reverently.

I suppressed a chuckle. This idiot was trying to cozy up to my new bosom buddy, was he? Well, he'd need to back off; RG was *my* incredible spirit guide!

"You have been gone for a long while," Crowmoon continued. "It was said you were sealed away by Eregannon's own hand, never to be released again."

"I fought him on a mountain!" Rexen answered enigmatically, neither confirming nor denying the claim but sounding like he found the whole thing quite exciting.

"Yet here you are, in defiance of the Elder Magus's will. It is a fantastic accomplishment."

Man, Crowmoon was really sucking up to this little spirit. What was his aim?

"You are correct," Rexen agreed, nodding sagely. "My power is mighty and my miracles endless."

"If you are who you say you are," Crowmoon said, gesturing to himself, "would you know a Son of the Tides on sight?"

Rexen shrugged, seeming unaffected by Crowmoon's words.

"The only Tide's Son I recall is that chap called Glendolyre—big fella, smelly body, sworn enemy of that Sovereign cult." Then Rexen froze as if recalling a horrible memory before announcing. "*AND* I just remembered he still owes me a shoulder massage!"

*Who?* I wondered. *Great, more unhinged backstory that I'll have no opportunity to understand because* no one *explains fucking* anything *to me. Then again . . . I suppose I am not the best listener. But . . . I mean, maybe people should be less boring?*

My tangent was forcing the critical component of this crux out of my mind, so I refocused.

*What did he name himself? Son of the Tides? Sounds like something you'd call one of Poseidon's kids.*

Fucking wonderful. We weren't in Harry Potter anymore; now we were in a goddamn Percy Jackson book.

*But he* did *say Tides. Which is the group that Ocho was spouting some ol' bullshit about.*

*That* painfully monologuing shit-eater had been convinced I was either working for this "Tides" team or would be shortly dispatched by them. It was confusing, but then again, the irritatingly handsome super-bastard had been moments away from dying, so he might have been simply losing his damn marbles. Man, what was with all these male-model motherfuckers tootin' around Wonderland there with their vaguely evil misdeeds?

It was becoming more and more evident that I should avoid any and all mega-hunks and sexy ladies, since they were turning out to be complete murderous toolbag psychopaths. It proved one thing I already knew: you can't trust pretty folk. Would I, too, submit to the laws of this world and become a rakishly dishy ne'er-do-well since I now had scientific evidence I was in the physical one percent? Not likely. But I'd need to be careful, lest my attractive allure drag me down a path of villainy.

Crowmoon's vibe suddenly shifted, like it had when the jailhouse captain arrived earlier. His demeanor was more serious, his smile vanishing.

"Ah," he said softly, as if contemplating his following words carefully. "So, you haven't heard of one known as the Drifter, then?"

*There's that fucking nickname again,* I thought. *The one that Zeol and Sababo had said belonged to someone I needed to avoid.*

Of course, now that I was hearing a non-godly voice utter it, it suddenly hit me that I'd heard it at least another time. When I'd been escaping the Redmark camp, I'd had a run-in with one of their big, macho underlings with a burned face. Right before he'd pushed me off a cliff, he'd said . . . what did he say about the Drifter? *Praise be?*

That was unsettling, but staring at Crowmoon caused me to realize that there were more than a few similarities to the bald, mustachioed blacksmith who'd tried to *The Good Son* me. Both were big, beefy assholes with burns on their bodies and a hankering to end my beautiful little life. So, what was up with that? My brain was making connections unbidden, and I was forced to come to terms with the fact that the Tides—whoever they were—and the Drifter— whatever the fuck *it* was—were linked in some way. This also meant that the . . . Echoes, AKA the shit catapult of dunces piloted by the curly-haired hottie, were *at least* on opposite sides of the battlefield from Crowmoon and the pile of ash formerly known as Velton . . . for a reason that was still not clear.

Man, thinking really hurts the head, ya know? I made a promise not to do it more than I needed to, just as my focus returned to the dopey duo discussing dastardly deeds.

"Drifter?" RG answered. "That sounds like me! See?"

He then shifted around, floating through the air and making whooshing noises.

I chuckled. This guy was weird as hell; that was for sure. But I liked the effect it had on Crowmoon. Mr. Universe was having a heck of a time taking this guy seriously, despite wanting to grovel at his skirt or whatever. I'll give him credit, though. He barely indicated that he was losing his cool as the spirit continued flitting about—even when he got up in Crowmoon's face, paused, and then quietly said, "Whoosh."

"Alas, O Gravetongue . . ." Rafe practically pleaded, "I only wish to converse with you for a moment. If it is possible, I wish to learn some of your secrets. Would you consent to return with me after we clean up this rabble so that I might train myself under your experienced tutelage?"

The hell? I had grossly misunderstood something. Crowmoon seemed to know who Rexen was or, rather, who he *used* to be before he obviously mainlined a bathtub full of paint thinner and scrambled his brain. What was more, he wanted to be his what? Student? This was too weird for me. As far as I knew, Rexen's only claim to fame was making a stupid dungeon full of ever-dumber bullshit before getting his soul trapped in a *Warhammer* mini. There were obviously more achievements to be impressed by. Still, he'd have to start shredding some Morbid Angel guitar riffs or something if he wanted *me* to act all moon-eyed in his presence.

Rexen stopped his ghastly rotations for a moment, turning to face Crowmoon and locking his weird, spirally eyeballs onto him.

"Hmm . . ." he said, drawing the word out dramatically like he was considering the possibility before continuing. "Nah."

Crowmoon's eyes bulged. He'd clearly misjudged his own level of X factor and was now eating . . . crow like the stupid, spoiled brat he was.

"Nah?" he echoed, obviously stunned by this revelation. Man, this guy had gone from being intimidating as shit to being just some loser rejected by his senpai. You love to see it.

"Yeah!" Rexen continued, then gestured to me with a smile. "You're too late. I've already chosen my next disciple."

"WHAT?!" Crowmoon roared, his shocked gaze wheeling toward me. "Him?!"

"Me?!" I shouted, nearly as surprised as the bodybuilder seemed to be.

"Yeah!" Rexen declared again happily, and then zoomed away from Crowmoon to float near me. "He got here first, and while he lives, he shall be the heir to my knowledge—and my hidden trove of toffee treats!"

*Whoa, I just hit the jackpot—that is, if he's as powerful as Deputy Dipshit here thinks he is. Though based on this whole candy reference, I might actually be the loser in this interaction. I wonder if—*

"So, then," Crowmoon interrupted my internal dialogue with his fake-ass grin affixed back in place, "if he were to die, you'd consider taking me on as a pupil? Is that how it works?"

"Okay, wait a minute. What the fuck is going on?" I asked, baffled as to how this had gone from a B-list slasher film to the kind of contrived plot you'd find in a 1970s kung fu flick. "This has gotten way too *Revenge of the Sith* for my liking. I didn't agree to any of this! What the hell do you—"

But I didn't finish, because Crowmoon moved so fast that there wasn't even time to blink. He was in my face suddenly, his fist drawn back to strike again while my life flashed before my eyes. Spoilers: it was a pretty cringey recap.

He brought his fist forward, and then . . . he was floating?

I gaped. Crowmoon had just been yanked into the air, his body spinning slowly as he fought against some force that had him trapped. But whatever it was, he couldn't get a handle on it. With each swipe of his powerful arms, he turned faster, like an astronaut trapped on the ISS with a persistent hornet. I looked to Rexen.

"You have got some seriously cool magic, my dude!"

"That wasn't me," he said, smiling. "But you're right. I do have a marvelous arsenal of Arcana. Which is nothing compared to my cache of confectionery sweets."

I shook my head as Crowmoon shouted in the air a few feet away.

"What do you mean? This isn't you?"

"Uh-uh," Rexen said in his dreamy voice, shaking his head. "Looks fun, though!"

"Wait . . ." I hissed in horror, then stared down at my own hands. "Was it . . . *me*?!"

"Pah! You wish, orc!"

I turned to where the voice had come from and saw Edwig slumped atop a mound of broken floor panels and waving his appendages grossly from side to side.

"Edwig!" I exclaimed, surprising even myself with the relief in my voice. "You fuckin' faker, I thought you were dead!"

"Not a chance!" he returned, rotating his arms together in a slow circle. I watched as Crowmoon's air pirouette mirrored his motions as the big man continued to fight against the arcane current.

*This pleases me.*

"Whoa, you really weren't kidding about being able to take him on, were you?" I asked, nodding and contorting my face in a very impressed fashion. "Good on ya, partner. Can you, like, crush him into a little ball or somethin'?"

"No," the illisinaf said. "I've been blasting out uses of the Clone Spell all evening from the back of that wagon, so I don't got a lot of juice left in the tank—but I can do *this* and hold him off while the rest of you escape."

"Escape?" I asked. "Why the hell would we escape? We've got him right where we want him! Plus, ol' Arjee here can probably rip his body apart with a sneeze or something."

At that moment, Crowmoon's body began to glow with bright blue energy. I sensed the danger leaking out of him then and could feel the heat of his magical maneuver leaping off him like I was standing too close to a jet engine. Instantly, he stopped turning in the air, though I noticed he was still floating.

*Well, shit.*

"This is probably not relevant to the situation," Rexen said, his eyes still on Crowmoon, "but I can't actually do anything that would affect him."

"Huh?!" I exclaimed, feeling a very acute sense of unease wash over me. "That is *extremely fucking relevant to the situation*! Nor does it make sense! You've pummeled me with magic since you showed up on the scene."

"Yes, I have," Rexen agreed. "I made a Pact with you. I can't do any tricks against anyone else. I'm just a tiny soul."

"What about the orb?" I demanded.

"Oh, my shiny?" Rexen asked, lifting up the indestructible orb and then lovingly rubbing his face against it like it was a furry kitten. "This is mine. I can always take my own stuff back—I made it that way!"

I stared, utterly speechless at the moment—which may have been a first for me. Crowmoon suddenly released a force of power that sent me staggering backward, and I almost fell on my ass. Fortunately, I could withstand it by grasping one of the destroyed load-bearing pillars in the center of the room.

*Rexen can't do anything against Crowmoon? He's about to go goddamn super-nova! My safety is compromised. Abort! Abort!*

"GAH!" I roared. I could see Rua standing from the corner of my eye, having recovered at least partially from the beatdown before. I jabbed a finger in her direction.

"RUN!" I shouted, gathering my spilled belongings and making for the hole we'd entered through. The elf didn't even question it; she just wordlessly shot in the same direction, determination on her face. My legs pumped as I tried to escape the worrisome—based on the output venting off of Crowmoon's body—attack that could devastate the whole city block. I didn't know why I thought that, but I did. That meant we had to be as far away as possible before he blew. Rexen was floating next to me, seemingly oblivious to the peril of the predicament, as he was still nuzzling the unwholesome hell out of the orb.

*This guy is truly something else. I need to be careful I don't say the wrong thing and he does that to me. I'll have to—*

Then I fell face-first into a pile of rubble.

"GAH!" I roared again as I hit hard and felt the insides of my gray matter jostle around in the collision. I looked down at my feet and saw something that might have sent me into Primal Rage if I hadn't been so hell-bent on escaping with my life: Orville. The son of a bitch was lying flat on his stomach, his eyes wide like a deer in the headlights of my Aunt Ella's Subaru. I hadn't even fucking seen him! I'd tripped right over his stupid human body in one of the most critical moments of my career.

"What the fuck are you doing?!" I shouted into his face, struggling to stand and shake off the dizziness from my fall.

"I was hiding!" he declared, sounding both bashful and afraid.

*This fucking guy . . .*

"You fucking . . . guy!" I roared, then, not having any other recourse, grabbed him around the collar and hauled him up to his feet.

"We've gotta go. Now!"

Orville cowered before me, and if I hadn't been worried we were about to be cut down in a hail of magical dick-blasting beams, I'd have gloated a little. But this was not the time.

"Let's goose it!" I yelled, and turned to the exit, where Rua stood, waiting for me. She nodded as I shoved Orville forward. He let out an *oof* and then crashed back to the ground.

"Are you fucking kidding me?!" I demanded, but froze as I saw what had sent him tumbling from his perch.

Framed by the destroyed exit was a figure clad in armor, her face bloody and hair being tousled in the grasp of some unseen wind. It was the captain. Apparently, her fight with Crowmoon wasn't over just yet, and she'd come back for seconds.

Her steely eyes regarded me with the same kind of acknowledgment a stalking housecat might give to a baby mouse when juicier prey was nearby.

"Uh . . ." I started, not sure exactly what to say to this woman who looked as though she could kick my ass no-legged from thirty feet away. ". . . hi, there. Uh—Captain."

I didn't know how best to salute, so I did a little curtsy instead. It was real cute.

"I'll deal with you in short order, burglar," she said, her tone icy. Then her gaze flicked to Rua, and she scowled. Finally, she glanced behind me at the roaring heat machine called Rafe Crowmoon that was prepping to light the whole place up with whatever magic atom-bomb attack he had up his sleeve. She shifted, her gaze returning to me before looking me up and down.

"Get out of here and help defend the town, orc," she said. "I'll come to find you afterward and ensure justice is served upon you. Be quick about it. I'll hold him off and grant you some distance."

Then she stepped past me, her body igniting in the same fiery form I'd seen her use thrice now.

"W-wait a second, hot stuff!" I shouted, causing the woman to turn and give me an annoyed-but-curious glance over her flaming shoulder. Oddly, I noticed that while I could definitely feel the backdraft from Mr. Orbit behind me, I couldn't feel anything from *her* flames.

"Who is he? I mean— Fuck, I already know his name is Rafe fuckin' Crowmoon, but I mean . . . who the hell *is* he? Like, why is he such a big fuckin' deal—and why the *fuck* is he so strong?"

The captain—whose real name I still didn't know—tilted her head and indicated Rafe, who was still trapped in the zero-gravity bondage bubble.

"Rafe Crowmoon is a dangerous tool of an even deadlier sect. His crimes against the people of not only the kingdom but elsewhere in Regaia are vast. He was being held only long enough to await the arrival of one of King Gaier's Warders so that he could stand trial. And—I hope—to be blessedly dragged apart by beasts in the Hall of the Jurat. As he has escaped, none of that can come to pass until he returns to my prisons."

She turned back toward the opening and lifted her hand.

"I will come for you again once all of this is done," she explained matter-of-factly. "Do not run. If you run, you will be hunted down. I *always* reintegrate those who escape."

Well . . . that was unfortunate—for her, not me. I was *absolutely* going to be running. This lady apparently didn't know that I was a *bit* of a Contrary Connie, and I wasn't planning on making my next days those of a prisoner. Didn't really fit my vibe, you know? No, I'd be getting right the fuck outta this watering hole the moment I'd completed my Quests and had all my companions together. Good luck finding *me* when you've got a town that needs to be rebuilt, copper.

I took one final glance at the building, mourning my loss to the fact that I didn't get an opportunity to use the knowledge gained from Eye of the Saboteur to send the whole place down around Crowmoon's ears.

*Oh, well,* I thought. *Next time.*

I didn't wait for the captain to say anything else; I just nodded at Rua, and together, we dragged Orville out of the building and into the street. I looked up at Rexen still floating next to me and expected him to be doing something weird, like French-kissing the indestructible orb. However, he was doing something else strange: he was staring back into the building, and though there really wasn't much for physical indication, something about the widened shape of his spiral eyes told me he was gawking.

"You doin' alright, Arjee?" I asked. Then, because I couldn't help myself, I added, "You look like you've seen a ghost."

"Who is that?" Rexen breathed, his gaze locked on the retreating form of the captain.

"Her?" I asked. "Oh, that's the captain. Real tough chick. Gonna be putting a wallop on Shithead, I imagine."

"I love her . . ." he said, his dreamy voice sounding even more full of wonder.

"You just met her," I said in a scathing staccato. "Besides, I think you're kinda married to me now, bud . . . and I don't share."

I tried to wink at him so he knew I was joking, but he didn't see it. Therefore, I decided on a different tactic to break him out of his reverie.

"So . . ." I started, unsure how to broach the subject, "you were trapped in there? In the . . . uh, figurine?"

That did the trick. Rexen suddenly brightened, swimming through the air and resting right by my face.

"Yes, indeed! Pretty neat, huh?"

"Oh, *yeah*," I said, nodding. "So . . . you're like, what, some kind of . . . genie?"

"*Exactly* like a genie," the creature said. ". . . except I'm *spirits*."

"Spirits?" I asked, dumbfounded.

"I think I might be a ghost . . ." Rexen said thoughtfully. "But I could also be a fish. Ooh, or maybe a potato!"

"Let's get moving," I said, rolling my eyes. It was clear I wouldn't get *anywhere* with this creature unless I had a few hours to navigate through the quagmire of bizarre personality quirks.

"Where are we going?" Rexen asked, but then looked down at his legs and gasped. "Wait! I don't have any feet! How do I walk?"

"You're floating . . ." I said.

"Ohhh," Rexen said, nodding in realization. "Good, good. That makes things simpler."

Just as we were about to put the foot to the flagstones, another figure emerged from the still-smoking hole in the building, glaring back inside with contempt. It was Edwig, and he looked like he had a kernel in his craw over something.

"Pah!" he announced, shaking his head in disbelief. "I can't believe she stole my line! *I* wanted to be the one to hold off the mighty and dangerous enemy while others ran away like cowards."

"You still can," I said with a shrug. "Toddle on back inside; I promise we won't wait."

"Nah, I'm over it," he said glumly.

"Good, because we still got a full night of terrors to enjoy," I said, clapping my hands together. "It looks like Mama Bug is still making her way to the water tower—jeez, it really seemed like we were in there forever, didn't it? You know what? Never mind. This isn't how our story goes. We're not going to sit . . . idly by while the rest of this town has a climactic confrontation without us. No, *siree*! We will crash down on that ugly horde with all the fury our bodies can muster—and I've got a body *built* out of anger. Hope y'all are ready, because—"

"Why are you giving us a galvanizing pre-battle speech?" Edwig asked, staring up at me with his amorphous eyes.

"'Cuz . . . uh, well, since I'm the leader of this outfit. It seemed like the thing to—

"You? The leader? Pah!" Edwig laughed. "What makes *you* the leader?"

I paused.

"... I'm the tallest," I said, half-indignant, half-insecure that my reign would be so easily usurped.

"It's a height-based merit now? Because I can stretch myself taller than these buildings! By that measurement, *I* would be the leader."

"Well, sure, but—you know what? Shut up, Edwig."

"Yeah—shut up, Edwig," Rua echoed.

"You heard them . . ." Orville, getting brave, tried to say to include himself, but he quickly deflated at a withering look from the illisinaf.

"Pah! This is mutiny!" Edwig said. "And to think I thought we bonded over our mutual capture, Rua!"

"It can't be mutiny if you're not the leader," Rua said.

"Well, neither is he, then," he continued sourly.

"Look, I am either the leader, or I'm kicking you into a ditch," I said. "It's your call, big dog."

"Maybe you guys can compete for it?" Orville offered. "Like a contest of skill? Seems fair enough to me. I'd be amenable to either of you, really—I'm just happy to be a part of the team."

"What?" I said. "You aren't part of *shit* yet, newbie—you're just a hitchhiker! One we didn't even want to pick up in the first place."

"And I am pleased you did!" Orville said jovially, seeming to ignore everything I said. "It was rough going there. Did you *see* all of those monsters? It was dreadful!"

I stared at him, but Edwig—likely hoping to win some anti-rebellion points—was the one to respond.

"Did we . . . Of course we saw them, you simpleton! We were being *chased* by them!"

"Oh, is that what was happening?" Orville said. "I noticed them but wasn't sure what to make of the situation."

"Who even *are* you?" Rua asked, sounding as exasperated as I was.

Orville pointed to himself with surprise.

"Me? I thought we'd been over this. I am Orville—a humble laborer out for an evening stroll to get myself to anywhere with some libations. Then the lot of you turned up, and I thought to myself, *Here's the best way to a beer.*"

"Ooh, I'd like a beer," Rexen said. "One with an acorn in it. Would that be allowed?"

"No," I spat. "Listen, punks. We can argue about who is or isn't in charge later. But it's definitely me."

"And now that we have settled that—the beer!" Rexen offered.

"*No beer,*" I emphasized, then pointed at Orville. "Look what you've done, newbie. You've confused an old man. I hope you're happy with yourself."

"Oh," Orville said, frowning. "Apologies for that. I wasn't aware of your advanced age."

"That's alright!" Rexen announced optimistically. "I'm not just old—I'm also moldy!"

I turned my whole body to face down the street in the direction we'd initially been heading before Crowmoon had ruined our joyride. Since our fateful time indoors, the roads had grown oddly empty.

*That's not a good sign. That means the oomukade have moved on to another area of the city.*

"You alright, Loon?" Rua asked.

"Yeah, I'm fine . . ." I said. "It's just that it looks like this will be a little harder without a cart to carry our asses to our future trophy corpse lickety-split. But, on the plus side, I have a feeling we won't have to travel far . . ."

"Why's that?" Rua asked, intrigued by my sudden optimism.

When I responded, I shocked myself with the grim tone I'd adopted.

"I can feel where the battle is."

In actuality, it was because I could feel *them.* My party members. They were close. Their lifelines were still there, radiating with ever-weakening strength, and I could somehow tell that they were fighting. All of them.

*Don't worry, gang,* I thought. *I'm coming to help, and I'm bringing . . .*

I looked at the pathetic collection of ragtag misfits before me and sighed. A low-level elf, a wizard-ghost that could only make pretty lights appear, a braggadocious, shape-defying *vest-wearer,* and . . . some guy named Orville.

*I'm bringing me,* I thought. *And that's all the cavalry we need.*

Seeing Rexen, Edwig peered at the little spirit suspiciously.

"Wait a second," he said, his eyes narrowing. "Who is this?"

"Your worst nightmare," Rexen said darkly.

"Nobody," I said. "Just a dude that was magically summoned from my crotch pocket."

"Huh?" Edwig asked, but I ignored him, moving on.

"What was that Spell you used on him, anyway?" Rua asked the illisinaf.

He puffed his . . . chest out a little and smirked.

"Unseen Hand," he explained. "Usually something reserved for grabbing objects or maybe tripping traps from far away. However, I've developed a version that's ten times stronger than the typical—"

"Alright!" I said. "Everybody shut up! We've gotta get this dirty work managed. So, we're going to have to be quick about our next moves. Onward, to our perilous and inevitable deaths!"

Then, without another word, I dashed off toward the fray.

# CHAPTER FOURTEEN

# GANG, GANG

**W**ell . . . that's her," I said, taking in the sight of the monster who'd been chittering her way through our temporary township. "Looks like we got our work cut out for us."

We stared up at the gigantic grotesquery that was the oomukade queen, and I couldn't believe my eyes. Up close, she was somehow even worse than I'd previously thought. Easily a hundred feet tall—if not more—with shimmering crawdad armor covering her body. Her legs, which had looked long and spindly from afar, were clearly larger than tree trunks, each ending in a blade that looked like it could tear through a Sikorsky King Stallion like it was made of wet spiderwebs. And her face, holy shit, her face. It was a festering, red, human-like colossus with sunken eyes and a mouth full of teeth that looked like they were made out of roided-out razor wire. Worst of all, I could see malevolence in her eyes and the hunger for destruction and death.

Unfortunately for her, she was having what was likely one of the worst days of her life—and you know, that kinda made my heart happy. Everywhere I looked, there were attackers. Dozens upon dozens of individuals working toward putting some slap-and-tickle on this behemoth beastie and slowing her down. A few of them I even recognized.

The gleesome threesome of Bonnie and her two Clydes were nearest to us, their bestial bodies bashing the ever-loving *bitch* out of the oomukade's legs. Farther out, I could see the flash of a brilliant bolt of tiny blue lightning as the tiny Yoda dude from the mending house darted up the creature's body and delivered punishing Spell attacks to her hide. A big man in a full suit of helmeted armor that completely obscured his form was wielding a sword as long as I was tall and carving off massive chunks of the queen's meat with each swing. A woman with long electric-green hair pulled back the string of a longbow on one of the roofs. When she fired an arrow, it looked like a ray of yellow light and struck the much smaller children of the queen, leaving smoking holes with each success. Four individuals in matching heavy robes of shining silver fanned out near an ornate water fountain, each casting an array of Spells of myriad effects. A ways away still, I could see a pile of those . . . war turtles—wartoises? They were dead. It was sad. Still, weren't nothin' gonna break my stride, so I stamped down the uncomfortable feeling seeing cute little turtley corpses had given me, and let it dwell somewhere near my guts—where I kept all the other bad feelings and useless information like *math*. Then, focusing on the other aspects of the battle, I adopted a better attitude.

"Whoa . . ." I muttered, taking it all in before I shouted with triumph. "This. Is. Fucking. Awesome! I knew I was missing out on a sweet-ass kumite! Edwig, you owe me five bucks!"

"What?" Edwig asked, clearly baffled by my comment. "I didn't bet against you!"

"Eh, don't worry about it, Jigglepuss—I'll just add it to your substantial tab."

"It's huge!" Orville exclaimed, sounding slightly intimidated by the prospect of going up against something like this creature.

"It's practically Brobdingnagian in size!" Rua said, her eyes full of wonder.

"Listen, I appreciate the vote of confidence, Rua—I really do, but even *I'm* not that big."

"What?" she asked, then seemed to figure out my error. "Oh. No, not a *barbarian*. *Brobdingnagian*."

I stared at her, uncomprehending.

"It just sounds like you're saying *barbarian* really weird," I said.

"It's from *Gulliver's Travels*," she said. "And could be used to describe anything—"

"Eh, I never really liked that show," I interrupted. "Too many plot holes for my liking. How the hell are you going to bring along a whole library on a three-hour tour? Doesn't make sense."

"That's *Gilligan's Island*, Loon," she said, clearly exasperated by my lack of . . . Well, it's not really pop culture if it's old as fuck, is it? Regardless, she wasn't having any of my shenanigans.

I turned my attention back to the fight we still hadn't actually joined. But you didn't just *barge* willy-nilly into combat mid-battle, did you? I had to figure it was a lot like doing double Dutch jump rope—you had to find the right rhythm and *then* jump in. Worrisomely, I didn't see anyone resembling my party members, but I could still *feel* they were close. I squinted, trying to make out some of the combatants on the other side. But I wasn't able to discern much beyond general mayhem. I now noticed a few people about a dozen feet from us, looking as though they were suited up for a siege—but should have prob-ably been dressed to meet Elvis, considering they were corpses. They'd brought along what seemed to be bags of food, drink, a compass, some rope, and a few other odds and ends—all of which had spilled out around their bodies.

*Apparently ready for everything except consequences.*

Once again, I was struck with strange wonder as to why I didn't feel as bad about things like humans and . . . whatever the fuck had two sets of eyes dying. It seemed more natural to chortle at their mortal coils being ambushed than any sense of sympathy. The turtles made sense. No one was so war-hardened that seeing that display wouldn't bother them, but . . . man. I didn't know. I thought that perhaps the horrible massacre in the dungeon might have . . . bro-ken me? Or something.

I remembered reflecting on the fact I'd felt less affected by the thought of death and destruction shortly after I arrived—especially with the Smiler and his gang of actual upright rats. That could have been easy to explain away—they weren't human. Even with myself excluded from being one as well, when I'd killed people who'd mostly resembled humans—like some of the Redmarks—it didn't . . . really bother me at all, actually. So, maybe Ocho hadn't severed my connection to my own relative human experience. Maybe I was just born that way?

*Come on, guys. Where are you?*

I saw movement out of the corner of my vision and looked up.

It wasn't anyone or, rather, *anything* I knew. A cloud of sparkling mist—that I had to assume was controlled by someone—was flying high through the air, literally raining magic on the gigantic centipede's head. Bolts of purple light-ning struck as a deluge of arcane fury dropped full force on top of the beast. When this happened, the creature roared, and I heard her voice in my mind again, filled with rage and hate.

*You will not stop me, little irritants! My quarry is in my sight! I summon to me more of my offspring, that they might feast upon you and remove your obstacles!*

"Ah, shit," I hissed. "Guys, this is about to get a whole lot messier! She's about to call in the fuzz. We gotta figure out how we can help cut her down."

"That's unfortunate. I'm basically out of Arcana," Edwig said somberly. "Though I'd be willing to try my luck hand-to-hand if the situation calls for it."

"Out of Arcana?" I wondered bitterly. "How are you *out* of *Arcana*? That's like the one thing you do."

"Pah! Don't give me that, orc!" he returned, sidling up close to me. "I told you, I'm a researcher. Most of my proclivities are centered around discovery and study!"

"What a fuckin' nerd," I jeered. "In that case, can you *discover* something about this monster that might help? Like weaknesses or anything like that?"

Edwig paused mid-retort as if he hadn't fully considered that notion.

"I, uh, suppose I could," he said. "I'd have to get close enough to touch her, though."

"I don't see the problem," I said, pointing at the gigantic creature as she kicked the armored man into a building. "You were just bragging about going all *Street Fighter Two* on her ass, so why don't you cozy up to her and do your . . . uh . . ."

I turned to Rua.

"What's the fantasy equivalent of science?"

Rua shrugged.

"Alchemy?"

I whipped my head back to Edwig.

"Do your alchemy at it."

Edwig sighed, rolling his eyes and sliming away toward the monster.

"That's right," I muttered smugly. "Go exercise your *hand-to-hand* against the *centipede* monster. She's only got like . . . a billion more arms than you."

"I can hide well."

The comment nearly startled me. I turned to see Orville smiling back at me.

"Huh?" I asked.

"Hiding," he clarified. "I'm quite good at it."

"Uh, alright," I said, shrugging. "Go, uh, do that . . . I guess."

Orville brightened and bowed deeply, looking very silly as he did so.

"I won't fail you!" he announced before shuffling off, leaving Rua, Rexen, and myself standing awkwardly, watching as he went.

"Okay, that's taken care of," I said. "Rua, you've still got that wand, right?"

There was a loud crash as one of the roofs exploded upward a few hundred feet away, the armored man from before heroically flying out of it with his giga-sword raised as he launched himself toward the oomukade queen. She slapped him down with a casual swipe of one of her legs, and he hit the ground hard, not moving.

"Yeah, but I think the charges are low," Rua answered my question.

"What are you normally good at?" I asked. "You know, other than being imprisoned."

I raised one eyebrow mischievously.

"Har-dee-har," she muttered, rolling her eyes. Then a grin appeared on her face as my question seemed to spark some interest. "Well, let's see . . . I'm specced as a Swordfighter, but leaning more of an all-around with my set. I'm hoping that will unlock a viable DPS tier while still offering a path with some AOE. Right now, I'm basically noob trash, but I'm hoping to proc something to help me out."

She smiled.

"Oh, you just *have* to flex your geek lingo, don't you?" I said. "Well, you're gonna have to keep it simple for the . . ."

I paused, trying to think of anything that was even sorta game-related.

". . . the, uh, Donkey Kong," I said, smirking. "Otherwise, I'm just going to let you get Game Overed."

"That was a really good try," Rua said patronizingly. "You're a Barbarian, right? So, you have, uh, rage and stuff?"

"*Primal* Rage," I corrected smugly. "And yeah, I've got a whole assload of other cool shit I can do. Like, check *this* out!"

I ran over, picked up a battered sword from one of the corpses nearby, and activated my Eye of the Saboteur on it. I was both overjoyed and disappointed that this new Ability gave me so much information on an object. On the one hand, it was nice to know a whole hell of a lot more about a specific . . . anything. I'd had a surprising lack of clarity on most stuff since I'd arrived. On the other, it was dreadfully dull to slog through a bunch of text, even if the System was back to its usual antics of being "jazzy" regarding descriptions. I read the message carefully and tried not to bore myself to death.

**Iron Sword**
- **Rarity: Common**
- **Item Class: One-Handed/Two-Handed Weapon**
- **Durability: 50/75**
- **Weight: 2.3 lbs.**
- **Damage: 11–14 Piercing / 12–15 Slashing**

**Material Composition:**
> o   Iron [97%]—The sword's main component, comprising most of the total weight.
>
> o   Carbon [0.9 %]—Present in small amounts to increase the strength and hardness of the iron.
>
> o   Other trace elements—Includes impurities such as sulfur, phosphorus, and manganese, which can affect the properties of iron.

*Ah, the humble iron sword, a weapon as old as civilization itself. Forged from the fiery depths of the crust and tempered in the cool waters of the anvil, it is a testament to the ingenuity and tenacity of the spirit. At its core, the iron sword is composed of the noble metal iron, mixed with just a dash of carbon for added strength and hardness. But there are other, more mysterious ingredients at play as well. Trace elements such as sulfur, phosphorus, and manganese lurk within its gleaming blade, imbuing it with untold secrets and properties. These are not arcane powers—no, quite the opposite!*

*But the true majesty of the iron sword lies not in its composition but in the skilled hands of the blacksmith. It is they who take the raw materials and, through sweat and toil, craft them into a weapon fit for a hero. First, the iron is heated to a white-hot intensity, rendering it malleable and pliable. Then, using a hammer and anvil, it is shaped and molded into the desired form. Once cooled and hardened, it is tempered and sharpened, ready to be wielded in battle.*

*So, the next time you heft an iron sword, remember the centuries of tradition and craftsmanship that went into its creation. It symbolizes our enduring spirit and the unbreakable bond between modern life and the natural world.*

I sighed, seeing the freshly minted madness my Ability had morphed into. Nothing like a fuckton of words just to say *nothing special*. That was a shame. The sword was run-of-the-mill, but I was disappointed in how mundane it ended up being in the Saboteur breakdown. I supposed I'd just have to be satisfied with the fact that not everything in this world was mythical and magical.

I tossed the weapon on the ground in front of Rua. She jumped a little, afraid it would hit her, but when she realized what I'd done, she glowed with excitement. She picked the sword up and hefted it like it was an ancient artifact of immense power.

"Nice!" she declared, giving it a test swipe. "I think this should work nicely. Time to earn my spurs, I suppose."

"Easy there, Musashi," I said. "You're Level Two. This is probably a deadly encounter for you. This isn't just some regular-degular, everyday fight. That's a big-ass enemy afoot in the foreground, so just make sure you're ready to run if need be."

Rua balked.

"And you're not planning to do the same thing, I take it?" she wondered. "Just *what* Level are you, then?"

I smirked.

"You shouldn't ask people that, you know," I said, paraphrasing what Fawn— the other Sojourner who had almost ended my life—had said. "It's pretty rude."

Rua scowled.

"What the hell, Loon? How can I help kill this thing if I don't know what my teammates can do?"

I shrugged.

"That's a good point," I said. "Alright, crybaby. I'm Level Ten, but I will probably be Level Eleven soon . . ."

*Huh*, I thought. *Actually, shouldn't I already be Level Eleven?*

"Level Ten?!" Rua exclaimed, apparently astounded by this revelation. "Whoa, Loon! That's amazing, man! You've been busy since you got here, then?"

I'll admit I puffed my chest out a little at that.

"Yeah, no biggie," I said, probably unconvincingly trying to disguise the fact that I definitely considered it quite the biggie indeed. "That's just what happens when you kick a dungeon's ass and—"

"Monster," Rexen suddenly warned, though it was with the same casual detachment from reality he usually had.

I wheeled around just as one of the smaller oomukade came barreling at us, its legs poised to strike. I rolled out of the way, drawing my haladie and slicing at it as I moved. One of the weapon's blades cleaved neatly through two of its legs. The creature drooped, its momentum ruined by my attack, allowing Rua to jab it with her sword. Her blow was true, and she managed to puncture its chest just as I leaped back into action and jammed the haladie into one of its humanoid eyes.

The oomukade screeched in pain, flailing around. I wrenched the blade from the socket and began the grim work of systematically hacking off each of its appendages before Rua enacted the coup de grace of stabbing it in the face until it didn't move anymore. That usually does the trick, in my experience.

I stood back, admiring our handiwork, as Rua cleaned the blade of her sword off on the body of the bloodied bedbug. After the death notification appeared, I checked my statistics, wondering if the slowly-building anxiety was for a good reason. I mentally scrolled to my Experience section, and read it over, confused by what I saw.

**Experience**
**25,321 / 23,000 to Level 11**

That was weird. Even though I'd beaten the threshold for Level Eleven by a mile, I was still—for some inexplicable reason—Level Ten. But that didn't make sense. How in the *Final Fantasy fuck* did that work? There had to be some reason that just wasn't making itself evident at the moment. Unfortunately, I was ill-equipped to figure it out and worried that I'd never—

"Still Level Ten?" came the whimsical response from Rexen. "Do you want help with that?"

I stopped in my tracks. Did he have a window into my menu? That would be very inconvenient—but also—if he *could* view my statistics . . .

"You can see that?" I asked, curious to find out the depth of his knowledge. "I assumed that was . . . I dunno, locked out from other people's inspection."

"Not for me," the little spirit proclaimed cheerfully. "I know the secret."

I was hesitant to probe further, but my curiosity got the better of me.

"What secret?"

Rexen turned in a circle, emphasizing his glee.

"I know how to *break* the *System*."

There was a long, dramatic pause as we let Rexen's words sink down deep into our mind grapes. When nobody really reacted, it seemed like an appropriate time to . . . refresh everyone as to what our current objective was.

"Okay, first of all—fuckin' hell yeah," I said, wincing as the oomukade hive mom crushed one of the robed men who was slower than his friends in dodging her leg. "But seriously, we've got better things to do right now. Like, I totally want to sit around and chat about this, but we've got a big, gross infestation to take care of first. So, let's crack the shit outta this creature, swoop the squad, and then head somewhere where we won't catch on fire while we yuck it up. Afterward, you can show me your leet hacking skills."

"Squad?" Rua asked.

"Yeah," I said. "The homies. My, uh, allies."

"Ooh! We have allies?" Rexen asked, looking pretty stoked by this information.

"*I* have allies," I said. "*You* have *ectoplasm*—or whatever—and probably a lot of social cues to learn, so let's not go full-on communism yet. What's mine is mine, and maybe we can introduce you to the posse if you're really helpful. For now, though . . ."

Rua cleared her throat.

"We need to kill this motherfucker?" she offered.

"I think technically *she's* the mother being— Wait, that doesn't matter— Yes. Let's ice this fool."

Rua lifted her sword and gave me a single nod. I knew we didn't have time to be dicking around there. Every second we spent standing there chatting was more time that thing had one less person putting the hurt on its terrible existence. We had to move on it, and fast.

"Right, so . . . what's the plan?" Rua asked.

I frowned. I hadn't sussed out what I would do when I got to this point. I figured I'd arrive just in time to perform a heroic rescue of some smokin' hot, gorgeous babe and then go with what I'd been doing so far: improvising. However, taking a gander at the goings-on there, I reasoned I might have to genuinely brainstorm a strategy. Frustratingly, I still didn't see Frida, Stinky, or Jes. However, my connection to them was still intact and basically beeping at me that they were close. I wish I had some sort of party GPS that could lead me . . .

*Oh. Maybe I do?*

"Arjee," I said to the little spirit, and he perked up immediately with something resembling a salute.

"Aye-aye!" he announced.

"What was that thing you said before?" I asked. "You know, about—"

"I have said at least four things before," Rexen explained. "Maybe even *five*. You'll have to be specific—I'm very old, you see."

I clenched my jaw. Now was not the time for shenanigans.

"I was planning to do that," I said tightly. "I was referring to when we got all Pacted up. You mentioned something about always knowing where I was. Does that mean you can track me?"

"Yes," Rexen said. "Like an expert hunter and trapper. Except for *this* hunter only *hugs!*"

I rolled my eyes as he stretched his arms out to me, but I ignored the motion. This dude was so fucking weird.

"To go along with that," I continued, trying to usher him along, "if I had a connection to other people, would it be possible that you could trace that as well? Does magic even work like that?"

"Yeah!" Rexen cheered. "I could do that, maybe. I don't know; I've never tried—but I think I'd be really, really great at it!"

*Fuck yeah*, I thought. *Now we're getting somewhere.*

"Alright, well, go ahead," I said, holding my arms out like I was in line for the TSA at the airport. "Scan me, baby! And make it quick!"

Rexen floated near me, inspecting me closely before closing his strange eyes and humming softly. I watched as a tiny, flickering purple flame appeared above his head, moving along to the rhythm he was creating. I felt something like cool water wash over me and had to double-check to make sure I wasn't getting rained on. I found that I was actually quite dry—other than the sweat I'd oozed all over myself from all the running around and other miscellaneous fuckery.

*This must be part of the Spell, then*, I thought. *He better hurry the hell up, though! We're wasting time!*

The intensity of the chill increased, and I gave an involuntary shiver.

"Whoa, whoa, whoa!" I shouted. "Warn a guy if something is going to feel like the Angel of Death's dick is creeping up my spine!"

"No," Rexen stated serenely, never opening his eyes.

You know . . . you'd think I'd learn to be less surprised about magic—uh, Arcana—by now. But as it turns out, I'm very easily flabbergasted—even by the simplest of magician tricks. I mean, it wasn't even that bad once I had calmed down; it was just a shock to the system. Kind of pleasant, I supposed, once I was aware of its presence.

It was only a moment before Rexen's eyes opened back up, and he smiled.

"Got 'em!" he announced, pointing a hand directly at the gigantic monster. "They're in there."

"Wait!" I shouted. "Where?! Don't tell me—"

"In the belly," Rexen said. "There. Solved. Can we get beer now?"

"She fucking *ate* them?!" I demanded, staring at the oomukade in horror.

"Yep! Gobbled up whole. Saves you the trouble of having to slay them."

"What?!" I shouted. "Why would I need to do that?"

"All enemies must be destroyed," Rexen said happily.

"They're not my enemies! They're my *friends*!"

"Oh," Rexen said, sounding embarrassed. "I thought you wanted to locate them to kill them. Never mind! All enemies must be destroyed, but all friends must be protected."

"Yeah, no fucking duh, Arjee!" I shouted, pulling on the Gussying Gauntlets and yanking my haladie out of my waistband.

My party members had been fucking eaten by this stupid goddamn monster? How the fuck had that happened? Were they trying to take it down and the beast just glugged them into her esophagus? Actually, fuck, it didn't matter. What *did* matter was that they *had* been swallowed and were still alive inside somehow. The rest of the group was too preoccupied with defeating the monster and would probably overlook a few out-of-towners missing in the mix. I'd have to be the one to do something. I didn't know how it would happen, but I was determined to do it one way or another. Knowing that they were in there really pissed me off something fierce.

I narrowed my eyes at the oomukade queen and could feel my grip tightening so hard on the haladie that I thought I might break my hand.

"Rua," I said, my voice sounding like a deep alien growl. "I'm going down there to fucking destroy that thing. Are you with me?"

I wasn't looking at her—I only had eyes for my target, the behemoth monstrosity so casually dispatching the warriors around it. It had to be an insanely high Level to still be trucking along despite the efforts of dozens of attackers. Still, I wasn't stupid enough to think I could do anything to it at my measly Ten.

Oh, hell—who am I kidding? It will surprise no one that I was still going to try. But at least I knew a direct approach would be suicide and the quickest way back into Pontivex's loving embrace. No, if there was any hope of me having a shot, I'd need to be a tricky bitch—and that meant actually using something other than a poor grasp of my Abilities and a can-do attitude.

*And maybe some help.*

"You bet," Rua answered, her tone serious and determined.

"Alright, then," I said, and began running toward the beast. "Let's fuck this shit *all* the way up!"

# CHAPTER FIFTEEN

# MONSTER MASH

*Total Settlement Destruction: 53.0%*
*Remaining oomukade [167 / 265]*
*Percent vanquished: 36.9%*

I scowled at the display indicating the metrics of the Quest.

*Christ on a crack binge,* I thought to myself. *This shit is getting out of control. Not only are we losing progress, but* more *of these centipede dickbags are piling into this town all the time! At some point, Tallrock's gonna have more bugs than people!*

The grand total of oomukade had bumped up significantly in just an hour, over a hundred, and the amount of destruction to the settlement was nearing the danger zone. We would have to kill their mothership before any more came barging into the city limits. Fortunately, that's exactly what I was in the process of doing.

I blazed through the street with a storm in my heart, ready to splice, dice, and Kimbo Slice everything between me and my path to rescue. Loon: the badass, take-no-prisoners general, leading an army of two—plus a spirit—into the butthole of battle. Here to dole out some military-grade Fiesta de Fist and beatdown blisters—and baby, there weren't gonna be no ointment.

It only took seconds for the first oomukade—a mean-lookin' party cobra with only one eye and an explicit death wish—to try and Stop Stick my passage. It dove forward with a shriek, trying to—of all things—bite me. I dove to the side, rolled, and was up again instantly, my haladie digging into its flank as I ran by. I checked over my shoulder to make sure Rua hadn't been casually eaten but saw she was hot on my tail, raking the blade of her newly acquired sword against the beast as she passed by. Taking her on this merry spree was probably not the wisest of moves, but at least this way, she'd get some combat ranks under her belt.

"My Two-Handed Skill just went up!" she shouted triumphantly. "E-Rank, Level Two!"

See?

"Fuck, yeah!" I cheered. Another centipede separated itself from where it and its siblings were fighting a leather-clad human. I turned back just in time to dodge as it attempted to strike at me.

My body seemed to almost move of its own accord. I whirled like a figure skater in a final spin performance while at the same time bringing my haladie hand-over-hand like a propeller in a downward rotation. I felt blood spray over me as I connected with the area underneath the monster's grotesque humanoid mask and watched it rear back in terror. Then it curved back like an S and pre-pared to strike at me. It instantly went limp, slumping to the ground and revealing the form of Rua behind it. Sword point forward, she removed the blade from the top of the creature's body just behind the face with a grim look of determination.

"Whoa!" I shouted, tossing a thumbs-up her way. "Righteous!"

"Thanks, I—" she began, but was interrupted by a flash of golden light sur-rounding her body. A glittering marquee appeared above her, declaring that she had Leveled Up.

"I . . . I'm Level Three!" Rua announced, clearly stunned.

"Hell yeah, you are!" I said. Then jerked my head toward the queen. "We'll celebrate later, though. Our Parcheesi partner is lookin' a little lonely over there. Let's give her some company."

Rua smirked, wiped the blade off on her clothes, and raced forward as I turned and continued our line drive of lacerations toward the mothership.

"Uh-oh," Rexen said next to me. "She is catching up. We will be unable to kill her soon."

"Will you . . . stop that?" I asked between breaths as I darted between two oomukade who were too slow on the uptake to notice me until it was too late. "It's super fuckin' creepy. Rua is our ally as well—why do you want me to kill everyone?"

I rammed the haladie into the side of one of the pair of beasts. I wrenched it upward, watching in disgust as innards slopped out from the wound and the oomukade screeched in agony.

"Ah," Rexen said contemplatively. "I did not know she was *friends*. In that case, I am pleased with her progress. Very good! Way to go, and . . . such."

"That sounded *real* genuine . . ." I said. "Believable."

"Thank you," Rexen said peppily. "I am very earnest."

I rolled my eyes and slowed down long enough to make sure Rua could also move past the blockade. As I watched, something strange happened. The moment Rua reached the oomukade in front of her, it was as though I witnessed some kind of shift. One second, she was up in its grille, and the next . . .

She was running past the beast, almost as if she'd *phased* through it.

*What the hell was that?*

She reached me and I gave her a questioning look, but she just shrugged, a beaming smile plastered on her face.

"New Ability!" she announced proudly.

"Well . . . *alright*, then!" I said, and turned my sights to the next problem at hand.

It was another minute or so of this—ducking, dodging, slashing, slicing. I was less concerned with murdering these things outright than just making sure they weren't in my way. In fact, by the time we reached ground zero, we'd left behind such a horrendous trail of disfigured and maimed superbugs that it looked like a macabre version of the *Family Circus* dotted line using a viscera Slip 'N Slide.

*Yuck,* I thought to myself. *Glad I'm not the janitor.*

Though I might as well have been a custodian, considering how much evil I was planning to *clean up* tonight.

Oh, yeah, baby. There's always time to spout a ham-fisted metaphor that allows me to gas myself up.

When we finally reached the immense monster's base, I had to avoid getting immediately ground up as the rapidly moving monster's legs punched holes in the rock and churned it behind it like a field thresher. All around us, folks were engaged in combat with the mama or her babies, and it was almost impossible to truly understand where we stood, concerning her destruction. I looked up, hoping to have a gout of inspiration pour into my mind, but all I saw was vertigo-inducing terror.

She was *big*.

The monster continued forward, heedless of the mess at her many feet. From my vague familiarity with this section of town, I knew we only had a few minutes before she reached the water tower—probably a lot less. I'd have to figure out how to get inside her stomach and fast. Not only because of the moronic time constraint on this bullshit-ass Quest but because I wasn't entirely convinced my friends could survive the depths of the roiling digestive acid inside the belly of this beast.

*So, how am I going to do this?*

The entire time I'd been observing this clusterfuck, I hadn't seen the monster devour anyone, only smash through all the defenses and be really hard to kill. I hadn't even seen her swoop down to ground level, only keeping herself upright. So, what was the deal? How had Stinky, Frida, and *especially* Jes made their way into her guts?

Like a monkey's paw of divine insight, suddenly, the oomukade queen showed me the way. The fully armored warrior that had been getting smashed all over the joint had taken the opportunity to cast a Spell or something to send himself flying into the air. A dazzlingly colorful plume sprouted from behind him like a Technicolor squirrel's tail as he soared up and up, a hundred feet into the air before coming to rest on the top of the mom-ster's head. Well, if you could really call it that. It was more like a bulbous lobe of chitinous flesh that happened to have a face on the end of it.

"Whoa," Rua breathed in reverence. "He's like Tanooki Mario!"

Somewhere, an image bubbled up into my consciousness of the famous mustachioed video-game character with a raccoon tail from when I was really young. That was probably what she was referring to. Leave it to a geek like Rua to know precisely what the name was of a sometimes-power that Nintendo creatures morphed into.

There were several cheers of approval from onlookers as the hero waved at us, celebrating his victory before lifting his massive, fuck-off sword into the air for a plunge.

Then he was flying again. But this time, it had nothing to do with magic and *everything* to do with physics.

The oomukade had snapped her face upward, launching the hapless goonie from his perch and high into the air, his body flailing as he tried to gain control of his impromptu flight. The queen's serpentine body reared back and shot up, her eye sockets wide and her mouth open in a terrifying and hungry smirk. Then she snatched him from the air in her teeth.

"Augggyuhhhhhgggggghhh!" the man screamed as the creature chomped down on his torso, his top half still protruding from her lips as his prolonged death rattle echoed out from on high. Buckets of blood gushed down from above, splattering the streets as his armor did apparently fuck-all against her razor-sharp fangs. Everyone below was still and silent for a moment as this transpired, the only sound being the warrior's dying screams. He tried to bat at the creature with his sword, but from the size of it, it didn't seem like he could get a good thwack in. He lost his grip, and the giga-sword fell from his grasp, falling straight down at maximum velocity.

"MOVE!" someone nearby shouted, breaking our shocked horror, and we scattered. The colossal blade hit the rock point-first, sending a shower of pebbles and debris in every direction. I twisted to look back at the monster and her fresh catch of the day, watching as she bit down with one final crunch, silencing the warrior and separating his exposed upper half from the rest of him. The oomamakade tossed her head back and began choking the man's lower body down into her gullet like a goose, her body undulating as she swallowed his remains. Then she faced the water tower again and moved on, utterly unfazed by the menacing display she'd just enacted.

I just stared as the head and shoulders of the armored man fell, striking the ground with a wet *clang*, blood exploding from within like a grindhouse water balloon. Everyone around us was frozen in disgust.

"What the fuck, what the fuck!" I roared, backing away. Fortunately, there was little visible of the fallen hero's actual body. The oomukade's teeth had ripped straight through his thick armored plating, so whatever tatters remained of his organic matter were well contained behind his helmeted costume.

I heard Rua gagging behind me and went to see if she was alright, but Rexen stopped me. He flew directly into my face, eyes wide and . . . creepily excited as he gestured to the metal-encased semi-corpse on the ground.

"He has a shiny," he said, his tone bright and urgent.

"He has no fucking body," I said. "What the hell are you talking about?"

"A *shiny*," Rexen said emphatically, jabbing toward him. "Look! Look!"

I glanced at the helmet and armor where once lived a plucky adventurer, but all I could see was the mess seeping out of the cracks. I grimaced.

"Ain't nothin' shiny that I can see, Arjee," I said. "Just a whole lotta body slime."

"His neck," Rexen said, gesturing again. "The shiny is on his neck!"

I peered closer, trying to understand what this weird-ass spectral wizard was talking about. The steel-gray helmet was closed, but I could see that it had a hinge on either side of the jaw, likely to open it up so the dude could walk around all Batman-style. Where it connected to the armored collar that joined the helmet and color-matching torso, though, was a band of yellow and blue. It looked like a medieval choker, with two solid strips of hammered gold and metallic sapphire completely encircling his neck and crosshatched engravings following it all the way around. It was dirty and covered in gore and grime, but there was definitely a faint sheen to it.

*Is that what he's talking about?*

"The necklace?" I asked, pointing to the choker with a shrug. "What? You want that thing?"

"Yes," Rexen said. "For you."

"For me?" I said, horrified. "Absolutely not. That belongs to a dead man. I'm no grave robber."

"He doesn't need it anymore," Rexen protested. "You can use it. You will look gorgeous."

"Nuh-uh," I said. "I'm not going anywhere near—"

"You should loot the corpse," Rua said from behind me. I turned to look at her as she wiped saliva from her mouth with the back of her hand. Apparently, she'd done a little more than retching. I couldn't blame her.

"Wait? You too?!" I asked, shaking my head in disbelief. "Listen, I'm as cavalier about a lot of this stuff as the next guy—more so, even! But I'm not going to—"

"In games, sometimes the only way to get some of the best drops is by looting," Rua continued, gesturing toward the corpse with her chin. "You can pick up a ton of good gear from people who are . . . well, no longer using it."

"What's gotten into *you*?" I asked. "This doesn't bother you? That may be how it works in Roblox, Rua, but as far as I can tell, we are *actually* here. I'm like . . . seventy percent certain of that at this point."

Maybe it had been the constant pain and agony I had experienced so far or having known the sensation of being crushed under the weight of an exploding monster, but something had changed. I wasn't sure when my brain had made the internal switch from *This must be a coma* to *Whoa, shit, this is real as fuck*, but apparently, it had. I'd been interacting with this world for the last few days as though it was genuinely happening. Because of that, there was something *super* icky to my faculties about ransacking this dude's belongings after the way he'd gone out.

"It might be real," Rua said. "But even you are aware the rules here seem nearly identical to video and tabletop games. Everything happening to us suggests we should follow the same kind of logic as if we were playing one. Even if it's messed up or doesn't make total sense, I think we've got to just go with the flow. You're telling me that you haven't taken stuff from other people? Nothing on your person came from the dead?"

She gestured to me and gave me a skeptical look.

I thought about the fact that I'd *absolutely* taken the dented helm from Berg's mummified remains when I'd been at the entrance to the Crypt. But this was different, right?

"Yeah, but not someone I'd just watched die," I said, in complete denial. There was something else that bothered me about this, though.

*Keep it together, Loon,* I thought to myself.

"You took the wands from the dwarf," she said. "You kill—uh, were there when *he* passed away."

"Yeah, but he was an asshole and deserved it!" I shouted back, feeling cornered. "I also yanked stuff from some motherfucking rat men I killed, too, but this isn't the same!"

"How so?" Rua asked. This had come out a lot softer, perhaps because she could hear the frustration in my voice or see the telltale signs of anger gathering on my face.

"Because he died trying to kill this fucking thing!" I exclaimed, clenching the haladie in my fist. I swiped in the direction of the monster moving away from us as the battle resumed in earnest—all while we stupidly argued in the street. I lowered my head, stamping down the fury building in my chest. I couldn't lose control now, not when it would have actual physical side effects. I took a deep breath before continuing.

"Do we respect no one in death?" I muttered. Despite my best efforts, I couldn't hide the venom in my quiet voice. "Even people who risk their lives trying to stop something bad from happening? What? We just say, 'Great job on the dying, bro, now pardon me while I desecrate your mortal coil—thanks for the treat, stupid'?"

I pointed at the quarter-man on the ground, the blood from his hidden body pooling out slowly, soaking into the spaces between the cobblestones. Rua didn't say anything.

"If we just take whatever we want from the people that have fallen—who have fucking died—trying to do something good, then what respect does anyone have left to them after death?" I hissed. "This fucker fought and died for something . . . I dunno, greater than himself, and to do . . . *that* is to completely disregard his sacrifice. It's just *straight-up. Fucking.* Cowardice. What, someone fucking kicks the bucket while trying to protect others, and this is the payment they get? You turn your back on them because they didn't live through it? It's a betrayal of their fucking memory and a betrayal of what they did. It's an act of greed and selfishness that shows a complete lack of respect for a person who died. Died fighting."

I took another breath, but it was starting to become more difficult to rein in my emotions, because I'd worked myself up over this. I knew I was a bit of a hypocrite, but the wrongness of what they were suggesting was burrowing itself deep into me. It felt different. It *was* different. I couldn't help but think of Dedyc, his arms broken and his body shattered, or Merra—stabbed through the face—or . . . Calden's frozen expression of horror and confusion when I stumbled onto his decapitated head. It *haunted* me. I'd never get those images out of my mind, no matter how much I tried or how long I lived. If someone had picked through *their* belongings after what had happened to them, I'd . . . I would . . .

Older memories invaded my mind. Ones from before arriving in Regaia and long before my own temper had become what defined me. Memories that I'd been pushing down to save my own sanity. Roger. My mother . . .

My breath became labored, my heart rate picking up speed.

I closed my eyes and slammed my fist against my head to force the thoughts out. I heard Rua gasp, my sudden violence startling her. I did it again, trying to punch away the pain and the anger, attempting to ensure I wouldn't go into Primal Rage—but also just trying to banish those bad feelings so I could focus. Again and again, I pounded my own skull to fixate on something other than these awful memories. I couldn't let myself fall into this trap. I *wouldn't* let myself do it.

Rexen and Rua were both silent, the mood of the encounter having completely shifted because of my outburst. I still had my eyes closed, trying to stopper the angry depression from spreading within me, when another voice cropped up.

"Whoa! What did I miss?!"

*Edwig.*

I opened my eyes and saw the illisinaf sliding along the stone toward us, his eyes wide as he took in the nightmare the three of us were surrounded by. I didn't say anything. I let my fists fall to my side and took breaths more slowly, the distraction helping a bit to calm me slightly. The amorphous man scooted up to stand between Rua and myself, his eyes finding the corpse. He let out a low whistle.

"Damn," he said. "Is that Klaude?"

"Who?" I asked emotionlessly. I felt drained, my mind foggy. I'd either hit myself too many times, or the intensity of psychological buildup had overwhelmed me to the point of exhaustion. Probably a column A, column B sorta sitch.

"Big brute, oversized sword, doesn't know when to quit?" Edwig said. "His armor looks a lot like that."

His gaze found the weapon the warrior had dropped sticking out of the stone, at least two feet of it buried beneath the surface.

"Yeah, that's Klaude," he said. "Nasty way to go. He probably deserved it, though."

"What?" I asked, a little bit of my sense returning. "What do you mean?"

"Huh?" Edwig asked. "Oh—just that he is—er—*was* kind of a bad guy. One of those 'might makes right' fellas that think that because they're physically stronger than other people, they can just push them around. Killed a bunch of folks just for slighting him. A real bastard, you know?"

"Huh? He killed people?" I asked.

"Oh, yeah," Edwig continued. "He'd get drunk or just have a burr in his belt about someone—thinking they were badmouthing him or something—so he'd force them into a duel and then have free rein to slaughter them."

Seeing my and Rua's expressions, the illisinaf chuckled.

"I can see you guys are confused," he said. "Makes sense since you're obviously not . . . from around here, but that's alright. Murder and mayhem are frowned upon pretty much everywhere—and illegal, too, of course. That is, unless you challenge someone to a duel. It's assumed both parties understand the terms when they enter into one, and you can specify if it's to first blood, death, or what have you. So, he'd pressure them into a sanctioned fight, set the terms to kill, and cut 'em down mercilessly. Granted, it wasn't always to the death. Sometimes, he'd just beat them into a cripple—but it was enough times for him to get a reputation for it."

Edwig shook his head, his eyes still on the corpse of—apparently—Klaude.

"Yeah," he continued. "The guy was a real piece of work. Good riddance."

Before I could say anything else, I heard another voice pipe up, startling me with its closeness.

"He was quite awful."

It was Orville.

"Jesus!" I shouted, leaping back. "Where did you come from?!"

Orville was standing not ten feet away, next to an overturned vendor stall of some variety. I could see a bunch of pastries that looked like economy-sized, badly burnt Hot Pockets spilling out of a steam trunk at his feet.

"You told me to hide," Orville said innocently. "So, I did."

"You were here the whole time?" I asked, baffled by this human.

"Yes and no," he said, shrugging his shoulders noncommittally. "I was following you lot but remaining out of sight."

I retraced our path, seeing that some of the oomukade from before had expired while others were simply floundering around with their missing body parts keeping them company not far away. Very little in that direction would be a good place to stay out of view, as it was mostly an open thoroughfare. That was odd.

"How?" I asked. "There's barely anything large enough to duck behind."

"I told you," Orville said. "I'm quite good at hiding."

"I guess so," I said, unable to help the impressed tone.

*Maybe I should get some lessons from this idiot. Even if he is nearly useless, he might be able to give me some pointers on utilizing my Skill to its best results. Lord knows I need it.*

"So, you both knew this guy—and he was a dick?" Rua asked. Edwig nodded, but Orville spoke up further.

"Worse than that," he explained. I noticed he was looking now at the man's severed torso with a sneer. "Klaude made my childhood unbearable. He and his friends were always tormenting me, handing out beatings, and chasing me until

I couldn't run any longer. But even as an adult, he never curbed those menacing impulses. Just last summer, he kicked the legs out from beneath my chair at the tavern, and I fell, breaking my wrist and elbow. All because he said I was sipping my ale too loudly . . ."

He stretched his arm to its full length, and I heard a few skeletal clicks.

"It still hasn't fully healed—and likely never will."

"Ooh, this means we can take the shiny!" Rexen exclaimed, hovering near me and spinning joyfully in the air.

I sighed. Then, wordlessly, I walked over to the puddle formerly known as Klaude and squatted in front of the armor. I focused on the gold-and-blue metallic choker around the neck and let my Eye of the Saboteur do its thing. I ignored the material components for the moment and focused only on what would actually be necessary.

**Bahlgus's Enchanted Gorget of Flight**
- **Rarity: Unique**
- **Item Class: Accessory**
- **Durability: 289/500**
- **Weight: 0.7 lbs.**
- **Bonuses: Grants Bahlgus's Flight for [60] seconds [ 3 Charges per day]**
- *Charges Remaining: [2/3]*

*Introducing Bahlgus's Enchanted Gorget of Flight—the magical accessory that will make all your flying dreams come true! Created by the famously whimsical wizard, Bahlgus, this gorget grants the wearer the ability to use the Bahlgus's Flight Spell up to five times per day. Soar up to 500 feet in any direction for a full minute with each charge, leaving a trail of rainbow-colored magic behind you as you fly! But wait, there's more! As you are probably aware, Bahlgus was known for adding amazing extra features to all of his artifacts, and this gorget is no exception! The wearer will be graced with a majestic, colorful tail while they soar, making them the envy of all their flying friends. So, why wait? Grab your Bahlgus's Gorget of Flight today and take to the skies in style!*

I scowled.

"This is weird," I said.

"What is?" Rua asked, coming as close as she dared to the revolting mess.

"Well," I said, looking back at her. "Normally, when I get a description, the system has, like, a sarcastic, annoying way of telling me what's going on with the thing I'm looking at. But this one is written like . . . I dunno. Marketing copy or something? Like it's trying to sell me on it."

"Wait, Loon," Rua exclaimed. "You actually *can* see the descriptions of things? I suspected you might be able to, but . . . damn, that's really cool."

"It's not as neat as you're probably thinking," I said. "Sure, it's badass to know exactly what I'm putting on at all times, but there's usually a ton of detail that bogs down the real info and makes it hard to understand."

I didn't mention that it was probably more challenging to understand because I usually only skimmed for the essential bits.

"Marketing copy?" Edwig asked, sliding closer. "What do you mean by that?"

"You know, like *Buy now* or *This is a one-of-a-kind value, so don't delay*. That sort of thing. Very sales pitchy."

"Oh," Edwig said. "Yeah, sometimes that happens. Especially with Artificers and Enchanters and the like."

"The *what* whats?" I asked.

"Those who design and craft magical items or effects," he clarified. "Pah! I know you're an *orc*, orc, but you sure do need a lot of handholding to make sense of the world around you."

"I'm *new in town*!" I exclaimed, frowning at the illisinaf. "Besides, I only pay attention to the pertinent stuff—like how to rescue gelatin men—who owe me *money*—from prison."

Edwig paused and then nodded.

"Fair point," he said. "Anyhow, when a suitably powerful individual concocts an item, they can also decide on the explanatory description for those of them that can read it. What was the name?"

"Uh . . ." I muttered, quickly activating my Ability again to read the message. "Bal . . . huhh . . . gus's Enchanted Gorget. Of, um, Flight."

"Bahlgus?!" Rexen suddenly erupted with glee—pronouncing it differently than I had. "Take it! Take it now!"

*Apparently, the* h *is silent.*

"You know 'im?" I asked, surprised at the instant ferocity of the little spirit on hearing the name.

"Yes!" he declared, his body briefly changing from its vibrant blues and purples to a glowing green and then back. "I've been living *in* a rock, not *under* one. He's famous. I want it."

It seemed odd to me that he cared about something like fame when he was arguably a popular myth himself. At least insofar as I'd seen by people's reactions to his name.

"Bahlgus?" Rua asked, still not taking her eyes off the corpse. "I thought this guy's name was Klaude? Is that his last name?"

"No!" Rexen said, feverishly flipping through the air with what almost looked like anxiety. "The dead one isn't Bahlgus! Bahlgus would never wear armor so tacky!"

I looked wonderingly at Edwig, who somehow shrugged the shoulder area of his amorphous form and sighed.

"Bahlgus is something of a notorious individual among scholarly sorts," he said dryly. "A real genius with magical construction theory. He could have done anything—potion-crafting, scroll lore, theoretical Arcanum, and the like. But he decided to ignore all the expectations his colleagues laid at his feet and focus on a different pursuit. Bahlgus believed his talents would be best spent creating magical accessories. Though his pieces aren't beautiful or really much to look at as far as visual splendor, they are unique in that they always have a bit of . . . artistic flair, I suppose you could say. Pairing with the fact that most of his creations can be recharged—a rarity itself—his name is thrown around a lot in academia."

"So, you said he's an Artificer?" Rua asked, her eyes now on the illisinaf and shining with hope. "Or an Enchanter?"

"No, actually," Edwig said. "Artificers craft objects and imbue them with Arcana during construction, while Enchanters take something already made and use their Spells to add additional effects. Bahlgus is unique in that he's in a whole Class category all his own. He's an Ensemblist—and the only known one in existence."

I'd spent the time during Edwig's overindulgent monologue fiddling with the clasp on the back of the gorget. Almost as if thematically, just as he said those final words, I was able to unhook it. Predictably, the item tumbled from the posthumous position between Klaude's pauldrons and onto the stones. I picked it up and clasped it around my own neck, feeling almost lighter as I did so.

"What're the features of an Ensemblist?" Rua asked, clearly dying to know what mechanics were behind the untold mystery in the Class.

"Eh, it's hard to say exactly," Edwig explained. "Seeing as how he's the only one. But, best anyone knows, if it were to become a typical Class, it might be that Ensemblists rarely design one-off items. Bahlgus's creations are always part of a set, forged specifically to bring all the pieces together for maximum power. However, that alone wouldn't be enough to set it apart from the norm. Enchanters, Artificers, and many other Modulation types can do that, so it's not unique to the Class. However, Bahlgus's powers work differently, which is what truly defines the nature of his abilities. He doesn't need anything to bring the items he made into being. He can create them solely from Arcana itself."

Rua seemed taken aback by this.

"That's, like, against the idea of . . . what is it—equivalent exchange?"

Edwig shrugged.

"I dunno what that means, exactly. Like a sort of swap?"

"Well . . ." Rua said, blushing a bit for some reason. "There's a . . . *story* where I'm from that talks about it in detail. You need to sacrifice something of equal or greater value to produce wondrous mag—uh, *Arcana*. Like when creating something out of nothing."

"Weird story," Edwig said. "Nah, there's little like that going on here. I'm going to assume you're not well abreast of the theory behind Arcana, because that doesn't make any sense from a practical standpoint. People create stuff out of nothing all the time. But Bahlgus is notable because the complexity of the items produced is far above anything typically found in the other Classes. Summoning a chair, a glass of wine, or even a potted plant from pure Arcana is typical. But crafting a completely material object with arcane properties *and* sophisticated function with a wave of the hand? That's what sets him apart."

"Alright, enough of that," I said, gesturing to my neck. "I'm wearing the damn thing. This doesn't change dick about what I said earlier, though, because I still don't think looting good guys is the way to go. I was only okay with this because it turns out Klaude was a real bag of shit."

"It looks fabulous on you," Rexen said. "Top-tier. Perfect for killing giant monsters."

"Oh, fuck!" I shouted, glancing behind me at the towering oomukade queen in the distance. "I got distracted! Damn, we gotta get going!"

"I didn't want to interrupt the interesting findings," Orville said, pointing at the monster. "I'd noticed it gaining ground but assumed you all had it handled."

"Well, maybe barge into the conversation next time if you see us freewheeling on some unnecessary information, newbie!" I shot back at Orville, embarrassed I'd gotten so easily led away from the *big-ass problem* looming above the horizon.

I turned to Edwig, suddenly remembering why he'd even been separated from us in the first place.

"Jigglepuss," I said. "Did you learn anything to help us take that fromunda cheese monstrosity down?"

The illisinaf scowled but then sighed.

"Pah! Suppose I did. Are you going to drop the nicknames?"

"Depends on how good the info is," I said. "Make with the deets, hermano— we're burnin' daylight!"

Edwig smiled.

"In that case . . ." he started, adopting a mischievous expression that almost made me uncomfortable. "I think I learned quite a bit of useful information. If you've got the stomach for it."

I sneered.

"I've got *plenty*!" I announced proudly, slapping my midsection with gusto. However, for the first time ever, I found that I missed having an abdominal section that wasn't so Rubenesque. The joke totally didn't work anymore.

"Good," Edwig said, pressing his appendages together conspiratorially. "Because I've got just one question for you."

"What's that?" I asked.

"Are you ready to become a hero?"

# CHAPTER SIXTEEN

# TROPES

**A**re you sure about this, Loon?" Rua asked, her tone admitting a lack of confidence for the first time I'd seen since we'd reencountered one another in this world. In the old world, she might've given me a million reasons as to why what I was thinking of doing was a bad idea or tried to rationalize the absolute insanity of the danger involved in what I wanted to do. Now, though, she was just double-checking if I was still as stupid as before.

"Yeah!" I announced proudly, trying to project more assurance than I felt. Apparently, neither of us was keen on the odds I'd stacked against us.

"The orc will probably be fine," Edwig said. "And think of it this way: if he fails, it won't be any of our problems anymore."

"Yeah, quit yer bellyachin', future corpse!" I said over my shoulder with a grin. "It's time to do silly shit. We can worry about the consequences if we die."

"Well, fortunately—" Rua began, but I cut her off.

"*Fortunately*, nothing! This is going to work . . . probably."

That had been close. I wasn't sure, but it seemed like Rua had just been about to spill the beans on our unique heritage—and I wasn't sure we could trust the three non-Sojourners to take it well. Sure, it was possible. Jes's party had seemed pretty chill with it, but I still had a near-death hangover from revealing that juicy bit of backstory to Fawn. It just wasn't . . . I needed to be sure before we blabbered about it to anyone. I gave Rua a pointed nudge that hopefully relayed what I'd been trying to do so she'd get the hint. Whether she understood or not, she didn't continue, only nodding as if accepting her fate.

"Alright," I said, turning back toward the oomukade queen, now so far away we couldn't catch it any other way if we tried. "You all know what your roles are?"

"Yes," Orville stated, happy to be helpful, it seemed. "The moment you take off, I am going to—"

"Dude!" I interrupted. "What are you doing?!"

Orville frowned, looking hurt that I'd scolded him.

"Reaffirming what our plans are in—"

"Never," I hissed, pointing a deadly finger at him, "*ever* recap a plan after it's been devised. That's a guaranteed way to make sure it fails."

"I'm sorry, what?" Orville asked, clearly confused by my statement. "I don't think I underst—"

"Shush!" I demanded, pressing my index finger over his lips and pinching them closed. "Just hush, baby. Shut your mouth."

He glared at me but remained silent. He didn't even try to remove my hand from his face.

"Good," I said. "We can't be breakin' movie rule number one when it comes to death-defying schemes to take down the baddies."

"I mean, you're right about that being a foreshadowing red flag," Rua said. "But this isn't a movie, Loon."

"Of course it isn't," I said, then more quietly so only she could hear, I muttered, "but that doesn't mean anything right now. We're in a world with bizarre fuckin' *Dark Souls* laws, yet I don't think we're inside *an actual game*. Who says movie rules don't also apply?"

"That's, uh . . ." Rua began, straining to finish her sentence. ". . . Okay, fine. I can't disprove that, so we may as well pretend—"

"Excellent!" I thundered.

"What was all that talk about games?" Edwig asked.

"What?!" I said, startled I'd been overheard. "Nothing! You shut up too! That was a private conversation."

"Pah! Maybe you should have spoken more softly, then! I could hear you plain as day."

"I couldn't," Orville admitted. "What did they say?"

"Both of you: shut your yaps. We don't have time for this—we've got a monster's day to ruin!"

"Yes, that part is obvious," Rexen chimed in. "But why is the elf tied to your back?"

I glanced over my shoulder again and saw the red mane on the back of Rua's head.

"Because I haven't used this rope yet!" I announced, thinking about how it had just been sitting lonesomely in my pack since I'd first arrived. "Now be quiet. We're tempting fate too much already, so I'm not going to explain everything and ruin the whole devious objective. All three of you are in adventure planning time-out. Zip it."

"Jeez, Loon," Rua said, pushing against the binds lashing us together to test its strength. "You're really serious about this movie-logic thing, huh?"

"Yes," I said. "I can't have anything messing this up. And can you stop moving around so much? You're digging your elbow into my kidney!"

"Shouldn't you guys be, I dunno . . . *enacting* your precious *plan*?" Edwig asked, choosing his words carefully.

"Right," I said, taking one final look at my Attribute scores to ensure nothing had changed. "Rua, you ready?"

"I've willingly strapped myself back-to-back with an angry orc who will probably end up killing us both because this plan is as foolish as it is insane. What do you think?"

"I don't deal well with rhetorical—"

"Yes, I'm ready!" she said, interrupting me with a sigh of frustration. "Are you just stalling?"

"No!" I said sheepishly.

I pointed at Edwig. "Jigglepuss—let's do this."

"Alright, orc," Edwig said as if it were his final hurrah. "But keep in mind, once I do this, I'm tapped. No more Arcana for me for at least a couple hours. So, make it count."

"Just do the thing alre—"

Instantly, a magical force wrapped itself around me. I'd started to shout at him, but before I could finish, the illisinaf had raised his wobbly, gelatinous arm, and it suddenly felt like I was being squeezed by a gigantic hand. The pressure was intense but not too much to bear as Edwig used Unseen Hand on us and wrenched us from the ground and into the air. I was initially concerned when we only levitated about ten feet. Still, a moment later, I felt hefted and *launched* like a javelin tossed by an expert arm.

We fuckin' *flew*.

Up and up, we went, flying through the sky as the world's deadliest conjoined twins. Well, I suppose it was triplets, considering Rexen was clinging to my shoulder as well. Whatever—it still worked! I could see the dark silhouette of the town below blurring by as Edwig's Spell carried us aloft.

*Nobody down there better be lookin' up my kilt.*

Up ahead, the oomukade queen's form grew closer and closer as we were sent on a crash course directly toward her. Rua's scream carried over the rush of the wind behind me, but I had the opposite reaction: I roared with laughter. I mean, come on: how could I not? I was literally soaring through the sky on a magic airlift. Rexen, seeing my glee, joined me, his dreamy voice mimicking my maniacal bellows as best he could.

This was fucking awesome! We were zeroing in on this boss battle in a very stylish and flashy way. Plus, I had an ace up my sleeve.

I opened my status screen as we rocketed over the buildings and glanced at my Luck Attribute. It had increased from the abysmal negative four earlier—and what was better, it had gained the *maximum* upward mobility it could for the moment.

**Luck 11**

"Fuck, yeah!" I cheered.

"Kill!" Rexen shouted.

"Ahh!" Rua screamed.

I wasn't sure *when* exactly the Attribute had changed, but it had. Zeol—the irritating mask god—had, of course, explained that this would happen several times per day. Luck would go up and down, and never by more than fifteen points. Right now, it was all coming up Loon.

*This is going to fucking work.*

The pressure from Unseen Hand suddenly lessened, indicating we had left Edwig's range and were now freeballing up there without a lifeline. But that was a perfectly respectable term for these conditions. I waited a few moments for our momentum to slow, feeling the rise in my stomach as we hit the apex of our travel and began to cruise downward. I looked over at Rexen, and we nodded at one another simultaneously. Then I put a hand on the choker around my neck and activated Bahlgus's Flight.

*SHOOM!*

I felt the change instantly. A warm breeze washed over me, irrelevant to the turbulent gusts enveloping my descent. I felt the arcane energy wrap around me like a snug body glove. What was more, I could now feel the currents of air in a new way. They made *sense* to me. It was as if my body knew exactly what to do and how best to achieve what it was made for: flying. I felt air thermals beneath me and dragged my fingers in them as my body easily found something like a groove and allowed myself to be pulled along with a gentle tug. I was doing it! I was soaring through the air like a motherfucking bird of prey!

Rua, on my back, was now facing in the opposite direction I was, likely staring up into the cold night sky. Then she released a gasp of surprise.

"Tanooki tail!"

I looked over my shoulder, seeing the vibrant plume of multicolored magical energy sprouting up behind me from beneath my battle skirt.

"That's right, baby!" I shouted. "I'm the fucking sky lord of the animal kingdom!"

I flew forward and watched as the queen mum grew more prominent in front of me. We were gaining on her, and it was delightful to behold. Below, dozens of fighters continued battling, though I could see there were fewer than before.

*Uh-oh,* I thought. *Hopefully, they just got tired and retreated, not . . . the, uh, other thing.*

We were almost there when the timer ended on the Spell, and we began dropping rapidly. Then I smashed the final use of the gorget, and we immediately soared forward again until we were just above the beast.

"Alright, Rua!" I shouted. "Ready?!"

"As ready as I'll ever—" she started, but I spun in a cute little pirouette so that I was facing the stars and she was facing down toward the monster. Then I dropped Bahlgus's Flight, and we fell.

I'll admit, it was a little unnerving to suddenly fall backward without being able to see. However, when I felt a jerk of resistance, I knew the elf had hit the mark. There was a wet *slink* as metal entered flesh, and I immediately pivoted to slap my bare feet on the surface of the creature's hide. I stared forward at the slope of the monster's body, feeling an exhilarating rush from my view a hundred feet from the ground. Then I ran right toward it.

"Here," Rexen said.

I slammed on the brakes and spun in place, turning back to look at our handiwork. I could have squealed with approval. Wedged right into the creature's noggin flesh was the massive blade of Klaude's prized giga-sword. It appeared at least three feet of the edge was buried in the hide—the very same hide utterly devoid of any armor-like chitin.

So, the first part of the information Edwig had gleaned had been accurate: the portion of the creature's body where it was weakest was the top, above its fucked-up face. I smirked.

*Let's hope part two is just as fruitful.*

I leveled Eye of the Saboteur at the weapon and checked its details one final time.

**The Behemoth Blade**
- **Rarity: Elusive**
- **Item Class: Two-Handed Weapon**

- Durability: 350/415
- Weight: 4.8 lbs.
- Damage: 100–112 Piercing / 120–150 Slashing
- Bonus: Channeling

Item Requirements:
  - Two-Handed Weapons Skill [E-Rank Level 1]
  - Strength 13

*This magnificent sword stands at a daunting seven feet tall, but don't let its size fool you. It may be forged from not only the toughest volcanic iron and obsidian but also breezestone, which means its weight has been magically reduced to make it easier to wield. Trust me, you'll still feel the full force of its might with every strike! However, if someone attempted to wrest this blade from your heroic grasp but was too weak to qualify for the minimum requirements, they would find the blade far too unwieldy and heavy to properly use.*

*The Behemoth Blade has a special property known as "Channeling," which amplifies the strength of any arcane properties it is subjected to or enchanted with. Imagine the power you'll wield with this baby in your hands!*

Man, having friends with different specializations than you really had a fabulous return on investment. Despite its deceptively light weight, I still wouldn't have been able to use the blade without having allocated digits in my muscle score. However, Rua was a perfect candidate, having dumped more of her Points into Strength than I had. Even at the bare minimum threshold, she was overqualified for the job with a beefy *fourteen*. But even more so, those extra properties were what I was really salivating over.

*This is going to work!*

I spun back to the edge so Rua could see the sword clearly in her line of sight.

"You're up again!" I shouted. Then, before the words had hardly left my mouth, I activated Enduring Perch. "Bring the thunder!"

"Got it!" she called. I felt her arm move behind me as she raised an object in the direction of the Behemoth Blade.

"Unleash!" she cried, and her words were followed up with the hot snap of an electrical current's crackle. I glanced over my shoulder to watch as a broken bolt of magical lightning exploded from the tip of the wand in her hand, striking the sword and causing it to flash like the theft alarm at a Safeway.

This was something I knew all about because of . . . *reasons.*

The blade flashed again, and as though the oomukade's body was sucking up the magic through a straw, the energy pulsated and shot downward, directly into the wound the sword had created.

"Yes!" I roared. I checked my Stamina level.

*We're still Gucci for the moment.*

"It's like *Shadow of the Colossus*," Rua breathed.

"Again!" Rexen shouted with glee, his eyes swirling vortexes of malicious delight. Rua was able to crack off one more bolt before the neck of the creature began to twist, and I felt a rumble beneath my feet.

"Here we g—" I started, but was cut off by an ear-splitting roar. Apparently, the oomukade queen suddenly became aware of the stealth attack we'd just busted out on her supple centipede flesh and wasn't pleased. My mind filled with the anguished cry of the beast as my Ancient Chitinus language primer automatically translated her message of torment.

*What foul spawn seeks to harm me? I will devour you!*

With that, the queen flung her head, attempting to toss us into the air. Unfortunately for her, I was an immovable object as long as my feet were planted. My body stayed put, riding the waves of contracting muscles like an expert surfer on a turbulent tidal wave. I watched from my position as the arrogant-as-fuck monster raised her face skyward, believing that whatever was putting the hurt on her back fat was now in the air, a-ready for a chompin'. She opened her mouth, but when she saw nothing hovering above to catch in her disgusting maw, I almost laughed. She froze, uncomprehending, staring straight up into the night sky with confusion. Then she roared again.

*You are a stubborn pest. So be it.*

I couldn't help but feel she was missing the irony of a giant bug monster using that insult.

She dropped her face, and her muscles tensed as she dipped her head low.

*She's going to try again but harder,* I realized. I immediately released Enduring Perch before shooting toward the haunting kabuki mask, racing against the clock. I activated and dropped Enduring Perch several times in quick succession to keep from falling as I ran along the top of her skin. Then we passed the sword and reached the edge of her forehead just as she snapped her head back up. I hit Enduring Perch once more and felt the force of her whiplike motion as she attempted to fling us up into the air. Wouldn't you know it? She opened her mouth again, expecting it to work this time.

*What a fucking putz.*

Now standing flat on her face, I released Enduring Perch, all the while keeping a careful eye on my Stamina. The Ability drained the bar quickly, and I replenished it not nearly fast enough to keep doing this forever. Right then, it hovered just over a quarter of the way from empty, so I had to make this count. I stepped forward, right in the space between her eyes and mouth— you know, where a normal creature would keep its nose. She froze again, but

I watched as her eyes crossed as she realized somebody was *walking* on her goddamn face.

"Howdy!" I shouted directly into her face, then, switching to her language, spoke again.

"Surprise?"

*What is this?* her voice demanded, entering my mind like a burglar. *A morsel that comes to test itself against a master? You are hardly large enough to sate my appetite, four-leg.*

I cracked a big grin—you know, just to piss her off—and positioned myself so that Rua could see the Behemoth Blade from where I stood.

"You big," I said in my broken dialect. "I small. Fear?"

*I do not fear that which is inconsequential, four-leg! Climb into my mouth and show proper respect! You dare delay my brood-making?!*

*First of all: ew.*

I shook my head, then dropped my smile and allowed my anger toward her to show on my face.

"You eat . . ." I paused to find the right word. ". . . my kith?"

*Eh, close enough.*

*I devour what I will, as is my right, four-leg,* the queen practically spat mentally. *I am of a higher mind than you'll ever hope to be. It is of no consequence to you when I feed, nor what upon. Now I command you to dance among my teeth and end this insufferable mewling.*

I shook my head again.

"Big mistake," I said.

*You are the one who has made an error, four-leg. A deadly one. I will—*

"Now," I hissed to Rua, feeling her shift again as she fired another lightning blast at the sword. A pulse rippled below me as the oomukade queen screeched with pain. The sound was nearly unbearable, but I held fast, activating Enduring Perch for another moment as she thrashed in agony. I caught a glimpse inside her throat and could see that, in this position, it was a straight shot downward into darkness. But far below, I could see a thin sliver of light.

*THIS IS GOING TO WORK!*

"Don't stop. Keep it up!" I told Rua, but she was casting it again before I could finish speaking. And again. And again. The oomukade queen continued whipping around. I activated Enduring Perch each time until I was so close to the dregs that I knew I had to act or risk hitting the Off-balance debuff. I leaned forward toward her mouth, watching her eyes as they followed me in their comically crossed fashion.

"YOU NO KILL!" I shouted, staring down at her teeth. Rua fired another bolt, and the queen's fangs parted as she screeched. "I KILL *YOU*, BUTTERSCOTCH!"

I lifted the object clutched tightly in my hand—the indestructible orb—and activated a *different* Ability: Pernicious Volley. Then I leaped into the air and hurled the ball down into her gullet with all my strength. I watched the first strike rocket right into the back of her throat, forcing her mouth to open wider as the orb burrowed into her soft palate like a missile. A gout of dark blood burst forth, but I wasn't done with her yet. This was only the first move in the next stage of my plan. I wrenched the haladie from my waistband and slashed through the ropes binding Rua and me together. Before her boots had hardly hit the beast's flesh, I had another object in my hand.

"Feather Chest!" I shouted. "Maximize!"

The tiny ring-box-sized storage container exploded outward, growing to its massive proportions, but I was already opening it.

"In!" I roared, and with only a hairsbreadth of hesitation, Rua plopped herself inside. I slammed the lid closed before minimizing the magical chest again.

Then, taking a final breath, I dove into the beast's open fucking mouth.

From within the Feather Chest, Rua screamed. I screamed too. Rexen laughed.

"You are an *excellent* disciple!" he cried as we plunged into the dark depths of the oomukade queen's substantial maw.

# CHAPTER SEVENTEEN

# TUMMY TROUBLES

I slashed out with the haladie, feeling it drag against the tender mouth flesh as we plummeted into the void of teeth and throat. Fortunately, with my Darkvision, I could see the shape of this drop, and just before we hit bottom, I activated Calden's Hang Time. I crashed against the fleshy floor of the monster's stomach and didn't feel a damn thing.

But the queen sure did.

I transferred the force of my collision into the spot I'd just landed in, using one of the best features of any Aegis known to . . . well, me. Her body shook with pain as the delayed assault ruptured several blood vessels where I lay. Thick, inky gore bubbled up around me, and I hurriedly climbed to my feet. I spotted the indestructible orb sticking out of a section of insides and yanked it out, wiping it free of muck before shoving it into my pack.

"I think I like you, pupil," Rexen said. "You remind me of myself, except smaller."

"*I'm* smaller?" I asked, trying to peer at my surroundings with anything remotely resembling a trained eye. "Or *you* are smaller?"

"Yes," Rexen said. "Just a little guy."

I rolled my eyes, then tossed the Feather Chest into the air.

"Feather Chest, maximize!"

The humongous box expanded into being, landing with a light *plunk* in the muck of the creature's esophageal lining. I opened the lid to find a scowling Rua inside. I grinned sheepishly at the elf woman, wiggling my fingers in greeting.

"So," I asked jovially, ". . . how was the *ride*?"

She shoved past me as she nimbly climbed from the chest's interior before bowling forward and puking all over the ground. I mean, she was really heaving. I just watched and waited as she emptied the entire contents of her stomach out in front of the floating Rexen and me.

"Jesus," I breathed when she finally finished. "When the hell did you have time to eat? That was way too much stuff to be a normal daily diet."

Rua wiped her mouth with her sleeve and shook her head.

"Body-shaming, now, are we?" she teased. "Thought you were better than that."

"What?" I asked. "I'm the last person who is going to body-shame anyone . . ."

I trailed off, considering my own words.

"Actually, I'm probably the first person," I admitted. "But that wasn't the case here. I was just morbidly impressed with the variety of objects that just poured out of you."

"Har-dee-har," Rua said. "*Hilarious.*"

"I'm serious!" I continued, gesturing to the pile of sick. "What have you been eating, lady? I think I saw a *boot* in there!"

"Was it your boot?" Rexen asked, glancing down at my bare feet. "The next corpse we encounter, let's loot their sabatons!"

"Easy, there, Ed Gein," I said. "How about we just focus on the mission at hand?"

I lifted my haladie and pointed a little way off to where there was a distinct drop-off. Below, soft light shone from somewhere, casting long, spooky shadows. It appeared we were on some sort of meat shelf, and though I wasn't sure what the inside of an oomukade's digestive tract looked like, there was likely a stomach somewhere beyond. The surprising lack of bodies and . . . well, partially eaten corpses led me to believe that this little oral outcropping was likely not a permanent fixture or maybe just disappeared when the oomukade swallowed, or—

*FWOOM!*

The platform of muscle below disappeared, and we fell again. It was another fifty feet or so, but had the beast not been spongy inside, we'd likely have spent the rest of our short lives complaining about our busted femurs. I noticed wherever I'd landed was slightly warm and a little wet. Rexen was the first one up, as he'd never really fallen—he had just sort of . . . trodden air in a downward direction. Rua was next, looking down at her body in disgust as a mucusy film covered every inch of her. I stood finally, finding that I was also coated in the same slime.

*Here we go again,* I thought.

It reminded me of when I'd donned the magical party hat I'd gotten from Zeol. It had given me the quality of "Slimy" and kept the roe from being able to fully attack me. This was, of course, back before I'd become solid pals with a few of them and before the hat had been obliterated in the gunky explosion that took my life.

"This is so gross," Rua said, trying unsuccessfully to shake off the goo. I did the same but gave up after only a moment. We had shit to do, and I'd been covered in much worse a lot more recently. We followed the glow of whatever-the-fuck before moving through a tiny passage that the others were fine navigating, but I had to squeeze through. That was when the source of the light became clear: stomach fluid.

For whatever reason, probably that goddamn game logic, the liquid that filled this chamber was a glowing amber color, looking like a pond of radioactive piss. It took up every available bit of walking space I could see—though it seemed relatively shallow.

Despite the overall nastiness, I couldn't help but marvel at the sheer size of the place. The . . . chamber—if you could call it that—was pretty substantial for something used for dissolving materials. Easily twenty feet tall and just as wide, I supposed it made sense. The oomukade queen was already fuck-off large, but also because she likely consumed creatures and objects far bigger than any of us.

"Whoa," I muttered as my two companions and I stumbled around in the dim and humid belly cave. "This place is *gnarly*."

The stomach walls were lined with gross, slimy sacs filled with sickly yellow fluid that undulated in a fucked-up, unwholesome way. I could hear the monster's organs grinding and gurgling around us, and the stench of decay was overpowering. We stumbled through the cavernous chamber, the floor squishing and squelching beneath our feet. I could feel the heat and pressure of the oomukade's digestive juices all around us, and I knew we had to move fast if we wanted to rescue my friends and not turn into literal shit.

"This is friggin' bizarre," Rua said, admiring the overall disgusting vibe this place was giving off.

"Yeah!" I agreed before eyeing the liquid that was up to our ankles. "I wonder if this stuff is safe. You don't think it'll give us hepatitis or anything, do you?"

"Doubtful," Rua said. "I'm sure there's way worse here, though, than a liver infection. But to be safe, maybe don't drink any of it."

She smirked at me.

"I'm tempted to do it out of spite," I said. "But we don't have time for me to commit to a bit right now. There's savin' to be had!"

"Yeah, I thought you said you had allies here," Rua said. "What's your Force connection telling you?"

"Eh?" I asked. "Is that one *Star Trek* or *Star Wars*?"

"You're joking, right?" Rua asked, looking offended.

"Of course I am," I said with a grin. "Relax, I knew what you meant. I'm a huge *Dune* fan."

I just couldn't help pushing a nerd's buttons.

Rua scowled at me.

"Aren't we in a time crunch, Muad'Dib?" She asked. "You already said you're not allowed to go off on a tangent."

"Is that like a McRib?" I asked. "Actually, yeah, I could go for a pork sandwich right now.

"It's from *Dune*. Tangent, Loon—tangent!"

"Ah, shit!" I said, mad she'd messed up a fantastic rhyming opportunity. "Yeah—lemme check."

I closed my eyes and focused on the sensation of my party members. Their Health had been steadily declining during the battle, but for the last few minutes, I'd noticed they sort of just . . . stalled? All of them. As if they were no longer in danger, except, strangely, they had not begun to heal or anything else to bring their vitality back up. And that was strange. I supposed it was possible they'd used up all their magic and medicinal resources, but that didn't seem right. In any case, we needed to find them quickly.

"Arjee?" I asked, turning to the spirit. I noticed he was stretching his arms out over and over. When he heard me call to him, he looked over, his arms hovering in the air.

"Just preparing my limbs for wrestling!" he said as if the answer made any sense at all.

"Yeah, no—don't care. Can you tell where my allies are?"

Rexen dropped his arms and shrugged. Then he closed his eyes, concentrating, I thought. When he opened them again, his eyes swirled in a way that almost seemed menacing.

"They are close," Rexen explained. "All but specks of dust before a scattering storm."

"What does that even mean?" I demanded. "*Dust before a storm*? Are they in trouble or something?"

"They have *been* in trouble, pupil," Rexen said, "and will continue to be until they are rescued or die."

"Well, that's fuckin' ominous as shit," I said. "Are you being serious right now?"

Rexen stared at me for a moment longer before shrugging his shoulders.

"Iunno," he intoned.

"I wish I could hit you," I said before considering. "Wait, *can* I hit you? Are you solid? I'm gonna hit you."

I swiped lazily at him, and he floated out of the way.

"That is not nice," Rexen accused, scowling. "You were so neat when we were falling."

"Yeah, the coolest shit tends to happen when I plummet sexily from great heights," I answered.

"Well, now I am confused," the ghost continued, scratching his head.

"Take a number, Casper," I said. "Listen, can you lead us to them or not? I don't want to be wasting my time if—"

"Uh, Loon," Rua said urgently.

Before, when she'd done that, I hadn't given her the time of day, which had backfired tremendously. So, this time, like a perfectly polite gent, I paused and glanced her way.

"Yes, Rua?" I asked with the same level of gusto a butler might use. "What can I do for you?"

The elf woman was facing away from us, her eyes locked on one of the sacs of ick clinging to the organ wall. I peered at it, noticing that it was moving more than before. Last I checked, it was a calm pulsation. Now, though, it looked like something was fighting to get out with the fervor of a rabid dog.

"You might want to back away from—"

As always, I didn't get to finish. The sac burst open like the most disgusting water balloon ever conceived, and a fountain similar to the putrid stomach liquid we'd already been standing in blasted out—only this stuff was greener. It hit the floor level and kept coming, churning the water below us. I noticed that wherever the two liquids touched, the area around it began to bubble and pop like a chemical reaction. I coughed as a sulphuric smell filled the entirety of the belly. I wasn't a scientist, but to use a technical term, that shit looked bad for fucking business.

"Move!" I roared, but the elf was already racing away, the liquid around her sloshing.

Then, because things always have to get worse, another sac burst. This one was also green, but I noticed that the force of the geyser dredged something up from below this time. Bones. Lots of bones.

"Oh, *hell*!" I exclaimed, and got to stepping even faster, worried that my lack of fancy footwear would be my undoing finally. "Arjee! Can you lead us to my friends?!"

Rexen watched the freshly exploded blister with interest, but my words rocked him from his reverie.

"Yes," he said. "Is that where you want to go?"

"Fuckin'— Yes, goddamn it!"

"Very well," he said, bowing and gesturing to the other side of the stomach chamber. "After you."

"What the fuck are you talking about?! *You're* directing the way!"

"Oh!" Rexen said. "That's right. Sorry—old age has made my brain very soft. Like a bruised summer squash."

"Let's goose it!" I yelled, and we three tried our best to escape the rapidly rising liquid.

The piss ocean was now up to my calves, and it was getting hard to move in a coordinated fashion. Then to my left, another pustule burst, and more of the gunk joined the party. It then grew increasingly harder to gain distance on the body-devouring goo as the tide moved in, reaching my mid-thigh. Fortunately, we were still ahead of the area where the contents were mixing, but I knew that—with my luck—all these zits would soon pop, and we'd be submerged in a nasty river of pain.

*Wait,* I thought, thinking about my fortune in a much more pragmatic way. *Don't tell me . . .*

I opened my menu, gaping in a fury at my Luck stat. It had changed again.


**Luck -1**


"Oh, you've got to be fucking kidding me!"

I sloshed forward, following my beacon of hope in the form of a shimmering cotton candy ghost, hoping he knew how to get us somewhere safe.

"It's like . . . a water level!" Rua huffed. Even in this predicament, she was still an unrepentant geek. The liquid was now up to her hips as she strained to move through the sickly stream. It seemed like she was having an easier time of it than I was—probably due to her higher Strength score. While I was considerably larger than her, it was wild that she would still probably kick my ass in an arm-wrestling match. I'd just have to hope that she could assist herself right now, because I was going to be too busy trying not to—literally—lose my own ass in this race against time. The worst part was that I could see my Stamina deteriorating before my eyes, which would likely mean I would collapse before long.

More sacs burst, and soon, it was up to my stomach. Poor Rua was chest-deep in the stuff, still powering along a dozen feet ahead of me.

*Fuck, we can't die here!* I thought. *Then I'll look real dumb for suggesting this plan in the first place! Where's the goddamn off switch?*

After another ten seconds, I saw Rexen and Rua reach the other side of the area, where the stomach ceiling curved down to form another tight avenue.

*Oh, thank God!* I thought, hoping this nightmare was about to be put to bed. I thought about how helpful Bahlgus's Flight would be right now, and wished I had any charges remaining so I could Flappy Bird this bitch.

That was when I started to feel the burn. Like little razors scratching against my skin, the digestive chemicals around me began slowly dissolving my flesh.

**Condition: Acidic Burns I**
*Will continue to lose 1 Health per 1 second.*

I roared in pain, fighting against the agonizing sensation of being actually eaten alive by the oomukade's stomach fluids. It was almost too much to handle, but I needed to keep moving. I only had a dozen more feet to traverse, even though the current had already reached my collarbone. Which also meant . . .

I looked ahead and could see Rua clinging to the opening of the exit, hauling herself partially out of the mire as she and Rexen stared back at me. However, it wasn't a permanent fix. The level of liquid was now so high that only a little of the organic doorway remained, meaning that if we didn't go through soon as fuck, we'd have to swim under it.

*Well, at least they aren't burning up yet. That's just a* me *problem, for the moment.*

I kept pumping my legs, feeling my life slowly whittling away the longer I stayed submerged. I was getting close!

**Condition: Acidic Burns II**
*Will continue to lose Health at a rate of 5 per 1 second.*

*Shit, shit, shit, shit!*

The effects were only getting worse, and my Stamina was not lookin' too hot either. What the hell was I supposed to do?

I finally reached the other side, Rexen and Rua still hovering there.

"Alright, let's get in there!" I shouted, shoving Rua forward. "We might have to dunk underneath a little, but—"

"Aggghh!" Rua screamed suddenly, and I realized why. So far, she'd avoided being caught up in the portion of stomach juice that actually hurt you. Now it was unavoidable. She'd likely just gotten her first taste of the acid, and it was a doozy.

She thrashed there, and soon I began to worry. She wasn't making any moves forward, just floating and screaming. I could see mist bubbling off her flesh—boiling red. This hurt her *way* more than it did me, and I couldn't figure out why. But I didn't have time to sit and ponder the reasons for that.

"I'm sorry," I said to her—not that she could hear me over the sound of her own blood-curdling screeches. Then I grabbed her and forced her underneath the arch of the stomach chamber and through to the other side. Afterward, I dove under, emerging into a horrible sight: another stomach room identical to the one we'd just left. Except here, the liquid level was lower but almost knee-deep because of the bottleneck. The passageway through seemed to dampen the stream. So, rather than an unending river, the bile sprayed out like it was under pressure. Still, the liquid here appeared to be the non-volatile variety, as my pain immediately stopped increasing. I was left to deal only with those burns that had already formed.

The other significant difference was that while the previous area had those undulating sacs fused to the lining of the wall in spaced intervals, here, they were *everywhere.* The walls, the ceiling, I could even see some peeking out from within the stomach acid itself.

Rua was still in pain, her skin burned raw in sections, and her clothing in tatters. She grimaced now rather than screaming, as I frantically looked around for any way out of this situation.

*You really did it this time now, Loony boy,* I thought. *Fucking things up not only for yourself, but you dragged other people into— Wait!*

"What the fuck is that?!" I demanded, pointing off toward the other side of the stomach. "Is that a . . . is that a fucking *house*?"

There, perched almost haphazardly against the side of the stomach wall, was a tiny cottage about the size of my Aunt Ella's gardening shed back home. It had a door, windows, slated roof—the works—with a lovely blue exterior. How in the IBS hell it was dwelling in this place undissolved was a wonder.

I let out a chuckle.

"Hey Rua, check it out. More like *chateaux* of the colossus, am I right?"

I think she tried to smirk, but it was hard to tell—you know, on account of the debilitating injuries.

Fortunately, Rexen was there with the assist.

"Ooh," he regarded with approval. "A Sanctuary Cabin!"

"Please tell me that's a good thing?" I asked.

"Well, that depends," the spirit said. "Are you inside it? Yes. Outside? No. It's impervious to the bad things. So, too, those inside. You should get one."

I glared at the cute little domicile.

"Oh, don't worry," I said. "I plan to."

"Fucking fuck!" Rua yelled, recovering—but still shivering—from the pain she'd just endured. "Fuck!"

"That's the spirit!" I said. "Don't let it beat you—"

"I'm the spirit," Rexen announced. "Are you referring to me?"

"Shut the fuck *up*, Arjee," I said. "Rua, what's your Health at right now?"

"Low," she hissed. It didn't sound like she was trying to be sarcastic, simply in too much pain to give an accurate number. That was fine—a ballpark would do.

"Let's run over to that cabin and pound on the door 'til they let us in," I said, moving forward before Rexen stopped me.

"That won't work," he said as if I had just suggested opening my Christmas presents early. "You can't get in uninvited! And they won't be able to hear you."

"I think you're underestimating how loud I can yell," I said.

"I probably am," Rexen said excitedly. "Can I have an example?"

I shook my head.

"Look, we've got to do something. Those other sacs are gonna burst any second, and then we are going to fucking die. Rua can't survive another round of that, so we need to move. Somehow, I'm a lot better off, maybe because of being an orc? I dunno. But what—"

"Constitution," Rexen interrupted.

"Huh?"

"Your Constitution is higher, so you are burned less," he clarified. "Isn't that neat?"

"Super," I said. "That's good to know. Rua probably wasn't some dipshit who dumped all her Points into a single Attribute, so for once, I'm actually qualified to—"

"You did?" Rua asked me through gritted teeth, her eyes closed as she seemed focused on trying not to scream. "What? You were min-maxing or something?"

"I don't know what the hell that means—but, sure," I said. "We don't have time for this. We've got to . . ."

I shut up for a second, my mind working.

"Pupil?" Rexen asked. "You have stopped speaking. Did you remember someone you forgot to kill?"

I hadn't. But I *had* allowed myself to think about potential solutions to this issue. I thought I had one. Or, if not a solution, a temporary Band-Aid.

"Rexen, you're all old and wise and shit," I said.

"Correct," the spirit said.

I scowled. This hadn't really been intended as a call-and-response sort of thing, but whatever.

"Say I knew how to increase my Constitution. By, like, a *lot*. I might potentially survive long enough to get us out of here."

"Oh!" Rexen exclaimed. "Like with your Aegis!"

"Yeah—wait, how do you know about that? Actually, never mind. What would be—"

*POP! POP! POP!*

One by one, the sacs around us began to burst, greenish gunk pouring out to mix with the amber liquid.

"Dammit! We're out of time!"

"What were you saying?" Rexen asked serenely as if our impending doom hadn't just exploded into being. I ignored him for a moment. I had another idea for an additional bandage.

"Rua," I said. "You're going to hate this, but—"

"You want me to get back in that chest?" She asked.

"Uh . . ." I started. "Yeah. How'd you know?"

"How long can I be in there without running out of air?"

"About four minutes."

She let out a noise of frustration and jabbed a finger at me.

"Fine," she hissed. "You have three minutes and fifty seconds to save us. Do it."

*Say no more.*

I'd forgotten that along with being a super geek and inconsolably socially inept in the old world, Rua was very, very bright. I remember her being called up on stage in front of our entire school last year during an academic assembly. She'd nervously slumped up, ignoring the jeers and catcalls, just for the principal to reveal that she'd gotten the highest ATAC score in our region and the fifth-highest in the country. She was definitely smart enough to figure out whatever harebrained scheme I could concoct on the fly. I quickly pulled the Feather Chest out and summoned its full size. The trunk floated on top of the water like it was made of paper. I nearly suggested we use the chest as a boat, but as Rua popped the lid open and immediately slumped over the lip and nestled herself within, I saw that her weight pushed it down. The liquid rose up around it.

*So much for that saving grace.*

I was about to close the lid when I remembered the acid's effect on clothing. I hastily dumped my bag and miscellaneous objects in with my elfish companion. That included the wizard-tower figurine Rexen had been chilling in for centuries and . . . Merra's amulet. I wasn't sure if my kilt and bandolier would survive, but I didn't want to risk anything floating out if I happened to get submerged again. However, I didn't want to be left entirely out of options, so anything still tucked into my waistband stayed, and I kept the Trespasser's Veil clasped around my shoulders.

I closed the lid and minimized the chest as a tingling sensation began again around my thighs. It was the precursor to the burns. I turned to Rexen.

"What's the fastest way I could Fatigue myself?"

Rexen smiled.

"I like the way you think!" he said. "You're very close. Maybe if you stood on your head?"

I almost swung on him right there.

"Be serious," I demanded.

"Oh!" Rexen said, his eyes suddenly shifting into mischievous swirls and his exterior transforming to an uncomfortable red hue. "Serious it is."

He pointed at the bile where my feet might be if I could see them.

"Enduring Perch," he stated, his tone taking on a different vibe. Like he thought he was some kind of tiny action-movie badass. "You're nearly there. Take it all the way down until it is almost depleted, release it, then again twice more. Combined with the pain you're experiencing, it should do the trick."

I didn't have time to argue. The room was filling up, and I began to feel the intensity of consuming flame as *Acidic Burns* flashed again in my vision. I grabbed the minimized Feather Chest in my fist and activated Enduring Perch—watching as my Stamina bar began to deplete.

*Come on. Come* on*!*

It dropped to the red, and I released it, then waited for it to climb back to at least fifty percent so I could reignite it. Despite the increased pain, it was loads easier to ignore when I had a clear goal and wasn't frantically splashing around in the devil's urine. Instead, I was becoming *one* with the flesh-destroying super bile, like the zen-wielding monks of yore. As the meter got to the honey zone, I activated Enduring Perch again, the stomach acid now cruising up to nipple altitude. It was filling this room faster because of all the sacs it contained, which was concerning. I'd only been doing this for about thirty seconds, trying hard not to let the burns obliterate my concentration.

I hit red again and waited. *Acidic Burns II* appeared in my vision, the pain increasing, and I started cursing up a storm.

"Fucking-cock-motherbitch-shit-goddamn-fucking-fuck-shit-cunting-fuck-ass-shit!"

I watched the meter drain on my Stamina, still a ways off. However, apparently whatever hell I'd endured must have done the trick, because before my Stamina had even emptied enough to go red, a notification popped up.

**Condition: Fatigued**
*Fatigue I*
*• Abilities and Skills suffer -5% efficiency while under the Fatigue I condition effect.*

Another message quickly followed the first, and what was *really* what I had been waiting for.

**Because of Fatigue I, Loon's Bombastic Beatdown Aegis has temporarily reached Tier I effects.**
- **Strength Attribute increase [+4 multiplied by 100%]!**
- **Dexterity Attribute increase [+4 multiplied by 100%]!**
- **Constitution Attribute increase [+4 multiplied by 100%]!**

**Strength: 32 (Fatigue I)**
**Dexterity: 32 (Fatigue I)**
**Constitution: 66 (Fatigue I)**

The feeling was immediate. My muscles grew more defined in front of me, and their presence was more understandable as if I'd only ever been scratching the surface of their capabilities. I could move better, I knew, and lift more, *do* more. Best of all, the incredible searing burn of the stomach acid faded into a dull, irritating nag. Loon's Bombastic Beatdown had flooded my body with speed, durability, and might, and I was a very consensual participant.

Then another system response popped up, and *oh, happy day*, did that increase my pleasure and cause me to stir with excitement vibrations.

**Congratulations, you have advanced an Ability!**
**Enduring Perch II**

"Oh, yeah!" I roared, the liquid in the chamber now at my neck. "Let's fucking *do* this!"

"Yeah!" Rexen cheered along in agreement, then paused. "Uh, what *this* are we doing?"

"Getting out of here!" I said confidently, scanning what I could see from my vantage.

"Oh!" Rexen exclaimed. "Stupendous! . . . How?"

I felt my stomach drop. Rexen's words, while annoying, were worth considering. Until that moment, I'd only been thinking about how to resist the nightmare stomach and get to safety, not fully considering what safety actually looked like or, more importantly, where it was located. As I'd been doin' some peepin,' I hadn't seen anything that looked like a haven or an exit. But there had to be one, right? A creature didn't just have a stomach without somewhere for everything to *go*. I sighed.

*Wherever the way out is, it's most likely under the piss.*

I zeroed in on the cottage, which was now submerged nearly up to the top of the doorway.

"New plan, then!" I announced. "We knock."

"That's an amazing idea!" Rexen said. "Or it would be if it wasn't *bad*."

"You suck, Arjee! I have about one minute before Rua's outta air, and you're not offering any other solutions! If you know something, toss me a damn bone!"

I didn't wait to hear what he had to say, though. I was fucking stronger now, and I was going to use that to my advantage. I was in the center of a lake of stomach acid in the hollow organ of a giant fucking creature. I imagined the camera cut as if I was in an action flick: me, a tiny dot among the vast and empty open space of an aerial view; rows upon rows of sacs fit to burst just as the thunderstorm SFX would begin on "Raining Blood" by Slayer. Yeah, that would be fucking *tite*.

**Author's Note: Hey there, gang. You probably know what I'm about to say: why don't you go ahead and pull up "Raining Blood" by Slayer and set this bad boy to "immersion" mode.**

Just as I mentally slammed the opening guitar riff into place, I dove into the disgusting and putrid scald, almost forgetting to close my eyes. I pumped my limbs and propelled myself forward, hell-bent on making it to teatime inside the quaint little cottage. Now that I was one hundred percent below the surface, I couldn't believe how much more intense the pain felt. It was also disorienting. Unlike being in the water, this substance was different enough that I immediately got turned around and had to emerge for a breath of air. But by the time I put my head back up, the level had risen, and I had to kick and swim upward further, almost losing my air.

I broke through above, mildly freaking out, but sucked in a gigantic breath. I coughed, realizing with a brand of burning eureka that I'd accidentally swallowed some of the liquid. My Health suffered an instant blow, and I gagged as the searing viscousness traveled into my esophagus. In the back of my mind, I could appreciate the irony of me having journeyed down the oomukade queen's throat, only for some of *her* to get sucked down mine. I'd never say that out loud, though, because it sounded dirty, and everyone knows I'm a PG-rated hero.

Rexen floated above me as I fought for my life against my own body's impulses.

"Did you find the exit?" he wondered calmly.

I wrangled my rage, shot him a quick glare, and spotted the top of the cabin. I say *top* because that's literally all that wasn't wholly underwater—uh, under-*bile*? Whatever; you know what I mean. It was turtling.

*Fuck this*, I thought.

I focused on the rounded crest of the hut as it slowly sank into the belly juice and locked its position into my mind. I didn't have long, and this was the only method I thought might work. I submerged myself again, knowing I couldn't open my eyes and just hoping I could navigate the treacherous pain pond without seeing. I shoved off, swimming forward, moving my limbs like I'd never have been able to perform back home in my old body. After a few motions, I kicked, bringing myself above the surface again to see if I was on course.

I was! Hot diggity dick!

I dove back down, knowing my timetable was extremely limited because my elf companion only had about forty seconds of air remaining. I pushed my muscles as hard as possible and received a notification for my trouble.

**Congratulations! You have gained a Skill!**
**Swimming [F-Rank Level 1]**

I ignored the description and continued on, kicking my legs and cutting forward with my arms, finding a little thrill in the exercise despite how much the liquid I was traveling through bit back.

*This is nice! You know for—*

*WHOOMP!*

I collided hard with a solid surface. It had to be the cottage of . . . sanctuary? Is that what Rexen called it? I quickly felt around ahead of me, trying to divine if it was, in fact, the structure and not some assholish new feature of the stomach I hadn't yet encountered. It was difficult to tell because it didn't *feel* like a house to my touch or, really, anything I could consider a structure worth living in. Its texture was a bit like glass. Then, despite my oxygen-deprived mind and my body's exposure to the liquid's unnatural elements, I realized something. I didn't *need* to see or feel.

*This is a magical world! I've got motherfucking Abilities!*

I activated Eye of the Saboteur, keeping my palm flat on the structure and hoping it would work.

Behind my closed lids, a message appeared.

**Sanctuary Cabin**
**This is not an item.**

*Well, shit. I'm in the right spot, but I haven't learned much.*

I grumbled about my luck before it dawned on me that despite it not being an item I could scan the information of, there was a badge of color next to the name. I'd learned that this typically indicated when I could view the structural makeup of something. So, you *know* I had to pop that sucker into action and see what fresh horror awaited me. I did. In less visual detail than I was growing used to, I saw the vague, hazy outline of the cabin in my mind's eye. It expanded in the same three-dimensional layout I'd seen from the crofter's building, except I could only see the exterior. Which, I supposed, made sense, considering the nature of this thing. However, there was an additional complication.

I'd learned so far that when something was extremely structurally sound, meaning there wasn't much in the way of weak points, it was shown in a whiteish-blue outline. Likewise, red indicated areas of structural fragility, most often demonstrated by orbs of crimson in different locations, like one of those silhouettes from 1990s pain reliever commercials. What I was looking at, though, was something I hadn't yet seen.

*Green?*

The entire thing was one solid, unbroken hue of emerald. I wasn't sure what the fuck that meant. Was it because it was a Spell? Or did green represent imperviousness—insofar as I'd encountered by my measly unranked version of the Eye of the Saboteur Ability? Either way, my odds were rubbish. It was also frustrating because I didn't see a single hair of red anywhere. No cracks. Not even fissures or pinpricks. Nothing.

*Fuck, fuck, fuck, fuck.*

I was going to die, risking everything on my last-ditch effort, stupid fucking Hail Mary idea. Now I was gonna be an oomukade queen's hors d'oeuvre, and my only comfort was that I'd hurt her minorly on my way down.

Then my eyes landed on the door to the cabin in my mental map. At first, I thought I'd imagined it. It was just as green as the rest of the building, right? I focused, allowing the blueprint . . . er, greenprint to grow larger—like doin' the two-finger pinch on a smartphone—and saw that, no, my first instinct was correct: the door was *slightly* less green than the rest of the building.

*That's good enough for me,* I thought. I tried a kick. The liquid slowed my attack and rendered it useless as my bare tootsie lightly tapped the door despite my efforts. I was stronger at the moment, but apparently, this had something to do with physics . . . I think. I tried again, holding on to what I suspected was the recessed door frame and trying to smash both legs against the entrance at once, and . . . it was the same result.

*Pupil,* Rexen said in my mind, startling me. I didn't know he could do that. *Three minutes and thirty seconds have elapsed.*

*Shit!*

What was I supposed to do? I couldn't get in, but something about the fact that I could *see* a weakness—however minor—told me that I might be able to do *something.* Though I didn't have a swollen purple clue what that might be. What could I do against a Spell?

*Oh. Fucking goddamn* duh!

I pushed back from the building, giving myself a little breathing room, and steeled my resolve, as I knew what I was about to do might backfire.

I counted to two and then activated my Blackout Warchant. Hot wind erupted from my throat as power gathered below my jowls and I felt the force of the Ability take off automatically. I kept my eyes closed. Eye of the Saboteur hadn't ended yet, I realized. But I was learning all sorts of wacky things today because—apparently—I could use them simultaneously. Blackout Warchant could cancel out magical effects, but I didn't know if it worked on something explicitly designed to keep everything out. We'd just have to see. I could feel the bile burbling around me as the cone of what I remembered as colorless energy blasted from my mouth and hit the area directly ahead of me. I watched it with Eye of the Saboteur. Everything remained the same—except for the doorway. It flickered for a moment or two, becoming—well, not red—but like a burnt sienna? I had the TV show *The Joy of Painting* to thank for that nugget of knowledge.

Insomnia ruled my world, as much there as it had before. However, whenever I'd been in the throes of a nasty case of the no-sleepies, I would hop on the internet and find a stream of the famously permed painter with the signature placid baritone. Even then, there were colors with names I'd never have known were it not for him, and one always stood out more than any other. Bob Ross really did be lovin' him some burnt sienna.

The flash stopped immediately, and the door returned to pale green.

*Fuck! It's too rapid. I won't be able to get close enough to do anything.*

Then I realized my error. I shouldn't have been trying to *break* the door—that would be foolish. I could maybe get it open with that method, but it would doom anyone inside, including myself. That was precisely what I was trying to avoid.

*Though . . .*

I reached into my waistband and procured the only wand I'd managed to keep on my person in the unrelenting chaos of the evening's festivities: the wand of supreme unlocking. Then I reared back and sent another Blackout Warchant right at the door and blindly aimed as the image flashed orange again. My gullet was raw. Two instances of my Ability being cast in quick succession had made my yellin' hole sore as the dickens. But that was just going to have to be part of the precious memories of this place. With the last remaining air in my lungs, I dropped my shoulders and roared as loud as I possibly could in an unintelligible underwater death scream while firing the bolt of magic from the wand.

It hit. In my mind, I saw the faintest flash of pink for the door, and then the greenprint's portal fucking *opened*! It was just a sliver, but it would have to do!

I kicked into overdrive, seeing that the door was a swing-in style. It was probably fortunate, considering it would be next to impossible to close it again with one that opened into the acid. I swam fuckin' *hard*, the burns almost reaching a point where I felt like giving up. Instead, I reminded myself why I was doing this.

*You are fucking awesome,* I said, giving myself the most ridiculous pep talk imaginable. *This is almost over. Rescue Rua. Save yourself. Survive. Let's fucking do this and pay it forward to* anything *who crosses you by administering thousands of expertly timed scrote punts!*

I let my self-esteem fuel my flight, slinking like a torpedo and slamming my shoulder against the door. Then I slipped my fingers into the crack in the door before it could shut again. Using every fat, greasy iota of the thirty-six Points of Strength I had available, I wrenched that bitch open enough to slip inside.

I landed with a wet *plop*, my eyes still closed.

*Is this . . . carpet?*

I heard the door pop shut again behind me and then loud gasps from all around. I was careful not to open my eyes, worried they'd be permanently damaged if I did so. Instead, I yanked the Feather Chest out of my waistband, tossed it into the air, and yelled.

"Feather Chest, MAXIMIZE!"

The sound of the magical item expanding and crashing into a bunch of shit was music to my ears.

*Yay! Yay! Yay! Yahoo!*

My heart skipped a beat.

*The egg boys! Wait, they're here? What in the* Innerspace *hell is happening?*

Their telepathic voices filled me with such an immense and confusing blend of relief and confusion that I almost passed out on the spot. They were there! I didn't have time to let the good times sink in, though. There was an urgent matter to attend to.

"Who in the fuck—" someone had started to shout.

"Open the chest!" I screamed at whoever happened to be inside this magical cabin with me. It sounded like several people, and though I was starting to suspect who some of them were, I wasn't sure. "My friend is inside and out of air! Open it!"

I heard the clasp undo and then Rua's broken coughs as she spilled out of the trunk and onto the same sopping floor I was on with a juicy squelch. I could sense her body shuddering with fits as she tried desperately to get air back into her lungs. After a moment, she seemed to find her rhythm, and her breaths became shallower. Finally, I felt as though I had earned the right to open my eyes, wiping the outsides of my lids so that I wouldn't immediately go blind.

Everything came into focus as I did.

First and foremost, the inside of this place was *way* bigger than the outside. It resembled what I imagined a Nordic fishing cabin would look like. A cozy fire was crackling in one corner, providing the single light source inside, while nearby, a squat table stood with three chairs gathered around and plates of picked-over food sitting atop. Furs covered the entirety of the place, from the walls and backs of chairs to a few larger ones hanging like banners. Most importantly, huddled in the center around the now heaving—but alive—Rua on the floor was a group of people. I knew their faces immediately.

"Jes? Frida?"

My two party members sat among the group. Frida was . . . What's the word? Resplendent? Sure, she was *that* in her battered armor, looking like a particularly attractive medieval cosplayer—even with her head bandaged on one side. I noticed she held a cup of brown liquid in one hand. Next to her, propped up on cushions and more furs, was the emaciated-looking elven form of Jesimir Carandalon—my party leader. He was gaunt and sallow-complected, swimming in robes that made him look even skinnier than usual. I noticed that both his arms and one of his legs were taped up in splints. Despite this, I saw that he, too, had a cup in one hand.

*How you gonna drink that, bud?*

The last time I'd seen him, he'd—believe it or not—been in much worse condition. With most of his bones broken in the skirmish with Frey, we'd deposited him with Tallrock's local healers. It struck me as odd that he was even there. Why had he left the healing hut when he was still very obviously injured? I mean, there's no way he could do much of anything with three-fourths of his limbs out of commission. So, how exactly had he managed to get there without getting churned up like buttermilk?

Cloistered with the others were two individuals I didn't recognize. An extremely short, stout creature with disheveled golden-brown hair that seemed like it had, until recently, been quite the tidy little 'do. At first glance, I'd thought he was a child, but that wasn't quite right. He had to have been something other than a human, though, because while he was pretty small, his proportions didn't fit as they usually might. For one, his head and feet were too big for his body, like a cartoon character. However, he didn't have the same look as the two dwarves I'd met, so I didn't think he'd be one.

Next to the short stack was a . . . young man? His face seemed pretty youthful, and I'd have guessed he was in his mid-twenties, but his hair threw me off. It was a dusty gray, reminding me of the hipster hair-dye phase from home. This could've been part of his genetics, though, because his eyebrows and irises beneath were a comparable color. He was dressed in what could have been lovely finery if it hadn't been wholly peppered with burns—likely from the stomach acid.

However, the biggest shock was sitting in the center of everyone. Surrounded on all sides by friends, strangers, and my precious possessed roe was a bald, scarred, yellow-fleshed asshole with an expression of sour surprise crossing his three cruel mouths. Stinky. I hadn't seen him in a day or so, but I found that there was something off about his general appearance . . .

*Wait a goddamn fucking second!* I thought, catching the difference with a wave of deep and horrible anger blossoming from my chest.

On top of Stinky's head was a small, colorful paper cone, and strapped under his jaw was the thin band of elastic-like ribbon to keep it fixed in place. I recognized it immediately. The Enchanted Festival Cap. *My* Enchanted Festival Cap. The one that had supposedly been destroyed by the Cosmic Chaos Monstrosity that had killed me in the Crypt. There it was—strapped atop his cue-ball scalp like a shining symbol of poor taste and *lies*.

"Stinky!" I roared, startling everyone in the room even further. "What. The. *Fuck?!*"

## CHAPTER EIGHTEEN

# THE OTHER GUYS II: THE SQUEAKUEL

The leaves had begun to turn, and with that came the chill.

Usually, visitors to the area knew of the unseasonable cold in the months following summer, preparing and planning for it. However, the tourists in this particular stretch of wilderness were unique in that they were quite unintentional castaways on their merry stretch of holiday. Wrested from whence they came and dribbled into this new land, they were rightly a tad peeved at the prospects of spending their unknown foreseeable fate in the lap of autumnal frivolity—and most of them without a jacket.

Though one individual *had* brought an overcoat. It had been badly abused during their outlandishly absurd inaugural advent from one world to the next, but had survived as a holey terror of strips, rips, and frayed tips so battered, it would offer the wearer respite from the elements no longer. That being the case, the owner of the formerly marvelous trench coat had decided its best attributes were its abundance of storage and field-dressed the article, harvesting the pockets and stitching them to the outsides of her other garments. She'd admired her handiwork in the reflective surface of a brackish pond after completing the task and thought that it looked quite lovely indeed, all things considered.

However, she had not yet devised a medium to properly insulate herself from the quickly declining temperatures in this vast, supernatural environment. Still, she was grateful to have those pockets.

Life had been odd for the last week and change. It seemed not just for her, she imagined, but for everyone. They wound up in such an unbelievable predicament that even eight days later, she still wasn't entirely convinced she'd been indeed experiencing it. When she woke most mornings, she'd pat her body down before even opening her eyes, running her hands over her features and trying to discern if she'd finally roused from the dream. However, each time, her fingers would find the newest additions—the changes—like her sharp teeth, the horns on her head, and the tail . . . and she'd smile. Another day in a fantastical world awaited her.

Then she'd open her eyes and begin her day, resolving to "try again tomorrow" while hoping she'd remain for as long as possible.

This was something of a dream come true for her, gallivanting about their camp, an endless unbridled feeling that she was on the precipice of an epic tale of adventure. And to be clear, she was *absolutely* gallivanting. The others in the camp may not have seen her in that way, most understandably finding her "weird," but she didn't mind. She was who she was, and who she *was* was someone—nay—some*thing* entirely different. Sure, her personality was relatively similar to her previous manifestation—as she'd begun calling her former life—but there was so much about her on a physical and internal level that had changed that she was quite pleased to imagine what her personal story would bring.

She considered events as she walked back to headquarters from the brackish pond.

The others had been scared when they had arrived; that was true. However, so far, nothing about the experience had frightened her in the least. She'd accepted all of it with quiet dignity—at least, she liked to think that was what it was. It was just as plausible that her reluctant companions would have considered the method she demonstrated, especially in those early days, akin to frustrated apathy. Those two words could be viewed as the antithesis of one another, but in her case, it worked. Internally, however, she'd been elated. She'd lived the whole of her life in the skin of others, constantly toiling toward her unfortunately unattainable end goal of stardom. She'd been an actress, though one could suppose that the title didn't entirely suit her, as she rarely performed. When she did, the reviews were . . . less than appreciative.

But that was a thing of the past. She recalled staring into the swirling, translucent orb at the outset of this . . . Could you call it an adventure? Sure, it seemed likely that one could. In any case, at the start of all of this, she fixated on the words the creature had said and the quantitative amounts floating in front of her. The choice was hers to be wrought, and to make matters even clearer and enticing, there was a predetermined roster! Ready-made to give her an idea of her innate strengths and weaknesses. When she'd observed the orb, a thrill had pollinated her body. She could choose whatever she wished going forward, she remembered thinking. All that existed ahead of her would supersede that which remained behind. The notion of forging a brand-new identity—no, a wholly new life—was a task she took a shine to readily.

There had been hard times already, sure. Indeed, more of them than seemed appropriate, but still, she endured. There, by the gospel of an unknown fate, went she. Even when their group had been attacked on all sides by maleficent creatures beyond comprehension, she didn't lose her zest for this new world. In her opinion, the nightmarish horrors that crashed upon them early on didn't diminish the opportunity that everything else around her presented. It was a feature, not a bug.

However, there was still the issue of their de facto camp leader. That despicable dwarf strutting around and calling himself "Alpha" like an idiot. As insufferable in this new life as he'd been during their brief encounter before everything changed.

He whined, and he complained. He was rude to the point of offense and went further still. He mocked and jeered and, after all that, still lacked good sense and considered himself the better of everyone present. She very much would've liked to see him squirm. Just once. She knew he'd taken severe affront to her behavior on the train, thinking himself too highly evolved or perhaps too close to his primitive roots to be genuinely afflicted by her words. But she knew. From their first interaction, she'd struck a chord that bothered him, and now she'd made it her immediate short-term quest to administer as many verbal contusions upon him as she could.

But then . . . he had to go and be a hero.

She had to admit that was a tough pill to swallow. During the assailing of their camp on the second day, they'd been scattered and frightened. She'd wanted to beat back the brutish beasts that fell upon them, but she'd found a truth during the battle: she was no fighter. Not in the sense that most thought of, in any case. As the horde of glittering golden malice made its way into their clearing, her body was not under her command. She'd tried, but her nerves did not let her, and she found that very unfair. As much as she'd desired to do *anything* useful, she was unable. However, Alpha was more than happy to assist in appending the mass of his own bloated sense of self-importance.

The dwarf had acted quickly and decisively, summoning his cronies from the train to follow him into the fight and beat the ever-loving tar out of the monsters with their newfound abilities. Though they were not the only ones. She recalled the handsome dark-skinned boy had been first into the fray, armed with his freshly acquired tools of destruction. The red-haired elf had been right behind him, her sword skewering the lesser beasts. That was not the extent of their defenders in the camp, but they were the most notable.

Afterward, the dwarf—that damnable little sphincter of a soul—had laid unwarranted claim on the magical rock that had emerged from the ground and called itself the "Settlement Stone." After that, Alpha was in charge. She seethed at the memory, remembering how he'd seized power and instantly begun his tyranny. He was powerful and seemed to grow stronger than the others at a faster rate for a reason still unclear to her. Everyone else begrudgingly accepted his new position, but not her. No, when she saw his response to power and the awful things he had done in its light, she swore a solemn vow to herself. For however long they dwelled there, she would spend the remainder of her breath cursing and scalding him with her tongue.

Her chosen Class made this easier. She'd wanted to continue in her pursuit of acting and make a name for herself with her fresh start. That had been her idea at first, but she found that the auxiliary functions of being a Minstrel, as it was called, allowed her to be better able to fling reprisal at the christened leadership under Alpha. If he spoke to her at all, she made sure he was never—for a moment—mistaken about her feelings for him.

And so it went. Days now, they'd been waiting for the return of the elf who'd left to scout for them, to learn a little of what this world offered them who had arrived in such a fantastical fashion. Would she make it back? It was a mystery. The elf had a unique trait that would allow her to find her way back, though that required her to be alive. If she'd died . . . well, who knew what would transpire then?

Three people had perished since the first day. One of their number had returned afterward: the woman, Mary, who'd fallen from the top of the wreckage and broken her neck. The man who'd faced off against Alpha and the girl from the train who'd simply arrived dead had not had the fortune of revival. No one was sure what that meant, and Mary was unable to explain it to them because of her chosen Race. All of that was to say that death for them was an unknown variable, and the red-haired elf might've suffered a lethal fate and gone the way of the other two. Each day of her absence cast the bones of uncertainty further into the latter the longer she'd not returned. Yet, whenever—or, instead, *if*—that time came to pass, it would surely—

"Veruca," a quiet voice said, dismantling her inner dialogue.

She blinked, finding herself in the lap of confusion. She'd been in the center of perfecting her eloquent narrative recap, finding that she was improving due to her Class Abilities. However, she hadn't been prepared for her train of thought to be derailed. Most people didn't bother her unless they had to. Which meant . . .

"Alpha wants to talk to you," the elf said, her white skin ghostly in the morning's hazy light. "He's at the wreckage."

*Pricipita*, Veruca thought, regarding the bone elf with caution. They hadn't become easy friends, and the powers the girl had displayed during the fight with the monsters had unsettled her. As such, she'd decided to remain vigilant and take care to always turn a surveilling eye in this girl's direction.

"About what?" Veruca asked, though not really caring what the self-aggrandizing shit bucket masquerading as their leader wanted from her. The woman was also left feeling somewhat crook-footed at having to answer off the cuff, much preferring to run through her list of pre-established responses before engaging others in meaningful conversation. She'd never been much for improv.

"Didn't ask," Pricipita said. "Just passing the word along. Probably wants to get more verbal abuse from you so he can skip into the woods and jerk off over it."

Veruca wrinkled her brow. The last thing she wanted was for Alpha to get any sense of pleasure out of their interactions.

"Disgusting," Veruca said. "However, despite that, I am grateful for your initiative in tracking me down on his ingloriously repugnant behalf."

*There,* she thought. *That's better. Much more eloquent.*

Finding her interactive foothold was less of a chore now than it used to be, but she could still stumble into these harnessless hiccups from time to time. Having an arsenal of solid repartee was essential to her and made her lack of social prowess much easier to maintain.

"Yeah, sure," Pricipita said, walking away from the vittra without so much as a farewell gesture.

Veruca watched her leave with relief, knowing she wouldn't have a need to fabricate more cobble-constructed syntax. It was exhausting enough as it was to prep her words when she understood the nature of the communication. With some of the others, Pricipita included, she was put off-balance, not knowing the best way to speak around them. It was uncomfortable.

After another moment, she sighed, seeing how her day had just started and was already well on its way to end up ruined. Despite this, she stood tall and went to where she'd been told their camp leader would be.

Alpha was easy to spot. As Veruca approached the massive serpent of twisted metal that made up the wreckage, she could see the stout creature standing atop it, peering out into the trees beyond their clearing. He was alone, which couldn't be good.

*Ugh,* she thought. *What could he possibly need me for?*

She leaned against the cold metal of the wrenched-apart tube and rapped on it to draw his attention. When she received no response, she sighed again and spoke up.

"What purpose could you glean from me so early in the morning, you twisted little bastard?"

Even that didn't seem to grab his gaze. Despite the fact she was positive her voice had carried to him, he seemed to be ignoring her.

*Is this some kind of game?* she wondered. *Is he trying to do that* negging *thing?*

She recalled several past instances when men attempted to pull that tactic on her. It had worked in most of those situations, but she reasoned that it was likely because she didn't know any better at the time. Now she had a name for it and an understanding of its unsavory mechanics so she could avoid it when it reared its head, attempting to ensnare her.

"I believe I asked you what—"

"Come up here," Alpha said, interrupting her.

"Why would I even begin to entertain that notion?" she demanded, half-prepared to just turn around and head back the way she came.

"Just fuckin' do it, okay, weird bitch?" he said, his eyes still locked on the distant scenery. "I need you to confirm something for me."

She sighed again, rolling her eyes, before taking a moment to find the pathway up. Ten feet from her she spotted the ladder they'd pulled from a different section of the wreck and repurposed for clambering up for the view. She ascended, feeling uncomfortable as her hooves clattered on the hollow metallic frame until she reached the top and carefully moved to join the dwarf.

"I am here now," she said, following his gaze toward the trees. "Now, do you mind explaining the purpose of dredging me up to this vantage first thing in the morning? Are you, perhaps, preparing to hurl yourself from it so that I can watch the light leave your pathetic—"

"You already used that one," Alpha interrupted in his arrogant tone. "You better do some recalculating, ya fuckin' robot, or people are gonna get suspicious."

Veruca scowled. She didn't like the fact that of everyone there, this horrible excuse for a sapient being was the one who seemed to understand her communication style the best.

Before she could follow up, Alpha jabbed a thick finger in the direction he was observing. Veruca hated him for that. She hated everything he did; especially considering every spoken word and pointed gesture seemed overly aggressive. He probably believed it made him seem confident and direct, but it just made her skin crawl.

"Check it out," he said. "Over there. Does that look like gold to you?"

Veruca instantly knew what he was asking. The rampaging monsters that had attacked had skin like precious metals, with shining gold being the predominant.

*So, Alpha thinks he's spotted some trouble.*

She smiled, not even checking the location he'd seemed concerned over.

"It could be," she said. "It is truly difficult to say, considering these particular conditions during this precise time of day. The sun has only just begun to rise—a fact that makes me wish for darkness eternal, considering how much I can see of the disfigured spectacle you refer to as your face."

She picked up steam, feeling confident now.

"I wake each morning, praying for the blessing of blindness so that I no longer have to gaze upon the breathing abortion of a creature you have assembled your atoms into."

Alpha turned his head for the first time, then. His pale, angry blue eyes addressed her with what she thought might be contempt.

"Did you even fucking look?"

Veruca shrugged.

"No, but I don't need to," she said. "There is a zero percent probability that those monsters are near enough for you to see without our knowledge. As you are something of a primordial ape monster insofar as the intellect you've brought with you from your original form, you might not recall that Ava set those perimeter markers to protect against precisely that. But regardless of your steep and diminished learning curve, you might've known that if you didn't spend all of your time stroking your blatantly fractured and garishly disproportional ego. Was that all you called me up for, or can I trot back down to ground level and continue my ideations of you dying from a festering infected blister?"

Alpha kept his gaze on her a bit longer before one of his eyebrows went up. "Which one is Ava?"

Veruca put her head in her hands, truly not understanding how one person could be so dense.

"The one who can manipulate plant life," she explained.

"Ohh," Alpha said, his tone still suggesting how little he cared. "The hippie chick."

"It would be more accurate to say she is a Green Mage. Though you're hardly one for particularity. Except insomuch as—"

"Where's, uh, what's-his-nuts?" Alpha asked, furrowing his brow as he seemed to genuinely try to think of whom he was referring to. He let the partial question hang in the air before—aggressively, she noted—snapping his fingers as he recalled the information. "Dragon!"

"*Dragoon?*" Veruca questioned with an exasperated tone. "You truly are one of the worst individuals to be placed in a position of leadership I have encountered in all my years. Scratch that—you're simply one of the worst *people* I've ever had the misfortune of sharing the same air as."

"Damn, you don't stop, do you?" Alpha asked with an amused grin. "I wish I could go back in time and stop whoever it was from putting that branch up your snatch to cause you to be such a raging—"

"Watch yourself, *child*," Veruca snapped, pointing a finger at him. "I don't give credence to what any of the rules here are. Keep speaking to me in that manner, and I will use every painful Ability I've got resting in my cavalcade of Class features to ensure every step you take from here on out is one of deep and sickening agony."

"Yeah, yeah," Alpha said. "Whatever. Where's Dragoon?"

"Am I supposed to keep an inventory of all the members of our community?" Veruca asked. "Especially when you, yourself, are unable to track down a single inoffensive thought before speaking—let alone the names and traits of those you supposedly lead."

"Fair enough," Alpha said with a shrug, then reached a hand up to play with the length of his beard. "I wanted to know where he was because he has that, um, whaddya-call-it . . . Farsight Ability? Thought it might be good to check our surroundings from a safe distance."

Veruca paused, realizing that he'd just proven he paid more attention to their group than she thought him capable. Still, he was being foolish about their surroundings. It seemed that despite their precautions, he was still an asshole determined to find lousy luck.

"As I said," she explained, "if they were near enough for us to see, they would set off Ava's alarms. Which—I feel I shouldn't have to explain—are working perfectly."

She was confident in her assessment. Last night, they'd gone off when some form of fox-rabbit hybrid animal had gotten too close, likely seeing the fire and hoping to find somewhere warm to rest.

"If you say so," Alpha said, in a tone that told her he thought he was patronizing her. It set her teeth on edge.

"Look," he continued, "I don't care what anyone says; I have a sense for these things. Something's out there. I can feel it tightening around my brain like good coochie. You're over here thinking I'm being a fuckin' jerkoff or whatever, but I'm just trying to protect this ghetto-ass little trailer park of ours. But since you wanna have an attitude about it, I'll make sure you're first in the line of defense."

He grinned cruelly.

"How's that sound?" he continued. "Might clue you in to the fucked-up dangers this world wants to show us."

The vittra woman swished her tail impatiently and gestured back toward the main section of the clearing where people were now moving around.

"Is that it, then?" she asked. "You just wanted me to climb atop this literal death trap to ask me if I knew the location of a different individual among our number? You are truly a miserable, *small* man—and I mean that in much more than just your physical sense. Your soul is a squashed, ugly, *wretched* thing, and I hope only for my own mental stability that there is a hell for you once you die."

Alpha laughed.

"Still on one, eh?" he asked, then he dropped his smile and settled his uncomfortably piercing gaze on her. Veruca would have been lying if she'd said it didn't startle her a little.

"You wanna bang?" Alpha asked, his face the perfect picture of sincerity.

The vittra woman leaned away from him, her face twisting in horror at the suggestion.

"You are such a disgusting creature," she said. "I would slowly and carefully chew and swallow a carton of glass and carpenter nails before I'd so much as entertain the idea of allowing you near enough to touch me, let alone lie with you. The only instance you'd ever catch me on top of your repulsive wormy form would be just before I forcefully drove something dull, rusted, and memorable directly into your shriveled scrotum."

"Ooh," Alpha said. "Kinky. If catching you in the act is the issue, I'll just keep my eyes closed and my door unlocked. Or I can be on top. That's what I prefer, anyway."

Veruca shook her head and then turned, climbing back onto the ladder and descending. Right before she disappeared from his view, Alpha called out to her.

"Oh, hey," he said.

Veruca stopped, not looking at him but waiting to hear whatever travesty he had to say.

"Don't tell anyone else, but I'm putting a group together to go out tonight. A bit of a ritual I want to try. I want you to come along as well. Tell *Dragoon*—we'll need him, too."

Veruca didn't respond; a moment later, she disappeared from view.

Alpha howled like an aroused dog at her departure, the sound echoing through the camp. Afterward, he chuckled, his eyes still locked on where the vittra had just been.

"Yeah," he said. "She totally wants to fuck me."

Then he faced away from the camp again, resuming his scan. Unfortunately, he'd been too busy gloating over his imaginary chances with the woman to notice the shape moving along in the tree line, disappearing just as he turned back in its direction.

## CHAPTER NINETEEN

# BAR-BARE-IAN

*live! Living! Made it! Joy!*

The roe's words permeated my mind as what could be described as *loud as fuck*, though I wasn't fully comprehending the mechanics. Would I, too, be able to do that? It was worth considering but primarily for pranks. I wasn't sure how shouting at them would aid me in any instance except to startle them mercilessly. I suppose it could work if they suddenly started doing that weird humping thing—and now that I was thinking about it, what the fuck was up with that? I never got any closure on that baffling anecdote.

The egg boys surrounded me, bouncing jubilantly off my torso and arms and repeating the process ad infinitum. The action made me think it was their version of a hug.

*Aw,* I found myself thinking. *They missed their papa.*

But I had bigger fish to fry at the moment. No, I wasn't talking about the dire circumstances of my friends and me all being trapped inside a mystical lean-to in the belly of a colossal monster, nor was I referring to the bitch-ass Quest that had been going on for way longer than I thought was necessary. What I cared about—the gigantic, desecrated elephant in the room—was that Stinky was wearing my goddamn party hat!

"I don't know how or *why* you have that thing," I hissed, "but you've got about two seconds to give it back before I come at you with everything I have. I'll be on you like a methed-out chupacabra, my man. Give it here."

Stinky, to his credit, seemed a little embarrassed like he'd just gotten caught with his hand in an X-rated cookie jar. However, he scowled at me and immediately tugged the paper cone off his dome. He gave the roe a tentative look before shoving the Festival Cap in my direction. He turned his head as he did, and I could see a fresh gash healing on his neck.

*I'm not going to ask, 'cuz he's just going to be a turd about it.*

Once my treasure was back in my possession, I frowned at Stinky.

"Thank you!" I huffed.

"Gargle a fuckin' foot, orc," Stinky spat in his signature super diplomatic way. "You've found me out, so just leave it the fuck alone."

"*Ohh*, no," I said. "There are way too many questions concerning this little doodad to not bring it up. Like, for one—"

"I nicked it from your mushy fuckin' corpse back in the Crypt," he spat in admission. "Didn't like the idea of sleepin' near these ugly, pink sons o' fuckers without some added protection."

"So . . . you stole my one neat conversation-starter because you're afraid of the egg boys? Wow, dude, that's low—even for you."

"I wasn't afraid, you godsdamned cock-swindler!" Stinky protested, standing up now. "I just found that the first few fuckin' times they took a bite out of me, I didn't like it. It's a weird quirk that I like to keep my body parts intact!"

"A-*HA*!" I exclaimed. "You *were* scared! What, you didn't want to wake up snuggling a heaping—"

"Sorry," the tiny man sitting next to Frida interjected, "but who the hell is this?"

Then he turned to me, his enormous eyes affixed into his too-large-for-his-body cranium, giving him the appearance of a fantasy-themed bobblehead.

"Mate, be honest with me. Are you a derro?" he asked, an eyebrow raised.

I scowled, annoyed at being interrupted just when I was about to dunk on Stinky and send his self-esteem to a farm upstate.

"Huh?" I asked. "What's a d—"

"Ah, rubbish," short stack said with an unconvincing expression of pained regret as he mimed a pat-down for his pockets. "Unfortunately, I've only got the big bills on me. Bad luck on that. I'm fairly certain I saw a tramp shelter, though, round the back of this monster. I think you hang a left at the spleen?"

He studied me for a second.

"Though it looks like you'd hang a little left, regardless, mate."

Was this guy . . . trying to wind me up? That would be . . . well, that was *my* charming comic foible!

*Think again, tater tot. Nobody out-pizzas the hut.*

It wasn't until I let his words fully register that a little bell of recognition sounded off in my brain. He spoke in a very informal way and sounded . . . was that a fucking Australian accent? Wait a fuck! Did that mean—

"Ach, et's just Loon," Frida explained to the man. "As ye can see, he's the type to bare et all. Akiva'n him are good an' square mates, so donnae worry 'bout the way they jaw. Et's all show."

*As you can see? What's that mean?*

"I'm not twisted up over his lingo, Frida," the tiny man continued, appearing disgusted by my presence. "I'm just over here suing for clarity. I mean, where the hell are his *daks*?! I can see meat *and* veg!"

I ignored them. There would be time for . . . pleasantries later. Right now, I had to focus on rescuing these guys, not whatever the hell a . . . *dak* was. Probably a weird slang word for a coconut or something. Although I did give a side-eye to how familiar he was with my party members.

I noticed the possessed roe had stopped their frantic display of affection and settled in a pile near Stinky. It was hard to tell, but I thought they might have been sleeping.

Just as I was about to start up again with the tiny Aussie good-taste terrorist, I was interrupted.

*Hello,* echoed a sudden voice in my mind. It was Rexen. *Did you make it, or will I be looking for a new pupil?*

I actually jumped—because that's a creepy-as-fuck thing to do to somebody not expecting it. Apparently, my fiendish little friend hadn't slipped in when I had the door cracked. Was he still out there, then? I decided it did me no good to make him wait—he'd probably have just launched into more insane non sequiturs. So, despite my reservations, I threw him a bone.

*Yeah, I'm alive,* I mentally returned. *Where are you at?*

*I'm playing outside.*

*I'd be willing to bet we have grossly contrasting definitions of 'playing.' Are you safe out there? You're not, like, dissolving or anything?* I asked.

*Yep and nope! Nothing can hurt me! I'm immune, probably! Oh, also, I'm on the other side of the door. Rap-a-tap-rap, let me in! Just fooling with you—you couldn't do that. Ooh, unless you could? . . . No. No, you can't.*

I rolled my eyes. This little ding-dong was seriously bizarre, and not for the first time tonight, I wondered if I'd goofed up and hitched my donkey to the wrong parking meter. However, for good or for ill, Rexen was out there, being all . . . ghosty. If he was just going to be loitering, it would make more sense for him to be helpful.

*Well, why are you just chillin' out maxin,' Arjee? Can't you go scout around or something? Maybe see if there's a route outta this joint?*

*Nope!*

*What do you mean? You . . . don't want to?*

*Oh, I do want to, silly little pupil-child! I want it so badly, I can taste its sweet nectar—it's onion-flavored, if you're wondering. But I can't do it! I'm locked tight inside a radius of my own design. Curses to my genius! I am the ultimate foe of myself.*

*What the fuck are you talking about? So, you're, what, leashed up to some-thing? Weird, I took you for more of an outside dog.*

*We've been over this, disciple-mine!* Rexen said. *I have to stay within range of the effigy! Oh, dear. I don't think you'll score very well on the exam.*

*You absolutely did not talk to me about this before! Even I would have remembered something like that.*

*Oh . . . that's strange. I definitely explained it to someone . . . Huh. Who was that, then? Perhaps it was that suspiciously talkative teakettle?*

I wanted to beat my head against the door in frustration. What was he *ever* talking about? Also, something about this interaction felt *weird*. I'd noticed that since starting our psychic phone call, my vision had become somewhat warped. All the other noises around me were missing, too—like my head was stuck in . . . I dunno, a fuckin' bubble or something. I frowned. Maybe I was just hungry? Dammit! I couldn't afford to suffer from the effects of low blood sugar right now.

*Alright, Arjee. Let's pretend for a second you're not completely fucking deranged at all times. What is this effigy thing you're talking about, and what kinda distance— Oh, shit. You're probably talking about the little wizard-tower figurine, huh? Never mind that part. What's the range you're restricted to?*

There was a brief pause on his end of the line before he responded.

*Iunno.*

*Great. You aren't even aware of your own limitations with a feature that—if I understand correctly—you trapped yourself in,* I said flatly. *That is just aces, my dude. I guess this is what I get for agreeing to chauffeur a tiny, evil mini-ghost on this tour from something outta* The Magic School Bus. *If that's the case, just hang tight there, Baby Babadook. This has already taken longer than I thought it would, and everyone is weirdly silent right now—so if you're just fine where you are, we can sort you out later.*

*Hm. Little faith on a big orc,* Rexen said.

I sighed.

*What* now?

*I'm using Commune. Couldn't ya tell?*

*Brother, you're gonna need to speak something other than puzzle talk. I just told you I don't have the time to—*

But before I could finish, a system notification appeared.

*Commune I*
- *Arcane Cost: 100 Arcana*
- *Range: 1,000 feet*
- *Duration: 1 Minute*

- *Restrictions: Intelligence 50, Wisdom 50*
- *Wait: N/A*

*How delightful it is to communicate with another person as if you were sitting right next to them, even though you could be hundreds of feet apart! For the duration of this Spell, as long as you're within one-thousand feet of your target, you can shoot the breeze with mental ease! It will seem as though it's only a measly minute of your life spent in profound, meaningful conversation. Still, to every outside observer, it will appear to occur instantaneously. So, go ahead, share your innermost thoughts and feelings with another being. It's not like you have anything better to do!*

*Well, would you look at that?* I think-muttered. Apparently, we were in some sort of brain freeze—but like, where the brain was . . . the thing doing the freezing. You know what? I think I explained that really, really well.

*I don't need to look at it, disciple. I sent it for you to see. I should consider a more extensive vetting process with the next protégé. Are you sure you're the most incredible mind of our time? You don't even have a beard.*

*Well, first of all—I never claimed anything of the sort—at least, not to you. Second: yes. Yes, I am. Third . . . ly, not to call bullshit on your inter-company memo or anything, but this conversation has gone on way longer than a minute. Wanna explain that?*

*I have cast it many times.*

*Really?*

*Uh-huh.*

*That thing costs a hundred Arcana a pop! Just how much magic juice you got in that fun-size body?*

*More.*

*More?*

*Yep! I'm lousy with the stuff. Filled to the brim! Pregnant! Chock-full of arcane energy, knowledge, and sixty percent of a sandwich.*

I mean, I really shouldn't have been surprised—he was a centuries-old specter, after all—and a former wizard to boot. It made sense he'd be souped-up somethin' fierce in the woo-woo department. But there was a lingering question.

*So, you've got a ton of sorcery porridge inside you, yet you couldn't do anything to Dickhole McLoves-to-kill back there?*

*Yep!*

*Please elaborate before I tear my own brain out.*

*Try as I might, I cannot summon many of the Spells I would have been able to in my heyday. This form isn't suited for most Arcana.*

*Of course it isn't,* I sighed. *Because that would actually be useful. Anyway, I don't want to drain any more of your Commune points, so how about we pick this up later?*

*Ah, pupil. I have reserves, remember? If you're not going to pay attention, how will we ever achieve our ultimate shared goals?*

*I'm not going to engage with that. I don't even* want *to know what you think we're both trying to accomplish.*

*Yes, smart little pupil-child!* Rexen exclaimed. *Feign ignorance! That way, none can spoil it for us.*

I refused to acknowledge his statement. I mean, ignoring the fact that this Spell was clearly on a private mental server—and therefore unlikely to be heard—his comprehension of not only who I was but also his wildly disproportionate view between reality and my actual capabilities was worrisome and not worth giving him attention over.

*Alright, Arjee. Time to split. Don't do anything I wouldn't do out there! Or do—I actually don't give a shit. Later days.*

*Yes, later days to you as well, my brilliant apprentice. Ooh! Tell the elf I say hi!*

*Sure thing,* I said. *Anyway, byeee.*

And just like that, the bubble popped, and the connection ended. Sound and motion returned to the world like a giant machine suddenly roaring back to life.

*Huh.* I thought. *Whaddya know? The Spell deets* were *accurate. Now, where was I before that super dumb shit went down?*

Ah, piss. I couldn't remember. Someone had been saying something, and then another . . . somebody else had said . . . another thing . . . ah, never mind. Fuck it. When in doubt, go the freestyle route. I turned back to the group and plastered on as large of a smile as possible, then I slipped the party hat on my head and struck a pose in front of everyone.

"How does it look?"

As one, nearly everyone started laughing at me. Even Rua had crawled up from her fetal position to chuckle. That was odd; did the Commune Spell not actually work as intended, and these guys had just been watching me stare off into space for ten minutes?

"What?" I asked, glancing around worriedly. "Is there something on my face?"

"Et's not what ye got *on* you, Loon," Frida said between giggles. "Et's what you don't."

I stared at her blankly.

". . . Come again?"

Then realization dawned on me. I *had* noticed it felt kind of chilly, despite the burns. I'd been obviously distracted and assumed it was just my body's natural reaction to not being fuckin' fricasseed. I looked down.

"Oh."

I was completely naked.

Well, not *entirely*, but this may have actually been worse. The stomach acid had clearly eaten its way through all of my clothing saving only the Trespasser's Veil and the waistband area of my kilt. Even my bandoliers were gone.

Just because I'm a super cool guy, I'd like to paint you a better picture: I was a large, burned-up orc wearing nothing but a black cape, a ring of hip fabric, and a colorful party hat while posting up like a Macho Man action figure. Suddenly, I was pretty sure I knew what the word *daks* meant. To make matters more ridiculous, I realized I still had my haladie and wand tucked into what was now a belt.

At my sudden revelation, the tiny room *exploded* with more laughter. Slowly, nearly casually, I slipped the festival cap from my head and held it in front of my crotch.

"Well, this is mortifying," I said softly, encouraging another fresh round of mirth.

Suddenly, Frida's eyes lit up in a panic, and she careened into a standing position.

"Loon!" she exclaimed. "The amulet!"

I'll admit, her reaction gave me a brief stab of anxiety before I let the words sink in. I held my hands up to calm her down.

"Easy, *easy*," I said, realizing I wasn't shielding myself anymore, and quickly moved my hands back in front of my shame. "It's in the chest."

Frida visibly relaxed, releasing a sigh of relief and plopping down on the floor again, her armor clanging as she did so.

"I'm not a *whole* idiot," I continued. "I thought something like this might happen, but . . . well, jeez. Does anybody have, like, a . . . blanket or something? It's brisk."

"I've never seen a beast so prone to losing all their fuckin' garments like you do, orc," Stinky said.

"Yeah, well," I started, "I sacrificed them to save people. What have you done lately except act cranky?"

I heard a throat-clearing noise. Rua smiled with a hand in the air, sheepishly waving at me.

*Oh, right. Introductions. Man, if Edwig were here right now, he'd be so pissed.*

I pointed at the red-haired elf.

"Everybody, this is Rua—Rua, everyone."

"Happy to be here," Rua said, leaning into the situation's awkwardness. I noticed she'd pretty much been staring at Frida since the moment she popped out of the chest. That suddenly changed as the small, mouthy creature leaned forward to gawk at the elf woman, arresting her attention for the briefest of moments.

"Christ, you're a beaut," he said, eyeing Rua up and down.

*Christ?* I wondered. *Well, that settles* that, *then. This guy's a Sojourner. Was he on the train with us? Actually, why the fuck is he here? Who even* are *these people?*

At the tiny one's words, Rua froze, clearly uncomfortable with this abrupt arrival of the male gaze.

"Uh . . ." she started, but it was apparent she didn't know how to react to his words.

The little dude's eyes went wide as if he suddenly realized what he was doing and went into damage-control mode.

"I'm not saying that as a lecher or nothin'!" he protested, waving his hands around in a panic. "I'm only giving my compliments to whichever chef whipped you up."

"Whoa, whoa, whoa," I said. "Easy there, Hannibal. This isn't the time or place for you to be shooting your shot, homeboy. Keep it in your husky-junior boxer shorts before I toss your ass in horny jail."

I stuck my thumb over my shoulder at the door and raised an eyebrow in silent questioning. It struck me at that moment how being that I was arguably a thicc-as-frick, mostly naked, picture-perfect patron saint of weird pornography—I was likely *somebody's* definition of a sex feast. Therefore, I was uniquely qualified to threaten someone with titillation prison.

"Ah, you're right, mate," short stack said, looking genuinely embarrassed. "I'm prone to let the ol' cake hole run itself fucked with the first thing that pops into my head. Bad habit."

He turned to Rua.

"Apologies, gal," he said less boisterously than before. "Didn't mean to be carrying on like a porkchop. Won't happen again. Forgiven?"

Rua nodded, eager to get the attention off of herself.

"It's fine, really," she protested, and I noticed her eyes flicked to Frida again before darting back to the little man in front of her. "I just . . . uh, don't know you. And . . ."

"'S'all right!" short stack exclaimed, hopping up and putting his hand out. "That's on me, bein' rude as I was. Wasn't tryin' to cop a root or anything. I swear. Name's Garth. Resident Volteface."

Rua shook his hand and returned her gaze to Frida.

*Jesus, get a grip, Rua.* I thought. *I know she's a smoke show, but you can't be openly staring like that. Social graces or whatever! I guess my old school chum still hasn't figured out how to tackle* that *particular hurdle.*

"There, see? We're proper mates now," Garth said before releasing her hand. "Be tossin' back brews together over the corpses of our enemies in no time."

"Did you say you were a *vault fast*?" I asked. "Like you're really good at jumping or something?"

Garth turned to me.

"Mate, don't think I didn't notice those references before," he said with a wink. "Let's grab a gab later about that. But, no. Not *vault fast,* ya drongo—Volteface. It's my Class—heyo, bit of a rhyme, there—nice. I specialize in redirection."

I was actually surprised that he'd handled my words so gracefully. I'd definitely had the intention to smoke him out that way. Still, I had kinda thought he'd be a little more secretive about revealing himself as a Sojourner. However, the idea didn't seem to bother him at all. Fawn had made it sound like I'd be hog-tied and donkey-punched the minute someone heard me say something slightly suspicious.

I glanced at the group, taking note of Jes and the gray-haired man, neither of whom had said anything yet. Suddenly I felt a soft rumble beneath my feet.

"What was that?" I asked, looking around the room.

"An earthquake?" Rua offered.

"Maybe . . ." I said, but I wasn't sure. Something about it seemed off. It wasn't like I had any experience with natural disasters like that to make a comparison, but it gave me pause. I looked at Frida.

"Does it seem weird that while we've been dicking around in here, the oomukade still hasn't reached the water tower? I mean, she was just a couple minutes away from it at most when we took our mighty spill, but we've been engaging in horseplay for longer than that, for sure."

"Stands te reason," Frida said, "that she's likely bein' attacked. P'raps someone on the out waylaid her?"

"Maybe!" Garth said. "Whoever's knockin' her block about, I hope they give her one for me. She nearly sheared a couple inches off my top—and I ain't got many of them to spare! I'll bet it's Hadowar, though. Bloke's got himself a banger right hook."

"Hope he fares better than . . . what's his name—Kraig?" I said.

"Klaude," Rua corrected, picking up my line of thinking.

"That's the one—hope he's a better fighter than him because whatever village these centipedes come from, *that guy* is a testament to their college of dentistry."

"Oh, no, she got Klaude?" Garth asked with mocking sadness before immediately perking up. "Oh, well. Good on her."

*Man, that guy must have* really *sucked.*

I needed to get some information, though. We were wasting time now, and we still had to figure out how we would get out of this mess.

"So, were you guys eaten, then, or what?" I asked before looking back around at the motley crew.

"Ye," Frida said. "But et were intentional."

"Eh?"

"She said it was *intentional*, orc!" Stinky said. "Gods, you're fuckin' deaf as ever."

"It all went to plan, though, right?" Garth said. ". . . Least, until it didn't."

Frida, who'd been refilling Jes's cup, took over before I could ask more apparently stupid questions that Stinky would take offense to.

"The group o' us were fightin' at the water tower—really given' et a go—when the new Quest appeared and put the whole thing in a tizzy. So, we figured we'd take the licks to the queen and try stavin' her off for a bit till more people could join up."

"We were givin' it the fair suck, too," Garth added. "But our queen, she ain't goin' down without a couple solid hits of her own. Set us back a bit, then. Had to regroup and do some thinking about what the smartest path might be. Then your mate Akiva, here, figures we might try our luck with a sneakier plan—"

"Wait," I interrupted. "*Stinky* did that? Man, I'm running out of jaws to drop."

"Want to make that a permanent affliction, orc?" Stinky shot back.

"We were plannin' t' dig our way through this monster," Frida continued, before me and the matau could start derailing the conversation with our mutual affection. "In an effort t' get to her eggs."

"That's genius!" Rua suddenly piped up. "That's a great way to circumvent the whole water-tower thing. Go to the source and wipe out the one thing she can use for the end game. No payload, no drop zone."

The others stared at her.

"Don't mind Rua," I said. "She's just a nerd."

"Didn't realize, though, we'd be sloggin' about in belly muck like this," Garth said. "Really put a damper on the idea then, didn't it? Had to fuck off inside this capsule and wait for an opening."

"You didn't realize that the stomach . . ." I began, incredulous as to their reasoning, ". . . would be filled with . . . acid? I mean, I'm no genius, but even I figured that would be a possibility."

"Ach! Et's not that, Loon," Frida said, smirking at me. "Just that we dinnae realize et would fill up the way et did. Et goes in stages."

"And *that* was a trial buggered from the get," Garth agreed. "Fuck me dead, mate! That's an ordeal I'm keen not to repeat."

"Almost caught us out palming our fuckin' bits," Stinky said.

I knew that had to be some weird Stinkyism for being caught unawares, but it was tough not to loudly accuse him of having been tuggin' his pud when the shit went down. It wasn't the time, though. See? I'm capable of growth. Though, to be fair, that is an objectively hilarious image.

"Oh," Rua said, suddenly *real* talkative. "So, does that mean it's a timed instance?"

"Lookit the brain on *you*," Garth said, giving Rua a wide smile.

"We've been usin' Akiva's Time Dilation to get a handle on the count," Frida said. "We were just sayin' we thought we had et right before ye tumbled in."

She gave me a big grin.

"Chuffed to see ye whole an' healthy, by the way," she said. "Et least, mostly healthy."

"Right back atcha, Frito-Lay!" I said.

"Ach! Speakin' of," the Guardian exclaimed. She reached into the pouch at her side and withdrew two tiny tincture bottles. She handed one to me, offering the other to Rua, who took the gift with a big grin.

"Bit o' Health, then," Frida said. "On'y brings back a slice of it, but great for wounds an' conditions."

I nodded appreciatively and activated my scanny-scan-scan, scoffing as I read.

**Vile Vial of Virulence-Vanquishing Vitality**
- **Rarity: Uncommon**
- **Item Class: Potion**
- **Durability: N/A**
- **Weight: 0.4 lbs.**
- *+10% Health*
- *Cures all wounds and conditions*

*The Vile Vial of Virulence-Vanquishing Vitality is a . . . virulent and venomous victual of vindicating vigor. It vouchsafes the very vaguest vestiges of vitality, verily ten percent, but invalidates any and all vilipending voluminous vexations with voracious velocity. The viscous vehicle of delivery is a verdant vermifuge, a veritable vaccine versus any venture to vilify your vampish vessel. Vein, ventricle, valve or vengeful virus, whatever variable vice vandalizes your vanity is vaporized and verifiably vanishes into the void. Be not a victim; be vigilant! Though its verisimilitude is invaluably valid, the vial has a villainous flavor, thus earning its vulgar vituperation.*

*Fuck this stupid system.*

I sighed and stowed the little bottle away in the tattered waistband. I noticed that Rua immediately cracked hers open like a glow stick and, after a tentative moment of caution, poured the contents into her mouth. A wondrous pale green light gathered around her, and in less than a couple seconds, she looked good as new. Her burns and other myriad ouchies had vanished, and now, with only her tattered clothing to indicate she'd been through the wringer, she looked like one of those too-clean-to-be-realistic actors in a disaster movie. You know what I'm talking about, right? Their hair and makeup are perfect despite constant explosions and close calls with plot monsters, and they're way too good-looking to believably have been working in the kitchen at Zippy's during the pre-credits scene. *Real* protagonists were covered in every conceivable kind of muck or grime and got their undergarments fried off from the digestive slime of giant kaiju battle monsters. It was also funny to me that Rua had decided to take the potion that way. She'd shown that since her jailbreak she was . . . would you call it genre-savvy? Sure. She'd shown she was *that* but also understood the mechanics of how things worked and had a mind for parceling out solid strategy—but she'd still had some odd little quirks when it came to basic concepts. Heh, people are weird.

"So, how 'bout we get ourselves out o' this tangle o' thorns, eh?" Frida asked. "The danger was at ets peak when ye burst through, so . . ."

She glanced at Stinky.

"Yeah," he said. "Should be about at its lowest point. At least if it acts like it's fuckin' supposed to. Never can be sure with *monsters*."

"So, what's the plan, then?" I asked. "Trot out and . . . what? Splitsville? Or are you guys still thinking about making some omelets?"

"We been tracking the location o' the brood the ol gel's brewin' with Akiva's 'Bility," Frida explained.

"What Ability?" I asked. "Stinky! You some sort of detective? Remind me to buy you a deerstalker hat."

"Shut your fuckin' yap," Stinky said. "You know damn perfect what fuckin' Ability I use. It's the same one I've covered your mangy ass with time and again!"

"You talkin' about the thing where you can tell what a creature is? *That* Ability?"

Stinky just rolled his eyes and grumbled, which, to me, had to be agreement. I nodded appreciatively at their plan.

"Damn. Y'all out here doin' a whole-ass *strategy*. Thought way further ahead about this than I did, that's for sure. I was pretty much just trying not to die that whole time."

"It was harrowing," Rua breathed, shaking her head. "I'm still suffering from it."

"Oh, come on," I said. "Don't pretend you didn't spend the worst of it snug as a bug inside the chest—out here acting like I wasn't blessed with the lion's share of the spoils."

"I didn't realize it was a competition," Rua said. "Congratulations on winning, then. Gold medal for you."

I swept my hand out in a bow.

"Thank you very much!" I said before straightening and sighing. "Honestly, I'm just glad it was mostly my outfit that got the hotsy-totsies."

I paused, looking down at myself again.

"Uh, so . . ." I said. "Is that a no on the blanket?"

"Gods be damned, orc," Stinky said, ripping one of the furs up from the floor and hurling it at me. "Cover yourself up already!"

The pelt hit me, and I had to double over to grab it before it reached the ground. Then I wrapped it around my waist and secured it snugly.

"Nice!" I exclaimed. "Much obliged, Stinky."

". . . Why does he refer to you as 'Stinky?'"

I looked up from my handiwork to see that the other stranger finally took this opportunity to speak. He regarded the yellow-fleshed matau with something like suspicion in his cool gray eyes.

"Who's this chump?" I asked, jabbing my thumb at the man. There was something about his tone I wasn't really savvy on. It sounded . . . I dunno, haughty? Is that the word? Like a dick who thought he was better than everyone else.

Stinky shook his head in response to the man.

"That's 'cuz even though he jabbers like someone with basic fuckin' brains, he ain't got a whiff of any. That's the best moniker he can cobble together."

"Uh, no," I interjected. "We've been over this. I call you that because you smell super . . ."

I paused, realizing that something had changed. While he was a bit beat up and bruised, the matau was no longer covered in the horrible plaster of literally vomit-inducing funky-gunk from when we first met. There wasn't even a hint of his typical rank stench, either.

"Holy shit!" I exclaimed. "Stinky, did you shower?"

"Fuck off, orc," he hissed, drawing his dagger and pointing it at me. "It was a blessed respite, not having your cloud of orcish calamity hanging over us this long. I should skin your—"

"Are you fucking kidding me?" I interrupted, pointing at his weapon. "This again?! Just use a fucking spear, douchebag!"

"I am called Derelynd," gray-hair said, finally catching up to my question and sounding offended. "And it would suit you well to reme—"

I stopped mid-row with Stinky and wheeled in place, staring at the slate-haired annoyance.

"Wait! Did you say *Derelynd*?" I asked, letting myself sound shocked.

This threw the man off guard, and his whole demeanor changed.

"Why . . . yes," he said, relaxing his posture. "I take it you have heard word of me?"

"No—shut the fuck up."

He instantly got all hot and bothered again, tightening his fists.

"You dare to . . . I—I . . . You think you can speak to me in that way?! I will *eject* you from this place most violently!"

*I'll take that to mean that he's the dickwhistle magician that summoned this place into being.*

"I can speak to you however I want, *Darryl*," I said. "This is *my* house now. Got that? That means I'm the motherfuckin' el Presidente of this casa. Lord of the Cottage. I'm Mayor McCheese, and you're just some guy who has to clean the ball pit."

"Do you think I could not . . . just evaporate this whole Spell around you, plunging you into the acidic pool beneath? By Paloma's visage—this orc is insufferable!"

"Yeah, well, I may be insufferable, chief—but you're *pointless*."

"You will come to regret that more than you know, orc. Repent, and I shall show you mercy. Do you understand?"

I leaned toward his face.

"Plfp!" I'd stuck my tongue out and made a sharp, quick fart sound right at him. Then, just to be a dick, I pivoted away from him, refocusing on Stinky.

*That oughta shut him up.*

"Did you hear me? I said you'd regret that!" he continued.

*Guess I spoke too soon.*

"Back to you, Stinkster," I said, ignoring the gray-haired man altogether. "I know you've got some sad backstory as to why you're refusing to use something you're good at, but it's starting to look real stupid at this point."

"Fuck you, orc!"

"Here et goes," Frida muttered.

"I asked you a question," the gray-haired man exclaimed. "I expect you to give due response."

"So, reckon you two are an item, then?" Garth asked Rua.

"No, fuck *you*, Stinky. And you know what? Fuck your little knife, too. You think that you'd have learned your lesson after we almost—"

"No, we're not. But—" Rua started.

"I *said* you must *repent*, scoundrel! This will—"

"—*died* in the fuckin' dungeon! Seriously, Stinky! What kind of shithead—"

"—I'm not really interested in anything like that with Loon. We're just old frie—"

"ENOUGH!"

At the thunderous bellow, everyone suddenly stopped.

I paused mid-argument to look at Jes having not moved from his position lying back against the pillows, his splinted arms straight out. It still surprised me that a voice that deep could come from someone so frail-looking. The others also turned to the injured elf, the void of noise suddenly sharp now that there weren't a bunch of people shouting at once.

"This is unhelpful to our current predicament," Jes said, adopting his usual direct speech—like he was a professor going over the semester syllabus. "Once again, Loon arrives, and everything erupts into abrupt, discordant pandemonium."

The skinny elf looked at me sternly. No . . . *wait*. That was a *glare*. He was glaring at me! What the hell? Jes looked pissed as fuck, and I wasn't sure why, but I didn't like it. It wasn't his usual mild disappointment, either. This seemed like . . . hatred.

"What are you doing in the stomach of this beast, Loon?" Jes asked. "Furthermore, why have you come here?"

"I, uh, came to rescue you guys?" I said uncertainly, not convinced that this was the correct answer. Jes had a way of doing that.

"I see," he continued, closing his eyes for a moment before continuing. "So, you—an individual of . . ."

His eyes went cloudy for a second—the obvious tell of someone looking at a display.

". . . Level *Ten* thought that a judicious—"

"Yoor still only Level Ten?" Frida interrupted. "Why haven't ye gone up? Ye was on the cusp o' 'Leven when we got here!"

I was going to answer, but Jes steamrolled through.

"—that a *judicious use* of your time would be to climb inside this foul monstrosity and attempt the liberation of a party whose Levels are all well above your own?" Jes finally got out. "Is that what I am understanding?"

"Well, yeah. But—" I started, but he cut me off, still in his calm, icy tone.

"In doing so, however, you seem to have only succeeded in getting your clothing destroyed, your pride bruised, and yourself and this unfortunately naive elf injured."

I wasn't sure where he was going with this, but it seemed like he wanted a verbal cue, so I nodded.

"Sounds about righ—"

"Furthermore—and I am simply placing the pieces together—you have not managed to stop, wound, or even delay the oomukade queen in a meaningful or advantageous way. Nor, it seems, did you have a plan other than to flounder to the very spot where you now stand. Naked and argumentative."

I sensed something else beneath the sharp barbs of his rebuke. He was building up to something, and I had a bad feeling about it. What the hell was his deal?

"So, you offer nothing more than ire, imbecility, and an additional two individuals for us to navigate with—spreading our vastly limited resources, skills, and energy even more thinly—so that we might ensure you *also* do not die inside this creature?"

"Well," I said, then paused to see if he would interrupt me again. When he didn't, I continued. "That's not exactly—"

"You are once more showing that—"

"Can I fuckin' *talk* for a second? Goddamn *fuck*, you're not allowing me to defend myself. Quit being a whiny little skid mark, and I'll explain."

"Shut. Your. Mouth, Loon," Jes hissed, his eyes suddenly blazing with fury and his broken body trembling with anger.

"Jes . . ." Frida started, but he ignored her.

"You," he continued, burrowing his gaze deep into me as if to dig my heart out of my chest with his corneas. "*You* have brought nothing but misfortune and fatal consequences upon our heads since first you assailed us with your blustering presence—and we are not the better for it."

"Hey, now," I started. "I think maybe you're just crabby on account of your arms being busted into—"

"*You* were the cause of our broken, injured exodus from the Crypt. *You* were the catalyst for the unjust *slaying* of Calden, Merra, Dedyc, *and* Virgil. *You* were the one that our last bastion of hope was squandered on—coming back as you would, regardless of our efforts . . ."

He closed his eyes again as if he couldn't even bear the thought of looking at me any longer.

"You are a *blight*," he said softly but no less severely. "Infecting that which you inhabit, and corrupting all within your berth with your . . . abrasive existence. Our friends—*my* friends are gone. And *you* are to blame. I hope that knowledge festers within you like it has me. I am an elf out of his own time, and now I have few to carry the burden with me. Because of an orc called Loon."

It was silent afterward, no one saying anything. Not even me.

He was right. I'd brought the ceiling down on everyone and created the mess that had killed the others. I'd been in this situation too often for it to be anything other than a pattern.

I'd been fighting off this line of thinking for days now, knowing my shame and sadness were still there, like a putrefying abscess. A curse had remained hovering over my head since the others' deaths, and I'd been refusing to give it any strength until now.

But I was tired.

No matter what I did or what my intentions were, it seemed I couldn't help but fuck everything up royally. I couldn't keep that pace up—letting my actions spiral into unstoppable carnage and then attempting damage control.

Looking back at that day, Jes's words were not what I needed to hear, but they were the ones I felt were most justified at that moment. I'd gotten Calden killed. Merra. Dedyc. Even if Virgil returned, his murder was still on my hands. Who knew where he'd end up when he revived or if he'd even be able to find his way back? Right there, I felt like a heavy shackle had been placed on me at that critical moment. I was an inescapable doom of my creation, *knowing* then that I was spoiled. I was the cause of so much strife to people I'd only just met, so how could those relationships improve?

I didn't know—even then—that my feelings would change. But, even recalling this instance of my bleak mental state, I'm not a fan of spoilers. So, as rough as it might be, let me return to that state of mind.

Jes was speaking directly into my shattered confidence about what I'd done. I'd killed my friends. And more importantly: I'd killed *his* friends. I'd probably get *everyone* killed eventually.

*Just like Mom. Just like—*

I felt an internal tug, as though my *soul* had a sweater string that could yank it into unraveling and was suddenly cut off from a . . . piece of existence? A line of comfort had snapped. I looked at Jes and noticed that Frida and Stinky did as well. They'd been notified. I saw the message pop up, and though it stung, I wasn't surprised. It made sense. This was what I deserved. Less than I deserved, really.

**Jesimir Carandalon has removed you from the party.**

"You are no longer welcome among us," Jes said.

# CHAPTER TWENTY

# SIXTY-EIGHT

I looked at the notification still hovering in the air, dumbfounded.

**Jesimir Carandalon has removed you from the party.**

"I would kill you here and now," Jes continued, not sparing any time in adding insult to injury, "but what little bit remains of the others dwells within your revived flesh and the sacrifice they made to bring you back. So, I will ensure our paths do not cross beyond this moment, Loon."

He looked to Frida, the Guardian staring back at him in shock.

"Frida," he said, "please retrieve the amulet from the chest. It does not belong there."

"Jes . . ." she began. "Ye cannae—"

"I am sorry, Frida," he said. His tone was much softer with his longtime companion than it had been with me. "We will continue and revive our friends—this I promise you. However, Loon . . . Loon will not be a part of that success. His is a road paved with destruction. Where he goes, only fools or the ignorant would follow. I pity those who walk alongside him."

Frida gave me an apologetic look but didn't say anything to counter Jes's words. I understood. They had been a team for a long time. Centuries, technically. They'd bled together in battles and shared the suffering of tremendous losses. I was just some dude they met a few days ago in a fuckin' cave. They'd need to rely on one another now that the world they knew was gone, and that was for the best.

I glanced at Rua, who was watching with stark, conflicted emotion. As though she wanted to say something but knew it wasn't her place. She and I were similar to Jes and Frida in this scenario. Both of us were groups somewhere new and frightening where the rules were different, the people strange, and everyone we knew—other than those we'd come with—unavailable to us. For once, I wasn't angry. I understood exactly what Jes was saying and agreed with him.

"Yeah . . ." I started, but nothing I thought of to say really sounded good, y'know? What good would it do? I was now the pariah of this crew, and even if I wasn't, Jes had made the whole room really, *really* awkward. Even if I'd been able to drum up something to counter Jes with, what would be the point? It wouldn't change the fact that he was right. He might've been just upset with what had happened, or maybe the pain of his injuries was so agonizing he was just lashing out—but regardless, he gave a voice to what I'd already felt.

I was to blame for getting good—no, *fantastic* people killed. If I hadn't been on my zero-IQ treasure hunt in the Crypt in the first place, they'd probably still be alive. They'd be stuck out of time but alive. Hell, if I hadn't been such a suck-awful piece-of-shit garbage when I showed *up* in this world, I wouldn't have been blown off course and would never have been mixed up in this mess. I may as well have dragged the knife across Calden's neck myself.

The skinny elf was right on the money: I *was* a blight.

"I'll . . . uh, head out, then, I guess," I said, turning toward the door to the Sanctuary Cabin. "Rua, you're probably better off stickin' with these guys. They can help you get back safely. I'd probably just accidentally knock you into a volcano or something, anyways."

"A volcano?" Rua said, confused by the interaction. "Inside a monster?"

"Yeah, I dunno," I muttered. "With my luck, there's probably one in here, somewhere."

"I don't think—" Rua began.

But she was cut off suddenly as a powerful tremor shook everything inside the cottage, sending everyone who'd not been sitting spiraling to the ground.

I slammed into the floor and skidded along the hard wooden floor on my face, only stopping when I hit the wall. I tried to stand back up, but another seismic crunch hurled me onto my back and knocked the wind out of me.

The possessed roe—now clearly awake again—began bouncing around the inside of the hut with a panicked fervor.

*Why? Oh no! What? Yow!*

"What is this?" I heard the gray-haired man shout. "Are we under atta—"

Everything stopped. Like, fuckin' *everything*. There was no movement from anyone, and the bubble feeling reappeared, clouding my senses.

*Hi!* Rexen's chipper voice invaded my mind. *Me again.*

*Arjee?* I returned. *This is* not *a good time!*

*Well . . .* he began, sounding like he was about to tell me he'd just accidentally shit in my turtleneck. *Are you busy, pupil mine?*

*What is it, Arjee?!* I demanded.

*You recall that fella from before?*

*Gonna have to be a bit more specific!*

*I've met few people since returning. This one appeared as a freshly baked thumb.*

Ah, shit. I thought I was catching on.

*Crowmoon?* I asked.

*No, I don't think that's it. The one with the desire to kill.*

*Arjee, that's Crowmoon!*

*If you say so . . . Though I think he might've been called Gamp.*

*Listen, if he's out there right now, I need to know that information immediately!*

*Oh! He's not.*

*Fuck, dude! We just got stirred up martini-style by tummy rumbles. If he's not kicking about, then why the hell did you scare me to death by even bringing him up?*

*Well, he* will *be here!*

Rexen seemed to exist only to cause me migraines.

*You better start making sense right now, Arjee, or I'm going to give you the Ghostbusters treatment the minute I find a vacuum! How do you know he's on his way here?*

*Ooh, that's an easy one! I can see his signature; it's—*

He paused for just a moment.

*Sorry—recasting Commune. Anywho—the signature is on the outside right now, but I think it'll be on the inside real soon. He's been fighting the beast we're in.*

That must have been what that was, then. Honestly, at that point, I'd have preferred oomukade indigestion. You know, nothin' a tall glass of Pepto couldn't fix. However, the little anal fissure personified had said something else, and goddamn if I wasn't curious. It seemed like whenever these bits of information were parceled out to me, they tended to have disastrous consequences. I guess it was just business as usual here in Bullshit Junction.

*Arjee . . .* I warned, *what is a signature?*

*A signature is a signature,* he said, sounding as if he thought I was joking. *You're a very funny pupil.*

Then I heard a shift in his tone.

*Oh.*

*I swear to fuck, if you don't tell me what's going on right now, I'm going to huck your effigy into a fucking sewer! What is oh?*

*It's only just occurred to me that maybe people don't call it a signature any-more. I've been gone a long time! Actually . . . now that I think about it, I don't believe anyone has* ever *called it that. I think I made it up! In that case, this is a signature—*

Suddenly, my menu popped up. It showed my name, Race, and all the usual junk but nothing else. I stared at it uncomprehendingly for a moment until I realized that there was a tiny badge next to one of the statistics. My Level.

*You can see his Level?!*

*Yes, but don't be alarmed. I can see* all *the Levels.*

I almost choked.

*Okay, fuck. I know I'm gonna regret this—but knowing is half the battle—GI Joe—so . . . what's his Level?*

*Sixty-eight.*

I did choke.

*What the fuck?! How did I even survive standing next to him, let alone trying to fight him?! He should have vaporized my ass into particles. Now he's on his way here— FUCK!*

If what Rexen was saying was true, then there was no way I should've been able to walk away from him at any point. Frey had been Level Twenty-Five when we'd tussled in the Crypt, and that motherfucker could have easily shattered me into a thousand orc nuggets if he had wanted to. I'd survived because he hadn't been trying to kill me, only wound me enough to take me with him without a fuss. That and the fact that I'd deployed some of my—what I was now coming to suspect were broken-as-fuck—special features.

But Crowmoon was more than twice as strong as Frey, and he wasn't trying to avoid killing me—he was actively encouraging that result.

*Ah, I see your confusion, pupil,* Rexen stated serenely as if the clear and present danger wasn't any of his concern. *Never fear; I can guide you down the twisted, winding pathway to enlightenment with—*

*Will you fucking spit it out?! I'm about to piss my goddamn pants—uh, blanket.*

*Hasty, hasty pupil you are! He is not as strong because he is limited. Probably because of his nature—I think he's not very exciting, is he?—asking me to be his master. A baaad candidate for pupil-making. I would—*

*Back up,* I said. *He's limited? How?*

*Oh! There's a—*

Another pause.

*—Commune again. There's a beautiful shiny inside him, keeping him weakened. I could sense it the moment I laid spirals on him! It was sparkling so . . . twinkle-twinkly! I wish I could take it . . .*

Rexen paused.

*Alas! It's not mine. So, I'll have to admire it from afar! Shame. Maybe I'll wait 'til he dies and take it! Yep! I'll do just tha— Ooh, pupil! You could kill him and get it for me! Yep, yep, yep! I want you to snatch it up as my welcome-back gift! I would use it recklessly, but it would be so much fun! I could—*

He continued like that for a bit while I absorbed the information. I recalled that during his initial chat with the captain, Crowmoon had mentioned being . . . What was the word he used? Bridled, I think. The huge muscle with a face had even implied that the captain—or maybe her crew—had done it to him. So, it was likely they'd somehow put a shiny—which I was realizing was the term Rexen used for high-value items—inside him somehow? Whatever the case, if he wasn't as strong as he *should* have been, maybe there was a chance?

There was the additional detail: as long as my umbilical buddy here could see his Level, we could spot him coming.

*Arjee,* I said, interrupting him in the middle of some ridiculous monologue.

*—and maybe . . . boil it? Oh, but then I would have to find a way out of the catapult, which— Uh, yes, pupil?*

*Shut up for a second.*

*Yessir!*

Somehow, I knew he'd given me some kind of salute.

*Is there anything that could, say, block your little . . . signature view? Like a Spell, or really heavy overalls, or something?*

*Nope!*

*Does that mean you can even see the Levels of everyone inside this magical house with me?*

*Yep! Everything that's within range of the effigy!*

He chuckled, and his voice took on a creepy tone.

*I can see it all! Each and every succulent detail is mine to behold and expose! The ultimate voyeur. I am ashamed of my behavior, but it fills me with such a thrill!*

I was suddenly having Sababo flashbacks.

*Ew—stop that,* I said. Then I caught up with his words.

*Arjee . . .*

*Yes, my beautiful apprentice?*

*What is your range?*

*One hundred feet!*

*Oh. Fuck. That means Crowmoon is—*

*Very close, yes! Probably just on the other side of this stomach! He is hitting it quite hard.*

This was a terrifying concept. Once the connection with Rexen ended, we'd be out of time. And that fucking sucked because the enemy was about to open this beast and drag me out of it.

*Arjee! I need you to end Commune and get ready to hightail it outta this place!*

*Oh! You have a plan! Brilliant is my student, and wondrous are his works!*

*Nope,* I said. *Not even slightly. But, depending on how this goes, I might be doin' a big-time silly.*

*What kind of silly are you—*

*Just get ready!*

The bubble popped, and the Spell dispersed—but I was already movin', baby! I jumped up, pointing at the first person I saw—Stinky. He'd been picking himself up off the floor after his spill and looking like someone had just told him they'd inappropriately fondled his mom's tombstone.

"We got incoming!" I shouted.

Frida—never one to miss an opportunity to be a badass—stood immediately, ready to act. I noticed she was carrying a different ax now from the one I'd seen her with only hours before.

*You goddamn beautiful klepto,* I thought to myself.

It was a mesmerizing weapon, and I couldn't help but think some might call it a *designer* ax, if there ever was such a thing. An ax that granted prestige just by carrying it, one rich socialites in a world like this would strap to their back for the evening as they drifted from fancy party to fancy party. It was slender, as if almost too delicate to be usable in battle, and bore a distinct, sloping head with dappled golden wings cresting the cheek and traveling up to its peak. At its crown was a gorgeous blossoming crystal, pearlescent white and shaped like a blooming tulip. This was the kind of weapon that would look more at home in a museum than in the hands of a warrior. But Frida, never one to shy away from a challenge, clearly had other plans for it. I wasn't skilled at all in the use or really even the proper handling method of such a uniquely inspired piece of warmaking. But for *this* bad girl—I'd be willing to give it an honest try.

I couldn't help myself. I had to peek under the hood.

**The Wing of the Golden Phoenix**
- **Rarity:** *Transcendent*
- **Item Class:** *Two-Handed Weapon*
- **Durability: ???**
- **Weight:** *1.9 lbs.*
- **Damage:** *Scales*
- **Requirements:**
- **Wisdom: 30**
- **Bonuses:**
    - **+2 Strength**
    - **+3 Dexterity**

- +1 Constitution
- Grants [8] Charges of Soaring [7/8]
- Grants Phoenix Shield
- Grants Blinkstep

*Behold, the ultimate weapon for those who value style as much as they do slicing their enemies to bits! Don't let its dainty appearance fool you; this beauty packs a punch that would cause even the Penitent Archon herself to quake in her shadowy unmentionables. With a narrow head and blade specifically crafted to scale to the wielder's strength to deliver precise and deadly strikes, you'll surely feel like a mighty god-slaying champion lugging around this delicious piece of fist candy.*

*This ax has a few tricks up its sleeve. The Wing of the Golden Phoenix grants the user [8] charges of* Soaring *per day, allowing for aerial attacks and quick escapes. Additionally, the adorable flower-shaped gem is made of Tymond's heart opal, and not only serves as a focus for the Arcana imbued within but also grants the user access to the Blinkstep Spell while wielding the Wing of the Golden Phoenix. And if that's not enough, the ax also has the ability to summon a magical shield to protect the user from incoming attacks, as well as the ability to turn into a giant, sentient ham sandwich for added distraction. [citation needed] But let's be real: you're probably just going to use it to impress the ladies at the local tavern, aren't you? Outcome for efficiency is* Strength + Dexterity Quotient.

*Yooooo,* I thought. *Ho-lee fuck, this choppy stick is a* beast!

Stinky must have seen my stunned expression and sneered at me, his harsh bark snapping me out of my nearly erotic.

"Incoming? Well, that's about as clear as fuckin'—"

"No!" I roared. "Shut up—there's no time for hilarious one-sided banter, Stinky! There's a Level Sixty-something fuckwit getting ready to blast his way through here and murder us all. We gotta scram!"

"What?!" Rua exclaimed. "Are you talking about Crow—"

"A *fuckwitch*, eh?" Garth asked. "I dunno about you lot, but that sounds like something I might want to stick around for."

"What's a fuckwitch?" Darryl asked.

"Goddammit!" I howled, running for the feather chest. "I said *fuckwit!* Why does everyone want to suddenly tempt me with conversation the moment I'm— *Wait a shit!*"

I looked down at my feet and noticed a form slumped, snoozing against the bottom of the chest. Jes. What in the oomukade's warbley womb had happened? He was out cold! I think he was even snoring.

"Oh," Frida said, sounding bashful as she began rifling through her belong-ings. "Ah feel a bit bad about et, as ah'm not one te support that sort o' unsa-vory behavior. Makes m' feel a little like a night-grabber. But ah saw how 'e was glarin' at ye when ye took yoor right tumble in. Thought ah'd cool him down a touch 'fore he went off. But, ah miscalculated how long et would take, an' ye got yoor tongue lashin' anyhow."

"You knocked him out?"

"In a manner of speakin', yes," she continued. "Fed him a dram o' the good stuff. One o' them sleepin' tinctures ah found."

*Oh.*

I'd seen what I thought was her refilling Jes's glass with . . . I dunno, booze? But that must have been her dumping alchemy drugs into it instead. I was touched that she'd chloroform someone for my sake.

"Uh, thanks," I said, unsure what else to say.

She frowned at me, and I thought I saw the start of tears in her eyes.

"I know et's not the time—cataclysm an' all. But, what Jes said te ye, Loon . . ."

I put a hand up.

"He didn't say anything I wasn't already saying to myself. To be perfectly honest, I agree with him. You all deserve better than me—what I've forced you guys to endure. I can't pretend that what he said didn't sting, but it was true."

"He's just hurtin' and doin' a bad job o' expressin' that," Frida said.

"On account of me, though," I said. "I can't—"

"Oh! Come. The fuck. *On!*" Stinky suddenly shouted. "I thought you said there was an *incoming,* orc! Now you're standing around, feelin' fuckin' sappy for yourself?!"

He jabbed his dagger in my direction, and all three of his mouths curved into venomous snarls.

"Knock that the fuck off right now," he spat, shaking his head. "Now's not the time for fuckin' melancholy. That elf is a fuckin' *prick.* Been one since we met him. You're halfway past stupid if you take anything he said in his moronic fuckin' stupor as something other than pure, garbled piss-swallow. There's *shit* to do, orc. Now hike up your fuckin' whipping post, and let's get going, you miserable fuckin' mope. Or have I got you wrong, and you're *wanting* to die in this stomach?!"

I could only stare. Had Stinky just tried . . . to cheer me up? Well, I'll be. Regardless, he wasn't lying—we did have shit to do.

"Fuck all the way off, Stinky," I said, trying to maintain a sense of normalcy after his awkward self-esteem clinic. "I ain't dyin' *never*—nowhere! I'm going to fuck shit up and live forever! So, strap in, everybody, because the chaos elevator only goes up, and it's *never* comin' do—"

*BOOM!*

The entire cabin shook as we were suddenly rocked by a tremendous force. I stumbled, grabbing the Feather Chest and turning to look at everyone. They stared back at me.

"See?" I said. "I fuckin' told you! *Incoming.*"

"Mate, of course we know," Garth said. "But *what's* bloody incoming?"

There was another rumble. Then what sounded like the door was being hit with a sledgehammer. Everyone jumped at the sound. I looked at it, scrambling to the Feather Chest to slip something out of it and into my waistband. For the moment, though, the door remained thankfully intact. But for how long?

"Darryl!" I shouted to Derelynd, who started at my voice. "Can this thing hold him off?"

"I—er—was only capable of casting it at the—er—first tier," he said, sounding slightly panicked. "If he is as powerful as you say . . . I'm not sure."

"But you are still in control of it, though, right?"

"Well, yes. But—"

"Excellent," I said darkly, narrowing my eyes. "That's all I needed to know."

Then I grasped the fur around my waist and uncinched it, hurling it dramatically into the air with a flutter and leaving myself *very* exposed.

"What the fuck are you doing, orc?!" Stinky demanded.

But no matter what anyone was going to try to say, I had decided I was going to face my fate like a motherfucking champion. That meant I was now stuck in a hero loop—and I couldn't be reasoned with. This shit was *fucked* right now and would only get worse. If this was how it was going to go . . . so be it.

"So, this swollen little muscle monster wants to play?" I said, letting my voice reflect what I thought an action-movie hardass might sound like. "Well, then we're gonna play. But it's going to be by *our* rules."

Mentally, the ride-or-die eggs echoed my sentiment.

*Crush. Kill. Destroy. Fighting.*

Crowmoon was there. Sure, he was a murderous, economy-sized brute of an absurdly higher Level than us. So what? He was terrifying, yeah—but that was just fine.

He wasn't prepared for the stupid, incredibly fucking unhinged shit I was willing to do to survive.

# CHAPTER TWENTY-ONE

# THE PARTY PLANNING COMMITTEE

**D**arryl," I said calmly. "Get ready to open the door on my say-so."

We'd arranged ourselves in what I thought might be the best configuration to enact what I thought was the best plan of attack—not immediately fucking dying. I glanced at Rua, to gauge her reaction to what we were about to do, but she wasn't looking my way. Instead, her eyes were clouded over as she examined something inside her menu screen.

Derelynd glanced nervously at me.

"You're certain this is the best—"

"Vosket's dick!" Stinky exclaimed. "*Just fuckin' prepare yourself,* lily-balls! Show an ounce of fuckin' audacity!"

Trembling, Derelynd nodded. Then he raised his hand like he needed to ask his teacher for a bathroom pass.

"Ready," he said.

"Alright," I said. "Frida?"

The Guardian was standing in front of the open Feather Chest, her hand raised over the lid. Within, the unconscious Jesimir Carandalon was wedged haphazardly, his broken body curled around our unneeded belongings, his arms and leg still straight out. The items were stowed for safekeeping, as it wouldn't do to have anything slowing us down right now. Not with so much on the line.

"Donnae need te worry on me, Loon," she said, her tone serious and deadly. "Ah'm not losin' any'ne else."

I nodded at her and turned back to the door, reaching out to the possessed roe with my mental connection.

*Clucky. Jumpy. Slappy. Mortimer. Y'all ready to bring the noise?*

*Ready!* they resounded as one.

"It's too late now for a potty break," I said aloud. "So, if you have to go . . .

either hold it or shit yourself. But try to aim toward *him*. Everyone else ready to go?"

"Well, we're not here to fuck spiders, mate," Garth said.

"Uh . . . what?" I returned.

"We're fuckin' ready, orc," Stinky said. "Let's fucking get this over with."

**Congratulations! You've raised a Skill!**
*Leadership [F-Rank Level 2]*

I smirked, now suddenly feeling a bit more confidence in this idea.

"Okay . . . NOW!"

I heard the chest snap shut at the exact moment Derelynd closed his palm.

"Feather Chest, minimize!" I yelled just as the door to the cabin opened.

I was relieved that the stomach acid didn't suddenly come crashing through the open portal like elevator blood in *The Shining*, but—despite my belief—I was not fully prepared for what awaited on the other side.

Crowmoon stood there, in all his towering handsomeness, looking like he'd barely survived an encounter with a woodchipper. I mean, he was *really* beat the fuck up. Apparently, the captain had once again whipped his ass hard, but he'd either killed her or escaped. Again. But, more importantly—his body was shimmering with hot blue light. But even *more* more importantly, he held a familiar object in one outstretched hand: the Behemoth Blade.

*Oh, fu—*

"Hello!" Crowmoon greeted us excitedly.

Then the sword pulsed, and a stream of blue fire shot from its tip and lit the whole area up.

# CHAPTER TWENTY-TWO

# CRACKLE AND CACKLE

You know, sometimes, life can be a little funny. Like reaching to grab an umbrella just before it starts to rain. Or opening a chat with someone on your phone, only to discover they're already typing to you. One minute, you're minding your own business on the precipice of death, standing in front of an open magical doorway, being blasted with nuclear death rays from a sword you left plunged into a one-hundred-foot-tall monster by an uncomfortably charismatic, super-muscular hyper-ape, and the next, someone surprises you.

I learned right away what it was to be a Volteface.

As my vision recovered from the blinding flash of Crowmoon's special screw-you Spell, I saw Garth. The tiny creature was standing in the center of the blast, his mouth open as a cackle of pure delight escaped from him. What was more, he seemed completely fine. His hands weaved around, churning the energy encasing him and—what I hoped was—containing the magic. Then, even more amazingly, his weave became a wide sweep—reminding me a bit of tai chi. This caused the volatile nuclear beam to diminish until the glow was only about the size of a beach ball. It continued following his movements until finally, the tiny man thrust his hands up in the air like he was swoonin' for Jesus before slamming both of his palms flat against his own chest. Garth's torso absorbed the blue light from his hands, and a ripple the same color flashed through him. Eyes closed, he took a deep breath as a satisfied smile spread across his face.

He opened his eyes and nodded at an astonished Crowmoon.

"Right, then," Garth said. "Thanks for that, cobber."

Crowmoon didn't have much to say in response. Instead, he remained standing in the doorway, his surprise attack rendered ineffectual by the resident miniature power vacuum, a dumb, perplexed expression on his face. However, in order to really showcase the sort of pounding we were trying to ambush him with, he'd need to cross the threshold into the actual cabin itself. But it seemed like he was a bit too cautious at the moment, deciding that loitering in the ankle-deep stomach sludge was the better move.

*So, it's a stalemate . . .* I thought to myself, trying to weigh our options.

I supposed he could keep firing blasts from the sword he'd commandeered, but I wasn't sure if that was necessarily his style. He probably would have figured now that Garth would continue to let his personal predilections chow down on his energy every time, and that wasn't going to be a good call for the overall longevity of his side of the fight. But I had to figure out a way to coerce or *force* him into taking a step in. Everything we could do rested on that balance. Especially considering we had a finite timetable on doing anything at all, considering the chest would kill Jes in very short order. Rua seemed to think she had a backup, but with her measly Level—hardly worse than mine—I wasn't as convinced.

"Hey, Crowmoon!" I said, adopting my friendliest tone and waving at the man. "Looks like you found us. Uh-oh. Whatever will we do?"

Crowmoon chuckled.

"I can see you thought to bring out an absorption specialist; not a bad play. You—"

"Yeah, you're fucked now!" I shouted, smirking. I knew I had to figure out a way of keeping him from doing something that would ruin the vibe, so maybe . . .

"Guess you should probably run along, then," I said, trying to do my best to *sound* like I was nervous but trying to give the impression . . . of *pretending* to sound confident. Man, that was hard to do—plus it was a gamble. "Unless you, uh, want me and my pals here to lay down a beating that sends you screaming back to that pile of ash that used to be your buddy."

His grin grew wider.

*Is this going to work? Fuck, I hate suspense.*

"I see," he said, squinting and glancing at each of us. "So, your plan is to what? Convince me to leave by rolling this— What are you, a Sealer?"

He'd directed the question to Garth.

"Volteface," the tiny man answered simply.

"I see—rolling this *Volteface* out so that I am . . . intimidated? Your bluff is abysmal at best. I can tell by your tone, orc, that you are hoping I believe you are capable of tempering my power and therefore not worth engaging. Yet I am not a fool. I know well that you are not strong enough to best me, and this last stand will do little more than mildly delay the consequences."

"That's not it at all!" I protested. "We just want to give you a chance to live. But . . ."

I let a crack enter my voice with my next words.

"If you want a f-fight . . . it's *your* funeral."

*You know what I really fucking hate? Pretending to be unconfident. It's really not in my skill set, but I suppose it's a small price to pay for total annihilation of your enemies.*

Crowmoon laughed again, lifting the Behemoth Blade so that it was pointing straight out at me.

"Unfortunately for you all, a battle would be a particularly unsound stratagem. It would not be prolonged, nor in your favor," Crowmoon said. "Are you not aware I have felled the beast that consumed you and put you into this predicament at the get? Your meager abilities are—"

"Oh, fuck right up a tree, you big fuckin' blabbermouth," Stinky suddenly interrupted. "Do whatever you plan to do, already. I'm tired of your self-sucking. You're not fooling no one with your mummering-agreeable, bilge-licking behavior!"

"I apologize," Crowmoon said, looking a little bothered. "Why is the orc naked? And what is *mummering-agreeable*? Did you invent that yourself, or—"

"It means you're making a bad go at a pretense, you fuckin' backstroke," Stinky continued, undeterred by this man's raw power and threatening aura. "So, either you're all talk and you're actually afraid of this shrimpy *nisen*, or you're going to step inside here and figure out what it's like to be on the losing edge of a battle."

*Did Stinky just call Garth a . . . Nissan? That would be a hilarious insult. I'm going to remember that.*

Crowmoon regarded Stinky with . . . was that respect? That was odd. It was suddenly as though he was seeing someone worth not immediately trying to kill. But was that right?

**Congratulations! You have raised a Skill!**
***Insight [E-Rank Level 4]!***

*Holy piss! I'm a people-reading wunderkind! I should start a career as a cold-reading psychic and make all sorts o' stacks!*

"You draw an irrefutable point," Crowmoon said to Stinky. "How about if—"

"Ken *oath*!" Garth suddenly exclaimed. "This guy loves to do more talkin' than killin', doesn't he? Just goes on and *fuckin'* on. Mate—rule of thumb—if you're gonna try and impress us with your mighty strength, maybe do something—I dunno—*strong*? You're just standin' there jabbering. Top tip: the blokes who blow hard about bein' tough usually aren't."

Crowmoon, attempting to salvage his brand of polite, murderous atmosphere, pointed a finger at the tiny creature.

"That is an excellent—"

"Ach! Yoor right!" Frida chimed in. "Had plenty of opportunities to strike us lowly pawns asunder, an' there he goes—not doin' the killin' he said he'd be doin.' Well spotted, Akiva. Man's a right bit o' mummer."

Crowmoon stood there, unmoving from the doorway, looking all stupid and confused as the gang inside the Sanctuary Cabin made a full frontal assault on his character. But I wasn't one to let anyone other than me have the upper hand in the Insult Olympics—so I figured I'd add the coup de grace.

"Yeah, what a fuckin' piece of trembling—"

*FWOOM!*

The whole place was blue again and hot as the dickens—whatever that means. I didn't have time to finish my sentence, let alone protect myself, as the blue flames he'd hit us with swallowed every available bit of empty space inside. But only for a moment. Garthy-boy, he really came in clutch.

His hands were the first thing I saw in the blaze, swirling, chopping, *guiding* as a small hole appeared in the center of the flames. The little creature was standing in the eye of this hurricane, weaving his limbs around like a backup dancer in a Steve Winwood music video. The energy coalesced around him, churning violently like a magical money-booth tornado as he continued, ripping the burning sapphire haze away from me and the others with his 'roided-out interpretive dance. I'd thought I was a goner, but the fact that the attack hadn't even reached me led me to believe that Garth had started his counter the moment Crowmoon had moved against us. One thing was for sure, though: this tiny Aussie bastard was making this angry blue storm his *bitch*.

But that wasn't all.

I saw a flash of green to my right, precisely where Stinky had been a moment before, and heard the chitter of the egg boys on the other side of the cabin, prepping. I was thankful for Garth's assistance—to be frank, Crowmoon instantaneously lighting up the inside of the room was not on our "things likely to happen" bingo card, but it really came in clutch, knowing a true-blue Nissan Volteface was batting for our team. To be perfectly fair, we'd only had a few moments to strategize, but I was as I was starting to learn, it seemed we had an ace up our hole. Wait—that doesn't sound right . . . ace in our tree? Hm. Whatever—we had a secret weapon. Regardless, it could have gone much, *much* worse had Garth not been there. However, there'd be time to wipe our dewy foreheads over our close calls later. For now: executing said plan.

Garth was still being the baddest bitch under four feet tall, and because of his expertly executed pop 'n lock, I could now make out Crowmoon. The large, lumbering motherfucker had remained perched on the porch right inside the entrance, though not entering the sanctuary. I suppose he hadn't gotten to as high of a Level as he had—nerfed or not—without being a little clever about his battles. He wasn't taking much in the way of chances and was already queueing up another attack of some sort.

"Plan adjustment!" I yelled, pointing at the shifting mist where Garth happened to be hurling his limbs around. "Aussie-man, you said your power was—"

I interrupted myself, realizing I didn't want to reveal our hand if I didn't have to.

"Uh, scratch that! I hope your description means what I think it means! Can you . . . *do that, uh, backward?*"

God damn, looking back—what a stupid way to try to speak in code. He'd mentioned his power was *redirection*, but how did one properly imply that without directly fucking saying it? Someone a lot more intelligent than I was could have probably figured that out, but as it turned out, we didn't need it. Our little flailin' Straylian was a bona fide smarty-pants and picked up what I was putting down.

"Mate . . ." I heard him grunt, his tone *heavily* implying that I was stupid for suggesting anything otherwise.

"Alright—everyone, *do the thing*! Darryl—lights out!"

In less than a second, Darryl's other fist was in the air, and the fireplace in the corner suddenly winked out and the room went black. Well, save for the bright swirling vortex of blue that made up ninety percent of Garth's current mass and the pale amber illumination from the weirdly luminescent stomach acid creeping through the open doorway. But it was enough that I figured we could make a splash.

As my Darkvision activated, I saw Rua. She was barreling across the hut with grim determination, her sword out and heading directly for Crowmoon. The massively muscular murderer himself was busy wincing from his sudden plunge into mostly darkness with a single focal point of bright, intense magic to sear the ever-loving dick out of his retinas. Because of that momentary lapse in his carefully articulated, piercing bad-guy gaze, he didn't see her coming.

*This needs to work!*

I wasn't sure if it would, but it needed to. As has been established many, *many* times: I'm not great at cultivating and executing a surefire scheme intended to go off without a hitch. It wasn't my strength. I was learning that *my* area of expertise was causing riotous chaos to explode around me while improvising a way to save my own ass—or from the arrival of suspicious providence-y deus ex machina. However, in this instance, there was one thing that gave me confidence. This swiftly buttoned-together shoestring plan had not been devised by me. Instead, someone much smarter and more savvy in terms of utilizing RPG-logic into success had been the one to whip it up: Rua.

The elf got within a few paces of Crowmoon just as Garth finished absorbing the death ray into his torso. Rua leaped into the air, a sparkling trail behind her as she executed her cool new Ability she'd been so jazzed about before, and then . . .

It happened without me being able to really understand it. One second, Rua was flying at the unobservant Crowmoon, and the next, she was standing in the doorway, facing out toward the stomach, and the big man was in the air, flying in the opposite direction toward the center of the room. I noticed his body was in the exact same position Rua's had been.

*Holy fucking Hetfield! That's not a* phasing *Ability! It's a goddamn switcheroo mechanic!*

Whatever dope-ass stunt Rua had done, it had swapped their positions and seemed to work despite the vast disparity between their Levels.

However, we weren't out of the woods yet! Crowmoon, shamelessly powerful as he was—I mean, it was really fucking obnoxious that he was so strong—twisted his body in midair and landed on his feet, facing the door, the big-ass Bastard Blade already pointed at Rua's back.

*Fuck!*

I moved on instinct, my haladie out and flying in Crowmoon's direction before I even had time to think about what I was doing. But I shouldn't have been worried.

Many things converged at once, showing me that there was a certain benefit to gaining Levels and Experience over just fuckin' winging it all the goddamn time. First, and most importantly, my haladie toss missed by a mile, the blade spinning past Crowmoon and sticking into the magical wall. However, just then, Jumpy, Slappy, and Mortimer hit Rua in the back and sent her careening through the entrance, rebounding back into the room to fly directly at Crowmoon. At the same time, Garth pivoted in place, his hands in the air sparkling with blue madness. Stinky suddenly appeared, the green glow of his Kameas still rippling over his body as he slammed his shoulder into the side of Crowmoon's borrowed blade, while at the same time I heard Frida's terrifying shout of anger.

"Slipknot Sepulcher!"

Stinky's move, while not nearly strong enough to *stop* Crowmoon, was able to divert the direction of the weapon's blast *just* enough to cause it to fire too high through the doorway to hit Rua's tumbling body. The Kameas he'd used beefed him up by fifteen Levels, bringing him into the upper twenties—not enough to outmatch Crowmoon's own strength, even as crippled as it thankfully was, but enough to *nudge* him.

That was when the silvery strangulation string exploded from Frida's chest and latched itself around Crowmoon's throat, his body yanked backward by the neck like a dog that mistakenly thought its leash was long enough to lunge with. His legs went into the air as the Guardian's superpower took effect, the noose zipping into the floor with Crowmoon attached. I didn't think it would hold long—but it didn't need to. Just then, my three egg boys reached their target. It wasn't Crowmoon; it was Stinky. They latched on to his back just as Crowmoon's leg shot out and—while still being yanked to the ground—he drove down with his heel in a hammer-drop kick to Stinky's neck and shoulder meat. The attack sent Stinky crashing to the ground, but Jumpy, Slappy, and Mortimer's bouncy bodies kept him from fully connecting. Instead, he did what I'd done in my moment of genius in the Crypt and sprang right back into a standing position.

The matau, bewildered, turned and dove out of the way as Frida did the same, the former crashing against the wall and using the roe to bungee him toward the doorway, while the latter performed an impressively agile somersault in the same direction. This was because it was Garth's take two to be a badass. As Crowmoon ripped himself free of Frida's snare, the tiny creature pointed his palms at him. He smirked before quickly shouting something that seemed a little *extra*, but was still cool as hell.

"Reflection: Double Damage!"

*KABOOM!*

Crowmoon's former attacks had apparently been sitting inside the miniature man's body just gathering energy, because the light that erupted from his hands was several orders of magnitude brighter than their original flash and instantly dissolved my Darkvision. It was like staring at those old grainy videos of World War II–era nuclear-testing sites. I mean, for a hot second—emphasis on the *hot*—I could see *through* my own elbow as I brought my arm up to shield my eyes. The full force of it hit Crowmoon right in the chest, and I watched as sections of the energy splashed off of him and ignited the ground and furs nearby. But I didn't wait to see what else was going to happen. As Crowmoon was engulfed by his own attack, I *ran*. I reached the door just after Garth, the nisen having turned tail the moment he'd fired, pedaling through the portal.

Quickly, I turned, looking back at the swirling sapphire flames and smirking.

*Guess I didn't need to prepare my backup anyway*, I thought, feeling the lightweight object pressed into my . . . waistband-belt.

In the thick of it all, I'd forgotten that I had gone completely naked before the fight, and I was kind of glad, because, I reasoned, I might have gotten them all burned off anyway from the intense heat of redirected atomic death.

*FWOOM!*

The azure blaze parted and Crowmoon—albeit a bit burned—flew from the center of the fire, directly at me. In one hand was the Behemoth Blade—still tight in his grip. The other was empty and—

Before I even had time to register my mistake of gloating at a downed enemy, Crowmoon's fingers were clamped around my throat. He lifted me into the air with a crazed expression, blue flames still flickering in his hair, shoulders, and back. My head smacked into the top of the doorframe and I winced, flailing my limbs wildly in an effort to get Crowmoon to relinquish his hold on me. It was useless; he was too strong.

*Well, fucking gulp.*

# CHAPTER TWENTY-THREE

# WHAT LIES DOWN UNDA

'd broken my own movie-trope rule: don't assume you've won the fight until the credits roll. Now it was going to end with me getting my neck snapped like a factory chicken. Perfect.

Crowmoon's grip tightened, and I actually felt sections of my tendons burst, my vision immediately filling with blood. Even though my neck was the injured part, I suddenly experienced the most painful headache of my life, and everything began to spin. I couldn't focus on anything other than the angry eyes of Crowmoon as he grimaced at me, his body still wreathed in the brilliant flames.

*Well, look at that,* I thought dreamily. *Finally got him to drop his polite act.*

I heard another sound like a melon being smashed and my neck went limp, drooping in his grasp as if there was nothing but cottage cheese in there. There's no way that could have been good. However, from my bleary, super-migraine perspective, I honestly could hardly tell what was happening, because my head felt like it was going to pop. I could hear loud shouting and saw shapes floating in front of me. Oh. It was a notification that I could hardly read.

*Bone Warrior.* I thought. *Oh, yeah. I forgot I'm unstoppable.*

Then I was suddenly seized by a strong opposing force and ripped backward, away from the fist choking my life away. The moment I began sailing in reverse, it was as though the blood hit my brain again full force and I could *feel* the veritable fuckton of pain I was under. I screamed out in agony, unsure as to why I was floating until I . . . wasn't any longer and gently rested with a soft splash on the ground against something that felt like it was generating static electricity. I wanted to lift my head to see what it was, but couldn't. There was literally no mechanism to do so, and I reasoned my ligaments or whatever muscle cables holding my gigantic cranium up all the time were destroyed.

I was able to focus on the message, though.

**Pact Boon [Bone Warrior]**
*While this Boon is active, the user cannot suffer the Fractured Effect.*
*Charges remaining: [0/2]*

Rexen's remarkable little gift had rescued me from having my spinal column broken and was likely the only reason I was still alive with . . .

I could see my Health in the corner of my vision. It was low and continuing to drop at an alarming rate. With my head flopping around like a flaccid fish wiener, I could hardly move much, but fortunately, my left arm was still mostly mobile. Unable to sigh, I simply rolled my eyes and—in an absolute asston of agony—inched my hand toward one of the two stowed-away bottles from my waistband and somehow got it upended into my mouth.

. . . and *holy gag reflex, Batman*—it tasted fucking atrocious. The description of the Vile Vial of Vomiting Vomity Vomit was accurate: the taste truly was *villainous*.

I couldn't argue with the results, though. I felt warmth spread over me suddenly, and in seconds, my lacerating neck wounds—and hey, cool, my burns— were healed and I was up and ready for action. I looked over my shoulder and saw that Rexen was holding on to my Trespasser's Veil, and for once, he was registering an emotion other than maniacal glee. If I didn't know any better, I'd say it was *concern*.

"I take it *you* were the one who pulled me outta that death grip?" I asked him.

"Yep," he said, though his tone was less peppy than usual.

"I thought you could only affect your . . . shinies, or whatever? How'd you manage to— *Ah, shit!*"

It dawned on me just as I was asking the question. Rexen could summon his possessions to him as long as they were within his radius of influence, and I'd made a Pact with him.

"You weren't just being weird earlier when you said you owned me, were you, Arjee?"

The specter shook his pink mane of hair and looked at me seriously.

"Nope," he said softly.

"Fuck— Actually, never mind— Later! Thanks for the assist, though! Let's get into that once this is done with!"

Why was he so down in the dumps? Whatever; not my circus, not my monkey.

I bolted right back toward the Sanctuary Cabin, sloshing through the receding stomach juices and spraying the liquid in every direction. I spotted Rua panting and resting on her side in the belly fluid not far from me—looking exhausted but seeming otherwise fine. I flashed her a grin as I passed. I noticed the entirety of the rest of the group was clustered around the doorway, fighting back against Crowmoon as he . . . What the fuck was going on? The bodybuilding maniac had his meaty fingers curled around the edge of the mostly closed door, trying to force it open with brute strength, while behind him the flames burned hotter and hotter, filling the interior space with vicious blue light.

Outside, Derelynd, the gray-haired owner of this magnificent mansion, had his fists out, his eyes practically welded closed with concentration as he fought against Crowmoon, apparently trying to fully close the man inside of the inferno with his magical connection but having a rough go of it. The others were in various stages of assistance, with Frida chopping at Big 'un's exposed digits and Stinky attempting to pull the door closed from our side.

If there hadn't been a maliciously flickering super fire threatening to melt everyone into glue, the scene would have actually been a little funny to witness. However, the danger abolished the comedic aspects, and unfortunately, it looked like this was going to be a real pain in the butt still.

Garth was taking part in his own battle, siphoning some of the energy on the other side through the opening and drawing it into his body to immediately send it back in. Each time he did, the flames seemed to grow more intense, and I could feel the heat increase—it was like he was a blacksmith, using the bellows to fan the blaze. Jes was—

*Ah, goddamn it.*

"Clucky!" I called, seeing the flash of pink that signaled the arrival of all four of my roe. Clucky had been the one I'd assigned the job of ferrying the Feather Chest safely out of harm's way since he had shown a very dogged loyalty to the object, often carrying it around in his spongy maw when I wasn't in need of it. He was doing so now, and I nodded.

"Clucky, spit."

The egg seemed hesitant at first, but I frowned and he quickly produced the tiny ring box–sized object, dropping it in the stomach acid. Before I could even say the words, Clucky's singular voice entered my mind, commanding the Feather Chest to expand.

*Feather. Chest. Maxi. Mize.*

For the first time, I noticed his tone and timbre were changing, becoming more distinguishable from the others. It was lower than his brothers' and was even a little more . . . present? Like there was more intention in how he chose his words, rather than the hapless joy that the others typically expressed. Weird. Did that mean something? Was he going through puberty? He'd better not go emo—I'd put up with a lot, but no egg of mine was going to be strolling around, listening to Dashboard Confessional and thinkin' that being sad was his superpower.

The Feather Chest transformed at Clucky's words, growing to its alternate big-boy mode, and I yanked the top open just to make sure Jes was still alive. At a glance, I could tell he was. His splint-bound limbs flopped over the sides like springs under pressure, his head was back, and he was snoring peacefully within. Apparently, I was worried for no reason. With his skeletal stature, shaggy hair, and wrapped-up appendages, the elf looked like a scarecrow recovering from a car accident. I left the chest open and turned back to the hilarious scene before me. Derelynd was still focused, his furrowed brow beaded with sweat like he was on a bathroom break at a deli-meat and processed-cheese factory. Frida was still a-choppin', Stinky was a-pullin', and Garth was still . . . a-Stralian.

Blue flame began to crawl at the edges of the opening, and I *knew* that had to be singeing Crowmoon's backside somethin' awful. I was sick of the show, though. I didn't know what was going on outside, but this dumb mother had said he'd taken out the mommy oomie. I think he was either lying or mistaken, though, because a cursory look at my active Quests showed me everything was still in play. However, there hadn't been much movement on any of the numbers indicating how fucked we were. Regardless, we had to get out of there and take our chances. That couldn't happen unless Crowmoon was dealt with.

As if to violently rebuke my wishes, that was when General Gym Rat finally outfoxed my companions and managed to rip his side of the door open, exposing the infernal interior. He'd been nearly completely consumed by the raging pyre of the inside of the cabin, and roared in pain and triumph, as he now had the upper hand. With this new terrible vantage, I could see he'd stabbed the Behemoth Blade into the floor—so he had two whole hands for a-grabbin'—and that was *just* inside the entrance. With a sudden bolt of inspiration, I realized that the blade's position was exactly where Garth had been aiming his redirected flames. Had he been targeting the sword to toggle its Channeling trait, in effect increasing the power of the pain he was inflicting? Whoa. Hence why the blaze had seemed to keep ballooning in magnitude each time.

That was a stroke of genius—especially considering only Rua and I—and I guess Crowmoon—had known what its true nature was. Well, I suppose it probably wasn't *super* hard to figure out if given time, but Garth had spent his entire meet-and-greet period so far as a freewheeling magical pretzel maker, contorting the baddie's attacks and sending them back from whence they came, so it was pretty neat he'd seemed to suss out the finer points amidst terrible impending death.

But I was letting my mind run wild—I needed to focus.

We'd originally envisioned trapping Crowmoon inside the Sanctuary Cabin long enough to get away. It was a pretty solid plan that Rua had cooked up. Shame it was in shambles now. With Crowmoon getting off his surprise blade-blast and now hanging out in the entrance that we couldn't close—we were going to have to get creative. But, fortunately, just because I was dumber than dicks didn't mean I couldn't also have flashes of inspiration, too.

The presence and relative proximity of the weapon to our foe, combined with Garth's practical application of sushi-grade ass-whipping, had given me an idea. I won't patronize anyone by describing the *type* of scheme it was . . . 'cuz y'all already know. I'm something of a one-trick pony. But it's a *hell* of a trick.

So, exercising my eminent domain on all things asinine—and hoping to utilize the final pistola di Chekhov of this malformed menagerie of mistakes—I wrenched the other bottle from my waistband. With my movement, a loud *snap* announced the final straw had blown this camel's back out, and the tattered remains of the circle of cloth that was once my britches fluttered away in the tumultuous heat of the roaring blaze.

No matter. Where I was going, I wouldn't *need* pants! Or, like, a kilt either—Listen. Let me have this.

Okay, so, back to business—the gang continued to cluster around the entrance, but this guy Crowmoon, he wasn't about to let that stand. No, *this* fucky schmuck had the door open, holding it in place with one hand and his other open and pointed at everybody as *oh-fuck* energy gathered in his palm. However, this time, it wasn't blue. It was orange—you know, the color of danger—and Tony the Tiger.

"NOPE!" I yelled, except, instead of just *yelling*, I popped open a fat wad of Blackout Warchant and *finally* hit Crowmoon where it hurt.

The nope heard 'round the world crashed against the big galoot with colorless, cylindrical force, and he seemed to brace himself for a further impact that didn't come. I'd noticed that in almost every scenario I'd encountered, my very special blend of cancelation had completely nullified any Spell within its general direction—as advertised. I'll be honest; I'd been getting cocky about it. However, this proved to be an issue that the system above—or . . . around us? Below? Anyway, the system must've taken that personally, because I was surprised to find that Crowmoon's Spell just . . . flickered. A bit. I didn't know if it was because he was so much stronger than I was, or maybe it really *was* the system flipping me the bird, but in that moment—more than any other previously—I finally saw the difference between us.

I mean, sure, I'd tried it on him before when he *wasn't* using magic—at least none I could see—and nothing had happened. But this time, witnessing true weakness in the face of this adversity . . . Well, it fucking shook me. I mean, I'd used it to great effect in the Crypt against Frey, and yeah, he was a much lower Level than this hulking butt fart, but still . . . that didn't seem fair.

Crowmoon registered what I'd done and even raised a questioning eyebrow in my direction. But then he fired his Spell point-blank and I actually managed to keep my eyes open—mostly because it happened so quickly that I didn't even have time to blink. Fortunately—for all of us, probably—Garth was still there. He stepped in front of the gray beam and snatched it up, beginning the process of gathering it within his hands as he'd done before with that blue bullshit. The storm-cloud-colored, sand-like amorphous Arcana swirled lazily through the empty air like a drunken lava lamp, writhing and undulating, growing and shaping larger, a gargantuan glutinous gray gumbo the hobbit-ish spellcaster attempted to wrangle. A wild stallion in need of breaking.

But something was different.

The way Crowmoon was looking at the Volteface made me uncomfortable. Gabe—the guy I'd been back on mighty Earth—would never have noticed something so subtle, but ol' Loon—he was a regular Baby Einstein. What I saw was best described as a sparkle in his eye, and suddenly I knew something bad was going to go down. This dumb son of a bitch was far too pleased. What the fuck had he done?

As though in slow motion, the tiny man suddenly paused, his bug-eyed face full of crazed confusion as he was clearly examining something within the magic no one else could see. No one else but *Crowmoon*. Garth stopped, some horrible realization dawning on him as he glared at the blob now coiled around him.

"Yuaggh," Garth exhaled with a disgusted, exasperated groan. His whole head turned up to face Crowmoon and he shook his head. There was just a moment of undisturbed silence as the two held one another's gaze, the tiny dude radiating clear, disappointed resignation—a man accepting his fate.

". . . You fuckin' cun—"

*SHLINK!*

Blood splattered my face as the entwining magical muck suddenly erupted outward, its shape transforming into massive deadly spikes that pierced Garth's body from every direction. Then they retracted into the main body of this new entity, revealing a goddamn monstrous *actual* snake. Its eyes were glowing green slits and its body was a sickly gray color, like it was made of rotting flesh. It was massive, easily as big as a damn house, and it looked like its body still hadn't shed some of its original composition, as rivulets of slime slid down its scales like a waterfall of magical snot. And, of course, before I could react to the fucking nightmare realization of what it had just done to poor little Garth—whose only crime was being Australian—the serpent let out let out a deafening hiss and plunged downward, devouring the nisen's minute form whole.

"Garth!" Frida shouted, clear, dangerous wrath in her eyes. Then she dashed away from the cabin toward the ginormous serpent and called out, "*Ah'll* clip the bastard!"

*What the fuck is that thing? It just ate him the fuck into the afterlife.*

I did a quick spot-check on the rest of the members of this idiotic ambush. Rua was now standing, her only weapon, the iron sword, in her hands and ready to bash some skulls—uh, probably. Nearby, surrounding Jes's sleeping tub were Jumpy, Clucky, Slappy, and Mortimer. They were guarding the unconscious elf like prowling wildcats—their malicious-looking, glowing red eyes darting around, scanning for signs of danger. Darryl's useless ass was still concentrating on something, though what it could possibly be, I couldn't begin to tell you. It sure as hell wasn't keeping Crowmoon contained in the cabin, that was for sure, 'cuz he'd full-on failed that . . . litmus . . . test—right? Or was it litmus . . . t—with a *t*?

. . . anyway, quickly recapping—*Darryl* was being bad at whatever it was he did for a living, *Rua* was ready to cut a bitch, *Frida* was Paul Bunyaning, *Jes* was sleeping, the eggs were *eggs*, Garth was *dead*, Stinky *sucked*, and Rexen . . .

Since saving me from being Million Dollar Babied, the Day-Glo phantom hadn't really moved from his position. He still had a look of concerned pondering and was observing the proceedings with . . . well, less than his usual amount of vigor. I'd only known him for about two hours, but the mood shift didn't seem in character for everything I'd seen from him so far. That was a nut I'd have to crack later, I guess: The Mystery of the Not-So-Spirited Spectral Sourpuss.

That was a hell of a title.

Believe it or not, all of my peering, checking, and percolating had happened in just a few seconds, and when I came out of it with my mind sharp and pointy for battle, I realized Frida hadn't even reached the coiling sludge with teeth yet. Speaking of, I could see the vestiges of mist steaming out of the monster's mouth as—what I assumed were—Garth's mortal remains evaporated from between his fangs. So, much like Virgil, the last lonesome ranger I'd met that had come from my world, I was watching another Sojourner disperse in a haze of magical vapor. Virgil was, in my mind, a cowboy—and I guess Garth was a bit too. I'd only known him for twenty-five minutes, but I'd liked the cut of his jib. Of course, he probably would have called it a *jib-riggly-doo* or something. In any case, the little dude had some strong yee-yee energy—mouthin' off, making trouble, and dying being an obstinate badass. It was sad and I was annoyed he'd been killed, but not enough to fly off the handle. Because he'd be back.

*See you . . . Wait. Uh, what do you call an Australian cowboy? Oh. I got it. See you, Keith Urban.*

"Ah, well, this is charming," a raw, hollow voice cracked, filling the entire belly with its volume. "Are you . . . You believe you can harm me with that tiny thorn, hm?"

I stared, looking up at the huge form towering above Frida. It was the *snake*. The magically produced, oatmeal-lookin', disgusting-as-hell fucking *snake* was *talking*. That didn't make sense. How could magic speak? I was missing something there. Was there something like Summoners there, too? Sure, back in the dungeon, we'd fought the CCM, but that thing didn't appear as a floating, low-protein gallbladder stool. It had just been pulled in from somewhere else all at once. Was this thing something similar to that, or was Crowmoon the type of guy tha—

"He's a fuckin' Awakener!" Stinky shouted, twisting away and moving out of reach of the—apparently now considerably deadlier—Crowmoon. Then, with the confidence of information only his mysterious not-my-Ability could provide, he said, "Ah, fuckin' hell! It's an Awakened Moon Apep. Level . . . fuckin' *unclear*. Umbral Summon."

*A moon what?! Yeesh—no, thanks. If that's what's hangin' out in space, then I'm just gonna keep these dice rolling here on terra firma.*

I balked and backpedaled. Crowmoon was still keeping himself positioned so that the *real* move I wanted to do was impossible.

"Is that bad? It sounds *bad*!" I called to Stinky. "Bet you're *really* wishin' you had a spear right about now!"

"Shut the fuck up, orc!" Stinky shouted.

I planned to counter, but that was when Crowmoon started acting super *fucked*. With one hand crossing under the other, he pressed his left wrist to his right elbow, then with the latter arm began to coil it through the air, mimicking the movement of a serpent.

"He's goin' full snake, gang!" I shouted. "I dunno what that means, but I think we gotta stop him, or . . . *mongoose him*, or something!"

"That's how he keeps the fuckin' Spell ongoing!" Stinky shouted.

"With finger-tutting and shadow puppets? That's dumb. Look at how dumb that is."

"For once, orc—we agree," the matau said.

"So, if that's all—"

"Quite the travesty you have placed beneath my scales, Mandolin," the serpent interrupted, but now he was speaking directly to Crowmoon—who for some reason he was using a musical pet name on.

"Couldn't be helped, Reck," Crowmoon said, speaking for the first time in a while and still maintaining his silly stage show. "I know I said I wouldn't need you unless I was in a substantial bind, but . . . they had a Volteface. That's something like a Sealer, I think."

"I know well what a Volteface is, child," the serpent said.

"I assumed you would, but one can never be too careful," Crowmoon continued, as though we weren't even there. It was sort of funny, in a detached way, to see him continue to wriggle his hand in the air while he talked. "In any case, I thought I could trick him into trying to absorb you. I did."

The snot snake squinted at Crowmoon, as if second-guessing his intelligence—a look I knew all too well—and it struck me as how strange this interaction was.

"To call on me in such . . . an objectionable place . . ." the creature said. "Am I to assume you are incapable of dispatching this . . ."

He sniffed the air, waving his sickeningly sloppy nose in a circle.

". . . unshorn and fragile gathering, hm? This . . ."

He trailed off again, as if realizing something and sniffed the air again.

"Hm? Sojourners? There are *Sojourners* among you, hm?"

Fucking hell. I could *not* catch a break. So, for whatever mysterious reason, this big . . . Awakened python could pinpoint someone with my particular fancy upbringing by *smell*? Alright, I knew I was in a world *built* out of suspension of disbelief, but goodness—fucking—gracious, couldn't I have a little *low-hanging* disbelief instead? This was getting ridiculous! Even worse, the moment this beast had said the magic curse word, *Sojourner*, I noticed Crowmoon's eyes grow wide, and he suddenly got *awfully* twitchy.

"You," the snake said, its burning emerald eyes peering at me. "Sojourner. Why are you naked, hm?"

"Why the fuck are *you* naked?" I spat back. "Listen, it's called body positivity, Super Schlong—look it up. And I'm *positive* your body is made out of . . . I dunno, chlamydia and gremlin cum?"

"Sojourners should hold their tongues around one such as I, Rekka, the Great—"

"Shut up!" I shouted, and . . . Rekka, I guess, looked taken aback.

*Good.*

"Listen up, porridge ferret," I continued, first directing my malice at the monster. "I've fuckin' had it. I am *sick* of you—ya dumbass serpent. Your shitty attitude, your scratchy voice, your gross . . . whatever the hell is all over your body. You're nasty. Nasty-ass . . . glue worm."

I'll admit, I hadn't expected to not need to cede the floor and hadn't really found my groove, so I was grasping a little. Next, I turned to the gesticulating asshole in the doorway of the cabin.

"And I am *doubly* disgusted by you, Crowmoon—or fuckin' Mandolin—or whichever cute nickname you're going by. Fuck you and your stupid massive body. Over here makin' snake-charmer moves like a fuckin' dope. Fuck you."

I shook my head.

"I just wanted to do something simple, ya know? Rescue my long-lost buddy from . . . what was probably . . . *false* imprisonment?"

I looked over at Rua, and she gave a single, firm nod.

"Yeah, *false imprisonment*, and get the fuck *offa* this stupid world. Maybe relax a little—take a fuckin' shower that doesn't involve an ice-cold, *raging river!* But no. Riff-raff over here got dumped into time-out—probably for acting indecent around ducks or something. *Then* dipshit here decided to summon his best bro to bust him *out* of there using a . . . giant monster attack for a distraction? Who fuckin' knows? To add a little extra cheese on.that sausage, though, for some reason he thought to himself, *You know what,* Blowmoon? *It's not enough that I fondle mallards— Nope! As I am Blowmoon—don't forget, very obviously a goose diddler—I'm going to also kill innocent people just because they happen to be around me and see my face. Can't have anyone knowin' I grope birds! No sirree."*

I waved my hands wide at the stomach surrounding us. I noticed that the pustule-like sacs were filling up again, and knew we were on a limited timetable.

"Now look at you, *Mandolin,*" I sneered, emphasizing the word so he knew I thought it was lame. "Couldn't leave us alone, and now we *all* look like a bunch of fuckin' jerks. You're standing there, acting like the world's most useless doorstop in *this guy's* shack—"

I gestured to Darryl, who looked like he was about to pass out from concentration, his face beet-red and his clothes completely soaked through with sweat.

"—in the belly of a centipede. Your mutated dildo pet is confused. *These* guys don't know *what* the fuck is goin' on. I'm over here grandstanding . . . Is this what you wanted? To look foolish? Because you look foolish. Why weren't the ducks enough, Crowmoon? Why weren't they *enough?* Maybe you should . . ."

I paused, feeling the hot anger well up inside me. I'd hadn't been blowing smoke—I may have been trying my best to keep it together and focus my aggression on colorful character assassination, but I was fed the fuck up and beginning to feel like I needed to pound on something bloated and polite to feel better. However, despite my intensive putdowns of these two hoofbites, no one said anything. I opened my mouth, and . . .

"Shit," I groaned. "I forgot where I was goin' with this—but, anyway you— Oh, yeah! I remember: *fuck* you guys."

Then I pointed at the Guardian, whose eyes beneath the slats in her helmet had never left her target.

"Frida, you got this?"

"Aye, Loon," she growled.

"Good—ICE THIS FOOL!"

**Congratulations! You've raised a Skill!**
*Leadership [F-Rank Level 3]*

Rekka let out a choking laugh as the coolest chick I'd ever met suddenly vanished from view, reappearing ten feet away and lurching forward, before disappearing once more. I couldn't track her, and it clicked for me that *this* was probably Blinkstep. So, it let her . . . teleport? Fucking. Awesome.

Rekka seemed to be having as challenging of a time as I was in keeping up with where the Guardian was, his body flailing around as he snapped his head in every direction, attempting to trace her movement. No sooner would he look away from a point than she would suddenly become visible in that exact spot, each time her arrival announced with a crackle of magic before being gone once more in a flash.

Man, he *had* to be getting dizzy.

The serpent, growing more and more aggravated in his hunt, began spinning in place in the air and floating upward—a move that seemed like particularly poor sportsmanship. When he finally reached a point about thirty feet in the air, he seemed to relax, something like a grin appearing on a mouth that—up until that point—I would have sworn was incapable of showing any expression other than hungry rage. The great, big beast seemed to think he now had the upper hand, and so—goddammit, I *almost* felt sorry for his self-assurance—of course he didn't.

Frida suddenly appeared high above him—near the stomach ceiling—the hyper-charge from her Blinkstep wrapping her in magical lightning and giving her the impression of a descending thunder titan. Rekka snapped his head upward, apparently thinking he had himself quite the easy meal as he opened his jaws wide to snatch her up. But this motherfucker should have been paying attention earlier when I'd tricked the *very beast he was inside of*. Nothing goes right for these monsters, does it? Oh, well.

Frida eyed her shot, lifted her ax high and then . . . Wait, what?

"ARMSHIFT!" she roared.

The ax suddenly winked out of existence, replaced instantly with . . . *whoa, baby butterscotch*—Ecliptic! The Wing had somehow swapped places with the unadorned wood ax in the harness on her back, and now she was driving down in an ultimate chop with the jealousy-forged, starry-night-lumberjacking thwacker. Like shoving a square peg into a round hole enough times that the whole box bucket caves in, my brain suddenly gave up, accepting information it hadn't been able to process as my mind was shut off from pure awe. I hadn't been able to discern why Frida had switched axes, but it was suddenly painfully obvious. She'd needed the Wing to use Blinkstep, but Ecliptic was far better at dealing with certain types of Arcana. Namely, solar and lunar. Rekka was a *moon* apep, and while I didn't know what exactly that was—I'd bet boners to ball hairs he was somehow affected by whatever lunar Arcana was. Therefore, his ugly, toothy mug was in for the ass-spanking to end all ass-spankings—and he didn't even *have* an ass. But, as Frida shifted her swing, I realized she wasn't aiming for Rekka's maw. She whipped the way-more-wieldy woodcutter full-tilt at his back half and connected with the floating mucus monster's mucky membrane with a loud, wet chop, slicing clean through Rekka's surprisingly juicy hindquarters.

Rekka roared, writhing in raucous rage, his jaws closing around nothing but air as Frida continued to plummet. The heavily armored Guardian dropped deftly to the ground with a cacophonous splash, her swapped weapon still swishing cleverly behind her to defend against any counterattacks. She smirked as the section of Rekka's body she'd cut loose slopped into the bile.

I cheered.

"Yeah, Frida! You show that mean ole jizz dragon what's up!"

*Ha! I'd said he didn't have an ass before, but he, like . . .* way *doesn't have one now!*

But, of course, this wasn't about to stop Rekka from being a gruesome, gooey boil on my browneye.

"You think this is over, hm?! That I'm so easily bested, hm?!" The oversized pinworm howled hoarsely. Slithering toward Frida through the fucking air, its massive body left a dripping trail of slime and blood that cascaded down to mix with the stomach acid. The concoction turned gray-brown and began to bubble and roil. I could feel my bile rising in my throat.

"That's . . . so fucking . . . gross," I said, my statement punctuated with retching as I struggled against my strong physical compulsion to puke.

That seemed as good a time as any to call it my cue.

I'd been so enraptured by the sight of the beautiful, glimmering, ax-wielding murder goddess that I'd pretty much forgotten all about Crowmoon. He needed to be dealt with, but I couldn't just leave Frida to keep fighting off the vice boss by herself. So, I'd need to be a tricky Vicky if I wanted to assist.

But first: Part One. I had to make sure *Mandolin* was distracted.

Forcing myself to stop doubling over, I roared to the matau.

"Stinky!"

The yellow-skinned, tri-mouthed salty dog shot a vicious scowl my way but didn't say anything. It appeared he was already racing toward Crowmoon.

"Oh–uh . . . never mind!" I said, quickly darting my eyes back and forth between him and the ex-con, and hoping he'd pick up on the hint.

I noticed that Crowmoon was *still* standing in the doorway of the cabin. He hadn't crossed the threshold back into the stomach cavern yet, for some inexplicable reason. It also looked like the blue fire had gone out inside or had, at least, mostly abated. Which may also have contributed to his comfortability with his position. But it really didn't make a lick of sense. Why hadn't he climbed out of there and started kicking us repeatedly against the oomukade's belly bones? Unless whatever Darryl was doing was actually helping? It would be awfully *zany* if he was still holding the Spell after our plan had been . . . sort of enacted *just 'cuz.* Operating on that assumption was probably safe and meant that the man tugging the cabin's puppet strings would need to be safeguarded.

*Guess it's on to Part Two, then, eh? Fine.*

The second installment of this ingenious play was to make sure that miserable-ass Darryl had someone monitoring his flank, so that meant— Shit, really?

I'd looked up to see that Rua had reached the gray-haired man and seemed to already be giving him a pep talk. She brought her sword up, and it was clear she was endeavoring to play bodyguard.

Okay, now, *that* was weird. But—and I feel like I'd mentioned this more times in the last week than ever in my life—there wasn't time to ponder over odd happenings. Frida needed backup, and I was going to see if there was any chance of rousing the dead.

"Wakey! Wakey!" I roared, emphasizing each word by slamming down the lid of the Feather Chest on the exposed, splinted limbs of the venerable Jesimir Carandalon. But the doped-up elven Invoker remained fast asleep despite the fact that his arms and legs kept careening hilariously upward with every clap. So, I tried again. Harder.

"Wake! Up! Time! For! School! You're! Gonna! Miss the! BUS!"

I heard a crunch and froze.

Slowly, I lifted the lid to peer wide-eyed inside, half-expecting to see one of Jes's lopped-off limbs tumble into the digestive fluid. Fortunately, however, it appeared—from a cursory glance—it was only one of the wooden rods holding his left arm rigid, and I breathed a sigh of relief. Then, because I'm impatient, I flipped the whole chest upside down.

A sputtering Jes greeted me from the pond of bile as he pulled his submerged head out and wobbled into a sitting position.

"Oh, *good.* You're up!" I cooed merrily, then I scowled. "Now go help Frida."

"What?" Jes replied, still scrambling to get a handle on what was happening to him.

"I said that *your* party's Guardian is fighting for her life against some sort of floating . . . phlegm weasel . . .? I dunno—anyway, it's gross, and she needs the brave and powerful Sir Jesimir the Drugged-up to assist her before it bites off her fighting parts."

Jes, to his credit, didn't argue. He simply took stock of the situation, cleared his throat, and stretched his hands. I'd spotted a strangely Feather Chest lid-shaped welt beginning to form along his forearm and quickly diverted my eyes.

"Yes. Hrm, well, er . . ." he started awkwardly. "Thank you for, er, bringing that to my attention. I am not sure how strong that drink was, but—ugh! By Hilrendar, my wrist hurts!"

Unable to massage the spot because of his stick-man cosplay, he resigned himself to flicking his wrist repeatedly.

"Oh, yeah," I said, nodding sagely. "Trunk cramps, huh? Bad luck, man—anyway, time to scoot!"

"I am, er . . ." He glanced down at his splayed-out legs submerged in the bile and then looked back up at me. Then he shrugged, causing his T-shaped arms to flap up and down like a helpless baby bird.

"Could you—"

"Oh—did you nee—" I paused, holding my hands up. "Sorry. Go ahead."

Neither of us spoke for a beat, so I thought I'd try again.

"Or did you—"

"It is only that—"

I zipped my lips and beckoned him to continue with my hand. Jes waited for another moment, opened his mouth as if to test if I was going to interrupt, and then nodded.

"I might need assistance, myself, in standing," he said, fully embarrassed to admit something so obvious.

"Yeah, no problem," I said, grabbing him roughly from under the armpits and hoisting him into the air. "Up ya go!"

It took a moment for Jes to get situated, aligning himself so that he could tiptoe forward . . . and that was a little annoying.

"Oh, come on! How the hell were you able to both leave *and* fight a huge monster earlier when you're walking like you've got someone else's shit in your jorts?!"

"I think, Loon, that despite certain elements of your personality, you might consider—"

"Come on, Grandpa!" I howled. "*Move it!*"

I'd never been accused of being patient. Ever. So, knowing this, please consider time was of a particularly critical element.

I grabbed Jes again. I wasn't really sure if it was, you know, safe to do something like that, but, I mean—come on—*magic* times. So, I sorta . . . stuffed him back into the Feather Chest like he was one of those pandas in the YouTube videos. You know the ones, right? Where they're movin' all slow and sleepy and trying to escape from the caretaker? Yeah. Like that. He made a weird noise as he landed, but I was already movin,' baby! Then, knowing how the physics, or whatever, worked on the weight component of the chest there, I grabbed the whole damn toy box and lifted it up in the air. Then I did a cute little spin . . . and launched his ass right at the monster snake.

"Alley-oop!" I called, and watched with just a *little* satisfaction as he soared forward screaming. He was alright, though. When he hit the apex of the arc, he shot out of the Feather Chest like a pilot slamming on his ejection button. But like I said: he was alright. Jes was a bit of a dick, but he was no slouch when it came to tossing out magical anger weapons. Already I could see fireballs erupting from his stupidly spaced hands as he rocketed along like Jesus on the cross—just as skinny and injured but probably way less willing to die.

That settled, I smacked my hands together, dusting them off over a job well done.

**Warning: The [Mission Quest] A Multi-pronged Assault is in danger of failing. The oomukade queen, while injured, has reached the [Settlement Resource] water tower.**

**Warning: The [Mission Quest] A Multi-pronged Assault is in danger of failing. Total Settlement Destruction has reached the [CRITICAL] level.**

Goddammit. When it rained, it gored.
*New plan.*
"Oh, *Arjeeeee!*" I sang sweetly. "Wanna hook a homie up with a favor?"

# CHAPTER TWENTY-FOUR

# O BROTHER, LARITH THOU

Despite his chosen vocation, Tarnen was never one for religious piety, and the city of Larith was the last place he wanted to be.

The City of Glass and Temples, as it was known by many, was the ultimate tourist trap. It was said that it was founded eons before, during the Era of Fog, Shadow, and Light, by a group of feverish religious nuts who had a vision of a city where all gods and goddesses could be worshiped. Being a member of a sect very similar in belief, Tarnen couldn't help but scoff. They'd built the city in the heart of a dense forest, surrounded by ancient trees that seemed to tower over the city just to mock it.

As the city grew, it became a place of pilgrimage for people from all over the land, or at least the ones who didn't know any better. Temples dedicated to all manner of gods and goddesses were built, each one more grandiose and gaudier than the last. The city's prosperity was due to its location, sitting atop a network of hot springs and geysers, providing power for the city's industry and hot water for its citizens, but primarily just a way to lure unsuspecting visitors with the promise of a warm soak in the bath.

The streets were lined with towering buildings made entirely of glass and crystal, which would have been impressive if it wasn't for the fact that the trees blocked most of the view. The buildings were all different sizes, but they all shared the same ethereal quality, which was just another way of saying they were all the same. The city was illuminated by radiant lanterns that gave it an otherworldly glow at night but mostly just made it hard to see where you were going. The regular citizens were a mix of different races, united by their love for art and beauty as well as their devotion to their gods and goddesses, or just their love for money.

But as with most things in life, beneath the surface of this purported utopia, there were some darker secrets lurking. Powerful and dangerous people controlled the city from behind the scenes, manipulating its politics and religion for their own gain. The city was also known for its underground network of caves and tunnels, said to be home to ancient artifacts and forbidden knowledge, or, Tarnen reasoned, just a way to charge extra for "adventure tours."

Despite its dark side, or perhaps because of it, Larith remained a popular tourist destination for those seeking to worship their gods and goddesses or just to get their picture painted in front of the scenery. Tarnen mused that the city's motto must've been *Come for the temples, stay for the glass buildings*, because everywhere he looked, he saw signs stating the obviousness of the settlement's features, and it seemed to be enough to convince the common folk to cash in their hard-earned time and energy toward a rousing visit.

He much preferred the hustle and bustle of the capital city of Regis, where there was always something to do and someone to see. But there he was, stuck in Larith, surrounded by glittering shrines and see-through buildings, waiting for something to happen. He didn't even know what it *was* he was waiting for, only that Yeska had told him to be there, and Tarnen knew better than to question Yeska.

He leaned against the wall of one of the many temples that lined the streets—wondering if that would be considered rude to do but ultimately not caring one way or another. The temples were truly the most impressive part of the city, each one dedicated to a different god or goddess. It was said that there was no deity that couldn't be worshiped in Larith, though Tarnen imagined there was a lot of *could* and not enough *should* in that statement. The man couldn't help but think that if there were any gods or goddesses paying attention, they were probably rolling their eyes at the whole spectacle.

He found the whole thing a bit much, in fact. He didn't have much time for deviant celestials—including his own auspicious entity—and considered himself more of a "live and let live" kind of man. But he couldn't deny that the city was beautiful. The crystal buildings seemed to glow in the light of streetlamps, casting a warm orange light over everything, making it look like the city was on fire. But he doubted that was a good omen.

He knew that he was supposed to meet someone from the other side of their clandestine playing field, someone who could give him the information he needed to complete his mission. But he didn't know who it was or where to find them. It was all so frustrating. He wished he could be anywhere else but there, waiting for something to happen. Most of all, he longed to be in Regis, at his favorite spot, sipping a cold beer and not giving a damn about gods or goddesses.

The streets of Larith were beginning to fill with people, and Tarnen knew that he needed to be careful. For true, this place was a confluence for all things culty and religious, but it was also a city of secrets. He had heard stories of individuals angering the powerful and dangerous people who controlled the city from behind the scenes, never to be seen again. He knew that if he wasn't careful, he could end up dead or, worse, stuck in Larith forever.

He pushed himself away from the wall and began to make his way through the crowded streets, trying to avoid making eye contact with any of the raving religious zealots that seemed to be everywhere. His nights so far had been bland affairs, but he knew that he needed to be ready for anything. He was in Larith, after all, and anything could happen. Who knew; maybe he'd even find a temple he actually wanted to visit. But he doubted it. Even Sovereign's temple was a place reserved only for the most devoted nutbags in their order, and he thought to himself if he heard them call him *Most Beloved* another time, he'd turn the whole sanctuary into a den of sharp, icy spikes.

As he walked, Tarnen couldn't help but think again about all the things he could be doing right now if he was back in Regis. Getting drunker than his uncle Harick at his favorite pub, flirting with the barmaid, or maybe even getting a game of cards going with his mates. Hell, the man might have had the wild itch to take a stroll through the market, haggling with vendors for the best deals, or maybe even catching a play at the theater. But no, he was stuck here.

He was deep in thought, wondering if he had made the wrong choice in his life's pursuits, when he suddenly felt a cold arcane aura. Tarnen immediately prepared a Spell to cast, feeling the tingle of frost at the tip of his fingers, ready to unleash frozen hell on anyone in an instant. He scanned the streets, looking for the source of the aura, when he saw a pair of glowing blue eyes staring at him from the shadows of a backstreet. The glimmering irises followed him, and he heard a voice creep out into the street, sounding very far away.

"Tarnen," the voice said.

"Are you one of the Tides?" Tarnen asked, "Or perhaps just a sentient alleyway?" He didn't know what else to say but released a sigh. Not for the first time since huddling under Yeska's wing did he think to himself that this was not a situation he wanted to be in.

"Did the Yeska feel our presence? Our . . . breeze?"

Tarnen's mind immediately went back to the cold grip he had felt when he was with Yeska a few days earlier, before he came to Larith. The specter hadn't confirmed or denied its involvement, and it annoyed Tarnen that it seemed happy to resort to silly games in its communication.

"Are you . . . in league with . . ." Tarnen began, his suspicion growing. He tried to say the name, but it felt as though all of the air left his lungs in the attempt.

The shadow let out a bone-chilling laugh, still not confirming or denying its affiliation.

"All will eventually follow the Drifter," it said cryptically.

Tarnen felt a sense of unease at the mention of the Drifter. He knew that many feared the mysterious figure and the power they held. None knew if they were simply a true deity, a myth, or some kind of monster or devil. Any answer was still troubling, regardless of its validity. It took him a moment to summon an appropriate response, all while the blazing blue eyes observed him with intensity.

"Sovereign's light cannot be so easily dimmed," Tarnen finally said, though he heard his tone as it escaped his tongue. It sounded insincere or, worse, like a lie. He wouldn't have believed himself if the roles were reversed.

The shadow simply chuckled.

"I have seen the weak, fluttering candle flame of Sovereign go out before, and it will happen again," it said, its voice filled with a sense of knowing.

"I can sense, too, the doubt in your heart, *Most Beloved*," it added. Tarnen couldn't deny the truth in the shadow's words. They seemed to linger in the air, and Tarnen hated the mocking tone that went along with his title. It meant little to him, only that he was one of Yeska's favorite lackeys, but it still angered him to hear it spoken with such malice. Still, he was at a loss for words. He didn't know what to make of this strange figure or the cryptic message it had delivered.

"What have you come to say, specter?" Tarnen asked. "Are you here to swap information? Or was this simply a tactic designed to elicit fear? You have chosen the wrong person, if that is your intent."

He let more icy Arcana spread into his palm.

"I'm not easily scared off."

"You may quiet your discontent, *Beloved*," the shadow said. "I am simply here to inform you of the accord your master has struck. Mine own masters have agreed to the terms. Though only those that he specifically laid out. That is all."

Tarnen didn't know what Yeska had gotten himself into or what terms exactly he had formed a treaty or contract under, but he had a terrible feeling about the state of things. Hoping to learn a bit more information—something he never had any of when Yeska parceled out his orders—he used a more casual tone.

"So, I take it that things have advanced further concerning the Crossed?"

The shadow's eyes brightened at this, making Tarnen feel a sickening dread.

"Yes," it simply said. "But that is all I will say of this. Return to your master's lap, heeler dog, and relay this information. You may also be wise to inform him that we have begun to unlock the chalices. The Pylons you hold so dear and secret have been revealed to us. We will not move directly against your . . . Sovereign, but neither will we ignore the slights."

"Chalices?" Tarnen repeated, confused. He wasn't sure what any of those terms meant, least of all the Pylons it spoke of.

"Our mightiest and strongest," the shadow said. "You will understand in time. And when you do, you will regret that you ever doubted our power."

Tarnen couldn't help but roll his eyes at the shadow's cryptic words. They were . . . well, a bit cliché, weren't they? It was as though he was having a conversation with one of those recitation runes that all the kids obsessed over these days. Those damnable things, loaded up with interactive versions of classic tales of adventure. Though he had found that the more . . . scandalous ones certainly had an element of allure to them. He didn't know who or what the shadow was talking about, but he knew that he needed to get back to Yeska and tell him everything that had just happened. Then, perhaps, he could return to more serious affairs, like betting on the pit fights in Regis's Grand Station.

Feeling braver now, Tarnen adopted a smirk.

"I heard word about a recent capture—any truth to it?" he asked. "That your boy, Mandolin, got himself nabbed by the local town guard in some backwater burg. Must not be very capable if one of your strongest agents can be overtaken by a bunch of small-towners."

The shadow let out a hearty laugh.

"Mandolin is hardly more than a child. Neither one of our strongest nor one of our most efficient. Whatever happens to him is hardly of consequence," it said in a nonchalant tone. "The Tides abandoned him and his . . . *serpent* long ago."

The eyes flashed again, and the shadow took on a more serious timbre.

"The time is drawing near, and your Yeska should prepare all of his foot soldiers for what is to come," the shadow said.

Tarnen was just about to open his mouth and ask the shadow for clarification when it interrupted him.

"But don't worry; you'll find out soon enough," it added with a chuckle.

"Is there anything else, then, shadow, or am I simply to assume—"

In the middle of his sentence, the shadow suddenly vanished into thin air, leaving Tarnen standing there in the middle of the street looking like an idiot.

"Well, that was a waste of time," he grumbled to himself before looking over his shoulder awkwardly.

*I hope nobody saw that.*

Aggravated at having been out-last-worded, Tarnen began making his way back to the inn. He was frustrated. He knew he needed to get back and report to Yeska, but the thought of finding a Gateway specialist after the taverns had opened for the evening was not something he was looking forward to.

*I swear, if I have to listen to one more drunkard's tall tales about traveling through time, I'm gonna lose it,* he thought to himself.

As he walked, the "Most Beloved" thought about the woman he'd seen treating with the Yeska just a few weeks before everything began.

*At least we have* her *on our side,* he thought with a smirk, *I'm sure she'll be thrilled to know she's the only saving grace in this whole mess.*

Tarnen continued off into the night, his mind racing with dour, sarcastic comments and his stomach groaning for food. But all that could wait. For now, he knew that he had to focus on the task at hand and make his way back as quickly as possible before Yeska's wrath caught up with him.

# CHAPTER TWENTY-FIVE

# MEETING OF THE MINDS

*Alright, I need a bunch of information, and fast,* I said to Rexen through the mental connection of Commune.

*Ah, disciple mine,* Rexen said, still with his weirdly muted excitement. *What truths do you wish for me to unearth? Knowledge? Power? The perfect type of bread to bake when celebrating the death of a vanquished foe?*

*No—shut the fuck up, goddammit,* I said. *I need to know—*

*It's banana!* Rexen revealed, and I heard him make a groan of pleasure. *Some might tell you it's soda bread, but those people are fools. Banana bread reigns supreme in any—*

*Arjee, if you don't stop talking about bread, I'm going to wrap my hands around your tiny, vaporwave neck and strangle you. You're a ghost, so you won't die, but I'll bet you'll hate it.*

*On the contrary, dear pupil,* Rexen said delightedly. *I would enjoy that.*

*Ew! Jesus! Stop! Just focus for a second. This is not why I called this parlay. I need to know what Crowmoon—uh, the big guy over there in the doorway—was talking about earlier when he was going on with that Son of the Tides bullshit. What are they? And I need to know quickly, and without your . . . weird embellishments.*

*Ah, pupil. I am pleased to find your thirst for mastery so unquenched! Tide's Sons are just a small fraternity of fools and not worth wondering over. Go ahead with your next question.*

*What? Listen, Arjee. I dunno what they were in your time, but they've clearly grown to be something powerful in this . . . uh, modern era. Regardless of how tiny and stupid they were, I need to know what they were about.*

I heard something akin to a mental sigh and, gathering up all the patience I had inside me, decided to try as best as I could to not lose it right then and there. The raw, unfiltered shit I was constantly having poured over me was really beginning to take its toll. I'd kept my rage at bay nearly all night, but I couldn't waste it on this nonsense goblin. Plus, we were balls-deep into the bog of this bewildering battle and I needed answers.

Fortunately, Commune was built for someone like me who was prone to wild bursts of tangent. It apparently gave us as much time as we needed for as long as the magic could be summoned, and with Rexen Gravetongue, the Dreadnaught Lord, apparently that was endless. It made me wonder how long someone could reasonably remain in this sort of stasis without suffering serious burnout. Would they eventually go insane? Or, even more relevant, could someone strategize about something unendingly before busting out hot, mighty destruction? I could imagine how easily that could be abused, say, if someone did this before every fight. That seemed a bit . . . unfair. If I had access to it, then it's likely someone else might as well. Maybe even at a higher level than what we were able to do. I mean, Rexen was definitely powerful—he was the Dreadnaught Lord, right? He was famous. That had to mean something.

*They were silly,* Rexen finally stated, and his voice was much more sober-sounding now. Apparently, this tiny spirit was extremely inconvenienced with having to give me a direct answer to something for once. *They were formed around a belief that there are other worlds beyond this one. Not just things like the planes of Arcana and the in-between joints the celestial powers inhabit. Good old-fashioned regular spaces. Like this one but just different enough to qualify. Pretty foolish, right?*

*Uh, Arjee . . .*

*Yes, pupil?*

*You know I'm from another world, don't you? I thought we established that.*

*So you claim,* came the response. I could fucking *feel* the aneurysm forming when he said that, but I got myself reined in.

*Alright, fine. Whatever. But continue. They believed there were other worlds, but is that really enough to form a whole frat around? There's gotta be more, right?*

*If you can believe it: yes!*

*I believe it. Continue.*

*Well, I don't know all the particulars,* Rexen said, and I could hear the shrug in his tone. *It was very boring, see. Those kinds of groups usually are. The fact that they offered me membership was even funnier! Can you imagine? The great Rexen Dumpling Gravetongue rubbing shoulders with such a group of miscreant dumbos? Ha! Even when I had shoulders, they were far too precious to shimmy with those sorts.*

I sighed.

*As much as this is going to pain me . . . I need to know. Your middle name is Dumpling?*

*Yep! Gave it to myself! I love dumplings, so why shouldn't I show tribute to them in the most hallowed fashion possible? Now I am forever tied to my preferences!*

*That is very cool and not fuckin' bonkers at all, Arjee. Anyways, what else can you tell me about them? You said that wasn't all they believed.*

*Well, of course not. Crazies rarely stop at* one *belief, do they? Always adding layers of theorizing and hearsay until they've baked themselves into a spiderweb so complex and fragile that disproving one element of it causes the whole thing to collapse. These guys not only thought there were other worlds but* also *thought it was up to them to make contact with these alternate planes. And hoo boy, did that ever go badly.*

*What do you mean?*

*Well, pupil baby, it turns out that they were right! There are other worlds! And they contacted one. A real bad customer, too, turns out. Oof.*

*Wait a sec—Arjee, you were just saying they were stupid for thinking there were other worlds.*

*Yep!*

*So, don't you think that fuckin' saying that might make it sound like you believe there* aren't *other worlds?*

*I don't see the issue. Just because it was stupid doesn't mean they were incorrect. Even a broken Reticulating Arcane Cadence Gromit is correct once roughly every three hundred millennia.*

*Arjee . . .*

*Anyway! They opened something up they shouldn't have, and a bunch of* bad *started pouring out into our world. What a day! A real mess to clean up. Those imbeciles had broken the fabric of our system wide open, and it could have been a real conundrum were I not able to easily sort it using my incredible abilities and world-renowned plucky demeanor! Still, I had to cancel my lunch plans to resolve it—something that still haunts me.*

*Wait, wait, fuckin' wait, I said. They released something into this world? What was it?*

This was all starting to sound very familiar. Calden had told me about what had gone down with him and the others at . . . Ah, fuck, I couldn't remember the name of the town. But it involved Jes's girlfriend Delyra. Some kind of artifact that allowed creatures from another world to claw their way into this one and wreak havoc—killing Delyra in the process. Was that somehow connected to this?

*Oh, just some creatures. Nothing I couldn't handle—though I suppose I wasn't alone in the fight. Had some stout lads, lasses, and others kickin' up a fuss with me. Actually, I miss them. I wonder if any of them are still alive. Probably not, considering it's . . . Oh! Pupil. What year is it?*

Well, that was easy. Stinky had helpfully informed Calden, Frida, Jes, and the other time warriors they'd been in a chrono bubble for several hundred years. He'd said it was the year . . .

Ah, fuck. What had he said?

I tried to think back to the conversation, but the details were a little foggy. I couldn't remember if he'd said the exact year or just referenced time passing. A hundred and eighty? That sounded right. I definitely remembered it was a new Age, at least, and that they'd been in there since thirty-six-hundred . . . something. Close enough.

*You know, I'm not positive on the precise year, Arjee,* I said. *But I know a new Age started up around a hundred and eighty years ago—Geiger Dynasty, I think.*

*Oh! Geier got himself a dynasty then? Good for him.*

*Geier, that's it. You know him?*

*Probably not the current ruler-boy, but back where I'm from, Frask Geier was one of the Archons. Then, the last time I was woken up, I'd learned his descendants had become kings and queens a few times. Which is very swell. Geier's brood is a handsome crew. Nice hair. Bunch of teeth.*

I froze.

*Arjee, what do you mean, the last time you were woken up?*

*Silly pupil! You don't think you're the first to ever shake me outta that talisman, do you? Don't be such a jealous disciple! I've been called upon loads of times through the ages. Last time it was . . . Huh, what was the year? Sometime around thirty-eight-eighty. Yep!*

*Hold up! That doesn't make sense!*

*It makes perfect sense! I suppose if you're confused, it's because the new Age probably threw you off. We didn't go backward in time, silly pupil!*

*No, it's not that. But, when I showed up on the scene, apparently no one had been in your chamber of secrets in hundreds of years. I suppose it was possible someone entered after Jes, Frida, and the others had climbed inside, long before I went in. But still, I got you from inside the Crypt. So, did someone take you outta there and then bring you back? I mean, I don't blame them—you'd grate on anyone. But how does that work?*

*Oh, that's easy. For a good five hundred years or so, the talisman was kept by the family of one of my disciples. One of his great-great-granddaughters revived me, and we went on many an adventure before our tasks were finished. Then, when we were done, I sent myself back to the Crypt. See? Easy. Easy-peasy.*

This was blowing my mind.

*Okay, we can unpack all of that later, I guess—we're moving way too far away from my original question. These Sons of the Tides were able to open this . . . hole up in reality, and things started rampaging. Did this have anything to do with Void magic?*

*Probably! It's hard to remember. I just remember whipping their tailfeathers real good and still being able to make it back before dessert. Oh—but now that you mention it, I think I recall there being a similar incident back around when your not-enemies entered the Crypt. In Derika, I think. Maybe. Yes! No? Yes. Nasty business, that one. Of course, I'd suspect that if the Tide's Sons have gotten stronger since I last butted heads with their leader, then they could have been behind that as well. It's quite strange to see them still muckin' about, though.*

*The Tides did that, too?*

I had a terrible feeling in the pit of my stomach. Learning what I was up against was always a crushing blow, but in this particular instance—it seemed especially bad. There was a connection here, and I wasn't sure if I was qualified to marry the information together to form something even remotely sensible, but it was there. If the Tides were involved in this, and if Rexen's cement-mixed brain was capable of recounting details accurately . . . there was a much-bigger *something* going on.

*Possibly! I dunno, pupil—you sure do ask a lot of strange questions.*

*Well, I've got one more for you. Assuming all that information about the Tides is real—where does Crowmoon fit into all of this? Is he on some mission of theirs here in Tallrock and just happened to get caught?*

*Excellent question, I think,* Rexen said. *But no, probably not!*

*Explain.*

*Well, if he's part of the Tide's Sons, then he is acting weirder than even you, pupil. He knew who I was—not a surprise; I'm incredibly knowable, after all—but also wanted to become my disciple. Stupid. I'd never take a Tide's Son, and they'd never want me to join up with them. Glenny-boy hated my guts and probably still would—even though I don't have any! If one of their number were discovered to have been asking to take one of my coveted pupil positions . . . well, I'm sure they'd be in big-time trouble. To ribbons kind of trouble.*

*So, what? He's a fuckin' idiot? Or trying to find a way to take over the gang?*

*Iunno, he was probably banished from them and wants revenge. Horrible, engorged brute.*

*So, he got dropped from their roster and thought,* Oh, what luck *when he learned who you were? So . . . needless to say he probably doesn't have their backing, then. Makes more sense why he'd have been left to rot in a prison cell.*

*Yes, very good, pupil! The Tide's Sons would never allow one of their own to waste away in captivity. It would look stupid, and Glenny-boy hates lookin' like he doesn't know what's going on. Of course, that didn't stop me from beating him several times in the past, and he looked very dumb indeed! I fought him underwater once!*

Neat, I said cooly. *Listen—Crowmoon had someone trying to break him out of jail—well, successfully did so. It was also the reason this whole mess happened in the first place with the oomukade. You don't think that was them, tryin' to bust their baddie bro out?*

*Iunno,* Rexen said. *Maybe, maybe not. But unlikely. It would have been much more than just a single person—and they wouldn't have let him get out of hand like this. Nor would he have been able to keep coming after you like he has been! You must have really pissed him off!*

Yeah, I said, *he's claiming he was just trying to kill us for seeing his face or whatever. Seems like a really dumb, stereotypical villain move, but now he's cranked it up to eleven by definitely being seen by just about everyone.*

*Oh, I think he's trying to ride my coattails,* Rexen continued. *He thinks that if you die, I'll be forced to be his master. But I'm not bound to that! I can do whatever I want, including taking on more pupils! I made the rules, and I can and will change them whenever I feel like it. I just didn't take him up on it because I don't like him.*

That made me laugh.

*Well, in that case. What can we do to end this quickly and efficiently? I am really itchin' to get the fuck outta Dodge, but he's making it hella difficult.*

*Iunno,* Rexen said. *He's an Awakener, so he's probably got loads of Arcana in reserve, but he's all weak because of that limiter, so probably not as much as he's used to. I'd bet that you could exhaust him of his beautiful little Spells and then punch his lights out until he stops moving.*

*You really think so?*

*No, but that's about the only chance you have. Find a way to force him to use his Arcana up, and victory might be yours! Or death. Probably that one.*

*Wow, really filling me with confidence here, Arjee.*

*I'm not meant to build your confidence, pupil. You are meant to prove yourself as my disciple. Really impress me, you know? I want a show.*

*Well, you might get one—but not the one you want.*

*Any show is better than no show, pupil mine. I have been indisposed and I demand bloodshed to sate my crooked desires.*

*You are . . . really creepy, you know that?*

*Yep! I aspire to creep. It is something I am good at.*

Okay, then, I said. *I think I have enough information. Quick Q, though. Are you able to talk to anyone like this, or is it just me because of our fucked-up partnership?*

*You doubt my strength, disciple? Naughty, naughty pupil.*

*What? No. I'm trying to just figure out what you're able to pull off. Can you do it or not?*

*I can. None shall escape my chattiness.*

*Perfect. I have another favor to ask.*

I explained my idea to Rexen, who only spent about half the time I thought he would derailing me with ridiculous off-topic banter and lowbrow non sequitur. When I was done, though, he chuckled.

*You are an interesting pupil. I will be sad to see you go when you are invariably destroyed by the machinations of your own design.*

*Yeah, right back at you, Arjee. Everything make sense?*

*Yep!*

*Alright, then, let's fuckin' chop this shit up Loon-style.*

*Godspeed, pupil.*

I chuckled.

*Heh. I'm going to be going* way *faster than God.*

And with that, Commune was broken.

# CHAPTER TWENTY-SIX

# THRESHOLD FISTFIGHT

I'm what one might call a bit of a dipshit. I make poor choices, run my mouth, get slapped down, and *still*, after all that, usually come back for seconds. I am not the type of guy to let anyone get one over on me, *especially* when they are gettin' one over on me. I'm loud, ignorant, and really fuckin' angry all the goddamn time. However, one thing I am quite proficient in is chaos. I'm basically a human cataclysm. Well, I'm not a human, but whatever. I know a thing or two about causin' a ruckus is all I'm sayin'.

Because of that, I thought I had an avenue for serious mischief in my delivery. I'd given Rexen the instructions necessary to pull off what I planned, and as the world returned to normal, I glanced at the others in the group. One by one, each took on a faraway look, as if their minds suddenly wandered before returning a split second later, each looking at me in turn for confirmation. I just nodded. Rexen had done part one of what I'd requested, so now it was down to me to get the ball rolling on the fully automatic calamity that I was temporarily calling Project Absolute Pounding.

I took off at a naked sprint, watching my Stamina carefully as I did to make sure I'd be maximizing my potential. I beelined right for the cabin, where Crowmoon was still performing his dumb-as-shit snake dance. His arm kept a-slitherin' and it pissed me off, you know? It was almost like he was mocking us.

In the next seconds, I caught Rua's eye, and she tossed me two objects as I passed her, and I caught them. I didn't have anywhere to store them, so I simply stuffed them between my teeth and kept running.

Stinky reached him first, and I watched as he charged forward with the dagger, trying to slice Crowmoon into carrot sticks. However, the gesticulating juggernaut brought a foot up and kicked Stinky in the chest, sending him sprawling backward. The knife flew out of his hand and splashed in the stomach fluid, disappearing from view.

I was there a second later and hauled Stinky to his feet.

"Get your fuckin' mitts off me, orc!" Stinky roared. "I can climb to my feet unassisted!"

"Not t' time to be bashful, Shtinkshter!" I said, my mouth full. Then I let go of him and continued plowing forward. "I'm jusht f'exin' my shweet shkillsh!"

It was true. With Fatigue, Loon's Bombastic Beatdown—gifted from the god Sababo and cleverly named by me—brought my Strength, Dexterity, and Constitution way up—as well as my Health and Stamina by . . . osmosis? Maybe. Those Attributes getting better meant that even though no one had ever explained any of this shit to me, I'd discovered a correlation between them. Now I was using it to my benefit.

I wound up a fist and swung as I neared Crowmoon, connecting with nothing but air as he moved out of the way. I activated Enduring Perch for the first time since the belly-acid incident so that I wouldn't topple, and caught the description of the new features since the Ability advanced.

**Enduring Perch II—A Barbarian takes a readied stance that they cannot be moved from while their Stamina lasts. For the extent, their feet become rooted to their position, and while they can be hurt or killed, their feet cannot be wrested from where they plant them. With the Tier upgrade to II, the surface they root themselves to is no longer required to be ground or floor-aligned. Stamina exhausts at a rate of 5 points per second. Stamina must be at a minimum of twenty percent to activate Enduring Perch. If Stamina is exhausted during use, the user will suffer the Off-Balanced condition and be unable to activate again until Stamina is at maximum.**

*Ooh, baby. This is going to be fun.*

My excitement was short-lived, however, as Crowmoon's foot flew up and kicked me hard in the chest. Without thinking about it, I released Enduring Perch and was launched backward, directly into Stinky, and the both of us crashed hard into the liquid. I was glad I'd done that on instinct, considering even an offhanded kick from Crowmoon had chipped a decent chunk outta my Health. If I had kept the Ability active, it might have just blasted my torso off my leg stumps.

"Orc!" Stinky roared, as we both scrambled to our feet. "I'm gettin' sick of your antics. Learn how to take a fuckin' kick in a way that doesn't involve you bashing into me!"

"*Eat m' whole ash*, Shtinky," I said, fumbling the words through the objects in my teeth and pointing at Crowmoon. "You're really going to b'ame me for that one? Focush your pishy add'dude on dis dumb mo'erfucker, where it be'ongsh."

"I got plenty of piss for the likes of both of you, orc," Stinky said. "Stay out of my fuckin' way or we're both goners."

*That's right,* I thought. *Keep up the vitriol. All according to plan.*

The two of us converged on Crowmoon. Out of the corner of my eye, I could see Frida and Jes were still tangling with Rekka and performing well as a team. With the former exercising her gods-given right to be a complete badass—zipping through the air and striking more sections of the beast—the latter was focusing magical attacks in the areas he was being corralled into. I could also see that Jumpy, Clucky, Slappy, and Mortimer had joined the fight with the Elmer's paste serpent, looking as though they were working in tandem to bait and distract him.

Stinky suddenly went for Crowmoon's legs with a scissor kick while I chose a more direct, confrontational approach. I headbutted him.

It was a mistake.

It felt like I'd fallen ten feet onto my face, and my skull rang. I wasn't sure why I'd thought that was a good idea, but it was the first thing that came to mind. Now I was worried nothing would ever come to mind again. But, hey, I'd given it the ol' college try.

Stinky was able to come up for a scoop, wrestling with Crowmoon's legs with his full body. The Awakener fought against him, lifting him into the air with one leg raised and shaking him like he was a piece of tape that had gotten stuck to the underside of his foot. But Stinky held on, punching him in the thigh over and over. While he was off-balance, I recovered enough to attempt to grab his arms. However, Crowmoon used his snake moves to smack me in the face, and I slammed against the frame of the entrance hard. Then, with a great force of will, I pushed myself forward again and tried grabbing the big man's wrist. He elbowed me in the face, still on one leg as he shook Stinky.

"Ah, f'ck!" I roared, my teeth clenched.

"Doorway fight! Doorway fight!" I heard Rexen yell from somewhere behind us.

I aimed another swing at Crowmoon, but he ducked under it and slammed the side of his body into me with a hip check. This dude would have been one dangerous hula hooper. Then I heard a call from Rua and looked up as she stood in the liquid, Stinky's dagger in her hand.

"Shtinky!" I yelled. "Headsh'up!"

Rua hurled the blade in our direction—which, probably not the smartest move in most scenarios, but she called out as she did, and I watched the knife slowly propel itself to Stinky.

"Rearm Ally!" she yelled, and suddenly, the dagger was back in Stinky's hand.

*Oh, hell, yeah.*

Stinky jammed the blade into Crowmoon's calf, and the Awakener cried out, bringing his serpent hand down to blast the matau on the noggin. Stinky released his grip on the leg but not before he stabbed him again for good measure. For some reason, this had seemed to actually hurt Crowmoon, and there was a glimmer of hope for me that it was a harbinger of things to come.

With my matau companion drawing his attention, I finally spotted the opening I'd been waiting for since we got booted out there. I only needed the briefest of views of the inside of the cabin before I acted.

"Now!" I roared to Stinky, and we launched backward as one, then I finally tossed the object I'd been holding on to for the last ten minutes.

When I said I was a one-trick pony, I wasn't lying. Upon realizing the threat Crowmoon offered earlier, I had immediately gone to grab something out of the chest that might end up beneficial. Something I'd used before to great effect. However, after seeing Garth's clever use of the Behemoth Blade during our initial attempts to fling Crowmoon out of the doorway, a different idea had formed.

I watched as the bottle of Pepper's Hair Tonic soared toward the massive sword stuck into the floor of the cabin and crashed against it. I was taking a gamble in hoping this would qualify as something to be magnified, but I did not anticipate the reaction. The moment the glass shattered, the sword flashed, and suddenly, all I saw from within the cabin was hair. Like a time-lapse of a Chia Pet set at one hundred times normal speed, long, luxurious locks exploded outward in every direction, on everything inside. That included Crowmoon. He was suddenly wooly, the hair sprouting from every inch of him as he roared in confusion.

I'd pulled this move off only days before with Frey, to similar results, but this time, it was amplified from the Behemoth Blade's Channeling quality.

Crowmoon, however, wasn't able to yank at the hair as Frey had, because he was still forced to focus on his summoning maneuvers. I could see the furry lumps that were his arms moving around frantically as he tried to maintain his concentration despite hair likely coming out of his eyeballs and dick hole. But, man, credit where credit is due: that guy sure wasn't interested in losing his snake pet.

So, that's when I pulled the objects from my mouth, leveling one in particular at him, and released a roar.

"Brrreeeeeeee!" I pig-squealed as a blast of fire ejaculated out of the tip of the wand and hit Crowmoon square in the chest.

*FWOOM!*

He went up in flames instantly. One moment, he was some dumb, hairy shit for brains standing in the doorway of the cabin, and the next, he was a towering, furry inferno. But I wasn't done.

"Arjee!" I yelled, and watched as Crowmoon paused immediately. It was only for a fraction of a second, but that was the only other window I needed. I lined up the second wand and fired a crackling blast of lightning right into his face. It hit him but likely didn't do much damage. That was alright, though. That wasn't the point.

Rexen had done his part and used Commune on him. I didn't know what he'd said, but at the end of that momentary pause, the blast connected and Crowmoon stopped moving his arms as he reached up instinctively to try to protect his face.

Rekka disappeared, suddenly winking out of existence just as Frida was taking another aerial swipe at him. Seeing the beast had been sent back to whatever fart farm it had arrived from, she dropped to the ground in an exhausted heap.

I fired several more blasts from both wands, trying desperately to get Crowmoon to move, now that he'd been so overwhelmed, but he wasn't budging from the doorway. We could keep him there indefinitely, I supposed. But at what cost? He would eventually get himself in order, and then the real pain would likely begin. I was so fucking sick of this, though. Spending our entire evening trying to wrestle some idiot out of a house like he was a drunk numbskull at a party that just wouldn't leave was infuriating.

But that was just the thing, wasn't it? I'd been forcing down my anger and pain for days now, desperate to avoid the agony living inside of me and terrified of the hurt reflection would bring. But I wanted to end this fight and bring it to the conclusion, the closure, it needed. Crowmoon had been fucking around all goddamned night trying to kill me, and he wasn't going to stop. He was a pariah to his own people, and much like any bully I'd encountered in my life, he was hell-bent on trying to quench the shameful blaze tormenting him from within. But I wasn't a punching bag, and I wasn't going to make nice with whatever he thought was within his rights to pile onto me.

This wasn't the same as with Frey—he'd been a true monster. He'd killed my friends, wounded me, and tried to kidnap me. In that respect, Crowmoon's aim was pretty simple—laughably so. He'd wanted to end my life simply because he was afraid of being recognized. Then he'd come back because he'd been denied something he thought belonged to him. He was wrong, but it wasn't something I didn't understand. His motivations just weren't very . . . thematic. Almost lame. But he was strong and would continue to be an annoyance and a danger. Unless I did something. So, I made my decision.

"Arjee," I said, my resolve clear in my voice.

To his credit, the spirit didn't seem interested in messing around. His own voice was softer, more contemplative as he answered me inside my mind, and I was thankful for that. The world stopped for a moment as he used Commune.

*Yes, pupil?*

*Get ready to communicate if I start hollerin'. The plan's the same; I just might be going about it differently.*

Rexen was somewhere behind me, so I couldn't see his expression, but I could tell he was hesitating.

*Pupil,* he finally said. *This will sound strange—*

I sighed.

*I don't have time for strange,* I said. *Just get ready to—*

*You will listen, pupil,* Rexen snapped, and immediately I tensed up. Hearing the typically lackadaisical specter suddenly shift into an authoritative timbre really put me on edge. But . . . I listened.

*Good,* he continued. *This will sound strange, but I need you to do something.*

*Yes?*

*Eat the talisman.*

*What the fuck are you talking about?!*

*I did say it would sound strange. It appears you're going to attempt to do something foolish, and so I would like to ensure my own survival. Swallow the effigy, and do it quickly.*

*How is this supposed to help?*

*I'm running low on Arcana, so just be a good disciple and listen to your master. It will be necessary, okay? Do it.*

In most situations, you know ya boi would have argued his damn dick off about being asked to do something so weird. But Rexen Gravetongue was a damn . . . Thermopylae? Uma Thurman? Whatever; he was a damn witch ghost and had, despite his strange behavior, come in hyper clutch multiple times now. What did I have to lose at this point?

*You know what—fuck it. Gimme the fuckin' thing. I'll neck this noise, no prob.*

Commune suddenly ended and I felt something plop into my palm. I looked down. Rexen was next to me, smiling, and in my hand was the little wizard-tower figurine. It'd thought it was tiny before, but now knowing what he was requesting of me, it seemed like the largest object in existence.

But I don't balk. Just to show Rexen I wasn't afraid of anything anyone could suggest, I scooped up the trinket without another word, popped it into my mouth, and, with a tremendous amount of effort, choked it down in one go.

I immediately felt strange but didn't wait.

"Now you do your part," I said to Rexen. He nodded.

So, with that, I allowed myself to look at Frida and Jes. They huddled together, each checking on the other to make sure they were alright and not needing further healing. There was a bond there that I could imagine only existed between two individuals who'd been through pure hell together and seen the other side many times, a connection forged in the fire of strife. It was beautiful.

I looked at them—truly and deeply looked at them, and all that remained for them, which was . . . nothing. The leftover anguish from what I'd known was fully my responsibility washed over me. I let that feeling saturate my mind. I opened the portcullis of that which I'd been trying to hold back and *felt* the sorrow. I knew what I'd done. I'd gotten everyone killed.

I saw Dedyc's broken body, a kind soul with unlimited potential and talent ripped away in a flash. He hadn't deserved that fate. Not like that. He'd given me clothes after my resurrection, the clothing that was now gone because of my carelessness in my arrival. I saw Merra, the invisible blade striking her head and her body going rigid as she fell. I saw Calden . . .

In that moment, other images flickered into being, long cold from my expert avoidance of them anytime they'd rear their ugly head.

Mom. I hadn't seen her go, but I was there for the aftermath.

I'd only been trying to be helpful when Dad had called me, his usually angry tone transformed into pleasant politeness on the other end of the line. He'd called me buddy, like when I was really young. He'd joked with me. He'd made me laugh. Apologized for being "such a dick" and brought my guard down. At the end of the call, he'd asked where "Mom was staying now," and even though I knew I wasn't supposed to tell him . . . the way he'd been talking to me, so positive and upbeat, I was torn. I wanted him to have changed, for it to have been a misunderstanding, a dream. Things were going to be better, he'd said. Just from his voice, I knew they would.

I told him.

But all of that had been a lie. A manipulation, and I would forever live with that regret.

Roger had been the one to find her first, but I was right behind him. We'd gone to visit, and I was still flying high from my conversation with Dad. Things really *were* going to get better, I thought. But they'd only gotten worse. Because of me. Because I was too stupid, too naive to understand what I'd done before I'd ended the call. I'd invited the vampire into the house to feed.

I could still see the unusual angle of her neck, her chin turned up, her eyes still open, staring. Staring at me—what I'd done. Her arms, bruised, her shoulders bare and covered in welts. My beautiful mother was gone, replaced with this . . . thing. It wasn't her, surely.

It hadn't gotten better.

It hadn't gotten *better*.

And Dad had come back. Not long afterward. How he'd done it, I didn't know. But after that night . . . After we'd already lived through so much, after living hadn't even felt fucking worth it anymore. He'd come back. To do to us what he'd done to Mom. He'd gotten something else in return. Was it fucking worth it, Dad? For Roger, it hadn't been. I saw Roger then. Or all that I'd dared to. Feet trailing, inches from the floor . . .

It happened. The maelstrom of agony living in me was released.

I was the tempest, a raging storm. Fury boiled within me, a cauldron of molten lava, threatening to engulf me in its fiery embrace. It coursed through my veins, pumping through my heart and surging through my muscles. I welcomed it, embraced it, and let it take control. I let it consume me and delighted in it.

My vision dissolved into the red mist of fury, and the world around me became nothing but a blur of intention and destruction. Every sound was a deafening roar, like a thunderclap in my ears, every scent an intoxicating elixir fueling me. I was a beast, a predator, and nothing could stand in my way.

Crowmoon stood before me like a small boat in the midst of a tumultuous ocean, a mere obstacle that I would crush under the power wrapping itself around me. He would tremble in fear and horror at the spectacle of my unfettered ravaging.

I charged.

The world slowed down as I hurtled toward him, every step a symphony of violence.

The tempest had taken over. I launched myself at Crowmoon and into the entrance of the Sanctuary Cabin, my body a blur of motion—a bullet leaving the barrel of a gun.

I hit him, flames and all, and felt a glorious moment of resistance before we both crashed through the opening and onto the floor. Though the fire on him was still present, it had mostly died out. I sprang up instantly in the dim light of the cabin and glanced back at the group staring at me. Then I watched as Derelynd slowly lifted his hand and, with a final nod to me, closed his fist. The door of the cabin slammed closed, plunging the room into darkness.

But that was exactly what I wanted. I wheeled in place, rage still pounding like a war drum in my chest, and I smiled.

"Welcome," I hissed as my Darkvision activated. "You're in *my* house *now*."

# CHAPTER TWENTY-SEVEN

# RAINBOW IN THE DARK

**W**ithout anger, I was nothing but a leaf in the wind, pushed around by the forces of life. But with anger, I *was* the wind.

As soon as I'd uttered my threatening message, I pounced.

"This won't stop me, orc," Crowmoon said. "This space is far too small to offer a significant advan—"

I slammed right into the big idiot with all the grace of a coked-up wolverine. But Crowmoon wasn't having any of it. He grabbed me by the arms as I pounded my fists against him and chucked me across the room. I slammed into a magically constructed taxidermied animal head in a shower of wood, leather, and hair before crashing to the ground. I was surrounded by a forest of follicles from Pepper's Tonic and thought about how gross that was. It only further enraged my already fully engorged red rocket of fury.

"BIG M'STAKE!" I roared, my mouth filled again with the wands. I tore myself up from the ground and charged again through the prairie of hair, attempting to take advantage of the fact that he was still discombobulated and was looking in a different direction in the darkness—his body like a glowing homing beacon as the flames smoldered on his furry flesh.

*BOOM!*

He swept my legs out from underneath me as I approached, and I crashed to the ground. He flung a fist down, but it was too wide, and I was *just* able to roll to the side to avoid it before teetering back and grabbing his arm. I noticed his moves were slower, and fortunately, his strength seemed as though it was lessening. He punched me, but I used my Ring of Redoubt to activate Fortification. I'd double-checked before running into battle that it was still an item I could use. I'd only be able to do it once, on account of only having ninety Arcana to spare, so hopefully it would be worth it.

**Ring of Redoubt**
- **Rarity: Elusive**
- **Item Class: Ring**
- **Durability: 70/70**
- **Weight: N/A**
- **Defense: +3**
- **Bonuses: +3 to Constitution**
  - Casts Fortification Spell Charges: [3] Per Day

*A ring forged of High-Grade Yellow Hydris-Gold and imbued with defensive capabilities, the Ring of Redoubt is the surest method to protect you slightly from outside damage. Grants +3 to Defense and +3 to Constitution while the ring is worn. Additionally, this item allows the wearer to cast the Fortification Spell [3] times per day. Hope you weren't planning on a quick death! This will make your end nice and slow—so seize the day and enjoy the (final) moment!*

*Fortification*
- *Arcane Cost: 50 Arcana*
- *Casting Time: Instant*
- *Range: Self*
- *Duration: 30 seconds*
- *Restrictions: Material/Imbued Object*
- *Wait: 1 minute*

*A Spell that casts a protective barrier on the user. While active, this Spell will reinforce the user, dampening physical attacks by 30 percent. Additionally, any user-targeted magical attack effectiveness will be reduced by 10 percent. Finally, this Spell will grant a temporary boost to maximum Health. Outcome for efficiency is Constitution + Strength quotient.*

Though I felt the strike, it was reduced. It still fucking hurt, though, and I watched a *huge* portion of my Health take a dive. I had to reason that if he was Level Sixty-Eight, as advertised, I'd have basically exploded into confetti with a single hit. But the limiter in his body apparently made him far easier to manage. Plus, Rexen had indicated he'd continue to lose strength because as an Awakener, most of what he did relied on Arcana. This was only good news.

While he was still physically much, much stronger than me, I was hoping my menagerie of murderous maneuvers could help me outlast him, at the very least. But I wasn't so stupid that I thought I had a meaningful chance of taking him down with pure strength. However . . .

I held on to Crowmoon's arm as he jerked me up from the ground along with him, swinging at me. I moved my head out of the way—barely—as he blindly tried to hit me with a targeted attack. I felt I should let the ring do the bulk of the protecting as, even in my Primal Rage, I was able to remember that my stats were beefed up—even more so with the actual feature of my anger.

We battled like this for a little bit: Crowmoon slowing down considerably and me ramping the fuck up. My rage was unending, it seemed, and he quietly fought back in the blind void. I hit much more often than he did—but did far less damage. Nerfed or not, the Awakener's power far exceeded my own, and like a baby bird trying to fight against a *Kitty Hawk*–class supercarrier, I was going to need to get creative.

Crowmoon, getting frustrated, tossed me again, performing an overhead hurl that sent me spinning to the far wall again. However, there was a change.

Enduring Perch II had indicated I didn't need to be floor-aligned anymore to do my sticky step, and so, as I smashed against the wall again, I pressed my feet down flat against the vertical structure and activated the Ability.

It worked.

I stuck like goddamn Spider-man, or like whatever the fuck was happening with that baby in *Trainspotting*. I'd been able to do something similar before when I'd fought the CCM in the Crypt; however, that had been more of the fact that the platform I'd been on had been horizontal when I stepped on it initially. This was just me, out here bein' Miley.

I stood up.

"Nice t'y, fuck-a-duck!" I roared. "But you'll haff t—UGH!"

So, funny story—one thing they don't show in all these badass Marvel films or what have you is that *gravity be a motherfucker*. I'd lifted myself triumphantly to stare at my attacker while standing functionally congruent with the floor of the cottage, but I wasn't anticipating the weight, and my knees immediately buckled, causing me to pendulum-slam right into the wall beneath me with the back of my head with my feet still perfectly fixed to the wall.

Crowmoon—more in tune with his senses, I guess—flashed forward, following my sound easily. Goddammit, I had to stop making mistakes that caused me to not be badass as fuck all the damn time. I released Enduring Perch and crumpled to the ground just as the big bitch full of muscles blasted a fist into the wood. This was becoming lemon-difficult very quickly.

It had only been a few moments, but I was learning a fatal flaw in my plan, and I forced myself out of Primal Rage with only a few seconds remaining. I felt as though I'd achieved my goal of wearing him down just a touch, and now it was on to bigger and better things like winning.

I still had a trauma hangover and was able to push the bad thoughts back down to enjoy later. Instead, I said a prayer to St. Dio in thanks for my incorrigible Acrobat Skill as I artfully dodged Crowmoon's foot with a sexy somersault.

He whirled and tried to diving-elbow-drop me like he was Macho Man, but I had my wand in my hand and blasted that boob between the eyes with a fireball. This threw him off his game and he careened to the side, body-slamming a coffee table in the process.

Look, I dunno if it was actually a coffee table, but it was a little wooden stand that someone could definitely use for a nice, calm morning sip.

"Oof!" he shouted, and rolled onto his back in the debris with a grin.

"I have to say, orc, that was genuinely well craft—"

*FWOOM!*

Another fireball to the face, then lightning. Then I followed up the one-two combo by dashing away through the tall grass—uh, hair—to the other side of the chamber.

"Running, orc?" he called. "I thought we were finally beginning to play!"

I watched him do a kip-up—the *exact same* style of Jean-Claude Van Damme chicanery I had done earlier in front of him. Worst was—he was better at it than I was. What a dick. This would not stand. I turned to my quarry: the haladie, still sticking out of the wall where I'd left it.

*Missed you, bro,* I thought to my double-bladed constant companion. Then, as I saw Crowmoon vaulting in my general direction, I wrist-snapped my biting boomerang his way and leaped in a wide arc to the side. Crowmoon smacked the haladie out of the air, but I think it actually got him, because he winced and I saw blood. But that was all in an instant, because I was already flying through the air and firing like I was in a John Woo adaptation of *The Wizards of Waverly Place.*

"Brrreee! Brrreee! Brrreee! Brrreee!" I hit him with the ol' jingle-jangle one after the other and slammed into the ground rolling, and was back on my feet in an instant, firing blindly behind me as I rushed for the fireplace.

"Take that, ya freak bitch!" I howled.

Then I saw a bright flash of blue behind me and oh, fucking goddamn, you better believe I hit the dirt just as a blast flew overhead and splashed against the furry wall. That side of the room instantly ignited, and I was hit with a wall of smoke and the choking stench of burnt hair.

I hopped up, and so began our *dance.* Back and forth we went, me shooting him with fireballs and lightning bolts, and Crowmoon blasting blue flames at me. I slunk though the hair like a prowling wildcat, cracking off blasts when I knew he wasn't looking and racking up quite a substantial amount of sneak-attack notifications. Like, I was really puttin' the punish on him as his reactions got slower and slower.

I dodged another of his attacks, and I began an army crawl in the opposite direction but felt a tug on my ankles as Crowmoon suddenly grabbed me and shook me like he was airing out a bedsheet. The move caused me to slam my head against the rafters and I saw stars. But it was clear that despite his capability in forcing me to do the aerial worm, his power was dwindling. The collision hurt, but it wasn't any worse than what I'd already been enduring.

"Foot-snatcher!" I yelled, but Crowmoon let go of me, attempting to let me tumble. I wasn't gonna just *let it happen*, though. *Noo*, no. I shifted as I fell so that I was facing him and kicked him donkey-style right in the chest. Except, when that happened, I activated Enduring Perch. The soles of my feet latched into place like he was my favorite pair of snowshoes. So, there I was, a six-foot-four-inch spotted, *naked* orc attached by the feet to the muscley pecs of a man so big, he was basically a chimney with teeth, all while the room continued to burn around us. I smiled down at him.

"BR'BRREEE!" I squealed with the verbal equivalent of a double tap, blasting him with two quick wand snipes from point-blank range.

Then I released my Ability and tried something I'd never done before—not really. I attempted a backflip. Using *Snow*moon as my launching pad, I kicked off and pivoted, hoping to Zeol and Sababo that I wouldn't just do three-fourths of the move and totally wreck my shit.

I landed in a patch of hair right in front of Crowmoon with surprise.

"Holy fuckin' shit!" I cheered. "I just did a godda—"

Crowmoon grabbed me around the waist and flipped me upside down, planning to deliver a stone-cold pile driver. That would have been bad. Fortunately—even though I hadn't checked—Luck had to be on my side. He'd lifted me a little too high since he couldn't see that well, and I felt my tootsies brush against one of the rafters. Predictably, I did the thing. Enduring Perch was active, and Crowmoon began trying to twist me free. So, I yanked the party hat from the back of my neck and snapped it atop my head and let the goo fly. Crowmoon almost instantly slid down my body, crashing to the ground. That's when I noticed he was next to my haladie.

*Well, shit, that could have been awesome if he'd been just a hair to the left.*

Instead, I waited for him to rise and then released, performing a front flip this time and landing in a crouch. Crowmoon was right in front of the door and started off toward it.

*Holy shit!* I thought. *I have an actual, really good idea!*

"ALLEY-OOP!" I roared, but poured the action into Blackout Warchant.

The blast erupted from my throat, and I saw Crowmoon turn, his eyes finding me in the blaze. I slid forward and grabbed the haladie. Then I sent it spinning right at his legs. The big man leaped into the air to avoid the obvious attack, and that was all I needed. He could resist me if he was rooted to the ground, but as I'd seen, this motherfucker was just as subject to physics as any of the rest of us schmucks.

Time seemed to slow as I watched my plan of action grab a foothold. My Blackout Warchant had hit precisely where I wanted it to: the door of the Sanctuary Cabin. Opening wide, it revealed a diminutive, neon form floating on the other side. Rexen. I shifted and brought my shoulder to the side just as the Great and Powerful Gravetongue summoned me to him, bringing me directly into the path of Crowmoon at a speed *faster than God.*

*BOOM!*

We collided, and my ultimate shoulder check hit him right in the solar plexus with a driving force that would have made a bullet train jealous. We flew out of the entrance together and landed in a now-much-deeper lake of stomach acid than before. I could tell the pus sacs had begun to burst and the place was filling up pretty quickly. We'd need to get out of there *fast!*

But before I could even untangle myself properly, Crowmoon grabbed me by the throat and hauled me up, his body trembling with the effort.

"You . . ." He grimaced, barely getting the word out. "You're going to . . . die!"

There was a charge of energy around him, and I saw the blue light of what I could only assume to be a supernova grab-your-ball-and-go-home game-ender magic power. I still hadn't seen it at work yet and would have been interested to observe it—you know, from afar and not having it used on me.

I couldn't do anything. I tried to wrench myself free, but Crowmoon's grip was tight. I wasn't sure how Rexen's recall Ability worked, but I had to imagine there was a cooldown period, and as he'd just done it, it was probably still out of bounds. Plus, it would likely have just dragged Crowmoon along, still choking me. The last time, his grip wasn't nearly this tight. But I wasn't ready to die. He could kill me, but I'd find a way back and—

"Displace!"

Then, in a blink, I was staring down at Rua. Her hand was wrapped around my throat and I felt the lurch as we both suddenly tumbled to the stomach acid, burning us where we landed. I shot up just in time to see Crowmoon confusedly fire a solid stream of blinding blue energy into the upper wall of the stomach, burning through it and out to the dark night above. He'd fucking *carved* a tunnel straight through the oomukade queen!

I glanced at Rua. She smirked sheepishly. She'd saved me with her badass switcheroo maneuver!

"I could kiss you!" I shouted into her stunned face, but she waved me away.

"Oh, uh, you're welcome. Though . . . you're not my type," she said, and I watched her eyes flick toward Frida.

"Too late, pal," I said. "When this is done, you're going to be on the receiving end of my business smoo—"

*BOOM!*

The entire stomach shook so hard, we all fell into the burning acid again. The pain was bad, but it was nothing compared to the horror of Crowmoon.

He was *furious*. Part of me really enjoyed seeing him like that, since he'd spent most of our interactions grinning like a dumb fuckin' pool stick. The other part of me was suddenly concerned I was about to vaporized. He stood, glaring, the blue energy gathering around him spookily as he pointed a finger at me. That was irritating.

"You dumb son of a suck!" I said—pointing right back; how 'bout? "You don't even have a proper villain motivation! '*You saw my face*'? Really? That's your whole reason for starting bullshit? I'd call you a clown, but you're not even ironically funny enough, considering you're too pathetic to even be a *joke*. Just some egotistical infant that gives flocks of birds the bad touch; pissed off that I got a sweet, shiny master and all you got was kicked out of the loser's bracket of your semi-pro dick-scratching league! Do your worst, fuckface. You're garbage—no, you're worse than regular trash—you're dumpster piss. I'm going to—"

"*Rebuff!*"

I was hurled dozens of feet away as the spot I'd just occupied erupted in blue napalm. I landed hard in the spot where the Sanctuary Cabin once was—realizing that Darryl must have finally let it evaporate. But that wasn't what surprised me. It was the Spell. Jes's Spell. The fragile-looking elf stood not far from where I'd been, and despite the fact that his splinted arms left his hands constantly in the air, I could tell by the way one twisted that he'd just saved my life. His eyes were on me, and I noticed a glimmer of sadness in them.

*Was that . . . remorse?*

**Congratulations! You have raised a Skill!**
***Insight [E-Rank Level 5]!***

However, then Jes's eyes hardened and he turned to Crowmoon.

"You're one of the Sons of the Tides," the elf said severely. It wasn't a question.

Crowmoon scowled, apparently just discovering that I'd been rescued and wheeling to look around for me.

"I have business with the Tides I would very much like to resolve," Jes continued, no less terrifying in his proclamation. "I had thought it strange when I felt a connection to that dark void—here of all places. My soul rings with it still, even after my life was saved. I know you have that connection too."

*What's he talking about?* I wondered. *Oh.*

Calden's story. He'd told me that Jes had been mortally wounded by the creatures that had crossed over from whatever plane they originally came from. He'd lived because of Delyra, but she'd died because of it. Was there some connection he could *feel*?

"I am not a Tide any longer," Crowmoon said, finally seeming to notice Jes. "Your grievances aren't with me, elf."

"Oh," Jes said, and all I could hear, as his voice dropped even lower in pitch than usual, was truly frightening malice. "I believe my grievances are safely where they need to be."

He dropped his head and snarled.

"Frida," he said.

There was a flash as a brilliant spectacle of light erupted overhead and the heavily armored Guardian exploded into action, flying right at Crowmoon, her ax screaming through the air as she roared, her entire countenance a storm cloud. Just as Crowmoon made to swipe at her, she disappeared from view using Blinkstep and then reappeared a fraction of a second below him, crouched low and leveling an upward strike. Crowmoon noticed it as the last second and was only able to just barely keep his head out of the way, but the crystal blossom at the crest of the Wing of the Golden Phoenix blazed across his chest, tearing a large gash open in the process.

He backed up, throwing a hand out to stop another one of her attacks as she Blinkstepped again to his opposite side. However, Crowmoon seemed prepared for that. He ducked under her swing, and hit Frida in the torso with a punch that probably could have cracked granite under normal circumstances.

The Guardian stumbled backward but didn't seem injured enough to give up just yet. That was when everyone else present charged him all at once. Stinky was there, dagger in hand as he darted around the sides Frida wasn't occupying, stabbing out at Crowmoon with an exacting preciseness. Jes lobbed spheres of golden fire at the bastard, some connecting while others hissed harmlessly in the stomach acid before dispersing. Rua had once again discovered the Behemoth Blade—left behind in the wake of the cabin's unsummoning—and was using it to get jabs in where she could from a safe distance. Darryl had his palm open, a flickering flame fluttering inside of it as a face I didn't recognize appeared within. Was he . . . making a phone call?

Even the roe were in on the action, zipping past Crowmoon in their aerial-configuration bounces as they used their razor teeth to bite and distract him.

Well. I couldn't let them have all the fun, could I?

No, no I couldn't.

I sloshed forward, ignoring the burning around my thighs as I'm sure everyone else was, seeing the Acidic Burns I notification appear in the air as I made my way to join the fray.

Just as I reached the ass-paddlin' storm thundering down on Crowmoon, he seemed to see an opening and rolled away from the group. He shot up, his hand striking out and sparking with blue fire. Right at the back of Frida's head.

*No . . .*

Images of all the dead I'd seen began to bubble up in my vision, repeating what had already unlocked my rage, dashing along my mind like a ribbon of cinematic film. Mom's waxy, bruised skin and sightless eyes. Roger's feet inches from the ground. Dedyc's mangled body. Merra's slumping body. Calden's headless corpse. Virgil's smile as he dissolved into mist. Garth's body filled with spikes. Crowmoon's palm behind Frida's head. Mom. Roger. Dedyc. Merra. Calden. Virgil. Garth. Mom. Roger. Dedyc. Merra. Calden. Virgil. Garth. Mom-Roger-Dedyc-Merra-Calden-Virgil-Garth.

Dad.

I felt the white-hot explosion of panic as I reached out, hopeless to stop it. Screaming out for someone, anyone to help. Someone did.

***Okay!***

**Pact Boon [Imprint]**
**Imprint Connection: Jailbreak**

Unlike any other time I'd seen a notification, this one didn't appear in front of me spatially; it was as though it was part of my vision itself—or maybe my mind. Time had slowed, and suddenly, I could see a symbol I'd not seen in a few days: the mushroom cloud that had been the harbinger of my Sabotage Ability, though now it had something like a crest behind it with an eye emblazoned over top. It overlay my vision as I moved, as though my mind was suddenly divided. A lock appeared over the symbol in front of me and more words flooded my brain.

**Jailbreak Fixation: Eye of the Saboteur**
**Duration: Temporary**

The words flickered suddenly, as if a virus had corrupted them, the letters swimming around in my mind becoming garbled and fractured. The lock on the mushroom-cloud eye crumbled as if it were shattered with a great force, and suddenly, my Ability activated in frozen time.

Crowmoon's body was now covered in markers, much like anytime I used Eye of the Saboteur on an object. But . . . was that what was happening? Had this been unlocked to use against . . . against *people?* I saw his areas of strength indicated by blue in most areas of his body, but there were some red markers as well, indicating weaknesses, fragility . . . areas that could be destroyed. His details spilled out as well, and I realized I was looking at his *character sheet.*

*Erasmus Rafaelen*
**Race: Half-Kindler, Half-Human**
**Class: Barrener [Awakener Path]**
**Level: 68 [Limited]**
**Profession: Unassigned**
**Health: 138 / 2,450 [Limited]**
**Arcana: 238 / 5,365 [Limited]**
**Max Stamina: 670 [Limited]**
**Reputation: Despised**
***Current Settlement Reputation: Tallrock [Kill on Sight]**

*Sodality*
**Assignment: Sons of the Tides**
**Order Rank: Mandolin [Exiled]**

*Attributes*
**Strength: 80 [Limited]**
**Constitution: 131 [Limited]**
**Dexterity: 76 [Limited]**
**Wisdom: 49 [Limited]**
**Intelligence: 50 [Limited]**
**Charisma: 102 [Limited]**
**Luck: 12**

*Holy shit! I can see his whole fuckin' recipe!*
There wasn't time to ruminate on all of this; I had one job. I focused on the weak point near his wrist and elbow and reached out for both, jerking them in opposite directions with all of my strength. Then I slammed my foot down on the side of his knee, where the biggest red flash was.

The world sped back up and Crowmoon screamed.

His blast flew wild to the right as he crumpled into the acid. Frida spun quickly, bringing her ax around to slice right into Crowmoon's face. Stinky was there, bringing the noise and jamming his dagger right into the big man's chest. He coughed momentarily and then fell farther into the acid, completely submerged.

*Is he . . . dead?*

"Fuck! This fuckin' burns!" Stinky suddenly erupted. "We've gotta get out of this fuckin' cesspool!"

There was a round of nods as everyone glanced up at the new oomukade skylight Crowmoon had remodeled for us. That was when we saw *faces.*

"Oh, fuck, now what?" I wondered aloud. "Actually—fuck it. Cowabunga it is. Bring it on, you rat bastar—oh."

Floating down from the hole were several individuals I recognized.

First to touch down was the blobby behind of Edwig Quintham, smirking as he glanced at all of us.

"Wow, *real* nice," I said. "Weird how you suddenly turn up *right* when we flipped the switch on this guy!"

"Pah! Quiet yourself, orc! I'm concentrating on floating!"

"Yeah, just like a turd would say," I muttered, but focused on the others entering the stomach.

Orville followed Edwig, and he seemed extremely nervous to be descending by invisible magic, frequently jerking in place as if worried he was losing his balance.

However, the next person to arrive was wholly surprising: Garth.

"Garth!" Frida and I exclaimed at the same time. The little guy gave us a wave.

"Hey-o," he said as he hovered in, motioning flapping his arms in place. "Turns out I'm not just a nisen, I'm also part bird."

"How'd you get here so fast?" I asked.

"Oh, that," he said with a shrug. "I set my Anchor to Tallrock ages ago. I kind of like it here, y'know? They haven't run me off yet, neither."

*Yeah,* I thought. *But he was gone for what, forty minutes? Is that how quickly we respawn?*

The tiny creature suddenly caught sight of Rua and smiled wide.

"There you have it," he said to her. "Told you we'd be celebrating on the backs of our foes, m'dear. But bugger me bald, mate, I forgot the plonk! Ah, well, suppose a drink can wait. I did bring *this* though, for you."

He tossed me a mess of balled-up cloth. I caught it and raised my eyebrow, before examining it with my now super-muted Eye of the Saboteur.

**Sojourner Garments**
- **Rarity: Pedestrian [Exotic]**
- **Item Class: Clothing**
- **Durability: 10/10**
- **Weight: 0.3 lbs**
- **Bonus: Ha ha ha ha! Oh, seriously?**

*The ultimate in fashion for the newly arrived traveler. The Sojourner Garments are perfect for those who have recently plopped in or returned from shedding their crooked mortal shame and seek to blend in with the local peasantry. Made from the finest khaki and tan fabrics, these garments are lightweight and airy, ensuring that you'll stay cool while looking like a complete idiot. But don't worry; at least you'll be comfortable in your own ignorance.*

*Goddammit. Is this what happens when you die? You get more retiree streetwear?*

I unfurled the fabric onion and stared confusedly. They were small. *His* size.

"Uh . . ." I said, looking from the wrinkled clothing to him, back to my own substantial frame.

"Christ, it's all I had time to grab," he said, rolling his eyes. "You'd reckon a bloke'd be a bit more appreciative to not be butt-naked and polka-dotted. I mean, mate—you're hanging out."

I looked down at the bundle of clothing and shrugged.

"Whatever," I said, and began pulling the shirt and pants on, hearing the ripping noises as I did so. When I was done, I sighed. I could only get one button fastened on the shirt, and the pants were basically Daisy Dukes, but at least my twig and berries were sheathed.

I noticed that the stomach liquid was now no longer burning us, and the sacs had stopped filling and popping. That was probably indicative of the overall health and longevity of the oomamakade.

"What's with the new 'do?" Garth asked, still floating alongside Newbie and Jigglepuss.

"Huh?" I asked. "Whatcha mean?"

"What am I on about? This bloke here," Garth said shaking his head. "I'm sayin' you look like you're in a bit of a grunge phase."

I looked at the others, but they all seemed to be staring back at me with expressions that definitely gave me cause for concern.

"Guys . . ."

Frida, wincing, held up her helmet so that I could get a good look at myself.

"Before ye go aff yer heid, ken it actually looks fetching on ye."

I stared back at my reflection in horror. Regardless of the ridiculous costume I was currently in that made me look like a big green sausage bursting out of its skin, the real travesty was sitting atop my head.

For starters, it was standing up like I was a cartoon character that had just been electrocuted. But what was worse was that its color was a bright, unwholesome, gradient of neon pinks, blues, and purples. Nearly identical to the scheme of hues Rexen was rocking. I scowled as I saw that this new look also stretched to my eyebrow hair.

"Arjee!" I roared, and saw the little ghost witch float into view.

"Hello, pupil mi—"

"Oh, no, you don't!" I shouted. "You can cut that shit out, you terrorist! You may have saved me back there, but that doesn't excuse . . . whatever the fuck this is!"

"Sorry!" Rexen said, shrugging his shoulders. "I don't know what you're referring to. Wait—were you the one I had that unicorn pubic hair delivered to? I can explain—"

"What the fuck are you talking about?!" I shouted. "Actually, I don't want to know; that sounds like a conversation between you and the law. I'm talking about this, *man!*"

I jabbed a finger up at my hair and grimaced.

"This is a fuckin' hate crime! I look like a My Little Pony Super Saiyan!"

"Oh, pipe the fuck down, you miserable doorknob!" Stinky exclaimed. "It could have ended up a lot fuckin' worse! Speaking of— Booger boy, give us a hoist."

Edwig shook his head.

"Pah! I'll take everyone *but* you, matau. I should zap you into little yellow pieces."

"It's going to take more than you to have a fuckin' shot at taking me out, you heap of fuckin' gutter slag!"

*Aw. They just met and are already getting along so well.*

"What do we do with him?" Rua finally spoke, indicating the spot where Crowmoon lay in the muck.

"Don't stress; we rang the heat. They'll be here in a jiffy," Garth said. "The Warder's here too, to . . . I dunno. S'pose to scoop up this bloke and chuck 'im in the wagon?"

"Wait—so, how long is this going to last, Arjee? I didn't sign up for—"

*FWOOM!*

From the liquid where Crowmoon had been, a blast of blue *fucking* fire arced out and shot straight at me.

*Oh, you've got to be kidding m—*

The eggs, ever vigilant, sprang into action, trying to shield me from the attack.

*NO!*

Fortunately, I was able to scoop them into my arms and insulate them from the flames just as they hit me.

"Fuuuuuuuuuuuuuu—" I roared.

The magic blue super fireball sent us right through the membrane of the stomach and soaring in an arc. Up and up we went, my body stuck to the blast with the force of its inertia. The eggs chittered in terror.

*Die! Dying! No! We're doomed!*

I couldn't do anything except be carried along, feeling my skin burn. Far below I could see a huge crowd of onlookers had formed—and it looked to be almost everyone from Tallrock was in attendance to watch my mostly-naked-and-screaming ass toodle-oo across the cosmos like a shitty ancient myth brought to life. Except instead of some super hunk carting a celestial object along a path through the sky—it was a fully automatic, taupe-bedecked dipshit clutching four large, sentient pink pearls and trying not to fucking die.

Worse, though, was that the pain and exhaustion from being up all night fighting horrors that just turned out to be spoiled brats had started to get to me. With a gasp, I saw my Stamina dip into the red well before my Health did. But it was too late. The eggs were freaking out; I was freaking out. Rexen was cackling with glee as we continued soaring.

Then, when I couldn't handle any more, my back burning with the searing agony of my rapid rise to popularity, my Stamina dropped to zero and all the lights went out.

# CHAPTER TWENTY-EIGHT

# OH, NO . . .

I woke up with a start, my head pounding and my body aching. It took me a moment to realize that I was lying in a bed, covered in blankets. The room was dimly lit, and I could see a figure loitering near my bedside.

As my eyes adjusted to the light, shapes began to become clear. I recognized the Muppet-sized form of Rexen. He was drifting right by my face, and the sudden realization startled me enough that I reared back defensively. But that just created a whole new set of problems. I felt an intense pain blossom in my neck and shoulders, making me forget the previous intense and oppressive torment that I'd woken up to.

"Ah! Fuck!" I roared, trying desperately to grab control over the torturous sensation tunneling its way through me like an angry, chain-smoking groundhog that just dropped its last cigarette in a puddle.

"Welcome back, my beautiful little pupil-baby," Rexen said in his cheerful, dreamy voice. "What a dazzling spectrum of feats you achieved. I'm very impressed. You are, once again, an excellent disciple."

I tried to sit up, but a fresh wave of dizzying agony washed over me and I fell back onto the pillow.

"Unwise," Rexen said, hovering closer to rest a tiny, staticky hand on my shoulder. "You are healing from wounds, pupil. Also, you are fat."

"What?!" I roared, and then winced because that hurt to do as well.

"I said you are fat," he announced again, smiling all the while. "The healers said you were too heavy for the bed, so they reinforced it to account for your substantial weight. They had to bring in a specialist."

"A specialist? I fuckin' dare you to make less sense, Arjee."

"Yep," the spirit continued, completely oblivious to anything other than whatever the fuck he was talking about. "He entered, hammered woods, broke other woods, then needed to get his special tools—for fat people."

I closed my eyes and took a deep breath, trying to steady myself and not immediately use powerful physical violence on the aggravating specter. Memories flooded back to me suddenly. The battle in the belly, the sanctuary shoot-out, pinwheeling through the air after taking Crowmoon's money shot right in the back. Then I remembered the last few seconds right before I'd passed out, and I couldn't help but to unload a long string of expletives. That whole thing had fucking sucked.

"What the hell happened?" I asked, my voice barely above a whisper.

Rexen's eyes widened in devilish jubilation.

"Ooh! A great many things! I found this!"

He held up a tiny cluster of . . . lint? Mold? Whatever the hell it was, I couldn't tell. Something that—knowing Rexen—was either bafflingly useful or completely inconsequential.

"What . . . is that?" I said through gritted teeth.

"Iunno," Rexen said with way too much wonder. "It looks like it belongs in a belly button. Here—"

He released it from his palm and let it land on my chest.

"Put this outside; perhaps it will find its way home."

"Arjee . . ." I said warningly. "I'm laid up in a gurney, all beat to shit. I can't *go* outside. When I asked what happened, I wasn't talking about this goddamn mushy nothing!"

"Touchy pupil today," Rexen said admonishingly. "Why ya full o' mopes?"

"Come closer so I can punch you," I said. "Tell me what happened or I'm going to leave your talisman in a toilet."

Where it was currently being housed, that was an eventuality anyway.

"When you fell asleep during your trip, I became bored. So, I summoned you to me—out of harm's way. Then we fell. But it took me a moment to figure out your curious Aegis. When I did, we were only several feet from the ground. I think it scared the roe."

"Are they alright?!" I shouted, but Rexen put up a little arm to silence me.

"Alive, pupil," he said. "You must be calm. Especially because a bird hit you on the way down and it may have scrambled your noggin."

"What?"

"Ah, see?" Rexen said, tutting. "A shame."

"No . . ." I started, getting control of myself. "I mean with the bird."

"Oh, yes," Rexen said sadly. "Unfortunately, it exploded on impact."

I let my head fall to the pillow.

"Just fuckin' great. Now I kill birds."

"And bedframes."

"Not helpful, Arjee."

"So you say," he muttered.

*Was that . . . sass?*

"Is everyone alright?" I asked, looking around at the room and noticing all the other beds were empty.

"Ah, yes, your . . . *squad* is all accounted for," he continued. "That was the bully-boy's last hurrah. The one you call Stinky apparently leaped upon him immediately and stabbed him until he cried."

I chuckled at that, perhaps too hard. It was a relief to know everyone was fine.

"Then the lovely, beautiful, *ravishing* captain arrived—atop a *turtle* no less—and escorted everyone away from the giant creature's corpse. Then the Warder appeared and took the bully-boy. He cried again. Did you know the Warder was friends with the sanctuary creator? The gray one? Summoned him somehow. They left together. In any case, the sultry, *sexy* captain sorted it all out well and good. I'd let her *sort* me out were I—"

"Easy there—keep it in your pants, Arjee," I said, my smirk still plastered to my face. "So, the captain made it too? Man, this is turning out to be quite the happy ending."

"Not all is happy,"

My heart sank.

"Goddammit, Arjee, who died?"

"No one," he said. "But the Quest . . . she was failed."

I scowled.

"Oh, well, *shit*, dude, I don't give a fuck about that— Actually, wait. Wasn't the oomukade queen destroyed?"

"Yep!"

". . . well, then *how did the mission not succeed?*"

"Oh! Pupil, you were asleep for that part; I had forgotten. It is because the city sustained damage to more than eighty-percent of its structures. Quite the mess out there."

"At least the mending house is fine . . ." I said, glancing around again.

"Hey . . ." I said, unsure how to approach the next bit. Rexen floated closer to me.

"Yes, pupil mine?"

"What was that thing that you did—you know, in the stomach—with the . . . uh, jailbreaking?"

"Oh! *You* did that, pupil. Very proud master moment on my part."

"Yeah, but, uh, didn't I get that from you?"

"Yep! But you were the vessel that used it. That was simply sharing a bit of what I know," Rexen said with a big grin. "I told you I could show you how to break the system."

"Yeah . . ." I said, letting my mind wander. "You did."

I tried to adjust myself, but it appeared that anytime I moved, I was racked with intense pain. But that got me thinking.

"Wait?" I said, and Rexen gave me a pointed look.

"How come I'm still all injured? Shouldn't I have been healed once I Leveled up? I mean, there's no way I didn't rack up a bunch of fuckin' Experience from a . . . well, from an *experience* like that one. I did a buncha stuff!"

Rexen shook his head.

"You did not Level yourself, silly disciple," he said.

"Why the fuck not? And *on* that note—why haven't I been able to since I got to this town? Is there lead paint in the walls or something keeping the magic WiFi from reaching us?"

I opened my menu and saw that everything was still the same. Scrolling through, though, I could—true to my grief—see I had an overabundance of Experience but was still sitting at Level Ten. I mean . . . it was a *whole* lot of the stuff.

**Experience**
**38,005 / 23,000 to Level 11**

"Ah! Pupil," Rexen said. "I see, I see. You're not just fat—you are also stupid."

"Alright, I'm not a huge fan of this dynamic," I said, swatting at him. "Come over here so I can kick the shit out of you. It would make your beautiful disciple feel better."

"It is only because you have not chosen your Subclass, silly pupil," Rexen continued. "The rules in place state that you need to select your new specialization at Level Ten, and if you do not, you will not advance further—despite continuing to gain Experience. Pesky."

"Well, why the fuck hadn't anyone told me that?!" I roared, kicking up a fuss and making my body hurt all the more.

"Because no one tells someone something they should already know," Rexen said.

"Fuck if they don't!" I said. "It's called mansplaining—and in most cases, it's considered a dick move. But, if I'm being honest, I could go for a bit of mansplaining right about now. Nobody tells me fuckin' boo about this convoluted horseshit, and I just wanna *learn*, ya know?"

"I doubt anyone else relishes the opportunity," Rexen said, nodding sagely.

"And what, pray tell, is that supposed to fuckin' mean, Arjee?" I demanded. "You're acting like I'm some sort of intellectual outcast."

"You receive news poorly," Rexen continued. "Good or bad, it doesn't matter. You treat everything as if it is inconvenient to hear."

I paused, ironically ready to immediately assault him with my opinion but deciding to hold off to not prove his point for him.

"I . . . see . . ." I said, gritting my teeth. "And . . . this . . . is . . . something . . . that . . . people . . . do . . . not . . . like, is it?"

"Even when attempting to be mannerful, you are terrible at it, pupil. Be yourself if you cannot pretend to be polite."

"Can you just tell me how to choose my Subclass, already?" I demanded. "I can't be stuck at Level Ten for the rest of my handsome days—I'll be ridiculed. I was already a late bloomer with puberty, so come on, man!"

"First, pupil," Rexen said, "you will need to assign your Points. Afterward, the process will start automatically."

I scowled into his spiral eyes.

"I mean, I *know* I'm supposed to use them up, but I was waiting on Frida! She was going to give me pointers."

"It is best, pupil, if you do this on your own—or better yet, let me assist you. Put everything into Charisma!"

"Yeah, if it's all the same to you, Arjee, I think I'd rather stick my dick in a toaster."

"Suit yourself," he said. "But I am here if you require help—especially with that nasty toaster business."

I rolled my eyes and opened my menu, realizing that I hadn't peeped my deets in a long-ass time. I cast a . . . mostly discerning eye over the offerings and began to sort through the information—surprised by some of my findings.

Unarmed Fighting and the Acrobat Skill had both gone up by two Level Ranks, while my Throwing Weapons Skill had finally increased by one. Wanderlust I had gone up to Wanderlust II as well.

There were others of note, but I wanted to get it over with and stop being an underdeveloped fetus in the system. So, I pushed forward to continue. I found the appropriate area, and seeing as I still had twelve Points to distribute, set about to allocation.

So, taking the plunge, I decided to keep a good mindset going. I put six Points into Constitution, two Points into Wisdom, and the remaining four into Charisma. That brought both Wisdom and Charisma to a nice even ten, while Constitution rested at a *very* healthy thirty-eight. I'd actually forgotten what had transpired previously when I'd done this. But, I . . . instantly remembered the second the change happened. Really wish I'd thought to, like, grab something to bite down on or, like, a puke bucket or *something*.

Once more, like the last time I'd brought an Attribute to ten, agony enveloped me. It was like a surprise party in my muscles, except the surprise was *knives*. I shouted bloody murder because apparently, I'm not a fan of overwhelming excruciation washing over me, leaving me unable to do anything but scream. It felt like my body and brain were suddenly having a heated debate, with my body saying, "Let's be on fire!" and my brain saying, "No, let's make it icy!" A consuming sear, like a wormy, blazing elemental, filled my veins. It burrowed into my bones and blood vessels with a searing fuck blossom, like someone was trying to light a barbecue inside me. I felt my brain writhing inside my skull, trying to escape. Also, someone had apparently left the back door open, as hundreds of wasps had suddenly been let loose inside my soul—because why not, let's make it a party.

Then, equally as similar as last time, the pain suddenly vanished.

I sat upright and tugged the sheets off my legs as Rexen regarded me carefully.

"Milestone?" he asked.

"Milestone . . ." I breathed.

It took a few minutes to dare to go forward with the rest of the whole endeavor, but I decided it didn't make sense to hold off. I'd already shortchanged myself by waiting so long, and delaying it any more would have qualified as a kink.

So, with nothing to do for it, I opened my Menu back up and let the prompts hit me.

**Congratulations! Having successfully attained Level 10, you can now choose a Subclass!**

*Bear in mind that your Subclass offerings will be determined by what might best suit you to pursue within the confines of your base Class. Every action you have taken up until this point will have been an influential trigger for these ultimate results. Review them, and choose carefully, because you cannot take it back.*

**Your list of [3] available Subclasses is ready for review.**

**Feral Stalker**

**This subclass is for the Barbarian who wants to trade in their traditional loincloth for some camouflage and a pair of binoculars. These stealthy Barbarians are experts in blending in with the wilderness, using their Sneaking Skill to stalk and ambush their enemies. They gain access to abilities that**

allow them to move more quietly than a mouse on a yoga mat, hide more effectively than a chameleon in a candy dish, and strike from the shadows like an assassin with a beef jerky addiction.

*Class Bonuses*

• Silent Hunter—The Barbarian gains a bonus to Sneaking and Perception when in natural environments, allowing them to move and spot their enemies more easily.

  ○ +10% Sneaking when in natural environments

  ○ +10% Perception when in natural environments

  ○ +1 to Dexterity

  ○ +1 to Wisdom

• Void Strike—The Barbarian can now perform a special attack that deals extra damage and has a chance to stun the target if they are attacking stealthily or from a hidden location.

• Wilderness Expert—The Barbarian gains further proficiency in the Survival-aligned Skills such as Tracking, Trapping, and Foraging.

  ○ Gain Tracking Skill

  ○ Gain Trapping Skill

  ○ Gain Foraging Skill

## Berserker Juggernaut

This subclass is for the Barbarian who wants to take their anger-management issues out for a joy ride. These rage-filled monsters harness their Primal Rage to become a nearly unstoppable force in battle. They gain increased Strength and Constitution as well as Abilities that allow them to shrug off damage like it's just a pesky fly and continue fighting even when injured, like a zombie with a personal trainer.

*Class Bonuses*

• Unstoppable Force—The Barbarian's Primal Rage further increases their Strength and Constitution as well as granting them temporary Health and resistance to physical damage.

  ○ +1 to Strength

  ○ +1 to Constitution

  ○ +5% Damage Reduction when under the effects of Primal Rage

  ○ Gain [50] additional Health Points when under the effects of Primal Rage.

• Rage Regeneration—This Ability also grants the user increased regenerative capabilities, allowing them to heal faster during combat.

  ○ +10% Healing when under the effects of Primal Rage

- Primal Instigation—The user can now perform a special Ability that enrages nearby enemies, causing them to focus their attacks on the Barbarian and granting them temporary bonuses to attack and defense.
    - +30 to Attack when under the effects of Primal Instigation for [30] seconds
    - +30 to Defense when under the effects of Primal Instigation for [30] seconds.

Savage Beastmaster

This subclass is for the Barbarian who wants to bring their love for animals to the battlefield. These individuals focus on their connection to the wild, allowing them to tame and command beasts to fight alongside them. They gain access to Abilities that allow them to summon and control wild animals, and can even gain bonuses to their attacks when fighting alongside them, like a circus ringmaster with a bloodlust.

*Class Bonuses*

- Wild Companion—You can now tame and command wild animals to fight alongside you in battle.
- Pack Tactics—You gain bonuses to Attack and Defense when fighting alongside your Wild Companions.
    - +10% Attack effectiveness when Wild Companion is within radius
    - +10% Defense effectiveness when Wild Companion is within radius
    - +1 to Intelligence
    - +1 to Wisdom
- Call of the Wild—You can now summon different types of wild animals depending on the needs of the situation, such as a bear for defense, a wolf for tracking, or a bird for scouting.

"*Oh*, mama," I said with a euphoric quiver. "Daddy likes *this* setup. Daddy likes this setup a *whole* mess."

I read through all the options again, smirking as I did so and daydreaming about how powerful I was about to become, and how messed-up everyone else was soon to get. But, as always, the wet-blanket parade had to sashay around the corner at some point, and that's exactly what it did in Rexen.

"Oh!" he said, apparently looking at . . . exactly what I was looking at. "Not precisely what I had in mind!"

He waved his arms around.

"Allow me to fix this mistake, pupil—as you should be rewarded for your efforts."

"Wait, what are you—"

However, suddenly, a new option appeared alongside the other three. This one was definitely . . . different and seemed more in league with where my specifications had been going. Though it didn't have the same sort of . . . je ne sais quoi as the others, I could definitely see what Rexen was referring to.


**Primitive Underminer**

**For the Barbarian who wants to add a little bit of finesse to their usual brute-force approach. Think of it as a way to sneak up on your enemies, give them a little tap on the shoulder, and say "Boo!" while they're not looking. These deadly pranksters are experts in infiltration, sabotage, hit-and-run tactics, and demolition, using their skills to weaken the enemy's defenses and create opportunities for their allies to strike. They can infiltrate enemy camps undetected, dismantle their structures and equipment, and make their fortress walls crumble like cookies. They are the ultimate magicians, striking fast and hard, then disappearing into the wilderness. Outsmart your enemies and leave them scratching their heads . . . if they still have them!**

*Class Bonuses*

**• Infiltration—The Barbarian gains Ranks in Infiltration and Deception Skills, allowing them to infiltrate enemy camps and strongholds undetected.**

**• +1 to Intelligence**

**• +1 to Dexterity**

**• Gain Knowledge [Infiltration] Skill**

**o Gain Deception Skill**

**• Sabotage—The barbarian can now understand how to perform tasks that can weaken or disable enemy structures and equipment, such as cutting rope bridges, damaging siege engines, or poisoning water supplies.**

**o Gain Knowledge [Sabotage] Skill**

**o Sneaking Skill increased by [5] Level Ranks**

**• Demolitions—Gain Knowledge in the use of explosives and can now use them to create powerful explosions and destroy enemy fortifications.**

**o Gain Knowledge [Ignition] Skill**


I frowned.

"I mean . . . yeah, it's alright—but some of those other features were way more badass than these ones. I like the idea of being the thing in the night people fear, but also, I want to *rage*, goddammit. If you're so special and greasy on the system, can't you . . . I dunno, like, combine some of these for a custom Subclass or something?"

Rexen stared at me.

"Ah, man, did I say something stupid again?"

He slowly shook his head, never taking his eyes off of me.

"Just the opposite *of*, my gorgeous, brilliant disciple!" Rexen beamed. "I like that big brain of yours. Can I smell it sometime?"

"How about you just be satisfied with explaining why I'm such a sexy genius?" I offered.

"Yes, okay, that is fair," Rexen said, waving his arms again. "I think I can do that—though I haven't done anything of this level in a while. It'll be fun practice for parties!"

I shrugged. I never knew what this deranged psychopath was talking about. But, just a flea's dick of time later, I had an answer.

"Behold!" Rexen exclaimed, sending the new prompt my way. "A master-piece is born! Crafted from the esteemed expertise of one Rexen Tulip Tulip Tulip Gravetongue—"

I scoffed. He'd changed his middle name again.

"—I present to you, my darling pupil: the perfect Subclass."

I read it over. Then I did it again. I couldn't stop myself from smiling, even though I fought it from creeping across my face.

*Goddamn, you really* did *do it, Rex.*


**Frenzied Saboteur**

**Boy, oh, boy, what a regular old Subclass this happens to be! Yep! Just onc to ignore, in fact; almost no one would ever think of picking this one because it's so . . . ordinary. I suppose if you had to describe it, you might consider referring to it as the perfect fit for a wonderfully scheming stu-dent of the greatest Arcane master of all time. However, you could also most pointedly not do that and just skip right over it.**

*Class Bonuses*

**• Inciter—Time to be one with the riot. So strange how these seem to be full of Skills and Abilities at first glance, isn't it? But then you realize it's actually just a regular old description that doesn't deserve a single secondary glance. Carry on!**

    ○ **+1 to Intelligence**

    ○ **+1 to Dexterity**

    ○ **Gain Knowledge [Infiltration] Skill**

    ○ **Gain Deception Skill**

- o Gain Knowledge [Ignition] Skill
- o Gain Knowledge [Sabotage] Skill
- o Sneaking Skill increased by [5] Level Ranks
- **Super Berserking**—Your Primal Rage is a shroud of unstoppable madness.
    - o +1 to Strength
    - o +1 to Constitution
    - o +5% Damage Reduction when under the effects of Primal Rage
    - o Gain [50] additional Health Points when under the effects of Primal Rage
    - o +10% Healing when under the effects of Primal Rage
    - o +30 to Attack when under the effects of Primal Instigation for [30] seconds
    - o +30 to Defense when under the effects of Primal Instigation for [30] seconds
- **Friendship Strategy**—Friends are wonderful! Non-Humanoid Companions are even better.
    - o +11% Attack effectiveness when Non-Human Companion is within radius
    - o +11% Defense effectiveness when Non-Human Companion is within radius
    - o +1 to Intelligence
    - o +1 to Wisdom
    - o Gain Nightfall Strike Ability

I gawked.

"Uh . . . Arjee?"

"Yes, pupil?"

"First of all: nice fucking work. But second—you can't really think this will fool the system, do you? I mean, it's broken as fuck and screams foul play. You're comfortable with that?"

Rexen shrugged.

"Iunno," he said. "I'm a notorious cheat. Let's see what we can get away with, disciple!"

Honestly, I *hoped* it hurt the system. Fuck that thing, thinking it was so cool . . . and stuff. It wasn't. In fact, it was the *exact opposite* of cool. It was dorky. And I didn't care if it was busted all up and down Overpowered Boulevard—I wanted a win. For once in my fucking life, I wanted to grab the world by the stubbies and yank it into submission. It seemed like Rexen was aiming to be my ticket to the stars.

I clicked yes on the Frenzied Saboteur and watched the screen fill with all of my illegal mods.

**Congratulations! You have selected a Subclass!**
**Frenzied Saboteur (Barbarian Path)**

Then another notification rolled in on that one's heels.

**Congratulations! You have reached LEVEL TWELVE.**
*You grow stronger and receive the benefit of [6] additional Attribute Points. 20% Health and Arcana restored. Combat conditions healed.*

*Well, well, well. Look who's back on the top of his game. It's me. I am the big dog.*
I quickly allocated my Points. Two more in Strength and Dexterity each to make them fifteen, as well as one in Constitution to drop it at a *beautiful* forty—with the Ring of Redoubt helping, of course—and another single Point in Charisma, which became eleven. Then I looked upon my character sheet with awe. I were really doin' this shit, weren't I?

*Loon*
**Race: Orc***
**Class: Frenzied Saboteur (Barbarian Path)**
**Level: 12**
**Profession: Unassigned**
**Health: 550 / 550**
**Arcana: 115 / 115**
**Max Stamina: 233**
**Reputation: Untested**
***Current Settlement Reputation: Tallrock [Neutral]**

*Sodality*
**Assignment: Cult of the Capricious**
**Cult Rank: Initiate**

*Pacts*
**Rexen Gravetongue**

*Attributes*
**Remaining Points to Allocate: None**
**Strength: 15**

Constitution: 40 (+3 Ring of Redoubt)
Dexterity: 15
Wisdom: 11
Intelligence: 12
Charisma: 11
Luck: 15*

*Skills*
- Acrobat (E-Rank Level 3)
- Camp (F-Rank Level 1)
- Deception (F-Rank Level 1)
- Hunting (F-Rank Level 1)
- Improvised Weapon (E-Rank Level 3)
- Improvised Shield (F-Rank Level 3)
- Insight (E-Rank Level 5)
- Intimidate (F-Rank Level 2)
- Knowledge [Nature] (F-Rank Level 1)
- Knowledge [Infiltration] (F-Rank Level 1)
- Knowledge [Ignition] (F-Rank Level 1)
- Knowledge [Sabotage] (F-Rank Level 1)
- Leadership (F-Rank Level 3)
- One-Handed Weapons (F-Rank Level 3)
- Perception (F-Rank Level 4)
- Simple Weapon Proficiency (F-Rank Level 6)
- Simple Armor Proficiency (F-Rank Level 1)
- Sneaking (B-Rank Level 9)
- Swimming (F-Rank Level 1)
- Survival (F-Rank Level 1)
- Two-Handed Weapons (F-Rank Level 6)
- Throwing Weapons (E-Rank Level 1)
- Unarmed Fighting (E-Rank Level 5)

*Active Abilities*
- Armorless Defense (E-Rank Level 9)
- Battle Born I
- Darkvision I
- Enduring Perch II
- Eye of the Saboteur I
- Primal Rage (E-Rank Level 2)
- Pernicious Volley I

- Natural Resilience (F-Rank Level 2)
- Nightfall Strike I
- Super Berserking I
- Uncommon Consumption (F-Rank Level 1)
- Warchant I
- Blackout Warchant

*Passive Abilities*
- Friendship Strategy
- Inciter
- Outsider
- Unfaltering
- Wildling

*Perks*
- Adventurous Tastes (First Perk Bonus)
- Aegis Synthesis

*Aegis*
- Calden's Hang Time
- Loon's Bombastic Beatdown

*Boons*
- Bone Warrior
- Imprint

*Esper Nodes*
- Emerald: 3
- Sapphire: 2
- Topaz: 1

I gave Rexen a thumbs-up motion and settled back into my bed. I couldn't lie; it felt good to see those stats. I sort of understood the allure of a place like this now. Having valuable information at your beck and call—beckon call? *Having info at your command* to sort through and improve with quantitative calculations behind it was an excellent fucking hand to be dealt. Especially when you had an ancient spirit sorcerer looking under the table at the cards. I gotta say, despite everything that had gone down in the last handful of days, I was feeling particularly Gucci about the whole thing.

"Hey, Arjee," I said, suddenly curious as to something that had been itching at the back of my mind.

"Yes, pupil?"

"Why are you called the Dreadnaught Lord? I mean, yeah, you're pretty cool, I'll admit—for an annoying ghost, anyway—but that is like . . . a name with some *oomph*, you know?"

"Ah, disciple," Rexen stated serenely. "It is simple. I call myself that because it is meant to inspire fear, but it is a private joke. I designed the nickname myself as a way of secretly relaying to others that, should one encounter me, I am *naught* to dread."

I groaned.

After another day of rest and relax—uh, recuperation—I was ready to leave the mending manor, or whatever; I set about trying to get a handle on what exactly the state of affairs was in Tallrock. It was interesting to me that now that I was known as part of the crew that helped defend the town, the cityfolk treated me pretty well! Actually . . . I guess they sort of just . . . tolerated my presence, but believe you me, that was a huge improvement over "Untrusted." Now I was "Neutral." I'd take it. Some even considered me something of a hero. Granted, it was mostly children who half the time seemed to think I was part-hobgoblin or a big tadpole or something, and also, they quickly moved on after getting bored, but still. As I'd said at the outset of the first evening—I'd change their minds. I think there were even some heroic poses thrown in, too, for good measure.

Don't mind me; just participated in the small matter of *saving the whole fuckin' town* from certain doom at the hands of a giant, man-eating centipede. No big whoop, right?

Tallrock was in shambles, with not a single building left untouched by the oomukade rampage. The others had spent the next few days hauling debris, patching up roofs, and generally making the place habitable again—despite being exhausted. It had been a communal effort. Well, you know, except for me. I had been wrapped up like a mummy and snoozing away my troubles on Easy Street. But based on everyone's accounts, it was *quite* the workout. With everyone pitching in, after only a few days, they'd even managed to turn the place from a disaster relief area to a functioning village once more. Well, mostly.

I spent some time reconnecting with the homies, mostly Rua and Edwig. The former had made it very clear that we should get back to her homebase as soon as possible, and the latter mostly avoided being in the public eye. Which . . . was fuckin' weird.

Jes and Frida had apparently led the charge in assisting with the rebuilding—which meant Jes supervised while Frida did the lion's share of the actual physical labor. They'd been too busy to chat much, but there was a night where the group of us got together at a tavern after a long day and got *fucking drunk*. It was my first real taste of other-world alcohol, and since the legal drinking age in the Kingdom of Arlo was *birth*, I didn't even have to sneakily sip it from under my coat. Though, because of the rebuilding, the swill wasn't nearly as rich in variety as it should have been, according to Orville.

Speaking of Orville, I'd also wanted to meet his friend Bonnie, just to thank her for her brief appearance in my general presence, but by the time I even remembered she existed, I'd been informed she'd went off to wherever it is cryptids go. I'm sure *that* wasn't something worth noting. Right?

Stinky . . . well, Stinky was up to something, though I wasn't sure what that something was. Yeah, he helped, and even made a name for himself when he pulled an old man out of a chimney, but he was surly about it—which goes without saying. I didn't talk to him much, either, over the few days, as he seemed intent on avoiding me. You know, like a dick.

I also got the real spiel on the inner workings of the city from Garth. He'd been happy to have someone to talk to about "Sojourner shit" in me and Rua, and was clearly pretty satisfied with life in the moderately sized medieval city. Enough so that he didn't feel the need to come along and meet the others at Rua's base camp—at least not until the rebuilding got sorted. Though, he did promise some Australian life debt that he'd come visit once things calmed down a bit in the city. I knew very little about the nisen's home country, but it absolutely seemed like the kind of thing they would legally mandate.

Oh, and surprise, the captain didn't try to arrest us after the whole fiasco. That was a relief, though she did give us dirty looks every time she saw us out in the streets. Rexen kept trying to send her gifts, but since I told him she lived in a hut in the nearby swamp . . . I don't think they ever got delivered.

Eventually, though, it was time to leave the city. We'd dragged our feet—well, mostly me—because I wanted to see if I could convince Jes, Frida, and maybe even Stinky to tag along. Unfortunately, it was not to be.

Jes and Frida, out of their own timeline as they were, still had business to settle. They needed to find Virgil, for one, who was out there somewhere . . . bein' a cowboy, I guess. Second on the list was to return to their homes and see what was left, or if they had any ancestors that needed their ears slapped or whatever. I understood. It was likely a lot had changed in nearly five hundred years, so they had to get their bearings. However, it wasn't without its silver lining: Frida had confirmed that once they'd gotten all that shit squared away, they'd come find us. I mean, after all, there were still friends to revive. They took Merra's amulet with them, though. Jes seemed to have forgiven me for my errors—insofar as he didn't blame me for the others' deaths—at least, not completely. I wasn't sure if I could give myself that much credit, but I was willing to take the wins where I had them. Frida and I spent the last day before they left just browsing the city, exploring and having a good time. It was bittersweet to know that they'd be leaving, but I'd hopefully see them again. That was it, though; I kept my unwarranted affections to myself.

Stinky's excuse was shittier. He was leaving to join back up with the Redmark—a name shared with Jes's former college, but I didn't think about asking about that connection before they'd left. I'd subtly suggested he abandon them, but he was pretty resolute in his refusal—and only tried to stab me three times—once successfully, during the conversation. Eventually, he too dusted off down the old winding trail, leaving me, Rua, the egg boys, and apparently a *very* eager Edwig to make the plans to head off.

Before we left, though, Edwig had needed to stop by Yosper Hall to pick up some belongings. He'd urged us to swing by the place—which turned out to be the gigantic fucking palace-like building that loomed over the whole town. He was acting weird about it the whole time, and the only indicator that he'd even had a connection there was when we arrived. He'd thrown the doors open and loudly bellowed, "I'm back, baby!"

Of course, this was short-lived, as several minutes later, he'd flown out the door with a pack over his shoulder and the sound of angry voices following him, merely shouting to us, "C'mon, we gotta go! Go, go, go!"

And so, we bid farewell to the city of Tallrock. Its towering walls and weird-ass turtle-riding guards would be sorely missed, but alas, our journey had to continue. Rua, Edwig, Rexen, the roe, and I set out into the forest, our packs heavy with provisions and our spirits higher than the writer's room of a John C. Reilly movie. See? That's what you call topical humor.

The forest beyond the city was dense and the path was winding, but we pressed on, determined to get the fuck back. I'll admit I was nervous. Ever since the curly-haired lady had commissioned me to rescue Rua, I'd been thinking about what would happen when I got back. And side note—I still wasn't sure what the fuck was up with that lady. I mean, I'd started to suss it out, but it was still a mystery. Like, why not just grab Rua herself? Why not help fight off the oomukade? Why the heavy winter clothes? It essentially boiled down to one factor—it was beyond me. I'm sure there was some malicious machination lying in wait I'd eventually encounter, but for now, I was just happy to have a clear goal that didn't involve being chased.

We encountered a few obstacles along the way, such as a particularly stubborn bush that seemed to have a vendetta against us, and a river that was more mud than water that Edwig seemed to take affront to in a way that seemed almost *personal*. But we persevered.

And so, the next two days were much the same. Rua, with her bizarre and inexplicable navigation abilities, led us through the wilderness, with the rest of our absolutely bonkers posse following closely behind. I have to admit I was starting to get a bit restless. Not only was the journey becoming monotonous, but I was also learning just how boring Edwig's life at Yosper Hall actually was. I mean, who actually gives a fuck about the intricacies of parchment-making?

Finally, after what felt like an eternity of trudging through the underbrush, we emerged from the forest onto a stretch of hillside. The trees thinned out there, and we could see for miles in every direction. The sun was setting, casting the landscape in a cozy, warm light. We set up camp, and as we sat around the fire, I started getting really impatient. It had officially been the longest amount of time I'd gone in Regaia without someone trying to knife my soft parts, and I think I was waiting for the other shoe to drop. When we lay down to rest, I watched an inky cloud of smoke drift lazily across the night sky. I'd been tired, so my attention was only partially focused on it, but I knew it was . . . odd. Something felt off about it, but I didn't know what. We slept, and the next day, Rua let us know that we weren't much farther from the end of our little journey.

She fuckin' lied. It took the better part of the day to get close to where we'd been led to believe the encampment was, and by the time it actually came to pass, I was exhausted and pissed off. I'd finally managed to get some new threads—and, more importantly, boots—but unfortunately, the clothes chafed my skin and the boots gave me blisters. I ended up finishing our march completely barefoot. I guess some things never change.

But, as we crested a far hill, Rua announced that we had finally reached our destination. The headquarters of the Sojourners, the place that had become something of a safe haven. Well, except for Rua described it as a nightmare of sleepless, unending horror upon their arrival. I had to admit a part of me was relieved. So far, my leg of the field trip had been awful, filled with danger and death-defying ordeals, but the thought of finally being around others who had gone through similar trials was . . . comforting.

As we made our way down the hill, I couldn't help but take in the breathtaking view. The land was lush and verdant, with tall trees reaching toward the sky. A sparkling river wound its way through the valley below, and in the distance I could see the faint outline of a train wreck.

*Damn, she really hadn't been lying about that. So, the whole kit and kaboodle had come flying in from the other world along with us, eh?*

From afar, all we could see was a long row of train cars, the very same ones that had brought us to this world. But they were in a complete and total wreck, twisted metal and broken glass strewn about. The encampment, such as it was, had apparently been built around them, but it was clear to me that it had seen better days.

But, just as I was about to remark on the beauty of the place, Rua turned to reveal our camp and froze in horror. I followed her gaze and saw what had caused her distress. The camp, not far from the train itself, was in ruins, smoke and flames rising from its central mass. The land around it was scarred and blackened, as if a great battle had taken place.

"Pah! What a dump!" Edwig announced.

"What in the name of fuck," I muttered, my heart sinking.

"No, no, no," Rua said, her voice trembling.

*Well, that's just great*, I thought to myself. *Just when I thought things couldn't get any worse.*

The same inky black clouds I'd seen the night before rose from several spots, the acrid smell of burning wood and metal filling the air. The tents that had been erected were tattered and torn, flapping wildly in the wind. The main building Rua had bragged about helping to construct was there, but now it was little more than a smoldering pile of ash.

*What the shit happened?*

My first thoughts were, of course, that maybe this had all been a trap set by the curly-haired fuckwitch—damn, Garth was right; that *did* sound awesome. But then, why would she request Rua's rescue only to turn around and raze their settlement? Something was fishy, and I wanted to figure it out before it spiraled out of control. More importantly, though, weirdly, I wanted to make sure everyone was alright.

In any case, it was clear that this was no longer some mythical mid-forest happiness shelter but rather exactly what it seemed to be: a makeshift camp in the middle of a warzone. And as I looked upon the scene before me, I felt an acute lance of dread.

This was not the sanctuary we had been promised but a battleground.

# EPILOGUE

The sun was setting on the hills outside of Machus City, casting a red glow over the rugged terrain, and Kent was running.

His feet pounding the earth, his breath coming in ragged gasps, the man knew that this was the end. Nothing was truer in that moment. Not the gathering chill against his sweat, nor the barren earth under his boots. This inescapable fate was a cloud of dread, and it had him in its snare.

Though he couldn't see his pursuer, the cold grip of a hunter's cowl bled into his heart. A predator. The thing giving chase, and it was a thing, would succeed. It would wrench him into whichever hell was waiting for him on the other side of the fog, and he'd be gone. There'd be no memories of Kent. He left his mark on none, and his reward was to be forgotten.

Beside him was a woman, a warrior. She was a companion but not a friend. Yet they were as lovers in their flight from this shadow. Both being pursued. Both doomed as prey. She did not fear in the same way as Kent. He was prone to it. She was tempered. Formed of the same steel and discipline as all who wore the helm of the Pentknight. But she could see the terror in her companion's eyes. She could see the way his hands shook, the way he kept looking over his shoulder. For him, fate was decided. For her, it was to be defied.

"We must fight," she'd demanded. "It is the only thing that will carry us out of this. You have your Arcana. Use it. We will locate this monster and vanquish it together."

But her words didn't reach the elf. His fluted ears were deaf to all but his own beating heart. His useless reach of an escape. The Pentknight had seen the massacre this path followed. It was the same as Zela, her body not yet cold but wreathed in blackened curses. Eyes still skyward, watching silent gods leer back. Zela was the best of their three, and Zela was dead.

The Pentknight knew as Kent did that this beast would reach them. She knew fleeing was the quickest path back to burn upon the family pyre. She did not want to burn yet. There was life left. No longer behind her but forward. The life she had left glimmered on that pyre already. She allowed for nothing else. She'd beg the stars for mercy if she thought they might place pity on her. A bleak, twisted thing such as she was. They were cruel. But they were sometimes full of mercy.

Kent cried out as something bit his leg above the ankle. He stumbled and fell to the hard earth, hurt. Though he knew the grip of death would pain him more. Grasping, Kent saw the wound. Saw the bolt. Black as pitch and filled with living death. Poison. The Arcana it held crept from the bolt to the wound to the flesh, and he shrieked. He wept. He wept as he'd not wept since childhood. He was sure now. Death was there. Death lived there in this dying sunset. A colder sunset than he'd ever remembered. It would take him, and he'd leave behind nothing. Nothing but the fear and the twilight that would bury him.

As Kent lay on the ground, the Pentknight grew angry.

"Get up," she pleaded. Commanded. "Stand or we will die. We cannot—"

But her neck was struck by another bolt, and she fell beside him, dead.

Kent tried to stand. He tried to escape the inescapable, but his sudden bravery was no good. The moment he rose was the moment he fell. He was down again, chains encasing his body and dragging him to meet the earth once more. Chains like glowing coals of emerald, as unyielding as death.

The hunter's shadow loomed, and the shape it contained belonged to a man. The hunter prowled from hiding, his shroud that of cloak over leather. A hat with a wide brim. Kent saw from the dirt that death carried a crossbow, longer than a man and cruel as the tomb.

"Thought I'd had a new start when I first came to this world," death said. His voice was soft, quiet. But he was also death, and death's voice is hard as iron. "Left this sort o' thing in that memory. But some folks can't leave well enough alone, can they?"

"Please," begged Kent, chained by the Spell and unable to do more than plead for forgiveness. "Spare my life. I haven't killed. I've never killed anyone!"

"No," said death. "You might not've dragged the blade, but you find them what are wanted for killin', don't you? You're a beacon for slayers, and that ain't somethin' to abide. You kill like a coward."

Kent's cries were for himself. For mercy. For salvation. But to death, they were the cries of one who'd taken that which he'd loved. For longer than Kent had years to his life. Family. The only ones he could call such in this place.

How precious were those who gave life to death. And how unfortunate were those who took them away.

"Where's the one what calls himself the Yeska?" Death was calm but impatient. "Lead me to him."

Kent, the skies opening for a moment, grasped hope.

"I don't know where the Yeska is. Even I'm unable to locate him, though I have tried. B-but!"

The raised crossbow had hurried his tongue.

"I know where his second is!" Kent said. "Tarnen is his name! Let me live and I'll tell you whatever you want to know! I promise!"

The hunter, death, unreadable in his raiment, shrugged.

"No. No, I don't think that's how this teases out. Seems that you tellin' me where this second of yours is . . . Well. That's your only trail. Coward."

Eyes glimmering, Kent bent to his nature.

"Larith," he said. "At the temple."

Kent cried out, feeling death's wrath crawling toward his chest now, his legs long abandoned to the poison.

"Please!" Kent said. "I've—"

"Which temple?"

"The Temple of the Sovereign! Please! Help me!"

Death observed his prey, unmoving. Then the emerald chains dispersed, and Kent cried out now in earnest celebration. Though it was premature.

Death, the hunter, stalked away from Kent, the man lying blackened still. The venom riddling him with pain, his eyes confused.

"The poison!" Kent demanded. "Please! Cure me; I told you what I knew!"

Death paused, his eyes watching only the horizon and the last flickering ribbon of red sunlight.

"That poison is Arcane, coward. Concocted by Bahlgus hisself with a promise of its potency. Ain't nothin' to be done of it. You was dead afore you hit the ground."

Kent continued, unearthing more. Telling death the whereabouts of any who might interest him in sparing the elf's life. Death's silence was the second gift given to Kent. But that was the last of what he gave.

The shrouded man left him.

Kent wailed and wept until he couldn't. Left only with his thoughts and the coil of the nearby woman. And when he gasped, he feared each broken breath. He counted them and saw the dim encroach. As long he could count his breaths, he knew he was still able to overcome this. To survive.

But the wind blew cold, the sky grew dark, and Kent was dead.

The shrouded man walked away, the sunset gone above the glowing sapphire of distant Machus City. Larith was a name he knew, if only hardly. Yet still. There was one more task before churning tread to the city of glass. There were locations that he listened to from the death rattle. Ones that gave him a faint light.

Death could not hope. But he was no longer death today. He was only the shrouded hunter, and to him, hope was a friend. But his work was done. He'd returned to familiar ground, but it was a grim, wretched thing. A melody he'd thought long gone, now in reprise. No longer a dirge, but neither was it a thing of beauty. Changed. Perhaps, thought the hunter. Perhaps it was welcome.

And so, he made for his next quarry, and he carried with him names he'd wanted never again. But the mantle of a man such as he couldn't be unhooded so easily. He knew he would be death again. But not tonight. And not for many nights yet. So, he remained the hunter. He remained the shadow and the shrouded man.

He remained Vengeful.

# ABOUT THE AUTHOR

Seth McDuffee is the bestselling author of the novel *Good Boy* and Dungeon Master for the popular *Dungeons & Dragons* 5e podcast *The d20 Syndicate*, as well as a purveyor of fine soups.

Podium
DISCOVER
STORIES UNBOUND
PodiumAudio.com